PROPHET REBORN

BOOK TWO

A sequel to *Perfect Prophet*

Hi there!

Thanks for taking time to check out my [illegible] novel. This book was an experiment, and I didn't invest in a huge marketing campaign, so I ask you one favor. If you like it, please find it online at your favorite book seller's site and write a review. Also, tell your friends!

Thanks for supporting my work!

DIANE M. JOHNSON

ISBN: 978-1-09831-446-0 (print)

ISBN: 978-1-09831-447-7 (ebook)

The story of two brothers brought together
by the devil and torn apart by God

Dedication

To the believers and non-believers, and to anyone looking to understand their place in the world. Special thanks to my beta readers, Kelsey C., Rosa T., and Zara Zachary S. for taking the time to read and share their thoughts.

Contents

Perfect Prophet

I SHOULD BE DEAD. THE THOUGHT NAGGED LUCAS AS he stared at Alec's perfect face smiling from the cover in the bookstore display. Tempered glass barricaded it from Lucas's touch. *At minimum, I should be cursed with a shit bag tucked under my shirt.*

Perfect Prophet. It was a narcissistic title for an autobiography. A *New York Times* Best Seller. A big deal. Former devil-rocking atheist becomes an instrument of God, an evangelical faith healer. An epic journey in faith. And Lucas was nothing. The shop's lights dimmed. It was closing time, and Lucas turned to face the sidewalk running along a four-lane road packed with weekend tourists and local club-goers. He walked, wondering what Alec was doing that night. It was probably a far better activity than what awaited Lucas.

Alec Lowell had saved Lucas before becoming the Christian superstar that the faithful now wanted him to be. It didn't happen in some church or during some nationally televised Christian hawker event. It happened in the woods of Wisconsin on a morning after the season's first snowfall. Lucas should have been dead. To be honest, God had ample reason to strike him where he stood, right here. Right now.

Or maybe God had forgiven Lucas. After all, he was kind of responsible for the Perfect Prophet's meteoric rise. A few months had gone by after Alec's debut at the Life Festival, a Christian event held annually in Orange County, California that sold out every year. The man, the one who had raised Lucas to be the leader of a new generation of classic satanic thought, had brought Lucas to the festival to kill Alec like the prophecies of the Black Book had foretold. The prophecies had been written by Brent Lowell, the father of the one who would rise up to either take charge of or destroy the New Church of Satan. Brent Lowell was Alec's father. He was also Lucas's father, but Alec was the one who rose up from the ashes of death to shatter the fledgling church into pieces.

Alec had also healed Lucas's hand, the one that had been intentionally maimed by the prophet Brent Lowell when Lucas was too young to have recollection of a father. Alec had done it on that morning in the Wisconsin woods when both of them should have been dead. The bullet had blown through Alec, leaving Lucas with the slug buried in his gut. They had laid beside each other, bleeding out together when Alec had taken hold of Lucas's withered hand that had been a useless claw for most of his life. Lucas had faded into black oblivion. When he had regained consciousness, Alec was gone and the hand was healed. Useful. He had found the strength to stagger to his feet and tend to the wound that oozed blood and juices from his intestines. Then he made his escape before anyone could find him.

It took time to heal from the shot, but Lucas did heal. He shouldn't have. He had sewn himself up with a fishing hook and line, a primitive butcher job. He wouldn't have been able to do it with one hand. And that hand, the one that had been surgically severed along its tendons to prove that he wasn't the destroyer of the classic satanic faith, was flexible and perfect except for the scar along the wrist.

The hand should have been the wake-up call, but it wasn't. Sepsis had set into the gut wound before Lucas had sought the aid of Fitzgerald Carver, his mentor within the new satanic church, who had yet to admit the church's defeat. According to Carver, Alec was meant to die and it was Lucas's destiny to kill him. Once Lucas healed, the two had attended the festival hosted by the charismatic televangelist Josiah Light. It was Alec's debut, and Dr. Carver had tickets and a plan.

The rest became history. Dr. Carver had smuggled a dagger into the event by disguising it as the handle of his cane, and when Alec stepped into the audience to lay healing hands on the faithful, Lucas set out to stab Alec through the heart. Brother kills brother. Carver had cited the story of Cain and Abel as misrepresented propaganda by the Judeo-Christian gatekeepers. Alec's former band mates from the Great might have called the entire idea of religion propaganda once, too.

They would have also cited the fantastical ideas of magic and miracles as fake. But Lucas knew otherwise. He had paralyzed Alec with satanic magic. As for miracles, Lucas needed only to look at his hand.

The moment came when Alec descended from the stage and the audience converged on him. Lucas was pulled in, Carver keeping close behind. When Lucas was in range with dagger gripped tight, he turned and plunged it through Carver's heart instead. Lucas escaped. It was his gift to disappear in a crowd, and headlines were made.

Lucas roamed the streets for weeks after killing Carver, gradually making his way from the Christian havens of Orange County to the filthy, sinful heart of Los Angeles. He left the bookstore and wandered into territory densely populated by the homeless, where he found a beacon of hope. A haven.

The gated storefront gave little impression of its claim in the window: Mission for Lost Souls. A challenge resided there: *Jesus saves. Ask us how.* When Lucas knocked on the glass window—on this street filled with addicts, gang members and the homeless—in the dead of night, he didn't necessarily find an answer to the question the sign proposed. But he did find hope, and she was ten years old.

The girl would have answered the door, but the man with the military vibe held her back. "Can we help you?" he asked through the barricaded door.

"It says Jesus saves." Lucas pointed out the challenge. "I'm asking how." The military man took his time to assess Lucas. Once satisfied, he opened up.

"I'm John David," he said as soon as he unlocked the door, but Lucas took note that he relocked it quickly once he was inside. The girl was Maggie, who went to find something for Lucas to eat. She returned with carrot sticks and water after John David sat Lucas down in a folding chair among several in a row. John David turned on a light.

The place was sparse, populated by more chairs and a couple of well-worn banquet tables that lined the back wall. A simple cross hung at the front behind a wooden pulpit. A black book sat atop the pulpit. Lucas assumed it was a Bible. An ancient TV was strung up in a corner of the room, adjacent to the hanging cross.

Maggie settled in a distant chair that John David signaled her to sit in, and Lucas posed the question one more time. "How can Jesus save me?"

"Do you want Him to save you?" John David placed a hand on Lucas's knee. Lucas didn't like that. When he didn't answer, John David persisted. "Maybe you feel like you're not worthy of His forgiveness." Lucas gave a nod, not as a confession but because he considered it a fair assessment.

"Jesus forgives everyone."

John David smiled proudly. Maggie must have been his daughter. "That's right. He chose to die for the sake of our shortcomings, for the shortcomings of the world. As long as He sees in you the intention to change, your sins will be forgiven."

"My intention to change," Lucas said with a snicker. "So, what? I need to confess my sins to you? Or to your priest?"

"Only to God," John David said.

"But through you. Or your priest."

John David freed an amused smile. "I take it you had a Catholic upbringing."

"No." The answer left disappointment on John David's face from his inaccurate assessment. Lucas knew much about the Catholics. The New Church of Satan had modeled their perverted rituals after Catholic ways. His oppressively Christian foster parents were Evangelicals, but he had left them at a young enough age to avoid the trappings of their church.

"God is the only one you need to confess to," John David said. "You know what your sins are. He knows too. There's no need for an intermediary."

Lucas found relief in hearing this, for his sins were a direct affront to God. He didn't offer to share them, and he let John David be frustrated by it.

John David tried a new tack. "Are you on the street? We don't normally offer shelter. We're not equipped for it. But we're having a service in the morning. You can spend the night this one time and find out more of what we offer then. Is that alright with you?"

Lucas gave him a shrug. The streets were cold, not that he couldn't survive a little chill. He'd survived Wisconsin winters in the woods often enough. But the idea of shelter and a warm blanket was enticing. John David directed Maggie to get just that, and Lucas found a corner near a heating duct for the night.

He was nudged awake early. "Help us set up for service?" John David offered Lucas a donut from a pink cardboard box. Maggie lined up more boxes on the back row of tables before she stacked napkins and cups alongside an insulated jug that Lucas assumed held water.

"John David," Maggie said. "We need more cups."

John David told her where to find them and, as Maggie bounced out of the room, Lucas thought that maybe she wasn't the man's daughter after all.

He accepted a donut. The first bite reminded him that he hadn't eaten much over the past couple of days, except from a dumpster dive outside a fast food place. The donut tasted like heaven. He wolfed it down, then filled a cup from the oversized jug. It contained juice.

Later, Lucas straightened chairs and distributed fliers to each seat. He noted the organization's name on the fliers. This Mission for Lost Souls was an outreach program for a church known as the Temple of Adonis, and Lucas wondered why a church that seemed to focus on helping people find Jesus would name itself after a mortal and tragic character from Greek mythology. It didn't seem well thought out. But he dismissed the thought as people filtered in.

The city streets were slick with rain, probably a factor in filling seats. Lucas recognized some of the crowd, although not by name. They were homeless, in need of physical and mental care, not words. Some were junkies. Some were just old and forgotten. Most were probably hungry. Lucas chose a chair near the back, close to the array of pastries that John David stood guard over. He sat and he listened, and he was amazed.

Maggie took to the lectern. She spoke about healing. She spoke about Jesus and a paralyzed man at a place called Capharnaum. Jesus had healed the man and told him that his sins were also forgiven, his soul freed from its own paralysis. "The Pharisees called it heresy," she said without a tremor of public-speaking fear. "They believed that his paralysis was a result of his sins. They were wrong.... Our body is nothing except a vessel of clay. It contains our soul, and with time it breaks down and returns to dust. But our soul will live on. If we tend to it like a garden, we can find entry into heaven." Maggie cast her eyes over disinterested listeners until they landed on Lucas. She smiled, and he squirmed. He felt connected to God.

But God was judging Lucas through Maggie's smiling eyes. The parable reminded him of Alec, and as Lucas flexed his left hand made whole by Alec's touch, he was reminded that he was incomplete. Unworthy. Ending up here in this hole in the wall that doubled as a church wasn't random. He supposed that nothing in life ever was.

He cast his gaze away and felt horrified about things that he had done to Alec, to Alec's son Jake. Lucas saw himself as a monster, one that, if Jesus had chosen to heal him in a place called Capharnaum, would never have been forgiven for his sins.

Maggie stepped away from the lectern. John David stepped away from the diabetic spread and put a stop to listeners rising from their seats. "Gentlemen. And ladies. Let's close with a prayer." The majority of listeners acquiesced. One or two headed for the food, until Lucas left his seat to stand guard over the table.

"Thank you for your diligence, Brother Lucas." John David asked the rest to bow their heads. "Repeat after me. Jesus knows me. Jesus loves me. Jesus died to set me free." Listeners mumbled in reply, and John David concluded with an amen. "Help yourselves to what we have in the back. And come find us if you wish to learn more about the Reverend Adonis and our mission."

The listeners plunged toward the donuts as Lucas stepped aside. "I'm proud of you," he heard John David say as he and Maggie made their way toward him. They stepped in to keep order to the handouts.

Lucas didn't belong here. He wanted to leave, but a fresh downpour delayed his decision. He sat in a chair apart from the activity, and he got lost in the rhythm of the rain.

A homeless moocher who was first in line settled near Lucas. He had several donuts and a cup of the juice that he downed in one gulp. He found the remote to the television and flipped it on to local Sunday morning programming. As fate would have it, they were treated to a sermon by mega church evangelist Josiah Light. "Is this your guy? Your Reverend Adonis?" he shouted.

John David scowled before he pounced on the man. He took away the remote and turned the TV off. "We don't live extravagantly off the needy and call it God's way."

The condemnation continued, but Lucas didn't hear it. His mind was set on the day when he had decided not to kill Alec. He wondered if Alec hadn't become like the Reverend Light by feeding on the hope of the hopeless for money. Maybe Lucas had been wrong to kill Dr. Carver.

Death to my son, the misguided one. New life for the unholy spirit. These were the words of the prophecy left by Lucas's father, the traitor high priest. Lucas had assumed that they were meant for Alec, an unholy atheist reborn into faith. Maybe he'd been wrong. Maybe they were meant for Lucas. It overwhelmed him, and he wondered if this was how Alec felt when he was pressed to choose between nothing and God. But it was different for Lucas. He had always believed in God, he just never believed that God was the right side.

Until he healed me.

Could an atheist profiting from his life-giving gift be a truthful messenger? Lucas didn't know, and instead of reaching out to John David and inviting a discussion from the man who wanted just that, Lucas found himself heading for the exit. He took fast steps toward the door.

"Where are you going?"

It was Maggie, and she was in his way. Lucas wasn't sure where she had come from. He had been alert to his immediate surroundings for most of his life. But here she was, blocking his escape with the most innocent smile he had ever seen. The kids he remembered from grade school and middle school had never seemed so innocent. Neither had Alec's son Jake when they were friends, although "friends" was a relative term. Kids, Lucas thought, were not as fragile and innocent as their parents chose to believe. Except maybe Maggie. She was challenging that notion.

"I—I don't…I don't belong here." He tried to dodge, but she managed to stay in his way.

"Anyone who finds us belongs here."

"I don't. I can't—" and she grabbed his hand, the one that had been healed.

"Seek the Lord, and He shall hear you and deliver you from all your fears." She refused to let go. His heart doubled its beat inside his chest.

"Get out of the way—"

The outburst alerted John David. He abandoned the guy who was convinced that the reverend Jonas Adonis was the Reverend Josiah Light and corralled Lucas into an embrace that freaked him out more. "Let me go! Don't—"

"It's alright. Whatever it is, we're here." John David wouldn't let go. He guided Lucas back to a chair to settle through his ragged attempt to breathe, and the homeless guy found the remote. The TV came back to life.

"Praise Jesus," Josiah Light proclaimed. "Praise Him. Hallelujah."

"Happy birthday, Marcus. You sonofabitch." Bourbon spilled over the rim of the shot glass resting atop Marcus Anthony Eddison's headstone. Alec took a swig from the bottle, knowing full well that this moment was another reason to visit the good people at Alcoholics Anonymous. He didn't really care. Mark wouldn't have cared, and this was supposed to be his day. Alec was almost twenty-nine. Marcus would have been thirty. He had died barely in time to be inducted into the Twenty-Seven Club, the one that commemorated the rising stars of rock and roll whose lives were cut short too soon: Cobain, Winehouse, Morrison, Brian Jones, Mia Zapata, all dead before their time should have been due.

Alec took another slug of his sin. His own time should have been due.... He found his guilty conscience and poured the rest of the bottle over the grave. "Enjoy it," he said. "You deserve it." He finished off the contents of the shot glass and leaned back against the marble. Goddamn, how did he get here? The former punk atheist finds a bullet, becomes a miracle, and finds God, fame, and happiness in the wake of tragedy. It was a lie. He was terrified most of the time. He was miserable, just like his born-again father.

His phone buzzed in his pocket. He pulled it out and shielded the screen from the sun. It was a text from his bodyguard Olsen, the one provided to him by the Reverend Light and his life-giving church, who stood a distance away at the roadside where Alec's limo driver, also provided by Light, waited. The message read, "2:00." Alec looked to his right, because he knew that Olsen wasn't referencing an appointment. He was referencing a location and, *oh shit. Fans.*

They could have been haters, for since his public admission that he did indeed believe that there might be a God, his loyal fan base from his days as a satanic rock rebel had become vocal bullies, especially on social media. But the woman approaching had flowers meant for a grave, and the other woman and man with her were hurrying their steps with wide eyes and open mouths. Alec threw a signal to Olsen to stay put and braced himself for the inevitable fan worship.

"Oh my God oh my God ohmyGod!" Alec pasted on a smile, and the woman with the flowers continued. "Can I hug you? You changed my life, ohmyGod!" She wrapped her arms around him before he had the chance to say no, and she let the embrace linger. "Oh my—I'm sorry. You're paying your respects, and here I am just...I'm sorry." She laughed in that anxious fangirl way and freed him.

"No, not at all," Alec said. "I'm glad you found...I don't know, a purpose I guess, because of me."

The woman beamed. The man thrust his hand out, hopeful for a shake. Alec obliged, and the man's second hand came in to grip Alec tight. "Wow. I can feel it. God works through you."

Alec nodded and thought about Mark, whom he had healed, now dead in the ground. He thought of Patrick, their band's drummer the "Mexicali leprechaun," as Mark had called him without ever entertaining the idea that the term might have been racist, who Alec had also healed, also now dead in the ground. He thought about Jake, his son, his sole reason for changing everything in his life, and how Jake now hated him. Alec pulled back, and the man let go of his hand. "I'm sorry," Alec said. "I have an appointment to keep. Two o'clock." He flashed his phone screen at them as if he needed to prove he wasn't lying, which he totally was.

The third fan grabbed his arm before he could leave. "Can we have an autograph?"

"I don't do autographs. Read the book—"

"—A selfie? Please?"

Alec gave in and smiled as three camera phones came out. He was asked when he would be back with Josiah Light, and Alec told them soon. "Yeah, soon. We're hitting the road, actually. So look for that." Then he escaped to the limo, where Olsen greeted him with an open door as the driver settled behind the wheel.

"I'm being paid to protect you, sir," Olsen said. "I can't do it from a distance—"

"—I get it, Olsen. Private time isn't an option anymore."

"Home, then?" the driver asked. He put the car in gear before Alec answered. The partition between driver and passenger went up, and Alec imagined the two of them having a good laugh at his expense. He was okay with that. He was every bit the insecure, self-centered celebrity that he supposed they believed he was, and there was nothing he could do but admit it. Alec stared out the tinted window. He wondered what God's point was. Nothing had changed. Nothing at all.

Paths to Healing

ALEC SHIVERED. BLOOD RUSHED THROUGH HIS HEAD as Lucas leered in his face. Barren tree branches cracked the overcast sky, and Alec found himself bound to an upside-down cross, bleeding from stab wounds and a bullet hole as Lucas spoke. It wasn't exactly what he said when Alec had first lived through this nightmare. This time it was apologetic in tone, an excuse. "We had to do this. It was written. I made you who you are. I saved you." And with that, Lucas plunged a knife through Alec's heart.

He startled awake, hyperventilating. Cleo startled awake too. She rolled over and caught Alec in an embrace, spooning against him and whispering in his ear until he found his rhythm. "I'm right here, hon." She continued with soft hushes, a mother soothing her child out of his fear until Alec shrugged out of the hold as if she was suffocating him. Alec scooted to the edge of the bed and sat there, shoulders hunched as he straight armed the mattress, his fingers clawed into its edge. The act of rejection was killing her. Every time. Cleo gave him a moment anyway before she posed the rhetorical question. "Are you alright, now?"

Alec glared over his shoulder. Stupid question, the glare said. He reached for his phone on the hotel suite's nightstand to call home, Cleo's cue to leave the room. Otherwise, she was going to lose her shit. She hated herself for being the other woman, the one whom Alec sought comfort from when he was on tour and away from home. She slipped out of bed and felt Alec's eyes follow the sway of her hips as she sauntered to the bathroom to quietly do her business and listen to the one-sided conversation.

"Hey, Jake," Alec said in a forced upbeat tone. "I thought you had school… Jake? Are you still… Lindy… I'm just checking in… Yeah, yeah good flight."

Cleo flushed. She rinsed her hands and found her toothbrush. She and Alec had talked about Jake's increasing desire to shut Alec out of his life, and she imagined that the kid's quick pass of the phone to his mom was proof. "I thought maybe lessons would help," Alec said once. "One on one with the guitar. Or maybe a drum kit because of Paddy. But he just pushes me away."

Cleo stared at herself under the harsh bathroom lighting and wished she could be as cavalier about her relationship with Alec as the kid was. She felt sorry for Alec and his woes as a father, she really did. But she understood Jake's side. It was hard to heal from a traumatic experience when the man who inadvertently caused it was barely holding it together himself.

"I wanted to say something," Cleo heard Alec say. "But he passed me off." Then, "No, no. He doesn't want to talk to me," followed by a self-loathing laugh. Cleo scrubbed her teeth. She paused when she heard him speak up again. "What," he said. "What do you want me to do from here?"

Cleo took the moment to spit before the last of the conversation snagged her attention. "Lindy," and that was it. Cleo rinsed her mouth. She checked to make sure the smile on her face looked genuine, then ventured back into the suite. Alec had his head in his hands, phone abandoned in the tangle of sheets at his waist.

"So how are things with the wife and kid?"

Alec pulled himself out of whatever despair he might have been floating in and filled in bits of the unheard conversation. "Jake starts school today so, you know. Lindy worries."

"He's a strong kid, hon. He'll get past this." Alec shrugged at her remark as if trying to convince himself that it was true. Then he pushed out of bed and slipped into his boxers. He set a path for the mini bar where he found juice and vodka to mix together. He downed it in one gulp, then rummaged through the little refrigerator for a second round.

"Hon, that's not going to help—"

He cut her off with another glare and a stern finger. "Don't."

She shook her head. She couldn't not. "Packed full of nutrition, hon. Breakfast of champions—"

"—I'm not judging you, alright?" He found the right bottle, then snapped open the cap and poured.

Cleo held her tongue. She was judging him, it was true. She let him take another gulp and then brood as she busied herself with fashion. She wanted something comfortable for the day's rehearsal, comfortable but clingy. And then it slipped out; the casual judgment that she couldn't keep in check. "How many commandments have you broken? Five? Six?"

"Rule number one? No other Gods before me. That one's a safe bet." He raised his glass and downed the rest of the drink.

Cleo laughed because it was funny. An atheist could never break God's first commandment. He had her with that one, and probably the one regarding idols. She went through a mental checklist of the other eight and decided that Alec was lucky to have atheism on his side. She continued to poke through her suitcase.

The vodka freed Alec's pent-up frustrations. "I didn't ask for this. People make me out to be some kind of... savior. I mean, what the actual fuck? And I just go with it, I'm leading them on because, I don't know. That's what they want. And I do it to support Lindy and Jake...And that doesn't matter because they're not happy. And I'm not happy. And—Jesus Christ, he's—the fucking prick is..." Alec caught his breath, and Cleo thought he was ramping down.

But no. He whipped his empty glass across the room. It struck the TV and shattered, the screen cracked. Before Cleo could follow up with something stupid like, *breaking things isn't going to solve your problems, hon*, he turned his back and hugged himself. One sob hiccupped out of him before he held the rest at bay.

Cleo headed for him. She hated these moments. Alec had always suffered from anxiety, and she had been able to overlook it when they were younger and irresponsible during their days as rock and roll punks with an agenda. Then he got shot, and Belinda and Jake returned to his life, and Cleo and Alec's friends-with-benefits relationship reverted to just friends. Until recently.

But this anxiety was fueled by something different. Part of it still stemmed from the trauma left by his brother, but now it was compounded by fame and responsibility, a responsibility to live up to the image that others wanted but that he failed to have faith in. Part of it was that, but this was something more. Cleo wrapped her arms around him, and he struggled out of her embrace. He didn't like to be touched unless it was on his terms.

And that was getting worse too.

"I'm sorry," Alec said. "I'm not being fair to you. I know that."

"You know?" The relationship had escalated into an affair only recently, and Cleo hated herself for allowing it to happen. She loved Alec. Okay, no. She did, but he was her mommy fix. She felt stronger when he was scared and needed comfort. *Come to me, hon. Mommy will make it better.* And when they had their arguments that led to bitter name-calling and the requisite fuck-yous while on the road with Josiah's Healing Tour, those ended with rough makeup sex. Sex that left Alec spent and able to sleep and that left Cleo whole.

Sex with the anxiety-burdened, always-terrified mess that was Alec Lowell left her feeling whole. That had never happened with Marcus or any other lover. But it didn't matter. It justified nothing, not when it came to the woman Alec really needed in his life. And Goddamn it, he was messing that up too. Cleo followed up *you know?* with, "Do you think I like being the thing that's tearing you and Lindy apart?"

"She doesn't know—"

"Is that supposed to make me feel better?" Alec fell silent. Cleo had struck the right nerve. "I know you're still scared, hon. I know it's the only reason why I'm here."

"Don't," he said again.

"Don't what? Walk away? We're using each other. And I know Lucas is still in here." She tapped his temple. "I can't change that. I want to, hon. I want you to get past it, but what can I do?"

Alec kept his eyes cast to the floor until he posed a different question. "Do you still think about Mark?"

"Fuck you." She thought about Mark every day.

Alec turned away, wounded. He checked out the remaining selections in the mini bar. "Stop," she said, preventing him from grabbing another bottle. When he pushed her aside, she lost her balance and hit the floor.

"Oh, shit," he said. When Alec reached down to help her to her feet, Cleo pushed back in kind.

"I'm alright! Don't bother."

They stood apart like rivals before a street fight until Alec broke. "When did I get so god damned needy?" He added a shrug to that, again with the self-loathing laugh.

Cleo stepped in, wrapped her fingers around his head; he allowed it this time, and she met his forehead with her own. "You are alive. We both are, by some miracle. And I know you don't think you deserve it. I feel the same way. But we can do this. We can move on."

Alec gave a sullen nod. He pulled her into an embrace, and she could feel him trembling. "It's okay, hon." She kissed his ear. He drew back to meet her lips. Instantaneous fire burned inside of her as Alec pressed close. She didn't resist. She never resisted with Alec, and they stumbled back against the dresser until she found herself seated on top of it with her legs spread and her negligee up in invitation.

Alec let his boxers slip to the floor where they threatened to trip him up as he slid inside her. Cleo wrapped her legs around his hips to steady him. They moved together. They breathed together, and Cleo heard herself moan as his warm breath tickled the fine hairs along her neck. Alec's presence inside of her made her feel whole again and almost content.

Almost.

Alec untangled his ankles from his boxers before he carried Cleo back to bed. They ravaged each other until they were spent, and as Alec lay draped over her with his cheek at her breast, she made a confession. "I think about them every day. Marcus and Paddy. I miss them."

Alec hugged her tighter.

Lucas took in the fresh pine aroma of the Sacred Temple of Adonis, a secluded camp along the Sangre de Cristo mountain range. The camp was named after its founder, Jonas Adonis and not some tragic Greek figure who symbolized death and rebirth. Lucas wasn't sure if it fell within the borders of Colorado or New Mexico, and his newfound brothers and sisters were of little help regarding that detail. It didn't matter. The place was disconnected from the outside world, a near dead zone for GPS and Wi-Fi devices, and Lucas was fine with it. Everyone was fine with it. Disconnecting from the outside world was expected here.

Temple leader Jonas Adonis had admitted that the place wasn't a temple at all, not in the purest sense. But it was. Members of the commune devoted the majority of their time to seeking ways to be closer to God. Everyone had their own personal copy of the Bible, and happening upon a man or woman in the midst of quiet reading was a daily occurrence. "It's more like a kibbutz," the reverend once said. Once Lucas learned what that was, he found it odd that a man with such deep Christian philosophies would model his deeply rooted Christian community after something so inherently Jewish.

The man was staunch in his beliefs. His dedication to worship and to living off the land as God had intended bordered on puritanical. At least Lucas perceived it that way. He knew much about the old-world Puritans and their confrontation of witches who practiced freethinking. If it had been an older era, and if Jonas Adonis had known of Lucas's prior intimacy with Satan worship, he surely would have been hanged. Or maybe pressed to death with boulders.

But that didn't happen. Lucas had taken John David's promise to heart. His sins were between him and his Maker and no one else. He wasn't enthused about the prospect of sharing them from within the confines of the confession box either. The cramped little enclosure made of wood and tin sat at the back of the other buildings, adjacent to the horse stables, and a padlock hung from a latch on its door. The temple was all for sharing your sins privately with God, but they weren't going to make it pleasant for you.

Lucas would be the first to admit that this new lifestyle could lead to boredom. He breathed it in deep then started his routine morning walkabout that began at the men's dormitory. The women's dormitory, on the opposite side of the commune's church and the reverend's private cabin, was also where the children lived. Married couples were not allowed to lie together because of temple rules. This was only temporary, and somewhat complicated, but Adonis had decreed it and that was all that mattered.

The rule didn't affect Lucas, so he didn't really care. But as he passed Lance and Carol, who were gathering eggs at the hen house, he wondered how they felt about that one. They had been married for some time, and rumor had it that they officially joined the temple after several failed attempts at having kids. Maggie had told Lucas about it when they were alone in the stables, where they often came together to talk.

Lance and Carol were a devout pair from Michigan. He was a skilled mechanic and she had trained as an EMT. They were valuable to the commune team, and they were married. But they couldn't sleep together. That was the rule. Lucas gave Lance and Carol a nod, and they nodded in kind before he continued on his way. It summed up his relationship with them; nods of acknowledgement and nothing more. He kept walking,

The camp itself had its own past. Again, Lucas had learned about it from Maggie who, as Lucas had originally expected, was John David's daughter. Again, temple rules forbid recognition of the relationship. There was only one Father, the Creator in heaven. The rest were his children: every single one.

The place had been a military facility more than a century ago and was even considered as a location for an internment camp before being abandoned by the government in favor of a more appealing location. What the appeal of the new location was, only the government knew. Adonis acquired two acres of the property, which was partially walled off on the side of the main entrance. A retractable gate made of corrugated metal rolled on a track at the entry point. The place had an infirmary and a garage that housed a small fleet of trucks, tools, and farming equipment. Then there was the stable, the hen house, the goat pen, and a greenhouse that allowed for year-round crops of fruits and vegetables. The place was entirely self sustainable.

The Reverend Adonis had been pleased when Lucas proved that he knew how to live off the land. His teenage years of fishing and camping in Wisconsin had been an asset, and his innate survival skills helped Reverend Adonis accept Lucas into the fold. But the man wasn't initially convinced. He was also a conundrum, a middle-forties throwback to the hippest male personas of the 1980s, and he played the role of the authoritative father figure. *So much for everyone being children*, Lucas thought. "John David found you at our mission? For lost souls. Is that what you are? Lost?"

"I've never been lost," Lucas had said. "I just realized I was wrong." Standing in the reverend's private cabin, he had taken in the things that the rest of the fellowship were not allowed to have including Internet and a wide-screen TV with access to premium channels not meant for the eyes of God's children.

"An epiphany," Adonis had said. "We'll give you a trial run. We'll see."

Lucas wondered what the reverend was doing on this chilly autumn morning before daily service. The people here catered to him like he was a god. Or a prophet. They hung on his every word. He was probably checking out his reflection in one of his many mirrors, making certain that his pale linen blazer with the cuffs pushed up to the elbows was draped just so, or that his crisp chinos had the perfect crease. Not a strand of hair seemed to stray from his perfectly trimmed head or, if it did, it was probably meant to stray. His five o'clock shadow was groomed to make one think that it was perpetually five o'clock. He was a modern-day depiction of Jesus, if Jesus was white, affluent, and of European descent. If Jesus had ever thought of living on a boat in Miami with an alligator for a pet, then Jonas Adonis was that man.

A conundrum. He had no pictures of himself, but he was fond of those mirrors.

Lucas continued past Adonis's private quarters and the church hall at the center of the camp and made his way toward the gun range at the back. He would find Todd there and maybe Zachary, and they would stop setting up their targets and checking their weapons in preparation for the day's practice sessions. They would greet Lucas with untrusting eyes and the obligatory head nods. "Brother Lucas," Todd would add, as if saying the name made him sound friendly. It didn't.

But the fact that Lucas knew how to use a gun was another point in his favor. He wasn't skilled in the use of the AR weapons that seemed to be the favorite choice among the guardians here, though. These people feared an apocalypse and they were going to be ready, and Lucas… well, being surrounded by the most devout of Christians with their guns to protect them in the middle of nowhere amused him.

In some weird way, God had plans to keep Lucas safe. Either that, or God was setting him up for some terrible retribution that would probably be terribly fitting. Lucas shrugged at that idea and continued on his morning walkabout.

"Brother Lucas," Todd said from the confines of the shooting range. He made steady eye contact. Lucas gave him a curt nod as he passed. He made a loop along the back of the commune lot that was open to a broad stretch of bureau-managed land. Then he rounded back toward the main compound, past the dog run where a pair of shepherds and a pair of foxhounds yapped to be set free. The foxhounds were for hunting. The shepherds were for security. The only times they were allowed to roam were during hunts or at night under the supervision of the night guard. Pent up in their daily prison, Lucas assumed that they barked because they wanted to be free. Or maybe they just didn't like Lucas. That was possible.

Saint scampered up to meet Lucas. That explained the barking. The knee-high, wire-haired mutt had the privilege of roaming, the benefit of being the teacher's pet—or reverend's pet to be more accurate. "Hey, boy," Lucas crouched to give the dog a rough scratch all about. Saint danced excitedly before he nipped at Lucas's nose.

Lucas chatted with Saint as the dog tried to trip him up along the rest of his route. "Are you ready for church? Ready to be enlightened? What does Jonas do all night in front of his big TV? Jerking off to some real housewives, I'll bet." He snickered at that. He didn't belong here. The reverend was right to be wary.

The dog wouldn't be found at morning service. But Reverend Adonis did call Saint his personal savior. He never explained why. The dog had taken a liking to Lucas, and this seemed to dissatisfy the reverend. And Lucas… well, he fostered the relationship with every morning walk.

He found a stick to throw and Saint bounded after it, giving Lucas the chance to take a few steps before Saint returned with the prize. Lucas rewarded him with another affectionate scuff up. He mused over the way he had tortured and killed dogs in the past as symbolic sacrifices to the devil. It had been worse than sinful. It was unforgivable. Dogs were loyal and obedient beasts with no purpose other than to please their master, like Christians were meant to be before their God. So Lucas had made examples of them. "If you only knew," he whispered while he continued to stroke the soft center of the animal's throat.

"Knew what?"

Lucas glanced to the left. Maggie had found him. He straightened up as Maggie freed her innocent smile. "Sister Maggie," he said in a way that sounded more like Todd's way of saying it than he preferred.

"Brother Lucas. What does Saint need to know?"

He skirted an answer. "I never had a dog. I had a cat—well, my foster mom did." He recalled the accidental death of the woman's awful cat, and he avoided further mention of that too. "Why is Saint so special to Jonas?"

"Because Saint saved him."

"I know that, but how?"

Maggie shrugged. "I don't know. He just did."

Lucas crouched to meet Maggie's height. "You know everything. You know everything you're not supposed to know." It was a well-deserved compliment. She had spilled things that no other brother or sister dared to spill. She talked about her father's unspoken relationship with Hannah, whom she didn't really like. She shared what she knew about Lance and Carol's miscarriage. She talked about Todd's discontent with John David being chosen to lead the camp's security operations. She even talked about Todd's secret distrust of a pair of women who he expected were lesbians, because that was a sin. Maggie was an endlessly running gossip machine, and she didn't even know it.

She blushed at the accolade as if it was a slight. Then she told Lucas what she knew. "He once said that Saint showed up when he was at his lowest. Saint was a stray. They were two lost souls that found each other. Except that he didn't find Saint. Saint found him… Maybe he was homeless once. Like you."

Lucas scoffed at that. "With what he wears?"

"He doesn't like socks. Maybe he didn't use to have any."

It was an odd logic that didn't explain the man's extravagances, but instead of pointing that out Lucas posed another possibility. "Maybe he's from Florida. Or California."

Maggie didn't have time to discuss it. The moment when Reverend Adonis stepped out onto his porch, her relaxed demeanor changed. "Saint," Adonis called out. "Inside! Come on."

The dog scampered to his master's command as Lucas straightened up. He felt Maggie grab his hand. "We're going to be late," she whispered as she dragged him to the place everyone was heading: the chapel.

Maggie sat among the children in front. Lucas kept to the back, even though Maggie tried to coax him closer. The back was where he felt comfortable during the reverend's sermons. He didn't budge.

And then Adonis emerged. He stepped through the double doors at the back of the chapel and passed through the aisle that separated the dozen wooden benches like Moses on a mission. He reached the lectern, and his gaze leveled over the heads of the congregation to settle on Lucas.

Adonis began. "There are those who disseminate Satan's wicked propaganda through books, through music and video, through the threads of social media strangling the life out of our world. They promote all the things that are sinful by calling them rights and freedoms!" He punctuated the last two terms with a vehemence that made them dirty ideas. Then he raised a leather-bound Bible above his head and shook it while quoting a passage that Lucas assumed he had memorized verbatim. "Ephesians 5:11. Have no fellowship with works of darkness. Reprove them."

Lucas's face burned from the reverend's scrutiny. The man's fiery approach to the Word reminded him of that Shatner captain from Star Trek. His pointed gaze continued to fall on Lucas, and he continued. "We must reject the unholy images, the blasphemous lyrics, the fiction that the Godless sow as truth. The promoters of this propaganda depict themselves as gods. They call themselves prophets. They lie. They are…satanic."

Again, the man's eyes fell upon Lucas. This sermon was meant for him. Everything was over. God had spoken. Things were about to go terribly wrong. Lucas lowered his head as if in serious and contemplative repentance, which was just as much a lie. He expected to be singled out with a pointed finger, to be exposed and to be banished.

Adonis's voice boomed. "Let no man deceive you with vain words, for these are the things that tempt the wrath of God!" A hush fell over the congregation. Lucas waited for the final shove that would send him to his fate.

It didn't come.

The reverend relinquished the pulpit to John David, who thanked him for his insight. "Go," John David said in closing. "Meditate on the Wisdom of God."

Lucas was the first one out the door.

Parishioners filtered out of the chapel as Reverend Adonis snagged Maggie's father and led him toward Adonis's private cabin. Maggie was curious about the urgency, but she was more interested in spending time with Lucas. If the truth were told, Maggie was a lonely soul and Lucas felt like a kindred spirit. She watched Lucas forge a path as Saint escaped the confines of the reverend's home and fell in behind him. She headed for the stables.

He was doing what Maggie expected to find him doing. The horses were out of their stalls, and Lucas pitched manure. Saint found a soft patch of hay to settle in. He raised his head to Maggie for attention, and Lucas paused from the dirty work. With a hint of irritation, he said, "You're back."

Maggie held up a book that she had with her, then climbed up on a hay bale where she sat and swung her legs with abandon. His irritation was just a game that he played. She would find him here, and he would work, and she would chat until he gave up pretending to be irritated by her presence and joined in. "I thought you might be lonely," she said.

"Maybe I like being lonely."

"Nobody likes being lonely." She saw right through his grumpy exterior. "John David says I need to practice my ministering, and he says that you need it most."

"Yeah? What else does he say?" There was a hint of worry in his question, and Maggie paused. She didn't know if she should tell Lucas what she had heard others in the commune say about him. Some people didn't trust him, mostly because he didn't participate in their Bible studies like he was expected to do. And John David, who had brought Lucas here with the best intentions, had begun to voice doubts too.

Maggie found a tactful reply. "He says that I should help you find the good in yourself."

Lucas motioned for her to carry on as he returned to clean-up duty.

Maggie opened her book to a marked page. "This is the story of the prodigal son—"

"—The prodigal son. Never heard that one." Maggie hesitated, feeling like he was making fun of her. She began to think that his usually fake, grumpy mood wasn't so fake today.

She paraphrased from the book. "A wealthy farmer had two sons. One asked for his share of an inheritance and left to explore the world—"

"—And he lost everything because he was a sinner. So he returned home seeking forgiveness, fully expecting a penance, but the father celebrated his return with a feast fit for kings."

"You said you never heard this story."

"I lied."

"Why?" When Lucas didn't answer, Maggie pressed on. "Anyone can return to the Lord."

"How about a murderer?" He continued to shovel manure.

"It doesn't say." Before Maggie could consider an answer, Lucas abandoned the shovel and hopped up beside her.

"It doesn't say because the prodigal son isn't a murderer." He pointed at the page. "You can't use this story as your argument for God's willingness to accept anyone—"

"—Jesus pardoned a murderer when he was on the cross." Her defense slipped out with an ease that even she found surprising. Lucas stared at her in silence. He finally admitted that she *knew her shit*, and she beamed at him. "You do, too," she said.

They let their feet dangle as they studied the cobwebbed corners of the stable. The horses and goats were in the corral, so the only noise came from Maggie's heels thumping the bale. Out of the corner of her eye, she noticed that Lucas was doing it again, his habit of taking his left hand into his right then shaping and molding it as if it was an unfamiliar piece of him. What intrigued her more was the scar across the wrist. It made her think of her mother. It was a thing that John David made her promise to never talk about, but here Lucas was with a scar across his wrist and a sadness that Maggie remembered from her mother.

"Why did you try to kill yourself?"

"What?" When she pointed out the scar, Lucas concealed it with his sleeve. "That wasn't…" He stuttered without completing the thought.

"Are you afraid to die?" The question freaked Lucas out. His eyes were swimming within a blank expression. She was sure he would avoid telling her. Instead, he found his wits and gave her the simplest answer possible.

"No. I'm not." He slipped off the bale and proceeded to strew fresh hay along the floor of the stall.

"What was it like?"

"I never tried to kill myself. I never said that."

"Then what happened?"

Lucas shook his head. "You're lucky to have a dad like John David."

"There's only one Father—"

"—Don't be led like that. He's your dad. Jonas's rule is stupid, and your dad looks out for you. Don't let anyone tell you he's less than that. My dad? He was—" Lucas stopped short.

"He was what?"

"He was a disappointment."

"Why—"

"—Don't you have something else to do?"

Maggie grew sullen. The other kids here that were her age weren't as dedicated to learning about the ways of God as she was. The adults, while impressed by her exemplary faith, still treated her like a child. The only person left was Lucas. He challenged her beliefs, but not in a way that suggested she might be a fool for believing in anything. Maggie had met plenty of those types on her visits to the missionary outposts. No, Lucas challenged her with new interpretations of what God's Word might mean. But not today. Today, Lucas just wanted her to go away.

She decided to share. "I found my mom in the bathtub, and she did that to her wrists. And she died. And Daddy—I mean John David, he was sad for a whole year."

Lucas stopped spreading hay. When Maggie's eyes met his, he said, "My mom died when I was young too."

Everything came together. They were friends because they shared things that they didn't even know they shared. "Did she cut her wrists too?"

"No," he said with a laugh. "Overdose." He seemed to read her confusion, so he clarified. "She took drugs. That's what I was told. I was too young to remember. Younger than you." Lucas returned to Maggie's side.

"So it was just you and your dad too?"

"My dad—my real dad wasn't around. I learned a lot about him, though. And then he… he died."

"How was he a disappointment?"

"He gave me this." Lucas tapped the scar. "He gave it to me, and he walked out of my life. Then my mom died, and other people took me in."

"See? God watched over you with the other people." Maggie smiled, hoping she had made Lucas feel better. He laughed again, but she could tell that it wasn't close to making him happy.

"I found out I had a brother. And a sister. Different mom." He began clenching and opening his hand again. He flexed its fingers, seeming fascinated by the feat. "They were raised by him and they hated him too."

"Why? What did he do?"

"He preached until the day he died."

"A preacher? Like Reverend Jonas?" Lucas didn't answer, still fascinated by the movement of his fingers. "Are you okay?"

"No one's ever asked me that." Lucas smiled again, and this time the smile seemed like he meant it. "I'm sorry about your mom. It's hard, those kinds of things. But it makes us stronger. Right?"

It was Maggie's turn to feel awkward. She didn't really like talking about the death of her mother, and she assumed that it was the same feeling Lucas had when she had brought up his father. The awkwardness got uncomfortable, so Maggie changed the subject. "Do you like it here? Do you like us?"

Lucas scrunched up his face in curiosity. "Don't you?"

"Sometimes I get bored."

With a shrug he said, "You're safe here."

"Safe is boring. I like when John David and I go places, and the people."

"People are the scariest things in the world."

"If people seem scary it's because they're the ones who are scared."

Lucas looked bored. "Did John David teach you that?"

"I figured it out by myself."

"Hmmm," escaped from Lucas.

Maggie dangled her feet as ideas floated through her head: ideas about her mission and the mission of the Temple. "Maybe your brother and sister would like it here—"

"—Nope." When Maggie asked why, Lucas said that his sister was dead and that his brother... Well, he didn't want to talk about the brother. He let his left hand crumple up into a claw before he spread out the fingers again in a wide span. When Maggie kept at him about his brother, he shut her down. "That's just how it is." He hopped down to the floor and returned to the stall. "You could help." He handed her a pitchfork to stab into loose hay before he took the shovel and set out to clean the manure from the second stall.

"Tell me another Jesus story," Lucas said. "Something that John David thinks I should learn from." Maggie could think of so many. She chose one from memory, and she preached. Lucas listened and nodded and challenged her with his own ideas, and Maggie enjoyed the company. She forgot about feeling lonely.

Music bled past Jake's earbuds. It was a new generation of new wave punk, and it was too loud even for Jake's taste. But the point was to annoy Mom, so he let the bass test the capacity of the buds to the point of assault. It was kind of stupid. His mom had grown up on music far more irritating than that of some wannabe anarchists longing to be compared to Green Day. When she reached over and pulled the left bud free, he thought that maybe she'd reached a limit.

"Turn it down. You'll need hearing aids before you're twenty."

Jake turned down the volume and was about to stuff the earbud back in place when Belinda prevented it. "I did what you said—"

"—How was the chat with Dad this morning?"

Jesus, not again. "Alec's an asshole." It was meant to irritate, like the music, and it did.

"He's your dad—"

"—Not really."

"Not really? Tell me what that means."

"He's not even here."

"That's why he calls—"

"—He's a freak, Mom. Everyone says so." He had said too much. His mother sighed.

"Who's everyone, kids in your class?"

"No." It sounded as unconvincing as it was. But the kids at school weren't the only ones saying it. They were saying what their parents were saying, which was what the social media trolls were saying, and that amounted to a world full of people who thought that Alec Lowell, the self-professed perfect prophet, was an attention-starved fake.

There was a time when Alec was cool, when he picked Jake up from school and they cursed and said what they really thought about Jake's third grade teachers. They would hang out, play recklessly at the parks in Ashland, then indulge in ice cream that would most definitely ruin Jake's appetite for dinner. Those were the days when Alec was Jake's best friend. His only friend.

Except for Lucas. Jake didn't want to remember his short-lived friendship with Lucas. Those memories haunted him as much as they haunted Alec, and Jake hated Lucas for making Alec into what he had become, a miserable TV Bible preacher who lied about his own joy.

It was true, Alec could heal people. Jake had firsthand experience with it when bullies left Jake with deep razor-blade cuts all over his face. Jake was eight, going on nine, and the bullies were much older, friends of Lucas. Alec held Jake for hours on that awful day, and the deep slice that had run from eyebrow to chin had healed without leaving a scar, or nerve or muscle damage. Alec was a god, a mutant with special powers, a superhero.

Except that he wasn't. How could a guy with the ability to heal himself and others be so freaking terrified? Of everything?

According to Alec's own account, he had healed former band mates Mark and Paddy too. But the claims were never proven, and Alec didn't own it. Alec once warned Jake not to show fear with tears or by cowering. It attracted the bullies, he said. It was exactly what Alec was now doing. He was a national bully magnet, and Jake hated Alec for it. To his core.

Now, Jake was in sixth grade in an upscale middle school, with no friends because he was the new kid. Kids here were too smart to believe in miracles and black magic. This was Los Angeles. It was Hollywood. Everyone knew how movie magic worked. The last thing they were going to believe was some washed-up former rock wannabe who now claimed he was a vessel for the healing power of God.

"He's trying," Belinda said. She parked in front of the school, where Jake watched other kids filter through the front gates. He didn't move to step out and join them. "Hey, you're going to be late."

Jake toughened up and reached for the door handle until his mom held him back. He gave her an annoyed glance even though he secretly wished that she had changed her mind; that he could stay home and zone out with some mindless video game. "I can talk to your teachers if kids are giving you trouble—"

"—Stop it, Mom. You'll make it worse."

"I won't—"

"—I don't even want to be here! They think he's fake. They call me Jesus boy!" He shut up after letting that slip.

Belinda nursed a headache. She seemed to have them often now. She moved on to give him more awful information. "We have a meeting with Father Grant later—"

"—What?—"

"—So be prepared."

"I'm not going back to religious fucking boot camp—"

"—Watch your mouth—"

"—So they can brainwash me to be one of the freaks."

"Jake—"

"—Alec's a freak, Mom. He didn't used to be."

His mother released a slow exhale before she told him how it was going to be. No excuses, no debates. "You will find me here after school, at this very spot. Understand?"

Jake stuffed his earbuds back in and pushed his way out the door. He kept his gaze down and headed toward the entrance. No eye contact and maybe no one would pick on him. He glanced back to find mom still at the curb. Guilt settled in the pit of his stomach. She was crying.

John David burst out of the door of Reverend Adonis's cabin. He bounded down the steps of a porch that extended across the front face of the building, and he felt the eyes of Reverend Adonis following him until he heard the door click closed. He headed for the stables.

Lucas and Maggie were laughing as they shoveled shit and spread hay. "Maggie. Go see Hannah." She stared with wide eyes, the kind that silently begged for forgiveness for something she wasn't sure she was guilty of. "Now."

Maggie set the pitchfork aside and left her father and Lucas alone. John David glanced over his shoulder to make sure she was headed in the right direction. Then he turned back to Lucas.

"We were discussing parables—"

"—Jonas wants to see you—"

"—Why?"

The click of an AR-15's safety came from behind. It made John David flinch. He checked over his shoulder, found temple brothers Zachary and Todd stepping in as back up. Zachary's Oracle was pointed at the ground, his finger tapping the trigger. Adonis must have told them. "Put the shovel down."

Lucas did with a slow and cautious move. He stepped ahead of John David who followed with Zachary and Todd trailing behind. When they reached the door to Adonis's cabin, John David reached ahead of Lucas and knocked. Adonis pulled it open and ushered Lucas and John David in. He shut the door in Zachary and Todd's faces.

Bless Me Father

"WOULD YOU BELIEVE ME IF I TOLD YOU THAT THE Lord Jesus Christ accepts you for who you are at this very moment?" Silence answered Josiah Light. He looked out at the packed venue, not an empty seat to be found. He waited for the reverent moment to sink in before he continued.

"God knows that we are sinners. He knows that we have tried and that we have failed to live to our highest potential, to live up to His lofty standards. We have failed, and still He accepts us. And I can see it, so many of you looking back at me with that hint of doubt in your eyes because you want it to be true, but you can't imagine it. You can't imagine taking back the husband or the wife who might have cheated on you. You can't imagine an employer taking you back after a major mistake, or a teacher accepting homework that you failed to put effort into. Life doesn't let us skate through with no repercussion for our choices, so why would our good lord and savior?"

The Reverend Light took a moment to flash his patented grin before he laid out the awful truth. "He wouldn't. He doesn't. That's what life is, our opportunity to keep trying. And God wants us to succeed, but He only accepts us for what we are when He sees us take steps to show Him that we are trying to do better."

Josiah cast his glance toward the wings of the stage. Alec was pacing again. He looked miserable, and Josiah wished that the man would pull that self-absorbed head out of his own ass and listen to his sermon. Just once. Josiah also realized that Alec was the reason for the Life Festival's sold out tour. Peddling faith was a thankless job. People were more prone to doubt, except when flat-out miracles were offered.

The reverend easily pondered these things while continuing to address his audience. He caught Cleo arriving beside Alec. Now there was a reason to seek God's forgiveness, and Alec should be doing just that. Josiah reminded himself how much he loved his wife every time Cleo was near. He watched Cleo give Alec her brief routine pep talk before she handed him a guitar. It was also Josiah's cue.

"I know I'm not the main attraction tonight. Heck, I'm not sure Alec is the main attraction. Isn't that right, Cleo?" He turned to the wings and grinned as Cleo stepped out just enough to be seen. The crowd whooped and laughed, and Cleo played along.

"I'm nothing but net, hon. A flawless swoosh!"

A not-so-holy catcall came from somewhere near the back, and Josiah singled it out by pointing in its direction. "I expect you, sir, to donate generously to our cause." More laughter.

Alec and Cleo stepped onto the stage. When the crowd saw Alec holding the acoustic, their applause grew. "You two are going to lead us with a hymn?"

Cleo stepped up to a mic waiting for her. "Feel free to sing along, hon."

Alec adjusted the acoustic's strap over his shoulder and leaned in. "Amazing Grace."

"Ladies and gentlemen, Alec Lowell. Cleo LeCroix." The lights dimmed to a single spotlight on the two, and Josiah Light retreated from the stage.

Cleo's vocal rendition was spiced honey, while Alec proved to be not much of a singer. He was fine, Josiah supposed, but his talent resided in his fingers. They traded verses, and while Cleo brought a passionate and soulful element to the lyrics, Alec's more fragile singing brought vulnerability.

Amazing Grace, how sweet the sound, Cleo sang before she belted out the second half, *that saved a wretch like me.*

Alec followed. *I once was lost, but now I'm found. Was blind, but now I see.* The audience listened, enthralled. The rendition was perfect. Josiah Light fancied himself a marketing genius even though he increasingly felt that taking Alec on as his main attraction was becoming more of a headache that it was worth. He hadn't originally felt this way. An atheist finds God after being the victim of a satanic cult because God chooses him to be a healer? Astounding. Whether it was true or not, the people wanted to be healed. Seats were filled, donations flowed in, and the people… The people testified. They believed, many of them did, that Alec's touch had improved their conditions or had flat out healed them. Whether true or not, they believed.

If only Alec believed in himself as much as the people believed in him. That was Josiah's problem with the man. The self-loathing, alcoholic adulterer was headed for a mental breakdown and a public scandal if he didn't change his ways. Josiah feared that the church he dedicated his entire life to would go down with him. Alec Lowell had once been an asset. He was quickly becoming a liability.

They finished the hymn. The audience cheered. The lights came up. Josiah exercised his jaw with a quick set of stretches before he found his perfect smile and stepped back out on the stage. He grabbed his microphone and met camera two with a wink. "Thank you, Cleo." Cleo gave the crowd a wave before she bolstered Alec with a hug. She left the stage. "They're all yours, Alec." Josiah took Alec's guitar and left the stage too.

He waited in the wings as a stagehand delivered a stool for Alec to sit on. He waited and listened and prayed that Alec would continue to hold it together.

And Alec did.

"How is everyone doing tonight?" Alec was met with whistles and cheers and garbled responses that were meant to mean that things were good. "That's good. That's good. Glad to hear it. That's the attitude we should all have. Every day, right? Every day. And I'll admit it. I myself find it hard to wake up some mornings and find my faith. I never believed. I grew up with the wrong teachers, seriously broken mentors, and I had no reason to believe that God, if there was a God, cared. I'm still haunted by…things that happened. That fear, it never completely goes away, and it undermines my faith."

Alec looked out and, with a tremble in his voice, he pulled the crowd in. "But then I show up here, and all of you people who believe in me; the ignorant former atheist death metal poster child for the devil—you come here believing in me, and it restores my faith." He paused then leaned close to the microphone. "So let's do this." He raised his hands like a conjuring wizard. The crowd went wild.

Reverend Adonis pointed the remote and turned off his Ultra HDTV flat screen. He turned to Lucas, who sat in the center of his fine leather couch, and he dropped a book in Lucas's lap. Alec's face leered from the cover.

"Have you heard of him?" Adonis asked, and Lucas remained silent. "Turn to page 172, near the middle." Lucas opened to the page. A photograph stared back at him, a soft-focus picture of a scrawny teen with a lopsided smile. He held up a fish on a hook with his crippled left hand.

"I seek salvation—"

"—Salvation from murder, or from courting Satan? *Do not I hate them, Oh Lord, that hate Thee? Nay, I count them mine enemies—*"

"*—Let the wicked forsake his way. Let him return to the Lord seeking mercy. He will be pardoned—*"

Adonis took the book and struck Lucas across the face with it. He shut down Lucas's biblical comeback without missing a beat. "Your knowledge of verse does not make you a repentant soul." He leaned closer. The faint scent of freshly washed skin filled Lucas's nostrils. "Did you do the things this man claims?"

Lucas massaged an ache in his jaw and remained silent. It earned him a shove from behind by John David. "Answer the question—"

"—You shut your mouth," Adonis said. John David backed down, ever the obedient soldier. "You're the one who brought him here! The devil's advocate. In my refuge!"

"Yes, sir."

Adonis settled down. He tried again. "Tell me."

When Lucas shrugged, Adonis took him by the wrist, the left one. Lucas yanked free with a violence that made Adonis back off. The urge to kill the man was there. He could do it if he had a knife or a gun in his possession, if John David wasn't in the room, because John David was always armed. He could stab Jonas in the throat or gut him like that fish on its hook in the photo.

But that wasn't who Lucas was anymore. No, he was seeking forgiveness for his sins. As Lucas held his left hand to his chest like something delicate and precious, Adonis persisted. "I'm confused. That photo is of you; Lucas the kid with the clawed left hand—"

"—Guess it's not me then."

"There are no lies here," John David said. Reverend Adonis stared him back into silence.

"Did you try to kill this man? In the name of Satan—"

"—I'll leave. I won't come back. I can disappear—"

"—What about this other man at the Life Festival? This Dr. Carver?"

"He wanted Alec dead. I stopped it."

Adonis shook his head. It was agonizing. Lucas found himself trying to justify his past, something he'd never felt the need to do. "I was misled. I was wrong. I seek forgiveness."

"My forgiveness? Hmmm." The reverend seemed amused by the plea, as Lucas felt his dark past tugging at him. His knowledge of the devil's black magic had made him capable of controlling people once, of making them sink to their knees. Taking possession of a thing that had changed the course of a person's life was the key. With Alec, it had been a bullet, *the bullet* that had made him famous. Alec had suffered. He could do it to Adonis if he could find a tangible thing that had enough significance to him. It was magic akin to voodoo to gain power over your victim.

Lucas glanced about the room for something, anything that might hold that kind of personal significance. Nothing stood out. Except for a dog's bed. *Oh, Saint was something special. Such a good dog. God, it was perfect.*

Stop it, he thought. *You're here to find the good in yourself, to lift your soul to perfection.* It was a momentous goal, one that he could never achieve. Not now.

Adonis bent down in a moment that seemed like outreach. "Do you believe him? Is his…gift…a sign?"

"You don't?"

Adonis breathed words into Lucas's ear. "Why would God choose such a dark and divisive soul over someone like me?"

Not what Lucas had expected. "I just…" A quiver in his voice surprised him and he cursed softly because of it. He tried again. "He saved me. I'm not sure he knows, but he did. I'm alive, and now I'm seeking guidance and redemption from you."

Adonis studied Lucas for an agonizingly long stretch before he rose and paced. John David broke the silence. "If I had known any of this, sir? I wouldn't have brought him here."

Adonis made a motion that suggested John David should hold his tongue when a mirror caught his attention. Or, more accurately, his own reflection caught his attention. If there was one thing Lucas learned during his stay at the temple, it was that Reverend Jonas Adonis was a vain man.

Adonis straightened his posture and smoothed down his clothes. He picked up on his thoughts. "Give me your hand." Lucas allowed it. Adonis caressed it from palm to wrist, his fingers brushing across the old scar there.

"We lay dying in the woods," Lucas said. "Both of us bleeding out. He took it, and he held it. And I passed out. I don't know for how long."

"So he's the Second Coming? He rose from the ashes that you created, and the Day of Judgment is nigh?"

"I don't—"

"—Get on your feet." Lucas stared up, not sure what was happening, when Adonis yanked him up by the collar. "On your feet!" Vehement words left a fine spray of spittle over Lucas's face. "Those who live and speak contrary to His doctrine serve NOT our Lord! They deceive the simple! FLESH AND BLOOD cannot inherit the kingdom of God! Neither does corruption inherit incorruption, FOR THE CORRUPTED ONE WILL PUT ON THE GUISE OF INCORRUPTION, THE MORTAL ONE THE GUISE OF IMMORTALITY! DO YOU UNDERSTAND!"

He truly didn't, but the mishmash of verse succeeded in making Lucas feel incompetent and small. "I seek forgiveness," he managed to say. "And refuge."

"Not here. Not from me." With that, Adonis signaled John David to take over.

John David took Lucas by the arm, as Lucas struggled and tried to plead his case. "Coming here changed me! I have no place to go. I will do anything to stay! For you—"

"—Would you kill for me?"

Lucas wasn't sure he had heard the question right. When he caught John David giving the slightest shake of his head in disapproval, he thought that it must have been a test. "No."

"Pity. Abraham was prepared to kill his own son on God's command."

Lucas had lost. There was nothing he could say that Reverend Adonis wouldn't counter.

Adonis continued. "You want the graces that accompany membership to my church? Prove your spiritual worth." He gave John David one final signal before John David led Lucas away.

Word had spread of Lucas's sins. The entire commune had stopped their activities in order to witness the exile. They watched from their safe distances as John David led the way to the men's quarters, Zachary taking the rear. *Like Jesus walking to his crucifixion*, Lucas thought.

In all honesty, Lucas didn't care what they thought. Most of them avoided him like the kids at school had done when he was under the care of his staunchly religious foster parents. Lucas knew their names: Todd, Hector, the secret lesbians Angela and Jonie, Hannah. They avoided him, and Lucas accepted it. He had actually preferred it.

Then he caught sight of Maggie. She watched from behind Hannah, the woman in charge of running the women's dorms. Hannah assigned duties and chores and made certain that those assignments were met. She was also the woman that John David would have been fucking if temple law had allowed it. Lucas was indifferent about Hannah, but the confusion and disappointment on Maggie's face was going to haunt him. He was beginning to understand how it felt to lose an actual friend. The only other relationship that had come close to being a friendship had been with Alec's son Jake. And that was truly sad.

They reached the men's dormitories where Zachary shoved Lucas through the door. The rooms inside were smaller than college rooms, more in keeping with the width of prison cells, but it was Lucas's private space and it had given him comfort. "Pack your things," John David said.

The closet had room for a week's worth of clothes at best, and still it looked empty. Lucas took a worn, half-filled back-pack off a hanger and began stuffing the other few items he had into it. The items still inside were from his past, things that he should have gotten rid of. A chalice, the bullet from Alec's crucifixion, lighter fluid, and a knife. It was wrong to still have them. Especially here. Zachary and John David whispered to each other before Zachary took his leave. Lucas slowed his pace.

"If you did anything to my daughter—"

"—She's not your daughter," Lucas said. "She's one of God's children—"

John David pulled his weapon so fast that Lucas dropped the pack. He kept still, hands raised. "She was the only one who took time to know me."

"What else!"

"Nothing else! She took the time. You raised her right." Lucas picked up the pack. He tried his best to pretend the gun wasn't still aimed at him, and he continued to gather his belongings. "She finds me, not the other way around. She shares things."

"Shares what?"

"Things about her mother."

Lucas glanced up. John David had turned the weapon down. "She shouldn't have said anything."

Lucas finished packing. John David marched him back outside where they met again with Zachary and Todd. Like sheepdogs, the three of them herded Lucas toward an extended-cab V6 truck parked at the gate, the same vehicle that John David had used to shuttle Lucas from Los Angeles to this place. John David ordered Lucas into the front seat, and when Zachary and Todd opened a door to climb into the back, John David intervened.

"I brought him here. It's my responsibility."

Zachary tried to remind John David that God would not hold him accountable, and Lucas let his tongue slip. "Because God forgives everyone. Right, Zach?"

"You can go to hell," Zachary said. The sentiment made Lucas snicker. There was never a doubt that hell would be his final destination. Maybe he would hasten his own delivery once John David turned him over to the authorities. Suicide. Just like Maggie's mother. Then the world would be a better place.

Zachary initiated a quick bro hug with John David, and Lucas mused about suggesting how gay they looked just to piss them off. Homosexuality was one of those sins after all. All things considered, Lucas should have realized that his stay here would be short lived. His satanic education taught him that sexual freedoms didn't hurt anyone as long as it wasn't forced or coerced. But here, God could forgive anyone, just not Lucas or sexually creative individuals.

Lucas glanced past the bromance toward Maggie again. Saint had found her. When she saw Lucas catch sight of her, she managed a wave. He looked away, and John David found his place behind the wheel.

"This place was good for me," Lucas said after a long drive in silence. Scenery whizzed past his window, unpopulated, rocky terrain with occasional thick patches of pine. There was no civilization in sight. "Where are you taking me?"

John David glanced at him. He pulled to the side of the road then hung his head over the wheel. Lucas tried the door. Locked. "I wanted to help you, Lucas. I still do, but…" He trailed off.

"The confession box wasn't good enough—"

"Shut your mouth!" John David reined in his frustration with a soft fist pound against his steering wheel. "I brought you here. I trusted you."

"How do I prove my spiritual worth," Lucas said. "How do I do that?"

John David didn't give him an answer. Instead… "I'm losing my faith in Reverend Adonis."

Lucas scoffed. He leaned in with his opinion. "I understand why you hang on his every word. He's passionate. He's good at it. But he preaches about the global conspiracy and the satanic agenda feeding it while he soaks it up. If he's so afraid of the evils of the outside world, why does he have satellite TV? And Internet?"

"He hates it," John David said. "He has to stay connected so that we can be prepared."

"For an apocalypse? Do you believe that?"

"Don't you?"

Lucas studied the amazed expression on John David's face. He supposed that this man, who had explored foreign countries torn apart by civil wars and who had been unable to prevent his own wife's suicide, had every reason to expect a coming apocalypse. But Lucas grew from a different experience. The devil's attempt to take over the world was disorganized at best, and Lucas was going to hell anyway. "It doesn't matter," Lucas said with a shrug. "I have no spiritual worth."

John David stared Lucas down. "My daughter—"

"—Seems like a reason to question the apocalypse." More uncomfortable silence. Lucas wanted it to be over, so he waved at the gun holstered at John David's hip. "Taking me to the police will cause you problems. They'll ask who you are, where you're from, how you know me, all the shit that will lead them to your safe haven that's supposed to be off the grid. Make it easy on yourself. Shoot me in the head. Dump me out there somewhere.

Then go hide from the end of the world like you're not already a victim of it."

John David pulled the pistol and aimed. Lucas resigned himself to his fitting end. The power latch unlocked. "Get out," John David said.

Lucas obliged, fully expecting John David to step out with him. He didn't. "Your will is strong, Lucas. I knew it when we first met. Maybe you have a purpose. You want to save yourself? Prove your spiritual worth? Save someone else."

John David reached across the seat, tossed Lucas his pack, and pulled the door shut. He put the truck in gear and made a U-turn in the opposite direction before he drove out of sight. Lucas continued to peer down the road, not sure what had just happened, not sure why he was still alive. He took in the two narrow lanes and surrounding wilderness. Some people, sophisticated city types, might have panicked. But not Lucas. He had survived in the middle of nowhere for half of his life.

He followed the highway for a short time, then wondered if John David might alert the authorities anyway, so he turned off into increasing wilderness that was better suited for his thoughts. He hadn't been worthy of this freedom and—while he should have been thankful, while he should have found a spot to drop to his knees and praise God for the second chance—he was too caught up in trying to understand why.

Your will is strong. Prove your worth. Save someone else.

He was flexing his left hand again. Even he realized that he did it too often, so he forced himself to stop. He happened across a trail marker that led to a path along a steady incline. It was a hiker's trail, but the time of year and the fact that it was a Wednesday made Lucas feel comfortable enough to take it without risk of running into people. He blew on his hands. They were getting cold as afternoon shadows grew long and the early autumn chill set in. He enjoyed the solitude. Then the mumble of conversation and the sudden jag of a woman's laugh alerted him to what was ahead.

Lucas rounded the bend to find a trio of hikers with backpacks and mountain bikes. They were about his age, in their early twenties. They snacked on granola and fruit, and when they looked up to see Lucas, they greeted him like a friend. "Hey there," said the girl with the tie-dyed headband that kept her hair out of her face. The other one had hair cropped short with a fade along the sides. The guy had a thick beard and an equally thick mane of hair that he kept together in a French braid down the center of his back. The one with the military cut said hi as well, while the guy gave a quick nod of acknowledgement with his mouth full of toasted oats and nuts.

Lucas kept walking until he heard a shout. It was the guy. "You heading for the lake?" Lucas could have ignored the question, kept walking, but this could be construed as suspicious behavior. He tried his best to seem nonchalant.

"Yeah," he said.

"Alone? At this time of day?"

Mind your own business, Lucas thought. He caught himself before he said it. "I'll be alright." He added a smile.

"That's a light-looking pack. Are you camping out?" The guy's questions were getting too specific, so Lucas turned and kept walking. He heard whispers that he tried to shut out, but he couldn't shut out the sound of approaching feet. He turned back, ready to defend himself. The one approaching him, the girl with the tie-dyed headband, stopped short. She held out their bag full of trail mix and an orange.

Without a word, she waited for him to take it. When he didn't, she introduced herself. "I'm Alice. That's Charlie and Jo." The other two waved. "We're done for the day. And, you know, sharing is caring." She shrugged with a genuine smile. Lucas took the offer and bowed his head.

"Dude, do you have a bedroll, or anything in that pack?" The guy's question was stupid, because Lucas's backpack was obviously too small for that kind of thing. Before Lucas could answer, Jo or Charlie, because he had no idea who was who, pulled a picnic blanket off the rack of one of the bikes and handed it over.

Lucas thanked them for their charity then watched them hop on their bikes and be on their way. "Stay safe, man," the guy shouted, and they were gone.

Lucas stood there, perplexed. His arms were loaded with warmth and sustenance from complete strangers, and he wasn't sure why. He supposed the strangers had felt sorry for him, but having them offer friendship simply for the sake of offering friendship was something he had never experienced, except for Maggie on that first night at the Los Angeles mission. She had been the first. These strangers were the second. John David had been cautious, and Reverend Adonis had been wary.

The trail took a downward turn. Lucas found a quiet lake by dusk. He cleared a patch of ground, then dug away the grass with a compact shovel from his pack. He laid out a ring of stones and scavenged for twigs and dry wood. Darkness fell before he got the fire started. He lit the kindling with a cigarette lighter and rubbed his hands over the fire's warmth. He rummaged through his pack for his knife and the chalice, rubbed his finger over the dent in the chalice left by a bullet. Alec's bandmate Mark had put it there. He dipped it in the lake for a drink, and he peeled the orange with the knife.

It was going to be a cold night. Lucas could feel it in his bones. He draped the picnic blanket over his shoulders and allowed the heat of the fire to radiate through him. He munched on granola, then decided to save it for the morning, and he marveled at the stars in the crisp, clear sky. It may have been cold, but the view was heaven.

Lucas prayed for forgiveness without expecting God to grant it. He prayed for guidance. His thoughts drifted to John David's suggestion. *Prove your spiritual worth. Save someone else,* and as Reverend Adonis's vile condemnation of Alec nagged him at the back of his mind, he began to realize. The Black Book prophecies of the New Church of Satan had been wrong. No, misinterpreted was a better way to put it. The more Lucas mulled it over, the more he understood. He knew exactly who needed to be saved.

"Hey! Jesus boy! Catch!" An apple took flight over the chasm between lunch tables. It bounced onto Jake's tray and knocked over his chocolate milk. Jake scrambled to get up before the spill reached his lap. He failed. He cursed. Laughter came from the bully and his friends. "I said catch it, not wear it!"

"Fuck you, shithead." Alec's contribution to Jake's upbringing served the moment, and the bully and his friends surrounded Jake.

"What did you call me?"

"Shithead." Jake followed up with a shove. The bully shoved back and the fight began.

They wound up in the principal's office after cafeteria monitors broke the two apart, but not before Jake got a good swing at the bully's face. The bully's eye looked rosy and puffed up while they sat on the office benches and waited.

The kid grumbled another taunt at Jake in his misery. "Your dad is lame."

"You don't know my dad," Jake said back. He regretted it, because—

"—Because your mom's a slut. So sad, Jesus boy."

"She's a nurse. She helps save people."

The bully hesitated from a comeback, but he found one. "All the people who stay sick because your dad is a fake?"

"At least he's not boring like your dad—"

"—My dad's a lawyer! He sues people—"

"—He should sue your mom for giving birth to you."

The bully was on his feet, and Jake cringed as he waited for a fatal blow. He remembered a time when Alec told him not to cry because it was a beacon for bullies. Now that he was older, he understood that some bullies showed up whether you cried or not. At least getting beat up because of a good taunt had some satisfaction to it. Jake shut his eyes, ready for the hit.

A door opened and Principal Vasquez stepped out. "Sit down, Reuben!"

Reuben slumped back onto his bench. Then the talk came, the rehash of what had happened, the accounts that had come from cafeteria aides and from other students that had left Principal Vasquez with a wealth of inaccurate and misleading information. It wasn't the first time Jake had gone through this scenario, and he was sure it wouldn't be the last.

Principal Vasquez droned on about the importance of supporting each other and how there was zero tolerance for this behavior. Both kids would be punished. Their parents were notified and a conference would be held once they arrived. Until then, Jake and Reuben would have to sit across from each other and stare. Vasquez said that he didn't want to hear a word from either of them and that he was leaving his door open. And Jake and the bully sat. And they stared.

"Are you as fucked up as they say you are?" Reuben finally asked in the softest voice possible. Jake stared in a different direction. He wasn't fucked up, although a full year of therapy with a licensed mental health counselor didn't encourage anyone to think differently. Reuben persisted. "Can you heal people too? Because you're the freaking Son of God and everything?"

Jake refused to take the bait. After an agonizing half hour of whispered taunts, Reuben's mother showed up. The bully's demeanor changed as soon as he spotted her approach. He covered his swollen eye and managed tears on cue. "Oh my God," the woman said as she bent down for a better look at the damage. Her hair and her style were high-class privileged. She turned to Jake. "Did you do this?" Jake sat straight, intimidated by her glare.

He was saved by his mom.

"Jake, are you okay?" Belinda saw the briefest hopeful expression on Jake's face as she approached. Then she was met by the high-strung, impeccably dressed woman who must have been the other boy's mom.

"Look what your kid did." Belinda noted the bigger kid's bruised face, and for a moment she expected she should have been proud. But the kid's mother didn't give Belinda time to enjoy it. She was rabid. "What kind of parent are you? I hope you're ready to cover his medical expenses." Belinda bent down to take a look at the boy's face. It only made the mother twice as protective. "Don't get near my son—"

"—I'm a nurse," Belinda said. "A little ice, and he'll be—"

The woman pulled Belinda back by the arm. She was fortunate, because if the principal hadn't stepped out, Belinda might have given the woman a black eye to match her son's.

"Ladies, please. We can talk about this in my office."

"Don't you have a nurse on duty? He should have ice on it." The principal gave Belinda an aggravated look. He called out to one of the secretaries down the hall to get Reuben some ice before he explained that a school nurse was only available three times a week due to budget cuts. Belinda crossed her arms at this. She noted that Reuben's mom did too.

"You're a nurse?" The woman softened, although her stance remained defiant.

Belinda took the high road and held out her hand. "I'm sorry this happened. I'm sure we can settle it." She glanced at Jake. That hopeful expression he had when she arrived was gone.

Principal Vasquez held a private conference with Belinda and Reuben's mother. He ran down the details of the fight. Reuben's mother got defensive. "Of course he's going to react. We don't use that language in our house." Belinda seriously doubted it, but she promised to have Jake apologize. She hoped that she could convince Jake to actually do it, because as she pieced together what happened, it was easy to determine that Reuben was the problem. Jake had stood up for himself. Belinda knew her kid. Jake hadn't lashed out because of a deeper problem like Vasquez subtly tried to suggest.

Principal Vasquez was aware of Jake's past trauma and had made his concerns clear. Jake's presence would be nothing but a headache for him and his school. This wasn't the first time that Belinda was called in. The situations were escalating, and this time the bully ended up bruised.

Vasquez called the boys into his office. They were forced to apologize to each other. Jake glared at Belinda while saying he was sorry. He hated her. She knew that. But she was the parent. She had always been the one to discipline Jake. She hated Alec for that, probably as much as Jake hated her at that moment. Then Vasquez laid out the school's no-tolerance rules for fighting. It consisted of lunchtime detention for the rest of the week: lunch in the study hall, no recess.

They were dismissed. Reuben's mother took her son out of school for the rest of the day. Principal Vasquez asked Belinda to stay behind. He asked Jake to wait in the hall. "He's not doing well," Vasquez said after Jake was vanquished back to the bench. "He's a smart kid. But he's not making friends. He's miserable here, Mrs. Lowell."

"No," she said. "You're not going to convince me to pull him out to be home schooled."

"No one would think you were a bad parent because of it—"

"—He needs social interaction. I can't keep him in isolation forever."

"Mrs. Lowell—"

"—Every time this happens it's because he was provoked. And instead of focusing on them, you focus on him."

"He doesn't try to fit in."

"He shouldn't have to! Fitting in? What kind of argument is that?"

"You're missing my point," Vasquez said with equivalent exasperation. "Kids who don't try to fit in somehow, in some way? They're the kids who become loners—"

"—He's a threat? Has he done anything to make you think he's that kid capable of that kind of terror?"

"Mrs. Lowell—"

"—He watched his father's torture. He was forced to witness that. It traumatized him. And you think that makes him the threat?"

"I'm saying that kids can be cruel. Your husband is a public figure, and yes, this school has had its share of kids with well-known parents. But Alec's notoriety is different. There are people who are religious and there are people who aren't. The kids pick up on the divisive nature of it. Especially here."

Belinda understood where the principal was coming from. She stood her ground anyway. After he threw up his arms and accepted her decision, Belinda left. She took Jake by the hand and led him away until he protested over the hand-holding part and yanked free. She signed Jake out of school for the afternoon, and they walked to the car in silence.

"I don't fit in, Mom," Jake said once they reached the car. Belinda's heart sank. He must have heard every detail of her conversation with Vasquez.

"Nobody thinks they fit in at your age. It's okay to feel that way."

"Reuben fits in."

"No, he doesn't. If he did, he wouldn't find it necessary to pick on someone small like you."

Jake was contemplative for a moment, but Belinda could see in his expression that he was still unsettled. "If you know it was him, why did you make me apologize?"

"Sometimes that's what you have to do. It makes you the bigger man."

"He's way bigger than me, Mom."

"You know what I mean." And she knew that he did. He shrugged in dissatisfaction before Belinda tried to show him the bright side. "At least you're out for the rest of the day. Come on, we'll get In 'n' Out then head to see Father Grant—"

"—What? No!" Jake had apparently forgotten about their meeting.

"We talked about this."

"Can't I skip it?"

"You're going. Get in the car." And like that, Belinda was the mean parent again. Jake threw open the door and slammed it once he got in.

Belinda crushed her fingers against her eyes. She had spent her morning tending to the homeless at a shelter that benefited from charitable donations from Josiah Light's Foundation. Reverend Light paid a team of health care professionals to administer basic services, and she visited several locations weekly. The phone call from Jake's school had put an abrupt end to that, and the drive was forty-five minutes with heavy midday traffic. No time for lunch, and then the confrontation with the bully Reuben's mom left Belinda hungry, jaded, and exhausted. The window of opportunity to be the comforting, best-friend parent had closed.

They drove in silence to the burger place. A single cheese with fries quelled a gurgle in Belinda's stomach, but it was too late. She was left with a mild headache, and Jake refused to offer much conversation while they ate. *He gets it from Alec*, Belinda thought. *All of his grumpy moodiness comes from Alec regardless of what that terrorist punk Lucas had done.*

When they were done, Belinda drove Jake to a small Catholic ministry that was well reviewed on the Internet. Father Grant led a youth group for middle and high school age kids who had suffered from traumatic experiences. Belinda chose it because it didn't have the kind of flash and notoriety that the Reverend Light's church had. She wanted to give Jake some anonymity from being Alec's son, and Father Grant understood. The group explored team-building exercises meant to instill trust in kids whose trust had been abused. They also studied the Bible and discussed how its lessons related to everyday problems.

Jake was encouraged to participate, but he wasn't forced, and Belinda was happy to hear from Father Grant that Jake was, in fact, involved. "Your son has a good head on his shoulders. He's skeptical of the idea of God, and I get that, but he's morally sound. You're doing the right thing by bringing him here." It's what Belinda needed to hear, and she squeezed the priest's outstretched hands in thanks.

"I will leave him in your hands, then." She glanced at Jake in the meeting hall, where he helped set up chairs with other kids, and she breathed. Everything was going to be fine.

Except it wasn't.

Rorie, a high school freshman three years older, bumped into Jake from behind with orders. "Hustle it up, Noob. The chairs go in a circle." Her smile offset her bossiness. The two were actually friends, in spite of the age difference and in spite of her retro punk style that made other parents uncomfortable. They often whispered about what a shame it was for Rorie to be heading down the wrong path; Jake had overheard a conversation or two. His own mom never said a word, and therefore Jake and Rorie had become friends; not best friends, but two damaged souls who gravitated to each other whenever they were at a meeting. They had similar tastes in music, although Jake never shared who his father was. He didn't need that kind of attention.

Rorie's attitude wasn't serious, but Jake pushed past her because he wasn't in the mood. "You okay?" She followed and took his chair before she set it down among the circle of others. When Jake didn't say anything, she shadowed him back to the stack and handed him two more. Other kids were setting up tables and putting out snacks under the supervision of other adults, and there was a general aura of good times to come, but not for Jake. Rorie was the only one who kept by his side.

She was a tall girl, too skinny to be considered healthy, with hair dyed neon red at the tips and evidence of face piercings that she was discreet enough to remove before meetings. Jake remembered that she had slipped once and left a nose ring in place until Father Grant subtly gave her a look and wiped at an imaginary sniffle. Rorie had removed it without a word. That was the thing about Father Grant. His discipline was quiet, and everyone respected him for it. Maybe it was because he was young for a priest. He was maybe thirty, at least close to Alec's age.

Rorie had singled Jake out as a comrade in arms when she had noticed the scar along Jake's palm, put there by Lucas. Jake wished it would fade like the one on his face had. He and Lucas had made a pact, becoming blood bound brothers. The scar was the nasty remnant of that relationship. "Where'd you get it?" Rorie asked when she had first seen it. He refused to tell her, and she had been kind enough to let it be. Jake supposed that Rorie could relate because of the scars on her own arms. She cut herself when she was feeling bad about…well, herself, and she had probably assumed that Jake did too. It was a thing she had talked about during circle time.

But Jake never talked about the scar. He barely talked about Alec, and never by name. If anyone besides Father Grant knew who Jake's father was, they never mentioned it, and Jake was fine with that. Having Alec as a dad was awkward. Even Alec hated the expectation that came with being who he was. Jake could tell.

He watched his mother leave before Father Grant clapped his hands together and headed for the chairs. "Alright. Circle of Terror time!" He called it that because everyone was terrified of sharing their faults, flaws, and fears. Other kids filtered over, and Rorie took her opportunity to whisper to Jake.

"Are you going to spill what's bothering you?"

"I got called Jesus boy at school."

Rorie screwed up her face and shrugged. "I've been called worse." They sat down together and, as the other kids took their seats, she whispered. "You don't have to tell anyone."

"Tell anyone what?"

"About coming here. That's why you got called Jesus boy."

Jake didn't elaborate, as Father Grant found the last remaining chair in the circle. He held out his hands for each teenager beside him to take. Hands came together to form a circuit. Heads bowed, and Father Grant led them in prayer. "Lord, grant me the serenity to accept the things I cannot change, the courage to change the things that I can and?" He waited for the rest of them to fill in the popular quote.

They came through with a shout. "The wisdom to know the difference!"

He broke from the hand holding to clap one more time. "Who wants to go first?" There were no takers, so Father Grant made a choice. "Jake? We haven't heard from you in a while. How are you adjusting in school? Are there good days? Bad? Or, as my good friend and arch nemesis Rabbi Shulman might say, maybe they're meh." There were a few chuckles, but not from Jake. Father Grant persisted. "There is no judgment here."

Jake stayed silent hoping that no one noticed the slight tremble running through him. Rorie nudged him. "Come on, Jesus boy. How did you get your name—"

"—Shut up—"

"—Rorie." Father Grant gave her the silent warning glare. It didn't help Jake's distaste from being singled out, but he stood. It was the rule. The speaker was supposed to stand when he or she had the floor.

"He called me a name. And I hit him."

"Alriiight," a kid said at the other side of the circle. It was Mason.

"Did it make you feel better?" Father Grant asked, ignoring the approval of Mason.

It really did. But that's not what Father Grant wanted to hear, so Jake lowered his gaze and lied. "No."

"Are you sure?" Jake looked back up. He caught Father Grant giving him a smile. "Come on, Jake. Of course it did. I've gotten to know you. All of us here, we've gotten to know you. I'd bet that every one of us believes that this bully deserved it. Unfortunately, I'm a man of the cloth, so making wagers on schoolyard fights isn't an acceptable thing for me to do." Grant was met with hesitant laughter, and Jake was relieved.

Grant wasn't finished. "But that's our cross to bear. Our burden, as Christians, is to strive to be the best possible incarnation of ourselves that we can be no matter how good it feels to be human. Jesus wouldn't hit the bully. He would hug the bully—"

"—Jesus is a joke." Jake's face went hot as Father Grant stared him down for the outburst. It angered Jake to be singled out over good Christian behavior. Jake didn't care about good

Christian behavior. He never did anything wrong, but here he was among a bunch of troubled kids who also didn't want to be here, being made an example of. He knew he should have kept his mouth shut at that point, but frustration fueled his tongue. "He doesn't care. He's not even real."

Father Grant gave a slight shake of the head. "Jake, you are a hard nut to crack. And I'm surprised that you, of all people, would feel that way."

Panic. Father Grant was going to spill it, who his father was, everything about Lucas. All of it. Jake fidgeted, and when Father Grant didn't proceed, Jake followed up with the stupidest response ever. "What."

"You still have the floor."

Jake sat down. Everyone's eyes were on him. Father Grant moved on, and Jake was at least grateful for that. The priest coaxed the next person in the circle to stand. The girl was even more nervous than Jake. She twisted her hands and revealed some dark moment from her week that was supposed to get brighter from sharing. Jake didn't hear what she said. Nor did he hear the next person in the circle, or the next. He shut himself out. Father Grant had crossed a line.

When circle of terror time was over, and the kids dispersed to work on team-building games, Jake popped in his earbuds. Father Grant had been pulled aside by a volunteer over some lame concern like there wasn't enough lemonade mix to add to the water cooler. If he hadn't been pulled away, he would have told Jake to give up the electronic device and go join one of the activities. Jake counted himself lucky on that front.

He chose to listen to the satanic-themed death metal from his father's former band. Jake was sure Father Grant would discipline him if he heard it. He wanted to blast it to see if it would give Father Grant a rise, because it was sometimes annoying how understanding Grant chose to be. Jake closed his eyes and bobbed his head to the epileptic beat. Paddy, the band's drummer had been responsible for that.

A pat on the shoulder made Jake pull his earbuds out, ready to give his phone up and to hear a lecture about rules.

"Way to nut up against the padre, Jake." It was Rorie. "I'm proud of you."

Jake said, "Why does he have to be a dick sometimes?"

"It's his job." They sat together, bored until Rorie said, "You never asked me about my mom."

"What?" Jake had vaguely remembered hearing bits of Rorie's update on her mother's mental state as her illness took its toll. "Oh, yeah." It was all he could think of to say. Rorie's mom had been struggling with some kind of rare cancer, something called Euroterial cancer or something like that. According to Rorie, it made her mom smell like pee. She rarely got out of bed. Rorie's mom wasn't expected to survive it, and her dad was no longer a part of her life. Her grandparents didn't understand her, the hair, the music, the piercings. They especially didn't understand the desire to cut herself, and they blamed it on a lack of religious discipline.

Jake supposed that he should be thankful that his mom's wild side was something she could control and that Alec hadn't abandoned his responsibility like many fathers seemed to do. But although Alec had physically been present during the parts of the year when he wasn't on tour, it never really felt like he was there. Not since they had left behind the horrors of Wisconsin.

"So are you going to ask?"

Jake shrugged. "How's your mom?"

Oddly enough, Rorie didn't give him a real answer. "I can't wait for it to be over. It's the waiting that kills us." They sat in awkward silence for a time before Rorie changed her demeanor and grabbed an earbud. "Whatcha listening to?" She popped the piece into her ear and bobbed her head to the beat, as Jake got his second unpleasant surprise for the afternoon. His ride home had arrived. It was Alec.

"Shit," Jake muttered as Alec stepped through the door and found Father Grant. The two had a brief conversation that made Father Grant straighten up in a wary stance before he thrust his hand out for Alec to shake. Alec stared at the offer but didn't take it.

What the hell is he doing here? It's always mom who picks me up. Paralysis crept up through Jake's toes. The rest of the youth group was about to find out who his dad was, and if they were familiar with the book, they would know about Jake's demons. Some would feel sorry for him. Others would think he was a fake, just like he thought God was fake. He ripped the earpiece out of Rorie's possession.

"Hey—"

"—Gotta go to the bathroom," Jake said. It wasn't really a lie. Jake thought it would be a good place to hide.

"Jake?" The shout came from Father Grant, and it carried across the hall to get everyone's attention. "Your ride is here."

Not all the kids reacted the way Jake had expected them to react. They glanced from Jake to Alec then went about their business without recognizing Alec as the celebrity that he was. A couple of the older kids commenced whispering, as if they were unsure about what they thought they knew. Rorie was wide eyed. "Is that your dad?" Jake's cringed silence propelled her to ask again. "He's your dad? Him?"

"I've got to go."

Rorie stopped him and got in his face. "He's your dad, and you didn't say anything?"

"—He's not what you think. He can't fix your mom. He won't." Jake pushed past, because Alec was waiting, and because he didn't want to answer for being the healer's son. He could feel Rorie's gaze burn through him as he approached Father Grant and his dad. It felt almost as bad as seeing Alec force a smile at him. Maybe Alec was happy to see Jake, but his eyes betrayed something more like fear or exhaustion, or both.

"Ready to come home?" Alec slipped an arm around Jake's shoulders that Jake would have shrugged out of if Father Grant hadn't been there. It wasn't that Jake hated his father's touch. Alec's embrace was an oddly comforting thing, especially coming from a man who seemed unable to deal most of the time. If Jake had the courage to shrug Alec off at that moment, it would have been because he hated the man Alec had become. At least he was getting out of participating in the rest of the afternoon's trust-building exercises.

Alec thanked Father Grant then led Jake out where a town car waited with Olsen standing at attention by the rear passenger door. "Where's Mom?" Jake asked as they closed in.

"What, no great to see you Dad, I've missed you?" Jake didn't appease him, and Alec sighed. "Tour's over. Our flight landed early. I offered to give your mom time for other things."

Olsen saluted Jake as they got closer. "Little man." Jake kind of liked Olsen. He got the feeling that if Olsen had shadowed him at school like he shadowed Alec in public, he wouldn't have the kind of problems he had with bullies like Reuben.

Olsen opened the door to let Jake, then Alec inside. When Jake glanced back at the church hall, he spotted Rorie, and others who had figured out who Alec was, getting their last glimpses of Jake's celebrity father. Father Grant corralled them back inside, and the spectacle was over. The door closed before Olsen found his place in the front beside the driver. Then Jake stared out his tinted window while Alec stared out of the other, both silent all the way home.

Exhaustion set in. It happened every time Alec returned from the week-long stints that Josiah Light booked across the country. Alec's battery was low, and he had nothing to give Jake. It wasn't fair. He desperately wanted to connect with his son. He just didn't know how, and he was too exhausted to try.

It was the people that drained him. Every touch took from him, and it left him depressed and confused and ragged. Alec realized this after his first Light Festival tour. Cleo found him in such a dead sleep that she thought he had overdosed on something. And when Alec had come out of that sleep, it was because of one of those fucking dreams. It fueled his exhaustion, the inability to fall into a dreamless stupor. When sleep overtook him, it often plunged him into nightmares.

He stared out the window, then glanced over at Jake to find him doing the same. When he opened his mouth to speak, nothing came out. Then he looked away, back out the window where he didn't have to deal.

Alec startled awake when their driver came to a halt at their home's security gate. He didn't remember dozing, but he was thankful that the nightmares hadn't come. He looked over at Jake, and this time they made eye contact. "What's going on between you and this Reuben kid?"

"He picks on me because of you."

Olsen glanced over his shoulder as the car pulled up to the house. He quickly cut into the conversation. "Need help with your luggage, Alec?"

"What? No, I'll be fine—"

Jake opened the car door, ran for the house before the driver could put it in park. "All kids are like this at his age," Olsen said. He stepped out in unison with Alec as the driver popped the trunk. "He'll grow out of it." He handed Alec a garment bag and a small suitcase before he returned to the front seat and the driver pulled away.

Alec was alone. He turned to the house, knowing that what waited for him inside wouldn't change that. Jake, Lindy, their presence wouldn't matter. Emptiness filled him as he stepped onto the porch. Then paralyzing pain ripped into his chest. He went down.

Deliverance

LUCAS WAS CURIOUS IF HE COULD STILL DO IT BY THE time he reached the town of Truth or Consequences, New Mexico. A truck driver found him hitchhiking off one of the more-travelled roads through the mountain passes, and the man dropped Lucas off in the town with the curious name. People weren't prone to pick up hitchhikers anymore. That era died out before Lucas was born. The few people who did offer rides were more apt to be looking for a return on the favor in some creepy way. That or they were the rare Good Samaritans who believed they were doing God's work.

Lucas hadn't been so lucky to hook up with a Good Samaritan. The driver was a closet homosexual, the kind who had probably been bludgeoned into believing that gay was wrong, so he hid it from his wife and kids and tried to force his repressed urges on strangers on the road. The guy kept a firm hand on the wheel while he draped the other into Lucas's lap. Lucas didn't protest. He didn't really care, but he needed money to help fund his journey to California, so he asked for it up front.

The guy's counteroffer involved a quick pull off to the side of the road and the suggestion to get out. "The ride is your payment, kid."

"First, I'm not a kid," Lucas said. "Second, you won't take me all the way to California, and I need to eat. You can afford fifty. You won't even miss it." The truck driver seemed impressed by Lucas's calm reasoning. He pulled back onto the road, and they ended up at a rundown motel in the town of Truth or Consequences.

The place was named after an old game show, and it seemed an appropriate spot for Lucas to reflect on the things he had done to get to this point in his life; the things he had done to Alec. Those things were far from the things he did with the lonely trucker who needed a release from his fake life with the wife and kids. Lucas took the trucker's manhood, and he allowed the trucker to take his throughout a night of fondling, kisses, and oral sex. The trucker was so taken with Lucas's gentle willingness that he treated him to a room service dinner and to an hour together at a private hot spring spa that the town was known for.

Lucas had never been pampered like this, certainly not when he was a satanic high priest under Dr. Carver, and as he lay there in the arms of the sleeping trucker, he mused at how easy it would be to kill the man. He had his knife in his backpack. He could have slit the man's throat in his sleep and walked away with more than fifty dollars. But Lucas vowed not to do that. Not this time. His spiritual allegiance had changed. That's when his thoughts shifted to the bigger plan.

Alec lived somewhere in the Los Angeles area, but where? Satanic conjuring would have helped; Lucas had the bullet, the one he had pulled out of Alec's chest during the botched sacrificial rite. He had the tools. He could still invade Alec's dreams. But he was seeking redemption for his sins, not approval. He was committed to saving another lost soul. He just wasn't sure how to find Alec now that he was hidden away.

By morning, the truck driver gave Lucas breakfast and his fifty dollars. It was a sturdy meal of eggs and sausage rolled in a tortilla. After they walked back to the truck, the driver embraced Lucas with a sincere thank you. He was headed to Louisiana, not a beneficial route for Lucas, but he called Lucas an angel before he left. An angel. Odd.

Lucas headed out on foot hoping to find a bus station in Truth or Consequences, and hoping that when the lonely truck driver reached for his wallet he would forgive Lucas for his sins.

The stolen money got Lucas to Phoenix. There were credit cards too, but Lucas didn't use them. If they had been cancelled for being lost or stolen, it could cause him trouble. He ditched the wallet and pocketed the last twenty odd dollars and change. He had to find more money or another free ride.

It was unbearably hot for mid autumn in Phoenix, so Lucas sought refuge in a public library where he could surf the Internet for free and soak up information on the perfect prophet. He found Alec's book listed in the computer catalog shelved with other biographies, if Lucas was interested. He decided not to tempt that kind of fate.

The Internet provided a wealth of other information. Alec's Wikipedia page confirmed that he was living in Los Angeles, but a more specific location was not to be found. Gossip websites hinted that Alec was still not really a believer even after all he had been through. The web pages for Josiah Light's church and the Reverend Light Foundation listed charities and organizations that they funded, but not information that would lead Lucas directly to Alec.

A pang in his stomach reminded Lucas that he hadn't eaten since breakfast, and the lack of fuel began to muddle his focus. He ended up surfing through posted videos of Alec doing his thing at Light's healing tour until closing time.

"Godwad." The softly spoken slur was accompanied by a snicker. Lucas checked over his shoulder to see two college-age guys at a table, their books, netbooks, and notes spread out between them. One smacked the other across the arm, a clear indication to shut up, although the one was still amused enough to smirk. Lucas could not have cared less. He kept watching Alec's turn as a miracle worker until the lights of the library flickered and an announcement came over the intercom. Fifteen minutes to closing.

Lucas slung his backpack over his shoulder and brushed past the college duo as they packed up their studies. He stepped into the night air that had turned surprisingly chilly and racked his brain over his next step. The college kids came out embroiled in a discussion about the multiverse, and how a theory involving strings failed to support it, or something like that. Lucas caught a piece of the conversation as they passed. It sounded like a debate about the fictional world of superheroes to him. The snarky one gave Lucas a pointed glance before he peeled away from his friend, got in his car, and drove off.

Lucas settled on a bus stop bench and thought about the things he could have done to the snarky one. The other one glanced at Lucas once he reached his own car. The guy fidgeted a moment. "You're not going anywhere."

"Fuck you." It just slipped out, and Lucas regretted it.

"Wow," the guy said. "Nice mouth you got there, Christian." He ducked down to slip into the driver's seat then came back up again. "Yeah know I'm sorry about Kirk. He's a hard-core atheist who doesn't think twice about the possibility of parallel worlds."

Lucas wasn't sure what the guy was getting at, and the guy followed with a dismissive shake of the head. "Forget it," he said. "You're not going to see the bus, man. The city shuts down service to this stop at seven. It's messed up, I know. Right?"

More kindness from a complete stranger. Lucas reluctantly said thanks and turned to leave. Then a thought struck him. "Hey, can I bum a ride?"

The guy paused with a grin. "GCU or Arizona State?" Lucas assumed that these were colleges, but he had no idea how to answer. The guy picked up on it with an apology. "You go to Arizona Community. My bad. There's nothing wrong with a JC."

Lucas had the feeling that this was a lie. It didn't matter. What did matter was that the kid probably had some money, and his car was right there for the taking. He didn't want to resort to criminal behavior to get to where he needed to go, but if Lucas's redemption involved saving someone else, maybe the means to achieve that goal didn't matter. Perfect examples of this were written in the Bible: human sacrifice, mass genocide. The Bible was a weird collection of contradictions. Its only consistent message was to trust in God to light the way. Strangers had given Lucas a handout. Accepting sexual solicitation from a man who was supposed to be an abomination got him a bath, free meals, and the ability to make it to Phoenix.

God had a strange way of leading Lucas on a path to redemption. "What school do you go to?" Lucas said. The guy gave him a funny look then told him that he was a junior at Arizona State. His name was Connor, and he was studying mechanical engineering. "Take me there," Lucas said.

Connor screwed up his face again. "You go to Arizona State? Why didn't you just say so?"

"I'm undeclared. It's kind of embarrassing."

Connor nodded. The story apparently seemed legit. "Hop in."

Lucas didn't resort to stealing Connor's car. They ended up talking about campus food and housing and the school's inability to make required classes available in a logical timeframe. Lucas faked his way through it. Then the conversation turned to religion and to Connor again apologizing for his friend's behavior. "You can live your life denying it without being an ass about it."

"I used to believe different things," Lucas said. "But I don't know. I've suddenly realized that I might have a purpose."

"What kind of purpose?" Lucas shrugged and left it at that. Then Connor asked, "Which dorms?"

"You can drop me off near yours. I can walk from there."

"Oh, I live off campus. Kirk and I, a bunch of other guys, we're having a party. Wanna come?"

For Lucas, a party meant food. He said sure. "But what about your roommate?"

"Kirk? He's an ass. But he's harmless."

Kirk was an ass. He wasn't harmless. As soon as they walked through the door, Connor's girl Janie met him with a kiss and a beer, and a whisper in his ear. "Hey, bae! Party's in full swing." Then, "Tell your bff to keep his hands to himself."

The warning was loud enough for Lucas to hear. Connor's response was typical. "He's going through a breakup. Cut him some slack."

"Who's this?" Janie gave Lucas silent appraisal. Connor introduced them then shouted across the room.

"Hey, Kirkinator! We have company! Best behavior, dude!" Lucas had the distinct suspicion that maybe Connor was an ass too. Kirk gave both of them a what-the-fuck look before he ignored them entirely. He returned his attention to a college party game that involved voting on the worst possible attributes of humanity to be deemed the winner.

"What do ya like, Luke? Vodka shots, tequila shots, beer…" Lucas opted for beer, any kind, before he found the table with snacks. It had chips and guac and a smorgasbord of cheap, microwaveable bite-sized junk. Lucas kept to himself as he observed the hilariously inappropriate game, and he understood why Dr. Carver had recruited so many college students into the satanic fold. The atmosphere was rife with freedoms, open discussions, and hedonistic ideas. Lucas had never thought of that before.

Kirk waved Lucas over to join the card game. "Hey Jesus freak! Becca is leaving because of some lame excuse about a morning chem test. Take her chair." He was drunk, and when the girl named Becca vacated her seat, Kirk made sure that his hand found the well-rounded curve of her ass filling out her stretch denims. She pushed him away with a roll of the eyes and offered Lucas the chair.

"Not if you're going to feel me up like that," Lucas said. Becca paused with a smile. Others whooped it up from the burn. Lucas had just made friends. Even Kirk seemed grudgingly impressed.

Lucas took the seat, and the game continued—more beer, more shots, more politically incorrect humor. A card was laid down with a fill in the blank challenge. *If ______ got caught masturbating, it would be to ______*. People laid down their choicest answers. Janie put down *Samuel L. Jackson* and *motherfucking snakes*. Connor added *William Shatner* and *an anal probe*. Kirk threw down *My ex* and *a mirror*.

Lucas studied his choices. The others waited until he paired two of his cards together; *Jesus Christ* and *your mother working the pole*.

An eruption of laughter. Kirk slapped Lucas on the back. "Dude, I misjudged you," and from that point Lucas understood that Kirk thought they were friends.

The night progressed, the drinks kept flowing, and Lucas ventured into casual conversation. "You split up with your girlfriend?"

"How do you know that? Shit, does everyone know?"

"Connor let it slip."

"Connor, you dick."

"Everybody knows, man," Connor said. The next card on the table read *A reason to embrace white supremacy*. Someone threw down the card *assault rifles*. Another one slid in *the high price of cocaine.* Someone else added *your Mexican gardener*. It was Kirk's turn to judge the answer cards. Lucas threw down *getting away with murder*.

Kirk cried out with a laugh. He chose Lucas's card.

"Why the split?" Lucas asked.

"You're getting a little personal on the first date, Jesus freak."

"I'm not a Jesus freak. Or a godwad. What happened?"

"Anyone who searches the Internet for Josiah Light word porn is a godwad."

"Dude," Connor said. "Maybe he's studying theology."

"Yeah, Kirk. Maybe he's more enlightened than you. Maybe you're going to hell."

"If there was ever a candidate," Connor said.

Kirk gave him an eye roll. "If anyone should burn in hell, it's the bitch in Manzanita Hall. Give me a blow torch and I'll help her along."

Janie stared Kirk down as she took Connor's hand. "Madison's a friend. If you can't be civil—"

"—I was right. I'm always right."

Silence suffocated the partying mood. Janie shoved her chair back and left the table. "That's right, share everything! Let her know every fucking word I said—"

"—Dude!" Connor was on his feet. "Sober up, man." He chased after Janie. They retreated together to a separate room.

Game over. The guests threw their cards down and made excuses to leave. They suddenly remembered that they had classes in the morning too. It left Kirk to brood with Lucas by his side. "Don't you have somewhere to go?" Kirk said.

"I'm not a Jesus freak." Kirk laughed. Lucas felt compelled to continue. "I was part of this Christian community, but they kicked me out because of my sins."

"Congratulations."

"I deserved it. I'm going to hell. I mean, we're all just meat. But there's a piece of me that's going to end up in hell." Lucas shrugged in contemplation of it, as Kirk shied away the slightest bit. "It's weird, because now that I'm free I feel like God is leading me to my act of redemption." Kirk continued to stare at him. "So, why the split?"

"Oh, we've been going at it for months, and I'm sorry if this offends your delicate Christian sensibilities, but I mean hot. And heavy. She's into stuff. Anything but butt stuff. Which is ridiculous, because she's always whining about not wanting to get pregnant, so if you want to avoid it, take it in the ass. And I decide I'm going to convince her."

Lucas could see where this was going. He gave Kirk a shake of the head hoping that he would get the hint to stop.

Kirk was too drunk to stop. "So at this frat, right? I caught her in the bathroom. We were so wasted, but I knew that if she just tried it, she might like it. I locked the door, bent her over the sink, and spread those cheeks. And I knew she liked it. She was juicy. So juicy up front. My fingers were dripping—"

"—So you raped her."

"It wasn't—" Kirk clenched his teeth like he was tired of that conclusion. "It wasn't that. We've done some wild shit before. It wasn't that."

Lucas shrugged. "It wasn't consent."

Kirk got pissed. "Why the hell am I telling you this? What the hell were your sins?"

Lucas smiled and poured Kirk a shot from a bottle that was near empty on the table. "Devil worship."

"Get the fuck out," Kirk downed the shot.

"I would," Lucas said still grinning. "But I need a ride."

"That's messed up. You're delusional."

"I'm in Manzanita Hall. I could show you how to curse someone." Kirk scoffed at the idea, but Lucas could see it. The guy was entertaining it, probably just for kicks.

"Let me find my keys."

Lucas had no intention of hurting Kirk's ex-girlfriend. He did have designs on the guy's car. He considered the possibility that Kirk was too drunk to drive and that he might die in a fiery crash, but Lucas decided he would be fine. His fate was his fate.

He followed Kirk out, making sure to grab an open bottle of leftover Desert Durum, a locally distilled favorite. The more drunk Kirk was, the more apt he was to make bad choices. They reached Kirk's nondescript Camry, silver in color, and Lucas felt even better. The plainer the car, the less likely it would be to spot once it went missing. Kirk slipped behind the wheel, and Lucas in the passenger seat where he wedged his backpack between his feet.

There was a parking lot across from Manzanita Hall, off of University Drive, and Lucas directed Kirk to park between someone's Prius and a Ford SUV. It was late, a weeknight, so there wasn't another soul to worry about. Lucas offered Kirk a swig from the bottle.

"Thanks, man," Lucas said. He motioned to get out then paused. "So, do you want to see it?"

Kirk took another swig. "See what?"

"The curse. The thing that I do."

Kirk scoffed again. "What do you need, chicken blood? A goat's head? A magic wand and some lizard eyes? Ooooohhhhwhhaaa! I'm all in for scaring the bitch, but curses? Come on." He took another gulp as Lucas opened his pack. Lucas pulled out his fancy dented chalice decorated with gargoyle like images, then handed it to Kirk who freed a fit of giggles. "Alright...We're doing this."

"Hold it against your chest." Kirk did. Lucas dug into his pack.

"I was wrong. You're not a Jesus freak. You're just a freak." Kirk fell into a fit of more giggles. "What's this gonna do? Can you make her pussy burn? Can you pass it to fucking Dani—"

Lucas ripped his knife through Kirk's throat and let it gush. The rest was a gurgle. He took hold of the chalice and let the blood flow into it while he clamped his other hand over Kirk's mouth and nose. Kirk's hands went up to claw at Lucas, but his seatbelt limited his fight, and Lucas didn't flinch from reflexes dulled by Desert Durum.

"I get it," Lucas whispered. "Sometimes we have to force people to see the light. We have to hurt them or make them do things before they understand, or because it's necessary for a greater cause. But you didn't do that. You raped the girl for your own pleasure. That's it. So maybe I'm here, maybe you're the sacrifice because God has brought me to you."

Kirk flopped and struggled and pissed his pants in the process, until the loss of blood and the absence of air killed him. Lucas freed Kirk's mouth and nose. He assessed the amount of blood collected in the chalice before he lowered it beneath the drenched crotch of Kirk's pants. He squeezed, letting urine mingle with the blood. Then he dropped in Alec's bullet, added a little lighter fluid, and gave a soft, memorized incantation in Latin before he set the contents on fire.

It worked. Alec was in a limo on a highway, and through the window, Lucas saw a sign that read Atlanta. He snuffed out the chalice fire.

It was disappointing to find Alec in Atlanta, but Lucas assumed that this was temporary. The Church of Josiah Light toured often, as Lucas had learned from the Internet. He was still going to Los Angeles, and when he got there he would try again.

He pulled his hood up over his head before he got out of the car. He took Kirk's body out of the driver's seat and rolled it under the SUV after he searched Kirk's pockets for a wallet and phone. He made sure to unlock the phone with Kirk's thumbprint and to remove the phone's passcode. It would come in handy for a short time until he had to ditch it.

The car had a GPS system, and Lucas entered in his destination before he pulled out of the lot. He wondered how the ex girlfriend would feel once the body was found, but that didn't matter. She would never have to worry about Kirk again, and Lucas thought that maybe, just maybe, he was an avenging angel. John David had been right. Lucas had a purpose, and fate was leading him to it.

"Where's your father?" Belinda asked as Jake skirted past her in the kitchen.

"I don't know." Jake kept going, and Belinda shouted after him before he could barricade himself in his room.

"Dinner's in ten! Don't make me find you." She was sure she heard a faint "whatever," before a door slammed shut. Belinda looked toward the entrance hall. Still no Alec. She called out his name then asked how the flight was, and when she got no answer she headed to meet him.

Alec came through the door with a thin sheen on his face and pallor in his cheeks. He dropped his luggage to the side as if the weight had winded him. "Are you alright?"

"Yeah," he said as if it was a silly question. "Long flight. I'm glad it's over."

"Anything else?"

He shrugged. "Like?"

And there it was, not home more than two minutes and the dance to skirt issues had begun. Cleo had called Belinda before they boarded the plane in Atlanta.. She had told Belinda about the episode in the limo. Alec had gone into paralysis with a pain in his chest that had made Cleo think he was having a heart attack or a stroke. And then he was fine. Alec had begged her not to say anything, but Cleo called Belinda anyway. "I had to, hon. You need to know." Belinda was grateful that Cleo felt compelled to share. But Cleo hadn't told her everything. Belinda was all too aware of that too.

Alec leaned in to share a kiss, but Belinda skirted that as quickly as he had skirted the details of the trip. "Thanks for offering to pick Jake up," she said. "Go rest. I can reheat your plate later." She headed back for the kitchen, hoping to hide her disappointment before he could catch it.

He caught hold of her hand before she could escape. "Hey," he said. He backed off when she met him with a glare. A soft curse escaped her lips when she realized she hadn't hidden it. Alec stumbled through what he wanted to say. "I—I tried to talk with him? But he shut me out."

"Okay." She watched him plead with his eyes for her to say more. She couldn't do it, not without starting a fight, not with Jake home. Alec left his bags at the door and retreated toward the parlor where there was a bar. It was weird to call it a parlor, but that's what the realtor had called it, so that's what it was.

She watched Alec drown his sorrows. He downed his first pour in one gulp. He refilled the glass, then went to the window, drew back the curtains the slightest bit and peered out.

This was not a good sign. The last time Alec thought he was being stalked, it turned out to be the truest definition of a living nightmare. He stepped away from the window, activated a computer on a nearby desk, and checked out the surveillance images from the cameras monitoring their property.

This was not good. Not good at all.

They ate together as a family. Therapists and counselors agreed that dinnertime was the perfect time to bond. But it seemed counterproductive to hold family time in silence. Alec had never been good at small talk. He had always preferred not to talk if he really had nothing to say.

The problem was that there was plenty to say that amounted to more than small talk. Alec was just afraid of it. The nightmares were old news, but the recent occasions of wakeful paralysis were a serious problem. His disintegrating relationship with Jake was a serious problem. His infidelity was a serious problem. And Lindy knew; once Alec walked through the door, he knew that she knew. She was waiting for him to confess it, but he wouldn't. He couldn't, because Lindy's stable presence in his life was a thing he was terrified to lose. He had failed her. She was the one who had been hesitant to make the relationship legit with a ring, but she agreed to it. He was her charity case, he knew that.

Alec fretted over which serious problem to tackle in order to break the stifling silence. He chose Jake. "I hear you got a good punch in on this kid at school." Alec caught Belinda looking up with an expression that said she was ready to jump in if he said the wrong thing.

"Yeah," Jake said.

"Well how did it start? I'm glad you stood up for yourself, but that comes with, you know, consequences—"

"—Why do you care? You don't have to deal with it."

"I do, Jake. Every day I do—"

"—You've got bodyguards and shit. They call me names because of you. Jesus Boy, the son of God. They ask me to do miracles, and when I don't, they laugh."

The blunt honesty wore Alec down. "I'm sorry. I mean it. There's nothing I can do about that—"

"—You can stop lying about it."

"Lying about what?"

"Believing in it."

Belinda jumped in to guide the conversation into smoother waters. "Bullying is what kids do to feel better about themselves. It has nothing to do with who you are or—"

"—I don't believe in..." Alec struggled with how to say it while vaguely aware of the fact that Lindy was glaring at him because he cut her off. She waited, and he tried again. "I'm not sure if Reverend Light's interpretation is...accurate." *Even words for a high school dropout who began his career playing death metal,* Alec thought. *Even words for an ambiguous answer.* And Jake wasn't buying it. That was clear.

"Am I done now? I've got homework—"

"—We're not—"

"—Yeah," Alec said cutting Belinda off again. "We're done."

Jake took his plate and slipped away to the kitchen before an argument could break. But Alec knew it was coming. He dipped his head down to shovel in a fork full of some healthy combination of Brussels sprouts and honey before the topic to spark it could be breached.

"Are we going to talk about Atlanta?" Okay, serious topic number two was on the table. As Alec took a breath to compose himself, Belinda nagged him for a quicker reply. "Cleo called from the airport—"

"—I'm fine! I'm sitting here having our therapy-mandated family dinner with these heart-fucking-healthy superfoods, and I am fine! I'm here, I'm breathing. I'm fine." He closed his eyes and took a breath because he was trembling, and he hated that. He felt Belinda's silent judgment as he regulated.

She tried again in an annoyingly calm tone. "She says you were paralyzed. The last time you had an episode that bad—"

"—I know, Lindy."

"Should I worry? Should you see someone—"

"—It's stress, and I'm tired, but I'm home. I can relax and recharge."

"And keep an eye on the surveillance cameras."

"He can't be both here and there." It was a thought not meant for Belinda's ears. She cocked her brow.

"It's happened more than once?"

"No—"

"—Don't lie to me. Don't sit there and tell me that everything's okay and that you're handling it. You haven't handled it well since it happened."

"I'm not lying—"

"—You're lying to me about everything." The edge in her voice made it clear that she wasn't just talking about panic attacks and nightmares. Without saying that she knew what she knew, she laid out his second worst nightmare. "Don't think for one second that Jake and I need you to survive. This house, the security?

It's nice. But we did it without you before. We can move, I can go back to my own name, maybe give Jake the chance to be a kid and not some reality show celebrity's son. I can support us without you. It might be better for him. It might be better for you."

Alec cupped his hands over his face and muttered into them. "I need you, Lindy."

"You need me?" He looked up again to find tears in her eyes. She threw her napkin at the center of the table then cleared both her plate and his without a word. He watched the unfinished Brussels sprouts roll around on the plate's surface before he noticed Jake listening from the doorway to the kitchen. The kid said nothing. He passed through. Alec heard him head up the stairs. A bedroom door slammed shut.

Later, Alec barricaded himself in a recording studio built in the basement of the house. He strummed his guitar and he played with tracks hoping that it would busy his mind and distract him from his problems. There was a comfortable sofa down here, and Alec expected to sleep on it. He didn't want to impose on Lindy. He didn't want to make it worse. He filled up on bourbon and distracted himself to exhaustion before he laid himself out across the couch face down.

Alec's hangover headache proved to be only mildly annoying when he woke in the morning. His mouth was dry. He had to recall where he was, and he was at least thankful for no nightmares.

A buzz alerted him to the soundboard where he had left his phone. Text after text waited for him. Several were from Cleo asking if he had made it home. Alec ignored those. There were a few from Josiah regarding upcoming services and future tour dates. The man was a non-stop machine when it came to his mission to spread the Word. Alec decided to get to those later. Then there were reminders from his publicist about local book signings.

He had forgotten about those. He threw out a text explaining that he had just gotten back in town and asked if he could reschedule. *Are you double booked?* came back the reply. *Because rescheduling causes problems for everyone.*

Have you read the book? he texted back. *I don't do...*

Before he could finish the word *autographs*, the publicist chimed in with an answer to his protest. She reminded him of his commitment and of his signature on certain contracts, and Alec caved. He said he would be there, then pocketed the phone and headed upstairs.

Belinda cleaned up breakfast as Jake finished stuffing his backpack with a bag lunch. The two glanced toward Alec without a word then went about their business. Alec filled a glass of water and took a gulp. He swished the second gulp around in his mouth to alleviate the cottony feel. Then he blocked the doorway before either of them could leave.

He took a breath. "I suck at this. I suck as a dad, as a husband. I suck at bringing people hope." Another breath. "I never said I'd be good at it, but I'm trying. I want to do better. I need to do better." There was a silent exchange between Belinda and Jake, one that he prayed would end in his favor. If God was indeed up there, and if He wanted Alec to continue on some spiritual path, He could at least give Alec a fucking sign that he might be able to save his own marriage.

"We'll talk later," Belinda said. "I need to get him to school."

"I'll take him." Alec caught panic in Jake's expression. "I can do that, right? I used to do it all the time."

"Are you okay with that, Jake?" It was obvious he wasn't, but he pushed past Alec like he didn't have a choice. "Are you going to call Olsen?"

"What? No. I'll take the truck."

"And you're okay with that?" He wasn't. Olsen provided a measure of comfort when Alec was in public, but Alec remembered how the youth group ogled Jake when he had stepped into the private car at the church. Alec lied again with a nod to Belinda's question, and she let it be. She closed in to pass through the doorway, and he stopped her.

Belinda looked into Alec's eyes and waited. He could feel the heat coming off of her, and he so wanted to pull her in, to embrace her and to never let go. "Thank you," he said. She held his gaze for a few seconds before she slipped past him.

Traffic was heavy. Jake fidgeted while Alec craned his neck to see what the holdup was. Alec's phone buzzed. The message on the Bluetooth-connected dashboard flashed a name. It said Claire. Jake motioned to answer it before Alec stopped him. "Just leave it." There was a hint of panic in his voice before he turned to Jake with a smile. "This is our time. We don't get that anymore."

It was an agonizing ride for Jake, even though they were only ten minutes from the school. Alec tried to do parent stuff, but he wasn't good at it. Alec told Jake that if he wanted his and his mom's help, he would have to open up and trust them. "I know I haven't been around because of this—this stupid tour. I don't like doing it. But that's what adulting is. Compromises. It's…I don't know." Alec sighed and glanced over, and when Jake stood his ground by keeping silent, Alec changed the subject.

"Is there some detour to get past this? Because this is fucking ridiculous—"

"—Traffic's like this every day. We're not late."

"You're right. I'm sorry. I just need to calm my a—my butt down and find my happy place." The family therapist had introduced Alec to that tactic. He took a few deep cleansing breaths as Jake thought about how weak it made him look.

They reached the school drop-off lane. A long line of cars crowded together to enter it, and while plenty of kids got out before their parents made it to the official drop off, Alec insisted that Jake stay put. "You know what would help you, Jake? Joining in. You should try out for track, or soccer. Or band. I could help you there… Find something to do that other kids like, too. Then you'll have something in common."

"Is that what you did?" They inched forward.

"What do you mean? It's how I met Marcus. And Paddy… and Claire."

"Claire?"

"Cleo. Don't tell her I shared that." Alec gave Jake a smirk. They inched forward some more.

"Is Mom leaving you?" It just came out. Jake was almost as surprised to hear himself say it as Alec was to hear it.

Alec stared out the windshield and shook his head. "I don't know, Jake. I really don't want that to happen."

"Are you with Cleo now?"

"What? No. I'm with your mom. My love will always be for your mom." It was an obvious lie. It made Jake all the more disgusted. Alec was quick to change the subject. "Do you need me to sign you in or—"

"—This isn't grade school—"

"—God damn it, Jake. Stop growing up." Alec let go of a pitiful laugh before he rubbed what might have been a tear out of his eye. "I love you. Don't ever forget that."

Jake unlatched his seatbelt and hurried out the door as soon as they reached the curb. *You do suck as a father*, Jake thought, because if it was true, if Alec loved him like he claimed, he would be there for him. Not just when it was convenient or when he was guilted into it, but every time Jake needed him. Alec couldn't do that because he was weak and afraid, and instead of standing up to the bullies, he hid from them. He hid behind Jake's mom and behind Olsen and behind Josiah Light. He did suck as a father.

Alec watched Jake head toward the entrance, past the sign that identified the school with its Huskies mascot, and he knew he had failed. That's when another punch of pain in his chest made him think that he'd just gotten shot. It radiated through him and made it impossible to catch his breath, impossible to move without making it worse. But he could whisper. He panted as he stared ahead with a soft prayer on his lips. "Please make it stop. Please. Make it stop."

And it was gone. Alec could breathe. The driver in line behind him blared her horn to suggest that he move. He caught Jake and other students looking to see what the hell was going on, and when Alec threw the truck in gear and swerved into traffic, he almost hit a school bus. He kept going for a block and a half before he pulled back to the side of the street and had a panic attack.

Regulate. Breathe. Find your fucking happy place. Calm settled in until he was caught by a jagged cough. It brought the taste of blood to his mouth. When he patted dry the spittle left on his lips with a napkin he had found in the center console, he confirmed it. Blood. More panic.

He called Cleo.

Lucas made good time reaching Los Angeles. He filled Kirk's gas tank at a station to the north of campus hoping that it would throw police off his trail once Kirk's body was found. He had used one of Kirk's credit cards to pay for it. Then he bought some food at another northerly location with the same card and made certain to get cash back. Kirk's PIN number was easy to ascertain. It was the same number he had used to secure his phone.

Once a credit card path had been set, Lucas ditched the card and the wallet before he backtracked and headed west. He switched plates with another silver Camry once he crossed the state line into California, and he kept the cell phone off when he didn't need it to reduce its chances of being traced. He kept it, thinking he could use its Wi-Fi connection to keep up on any news about a student found murdered in Arizona.

By late afternoon Lucas was hungry for more than just the snacks he had purchased earlier. He found a cheap diner in a dusty town within Riverside County, and he turned on Kirk's phone. There was indeed news about a student found dead at Arizona State University. Kirk's social media friends had clogged his feed with comments expressing their loss, their sorrow, and their despair. Connor's grief was brief. *Lost my best friend today.* Lucas chuckled about that. If Kirk was his best friend, then Connor also had a low opinion of women. Lucas decided it was time to get rid of the phone.

He found a dumpster in an alley, where he crushed the phone under his heel before tossing in the shattered remains. Lucas returned to Kirk's car. He sat behind the wheel and wondered about Alec. He pulled out the chalice.

What Lucas saw was an upscale stucco home, a rustic-looking door that was still fancier than any regular-looking door, and luggage. It wasn't much to go on, but Lucas was hopeful that wherever Alec was, it was home and hopefully not a home in Atlanta. He snuffed the chalice flames and started the car's engine.

He spent money on a cheap motel room in Anaheim once he reached Orange County, and he found another Silver Camry in front of a room that was far from his own, so he waited until past midnight and changed his plates again. Then Lucas settled in and watched the reruns of a crime and courtroom drama in syndication. He vaguely remembered the actual events that the show's writers had borrowed from. A teenager who had been a victim of online bullying was found dead in a park. The murderer wasn't the obvious person, it never is. Lucas had thoughts about his own preteen upbringing as a bullied kid while living with his agonizingly saintly foster parents. Things had changed when Dr. Carver had taken him away from that, when he made Lucas's disappearance look like a kidnapping and murder. Lucas's past was an unsolved crime case ripe for a courtroom drama. He stretched against the mattress and settled into sleep.

When morning came, he checked the parking lot. The other Camry was gone, its owner never noticed the switched plates. Maybe it was a rental, Lucas thought, and that worried him. He might need to change the plates again. He returned to the room and took a shower, then pulled out the chalice one more time. He used his own urine and blood for ingredients, and when he lit the contents he found what he was looking for.

The school had a name outside its main entrance doors. It had a mascot: a dog. Lucas could see Jake, of all people. He could also see another kid sneak up behind Jake and say something rude. He could tell by Jake's irritated reaction. A car horn echoed through his thoughts, and then a voice. *Please make it stop. Please. Make it stop.*

Lucas suffocated the flames, startled by the words. Alec's words. Lucas had never heard Alec speak when he had used the ritual to enter Alec's mind. Never. But Alec spoke, and it sounded like he was speaking directly to him. *Does he know? Can he see me? Could he hear me if I spoke to him?*

Suddenly Lucas felt self conscious about what he was doing. He didn't want to hurt Alec. He just wanted to complete his path toward redemption. *If you want to save yourself, save someone else.* John David's words had come from a higher source. Lucas's faith in this continued to grow with every step of his journey. Alec had saved him, but Alec was still lost. And Jake was being bullied. Lucas knew the telltale signs. Maybe it was too late to save Alec. Maybe God had other ideas.

He accidentally knocked the contents of the chalice over in his haste to find pen and paper. Once he found them, he wrote things down. He checked out of the motel and found another library. An Internet search found Jake's school in an upscale neighborhood. Every piece was coming together. It was coming together quickly. There were a few more things he needed to make this work, but his faith was strong. He left the library with a plan.

Belinda was secretly glad when Alec stepped up to take Jake to school that morning. Her day involved helping volunteer physicians give physicals to homeless teens at a shelter that partnered with Josiah Light's foundation. Belinda loved doing this, although it broke her heart to see so many kids on the streets. Many were smart beyond their years without being very smart at all. Their parents had failed them as much as they had failed their parents, and they weren't especially keen on taking advice from other adults. Many were also sexually active, because living on the streets taught you different things.

Each free physical came with a mandated perk from Josiah Light's Foundation: a group talk about the ramifications of sexual activity including pregnancy and the evils of abortion. Josiah had tapped Belinda for the job because, as he had told her, she was an excellent example of someone whose life had changed for the better after facing the difficult circumstance of being single and pregnant. While Belinda saw value in what Josiah Light was attempting to do, she didn't necessarily agree with his stand on the issue. She played devil's advocate to Light's teachings as diplomatically as possible.

She was in the midst of countering one of Josiah's sticky points about how having an abortion was an act against God's universal plan when her phone chirped in with an even less appropriate ringtone. It was the familiar AC/DC classic, *Highway to Hell.* Most of the teenagers were familiar enough to smirk. The caller-identified intruder was Cleo, the last person Belinda wanted to talk to. She dismissed the call.

Seconds later, her phone dinged in with a voice message, again from Cleo. Again, Belinda ignored it. When the text message came, Belinda put the phone in sleep mode, not bothering to read beyond the sender's name.

"It's important to understand that a step toward prevention is easier than steps toward termination." Belinda expected some kind of counter argument from Josiah at this moment, for the mere mention of *steps toward termination* was considered taboo. But Josiah's phone had also dinged in soon after Belinda had silenced hers, and now that he was engaged in texting, she took advantage of the moment. "But, everyone's circumstances are different—"

"—Belinda." He had been listening after all. Belinda continued with urgency.

"—When you're on the street and have nowhere else to turn—"

"—Belinda."

"—it's okay to consider every option, and to know where to go that's safe—"

"Belinda." She turned, expecting Josiah to be giving her a stern *that's enough* look. But it wasn't quite that. "Claire needs you to answer your phone. I'll take over from here."

Belinda pulled out her phone and found Cleo's text. *Alec is in the ER.* "Shit," she heard herself utter. As she hurried past, Josiah grabbed her by the arm.

"Keep me updated. My prayers are with you."

"He's fine, I think," Cleo said. She paced in the hallway outside of an emergency waiting room because of cell phone rules. "It's mostly a panic attack, hon. But he coughed up some blood, so he's here." Cleo dreaded meeting Belinda face to face, fearing that inevitable question, *why did he call you and not me*.

When Belinda arrived, she didn't ask the inevitable question. She went straight to the staff and asked about Alec's status, what tests were being run and his diagnosis. She seemed relieved and satisfied before she asked to be taken to Alec's bed.

Cleo trailed behind her. "He didn't want to worry you, hon," she said before the inevitable question came up. "But I knew better. Olsen's at the school—"

"—Olsen?" Belinda turned on Cleo sharply. "Why? Did this happen at school?"

"Jake's fine. He doesn't know. Alec had me call Olsen to be there."

"Jake doesn't get out until almost three—"

"—Alec wanted him there." Cleo fidgeted under Belinda's scrutiny. It was like the first time they had met all over again, in a hospital with Alec fearing for his life while the two of them danced around where they stood because of their relationships to him. The difference now was that there was more than awkwardness to be had. There was guilt.

The doctor reached a curtain before he realized that the women were no longer following him. He called out. "Right here, ladies."

Cleo let Belinda take the lead. They stepped behind the curtain and found Alec resting his eyes. His chest was exposed, revealing bullet scars and stabbing scars, and the doctor had him hooked up to a heart monitor that blipped steadily, if somewhat faster than it should.

"Alec?"

Cleo could see the slightest cringe from him as he sat up and tried to smile. "I'm okay—"

"—We're waiting on lab results," the doctor said. "But I don't see much to worry about. His vitals are strong, chest ex-rays look good. Blood pressure is a little bit high, but we've talked about what might be the cause of that." The doctor gave Alec a quick and confidential nod, which was funny because everyone surrounding Alec knew about his anxiety issues, herself and Belinda probably more than the doctor. It was a strong bet that Alec had a spanking new prescription for Zoloft or some other serotonin inhibitor that he would eventually complain about because it didn't work. Not on Alec. For him, the drugs never fully worked. He had often jokingly complained to Cleo that he couldn't even properly abuse them.

"What about the blood?" Belinda asked. "He was coughing up blood?"

The doctor scratched his head. "We thought maybe a lesion in the lung, given his history, but what can I say? He's a model of perfect health." But a follow up appointment would be necessary before the doctor's answers could be deemed conclusive. Alec was given permission to leave within a couple of hours.

"I don't need this to get out," Alec said.

The doctor reassured him that the hospital was quite aware of his celebrity status. "Our staff knows about discretion." That seemed to relax Alec more than anything. Until the doctor took his leave. Then he was stuck with the two women he was fucking. Cleo watched Alec take a hold of Belinda's hand while averting his gaze from her.

"You need to know something," Alec said.

Cleo braced herself. This was it. He was going to spill it, there would be a scene, and God damn, he had called her in his emergency, not Lindy. Yes, Belinda was the one he needed, but he had called Cleo. And now in his moment of weakness he was going to expose it, and there would be a whole scene that Cleo did not want to go through.

"It's happening again, Lindy. The paralysis, the feeling like he's in my head. It's not just nightmares. He's playing with me. And he's close."

Belinda bowed her head. "Is that why you sent Olsen to the school?"

"I don't want it to happen again."

"It won't." Lindy looked at Cleo. She looked right through her, and it made Cleo squirm. *She knows,* Cleo thought. *She's calm and she's rational, and she knows.* "Can you take him home?"

"What, hon?" Cleo wasn't sure she'd heard Lindy right.

"Olsen concealed carries. I'll need to speak with Jake's principal."

"Of course. It's straight home with him." Cleo offered a smile before she noted Belinda's abrupt break from Alec's grip on her hand. Belinda definitely knew, and Cleo was jealous of the fact that she could keep it together.

"I understand your concern," Principal Vasquez said, "but it's strict policy. He can't be here." Olsen stood behind Belinda looking every bit the part of a bodyguard with military training. Vasquez looked a little intimidated by his silent presence.

Belinda had explained the situation as best she could without being specific about the fact that Alec's fears were technically unsubstantiated. She couldn't justify the fact that her son might need armed protection based on a creepy feeling, so she kept it simple. "My husband received a threat—"

"—Take Jake out of school. His teachers can provide lesson plans until your situation improves, but I can't have a gun on campus."

"I'm trying so hard to get Jake to re-acclimate. He's getting better. I just—"

"—If getting better is defined by schoolyard fights at recess, I'm not sure you understand the term."

Belinda glared. She heard Olsen give in to a soft cough. The problem was that, as much as she hated to admit it, Principal Vasquez was right. She tried to rein in the glare before she used a different tactic. "My son needs the kind of everyday interaction that normal kids have to continue to get past what happened to him."

"Does having him here put the rest of the school in danger?"

She hedged on that one. "I don't think so."

"What if I stay outside," Olsen said. "Parked on the street, not on the premises. It would be better for Jake. He wouldn't have an obvious shadow." Belinda gave Olsen a smile. She liked his no-nonsense approach to things.

"I don't want our school to become a national headline."

"We know the potential threat. Olsen knows what he looks like. He's an outcast twenty-year-old kid—"

"—So, a stereotypical school shooter."

"I understand," Belinda said. She asked Olsen to wait outside at his car so she could address Vasquez in private. "Alec experiences post-traumatic stress," she told Vasquez once Olsen was gone. "To this day, he suffers from random panic attacks. He becomes convinced that something bad is going to happen based on...a dream or...the glance of a stranger in public. This is one of those things. So please, can you help me help him?"

The bell to end the last class rang, and Jake hurried into the halls to get jostled by other students eager to leave with him. He spotted Reuben coming from a different classroom, so he hunkered down hoping Reuben wouldn't catch sight of him. He breathed a sigh of relief once he made it past the main entrance doors into the afternoon sun. Jake smiled. He had made it through the day without a conflict with Reuben. Recess in detention had been agonizing. The two of them got to sit across from each other and pass each other the evil eye while pretending to eat lunch and do homework. But detention time was monitored, so there was nothing else Reuben could do.

Jake scanned the curb in search of his mom. Instead, he found Olsen, arms crossed and butt parked on the hood of Josiah Light's black luxury limo. Jake closed in slowly before Olsen hopped off the hood and pulled open the back door. "Make yourself comfortable, little man. Your mom's still in the office."

Jake heard whispers from passing kids. He followed their wide-eyed gazes as they noted Olsen's holstered gun, visible if you happened to be at the right angle. Jake couldn't decide if the kids were scared or impressed. Then he decided that it didn't matter because either way, it made him different again. A limo driver with a gun was not who drove the rest of the kids home. Jake scooted into the back seat hoping that more kids wouldn't see him, when his mom arrived.

Belinda intervened before Olsen could close the door. She poked her head in with a smile. "Your choice today. Ride with Olsen or ride with me?" Jake stayed put hoping that they would just close the door and go. Instead, Belinda held it open and had a conversation with Olsen. "You get to stay tomorrow. Bring something to read."

"Yes, ma'am."

Other kids passed by and peered inside, curious to see who was special enough for the ride. One of them was Reuben. That's when Jake scooted back over and yanked the door closed.

Cleo danced fingers across piano keys and mused over the strange course her life had taken. Once the favorite soloist in her Louisiana hometown Baptist church, she left because her parents refused to support the idea of a music career other than gospel, then found the ultimate rebellion in Los Angeles by hooking up with the young, jaded by Christianity bandmates of The Great. Literally. First it was Alec, who needed mothering in the worst possible way. Then it was Mark who, for all his misogynistic blowhard bluster, was still a lover and a protector. And Paddy had been adorable, the saint who Cleo had engaged with in a onetime drunken session of heavy petting. Cleo had taught Patrick a few things, probably the wrong things, but she wasn't ashamed. The kid had been seventeen at the time. He was all arms and legs under a mop of fine dark hair, a baby-faced Mexicali Leprechaun, as Marcus called him. Cleo was proud to have been his intimacy teacher.

Cleo had often grown tired of the endless debates over God, but she knew the band had talent, real talent. She had thought that one day, when they had all become famous and richly comfortable and satisfied with themselves, that their tune would change. It didn't play out that way, not exactly. Hers and Alec's tune had changed, sure. They were comfortably rich. But Alec was a neurotic mess. That hadn't changed. Or, maybe it was better to say that it had gotten worse. And Cleo, the most God-faithful member of the former satanic band, was losing her faith.

She had her reasons. And as Alec paced in the parlor of his rich, comfortable house, she was at least thankful that he had calmed down since when she had found him that morning. Alec had every reason to be the mess. *Every God damned reason,* and that was the problem.

Alec's pacing slowed, and he spilled what she knew he didn't want to say. "I'm not being fair to Lindy." He always called her Lindy. "It's up to me to make it work. To change—"

"—You're right, hon," Cleo said. It took him by surprise because, instead of trying to justify his decision, he fell into silence and resorted to pacing again. Cleo let her fingers play out a chord, then another. When the pacing got to the point of absurdity, she played a more familiar motif reserved for revelations in bad thriller movies.

"Stop that," Alec said. She got a smirk out of him, then patted the piano bench and he sat. "Jake asked me if we were getting a divorce."

This disturbed Cleo far more than learning that Belinda knew. She never wanted to be the woman that broke up a family. But here she was, that woman. "I will always love you, hon. But what we have? It comes from weakness. Maybe we're stronger together. I don't know. A piece of blank paper is flimsy and easy to shred, but a stack of paper bound together is inspiration, a story waiting to be told. Lindy, she's your binding. She's your glue. I get that."

She danced her fingers across a few keys as they sat in contemplation. Then Alec said what was going through her mind. "What the hell does that mean?" They burst out laughing.

"A work in progress, hon. Maybe I'll work it into a song."

"Good luck."

She shoved him. He shoved back, shoulder to shoulder, and when she turned into him, their faces came close enough to kiss. They lingered. Cleo could feel the heat coming off of him, radiating like a healing sauna. He rested his forehead against hers and bared his soul. "I'm so fucked up. And I know it, but I don't know how to fix it."

Her mommy instinct kicked in. He wasn't making this easy. What she wanted was to hold him and kiss him and tell him that she would make it better. And the kissing would lead to caressing and groping and sex, and neither of them would feel any better about it because of Lindy. Lindy didn't deserve Alec. But Alec needed Lindy far more than he needed Cleo. She settled for kissing him on the forehead. "This right here? Ending us? It's a start."

For a moment, Cleo thought they were going to ruin the good start by crushing against each other with absurd passion. Then she heard a door close from the hallway. It broke the spell. Jake peered in from the parlor entrance, and Alec straightened up. "Hey, Jake," he said with what Cleo decided was a little too much effort. "How was school?"

Cleo felt her face flush now that she knew what she knew, and when Jake ran off she felt like the bitch home wrecker again. She got to her feet. "I guess that's my cue to go confess my sins."

"Yeah," Alec said with a lack of enthusiasm. He hunkered over the piano and took over the random chord hopping.

Belinda was still in the hall when Cleo reached her. "He's all tucked in," Cleo said. "His pills are on the kitchen counter."

Belinda thanked her, and Cleo almost made it out the door before Belinda snagged her by the arm. Cleo braced herself for the fight she didn't want to have, and Belinda locked eyes with her. "I mean it," Belinda said. "Thank you."

That was it. The door closed between them, and Cleo headed for her car. Maybe it was all that needed to be said. Once Cleo slid behind the wheel of her sporty, space gray Tesla, she wondered how she and Alec would continue to work professionally together. Then she cried her eyes out.

Jake brooded in the back of the limo the next morning. Olsen kept the conversation light. Either he could read Jake's mood and respected Jake's privacy, or he didn't care. Jake liked Olsen. He decided to believe that the guy respected him. When they reached school, Olsen parked in a conspicuous place and gave Jake blunt instructions. "When classes are over, you'll find me right here. You come to that door and don't see me? You don't come out. You go to the office and you call me. Number's in your cell under Olsen." Olsen stopped traffic to let Jake cross before he returned to the limo.

Jake felt the eyes on him, the kids whispering about presidential treatment. He knew he would get teased throughout the day, and he did. Reuben asked if he thought the ride might be too rich for the Son of God. "Aren't you supposed to be humble and shit, Jesus Boy?" Then he shoved past him with a challenge. "Meet me in the bathrooms before detention. Just you and me."

Jake burned a glare through the back of Reuben's head. Did Reuben think he was an idiot? He continued to burn through math class. As the teacher droned on about equivalent ratios and how three over four was the same as six over eight, Jake began to think that if he didn't show up for Reuben's stupid challenge, then it would spread through school that he was a coward. That bothered him more than the potential of getting beat up. Showing the bully you were scared meant that the bully won.

The bell rang. Jake headed for the restrooms, the ones closest to detention hall that happened to be in the farthest building from math class. Reuben would get there first, and Jake knew this could be a problem. He pushed past the rest of the kids who were heading to the cafeteria and to the playground for recess.

When he reached the right building, he slipped into the boys' room and found it empty. There was one stall door that was closed. Taped on it was a piece of paper with the words OUT OF ORDER scrawled in marker. Jake looked under the door anyway. No feet. He slipped his book bag off his shoulder. It could be a weapon with a good swing. He waited.

Reuben didn't show. Bored and disappointed, Jake pulled a sharpie out of his pack and started to doodle on the bathroom tiles. He wrote REUBEN SUCKS DICK, and that made him feel better.

Jake's mind wandered to Alec. He wrote the word GOD and colored in the block lettering. He hated what Alec had become. Alec had once been the coolest dad ever, fun and adventurous and breaking the rules that were stupid. They used to share secrets that Mom didn't need to know, like skinned knees from dangerous falls and like slips when Alec swore.

Now Alec was nothing but a beaten-down coward. The more Jake thought about it, the more he scribbled. He vowed to himself that he wouldn't let Reuben do the same thing to him. He wouldn't let Reuben bully him and win.

He looked at his graffiti handiwork: DEAR GOD. FUCK YOU. SON OF GOD. Jake was satisfied with that. Then the passing bell rang, and Jake realized he was late for detention. He scrambled to gather his book bag and head out the door when a noise startled him from behind. The stall door with the OUT OF ORDER sign pulled open and Reuben stepped out. "Hey asshole! Catch," Reuben pushed past Jake in a high-speed escape.

Jake fumbled to catch a plastic zipper bag thrown at him when, BOOM! An explosion rocked the out-of-order stall. Jake cupped his hands over his ears in shock before he realized what was in the bag, fireworks. They were M80s. He was screwed.

He pushed through the bathroom door and ran, as the detention hall monitor rushed into the hallway, and as Reuben rushed toward her faking panic. "I'm scared," Jake heard Reuben shout before the teacher ushered him to safety. Concerned teachers filtered out to see what had happened. Jake escaped the building, but not before the detention hall monitor called out his name. He was really screwed.

Most of the school was outside for recess or in the cafeteria for nutrition break. Jake needed an escape, but the kids and staff outside didn't quite know what had happened yet. He kept walking, furiously tried to map out his escape from campus as a slower panic began to ripple through the rest of the staff and students. He couldn't leave through the main gate because Olsen would be there. The rest of the school was fenced in.

This is bad, Jake thought. *Really bad*. He might have been able to explain his side of it if he hadn't marked up the bathroom walls. He might have convinced Principal Vasquez that Reuben had framed him, but the graffiti would make the principal think otherwise. Jake knew this. His only option was to run, to avoid facing the consequences, kind of like what he imagined Alec would have done. Jake hated comparing himself to Alec at that moment, but it was true. He pushed those thoughts away and kept walking.

The auditorium beckoned ahead of him. It was the only other building that had direct access to the street outside the school, other than the main gate. Janitors stored supplies in the back rooms of the auditorium, so there was a chance that Jake could slip in from the school side of the building. As the campus loudspeakers clicked on, and as Principal Vasquez ordered everyone to shelter in place for a lockdown drill, Jake found an unlocked door to the auditorium. He slipped inside.

It was dark. Band practice took place in the mornings before first period, so the auditorium remained abandoned throughout most of the day. Jake stuffed the M80s into his book bag with a nagging thought that they were dangerous enough to be useful. It was a criminal thought, he knew, but Alec engaged in questionable behavior all the time. At least he used to. Then Jake hated himself because he just compared himself to Alec. Again.

Jake hurried toward the front stage, down the steps, up the aisles and to the foyer that led onto the street. He pushed the door open carefully. The coast was clear. Olsen was on the other end of the campus, so Jake wouldn't get caught by him. He slipped out and down the street into the residential neighborhood that bordered it. He was almost home free, because that's where he was going. A half-hour walk, he thought. He knew the way. He would suffer the consequences with mom, and the lack of consequences with Alec, and he would be okay with that.

He heard the faint wail of police sirens as he gained distance from the school, heard the choppy thump, thump, thump of helicopter blades. This was bad, but as he kept walking, his nerves told him that everything was going to work out. It was going to be okay.

His nerves kicked in again when he heard a car approach from behind. *Don't look,* he thought. *Stay calm*. His panic got the better of him, and he looked. A Toyota pulled to the curb. Jake felt his throat go dry as he looked ahead and kept walking. If it was a teacher or a school administrator, he figured they would shout at him soon enough. At least it wasn't the police. Or Olsen. It was probably someone who lived in the neighborhood coming home for lunch. A door opened and closed, and no one called out. Jake breathed. Kept walking. Everything was going to be okay.

Then the hand settled on Jake's shoulder. *Shit! It's over*. He let his book bag slip to the ground, ready for his punishment, when hot breath hit the back of his neck and a hand clamped over his mouth. The hand on his shoulder slipped forward and an arm snaked around to crush him tight. "Ssshhh, Jake. Ssshhh."

Jake's worst nightmare had found him. He struggled and kicked and tried to bite the hand over his mouth, but Lucas was too strong. Lucas kept Jake's mouth clamped and his nose pinched shut while the arm that kept Jake pinned moved up and around his throat. Jake kept struggling. He used up the air left in his lungs. He choked and clawed to break free and take in more air, but the opportunity never came. He passed out.

Lucas couldn't believe his luck. He found Jake's school listed on a district website. Satellite maps had given him a feel for the school's layout, so he took a day to drive there and observe the location. He hadn't found the place until school hours were over, but he supposed that was a good thing.

There was a main gate and a fence surrounding the perimeter, much different than the elementary school in Ashland, where Jake used to live. Lucas had to admit that the level of security disheartened him, but he was determined to find a way to reach

Jake. If God was guiding him down this path, then surely he'd find a way.

He set to work acquiring things he might need. He bought a gun from a shady dude in Venice Beach. He scored Ambien from a streetwalker in West Hollywood. At three in the morning, he had robbed an all-night service station with his newly acquired gun that had no bullets. The cash would help fill his tank for the trek back to the Temple. At four, he found another silver Camry to switch plates with.

By six, he found a place to park a short distance from the school. It was close enough to monitor the main entrance, but not so close to bring attention to himself. It was also located at a corner where he could scope out two sides of the school's perimeter. Lucas hadn't had a fully fledged plan that morning, but he had hoped to at least catch sight of Jake to confirm that this was indeed his school.

By eight, the street was clogged with parents and buses dropping kids off. Lucas spotted Jake's arrival, and again he was disheartened. The kid stepped out of a limo, and the driver was a menacing-looking type. Probably armed. The bodyguard also had no intention of leaving. Maybe God wasn't leading Lucas on this journey after all. He checked the time on the car dash. A second wave of kids arrived, the younger ones, kindergarteners through fifth grade, Lucas assumed. But he couldn't sit in the car all day without drawing attention to himself, so he got out and took a walk through the adjacent neighborhood.

It was a wealthier neighborhood. High walls and gated drives made Lucas worry about hidden cameras and a vigilant patrolling presence. He continued to lose faith in his half-baked plan. Even if he was able to abduct Jake, chances were high that he would be caught before he made it two blocks from the school.

After walking for a while, he thought it might be time to abandon the whole idea. It was about lunchtime when he returned to the Camry, fully intending to drive away and not look back. Lucas hadn't had breakfast and was feeling the pangs of hunger. He slid behind the wheel, about ready to put the car in drive, when the miracle happened: a commotion in the school. Kids in the playground that bordered the adjacent street paused. A loudspeaker announcement that Lucas could barely make out got the kids and their recess monitors moving. They were vacating the playground. The bodyguard couldn't see it. He was positioned to only see the face of the main entrance. But he heard the overhead speaker, and he was moving in, his hand reaching for what Lucas assumed was that gun under his coat. Something bad was going down. Very bad. He glanced down the adjacent street and spotted a solitary kid slipping out the door of the school's auditorium. The kid was Jake.

Not possible. Jake slipped down the street then turned into the adjacent neighborhood on that side of the school. Lucas turned his engine over.

Jake came to strapped into the passenger seat of the Toyota. Lucas jammed a pill into his mouth, and Jake struggled until he felt the barrel of a gun pressed against his throat. "Swallow it."

Jake burst into tears. His hand fumbled for the door handle until Lucas pushed the muzzle up under his chin.

"Swallow!" Lucas gave Jake a jerk, and the pill that had been rolling around in his mouth went down. Lucas drew Jake into as big a hug as the seatbelt restraints would allow. He stroked Jake's hair and whispered soothing words, and Jake could smell the scent of fast food in Lucas's clothes. It made him gag. "It's alright," Lucas said over and over. "I'm sorry I have to do this. It's alright."

Every ounce of Jake's being tried to refrain from crying. The sobs hiccupped out of him as he tried to find the belt buckle release without being obvious. But his arm was trapped by Lucas's weight, and he couldn't quite reach it. He felt dizzy as Lucas kept talking.

"Sometimes we have to do bad things to help lead people down the right path. You'll understand, Jake. It's for a greater cause."

The light-headed feeling was getting worse and, when the sound of helicopter blades hovered from somewhere above them, Lucas held Jake tight and still. He continued to stroke Jake's hair. *Like a dog. I'm his pet.* Jake drifted on fuzzy memories of Lucas's history of abuse. It gave him enough focus to lurch out of Lucas's grip until Lucas reined him in again.

"Stay still until they're gone," Lucas said, and Jake's arms got heavy. His eyes refused to stay open. The flapping helicopter blades were hypnotic. The beat of Lucas's heart in Jake's ear was steady, slow, not like Alec's whose heartbeat seemed to rival the machine gun report of one of Paddy O'Shaugnessey's drum sessions. Jake drifted on memories of Alec's hugs, when his ear had been pressed to Alec's chest. He wished that he was there, and that he had never been so mean to his dad. Alec loved him. Jake knew that, and as he drifted toward unconsciousness, he pretended that Alec was holding him. Because that made everything okay.

Acts of Contrition

HIS OWN FACE, FULL OF HOPE, BEAMED UP AT HIM. Alec pushed the book aside. A display full of the same books stood to his right, with that same face blown up to three times its normal size. Cleo popped gum from the seat to his left while she scrolled through social media threads on her phone. A pocket version of the *New Testament* rested on the table between them. Alec kept it handy to brush up on the scripture that he had blocked out of his mind from the days of his tortured youth. Fans were lined up behind a rope barrier not far away. They had books and posters and actual compact discs clutched in their sweaty hands.

Alec didn't want to be here, especially after the previous day's panic attack. But the event had been booked months ago, and the new meds seemed to have taken some of the edge off his anxiety. He ran his finger along the spine of the little *New Testament*, then flipped to a random page. *Maybe it's like a Tarot reading*, he thought; *pick a passage, see how it relates to the mess of one's life.*

He landed in Hebrews, 11:6: *Without faith it is impossible to please God. For those that come to Him must believe in Him and believe that He will reward those that seek Him.* Alec slapped the book shut and tossed it toward Cleo, feeling fucked.

Cleo looked up from her scrolling. "You okay, hon?"

"I don't do autographs. It's in the fucking book." His eyes landed on the waiting fans. Big mistake. They smiled and held his book out, and some of them held a hand up, palm open and fingers stretched to signify the power of his touch. Alec put on a smile and waved back, remembering the days when fans would greet him with a raised fist, pinky and index finger extended. Different times, neither one representing a happy point in his life. He didn't want to be here. He didn't fucking do autographs.

A shop employee stepped up to the rope that held the line back, and she let the first fan pass through. The woman approached on her toes, as if the floor had transformed into a bed of hot coals. She let out a squeal and held out the book. "I waited outside for hours."

"I'm humbled by people who do that. Thank you." He opened the book to the empty front leaf and he poised his pen. "What's your name?"

"Judy."

"And what's your story?"

Judy blinked. "My story?"

"What has brought you here, to this place in your life—besides me."

"Uhm." Judy twittered into a chuckle. She shifted from one set of toes to the other.

Alec tried again. "What inspires your faith, Judy?"

"I don't...I don't have anything."

Alec was disappointed. Josiah Light made it look so easy. He would ask these kinds of questions and he would coax out answers that seemed pointless or silly, or sometimes poignant and heartbreaking. "My mom inspired me when she beat cancer," or "My dog inspires me when he greets me with his wagging tail." Even "Chocolate inspires me because it tastes so damn good" would have been a fine answer. Reverend Light would relate each and every answer to the Glory of God, and his followers would eat it up.

Alec did not have this gift. *Maybe*, he thought, *it's because I'm still sorely lacking in faith.* As Judy continued to look perplexed, Alec began writing. He let her off the hook. "Well, Judy. My faith is inspired by people like you who buy the book. Half the profits go to a charity that helps victims of post-traumatic stress." He turned the book around for her to see his sentiment as he read it aloud. "People like you make me smile."

Judy barely restrained herself. She took the book and succeeded in squeezing his hand before he could retract it, and she thanked him. Judy plunked the book in front of Cleo, as Alec waved the next fan over. "Please don't sign bigger than Alec," she said.

"Hon, I couldn't even if I tried." Cleo snapped gum at Alec when he gave her an irritated glance.

Bits of energy slipped away from Alec with each fan he met. He smiled and thanked every one, and every one reacted to his touch as if it was a blessing from the goddamned Pope. His skin crawled from the mass of contact. It made him want to curl up inside himself and never be found. The anxiety meds that were supposed to help, the ones that were supposed to last for a good eight hours, began wearing off after two. He leaned into Cleo's ear between fan greetings, and he whispered his sentiments regarding the event. "Bogus fucking circus." He expected gentle chastisement from her, like she usually did. He expected her to tell him to look at the bright side, like a mother might say to an antsy child in church.

She didn't do that. If anything, what she said made him feel worse. "How did last night go with Lindy?"

Alec pulled away. He didn't want to talk about that either. "She forgives me." He motioned for the next fan in line. It was a lie. Belinda had technically said the words. She even let him share her bed and wrap his arms around her. But that was all. Nothing more. He had felt her rigid discomfort with him there. After Olsen took Jake to school, Alec and Belinda talked about their plans for the day and that was it. She got in her car and drove off to work with Josiah and homeless teens in need, and he had his driver take him to this scheduled book signing.

He would have preferred Olsen in the car with him, but Jake was the priority. Belinda had humored Alec by telling him that he had every right to worry. But then she had convinced him that maybe it was the stress. He was overworked and overtired and still suffering from that long-ago trauma.

He wondered if he would ever settle into a normal realm of emotional highs and lows instead of the mountain peaks and below-sea level plunges that defined the course of his days. Then the next fan, the bro, stepped up. "Alexander the Great! You rock, bro."

The bro slapped a CD jewel case on the table. It startled Alec to see it. The cover art was bloody and demonic. In it, Cleo sat on a devil's throne, her hair teased to extremes. The body suit she wore made her look nude beneath a thick sheen of dark blood. The guys, Marcus and Paddy, lay slain at her delicately crossed feet, and Alec lay draped across her lap, one arm slung over her shoulder, the other hanging limp to the floor as Cleo held a dagger beneath a gaping and bleeding hole in Alec's chest. Alec remembered that photo shoot. He remembered Marcus's glee over the gore of the bastardized version of Madonna and son after the crucifixion. Looking at it now made Alec nauseous.

The bro didn't seem to pick up on it. "I was there at Deathfest. Front and center. You, man, are one of the greats."

"Thanks," Alec said. He slashed his name across the plastic case and hoped that would be the end of the exchange. It wasn't.

"The Heartland Fundies don't get it. You are what you make yourself. God or demon."

"Riiight," Alec heard himself say. He slid the CD over to Cleo.

"The whole duality thing rocks. Keep with the program, bro, because some of us get it." He extended his fist—pinky and index finger up like horns, and he waited for Alec to reciprocate with a fist bump. At least the guy wasn't waiting for a miraculous touch. Alec obliged, and the guy grinned in victory. "See you in hell, bro."

"Yes, you will," Alec muttered. The guy missed it. He was too busy giving Cleo an appreciative once over as she finished scrawling her own signature across the case. He gave her a wink as she handed the case over.

"Not on a dare, hon," she said. The guy chuckled as if it was a compliment before he went on his way.

"Bogus fucking circus," Alec said again, and Cleo smiled. At least she was amused this time. When his phone buzzed in, Alec took it because if anything, it would give him the opportunity to stall before the next weirded-out fan accosted him. “Hello.”

It was Olsen.

Principal Vasquez waited for Belinda’s reaction, his arms crossed, as she took in Jake’s scrawl. The smoky remnants of gunpowder wafted from one toilet stall. Belinda knew what Vasquez was thinking. She was a bad parent raising a seriously troubled kid. She didn’t dignify his silent disapproval with an apology. She got to the heart of the more important matter. “No one’s found him?”

A police officer who stood at the open restroom door answered for Vasquez. “We’ve scoured the campus, ma’am. He’s not here.”

“Can someone explain how he left the school undetected after something like this?” She motioned to the smoky-smelling stall and gave Vasquez an equal look of disapproval.

“This is a no-tolerance offense,” Vasquez said without missing a beat. “This is grounds for expulsion.”

“And what about the other kid? What about Reuben—”

“—He says Jake did this. And he didn’t run—”

“—He was still involved.”

“I am fully aware of that, Mrs. Lowell. Measures are being taken.”

An argument between men closed in from the hallway. Belinda braced herself. Alec had arrived, and he was in full accusation mode. “You were here to prevent this,” she heard him say. “You were the fucking safety net! How did you let this happen?” His tirade was interrupted by occasional brief apologies and acceptance of failure from Olsen until the two of them reached the door. The officer there held up one hand, the other poised at the pistol on his belt.

"He's the dad," Olsen said. The officer stood down. Belinda watched Olsen pace in the hall, probably worried over his job, as Alec barged in and singled out the principal.

"You're Vasquez? Where's my son?" Alec's eyes drifted from Vasquez to the words on the wall. His aggressive demeanor diminished to self-loathing.

"It's nice to finally meet, Mr. Lowell." There was an edge to the word nice, as Vasquez offered his hand.

"Just tell me what happened," Alec said. "Tell me you're doing everything you can to find him."

"They've tracked his phone, sir," the officer at the door said. Olsen held up the display of his own phone to show a neighborhood map. "We have a patrol car on the way."

When Alec pulled out his own phone, Belinda intervened. "He's not answering. I've tried." Alec shoved the cellular back into his pocket. He took furtive glances at the message on the wall and he fidgeted as Vasquez squeezed past him.

"While the authorities are following up on your son's whereabouts, why don't we have a nice sit down in my office to discuss the ramifications here." Belinda followed Vasquez out.

Alec didn't move.

When Belinda doubled back to coax him along, he shrugged her off. "He didn't do this," he insisted. "Where would he get illegal fireworks? The other kid is lying. He didn't—" The message on the wall seemed to be the thing that briefly silenced him. Then, "He didn't do this."

The denial broke Belinda's calm. The writing on the wall defined it. Jake's problems stemmed from Alec's own inability to cope, and still Alec denied it. She had had enough. "Alec, I can't do this now. I can't deal with you. When we get through this? When we're done here? Don't come home."

A week had passed. Maggie wondered if she would ever see Lucas again. When she asked what Lucas had done to be sent away, John David kept it simple. "He lied."

"What did he lie about?"

She never got that answer. In fact, John David skirted the topic whenever she brought it up. It left Maggie disheartened. Lucas had been the only one she could talk with who thought it was alright to question things. John David was more strict. There was no questioning God's plan. She liked Lucas's blurred lines between right and wrong better. The idea of it interested Maggie to no end. It gave her hope that her mother had made it to heaven, even though she had committed suicide. Her mother had at least deserved that.

Then it happened. Maggie helped a work party, led by John David and Hannah, clear brush along the property's eastern perimeter on an early morning. Maggie was dressed in boots, jeans, and long sleeves, like everyone else. Her hands were covered by thick leather gloves that were a size too big. She felt awkward in the gloves, but it was important to keep covered because of snakes and spiders and scorpions.

Everyone was in good spirits, and Hannah encouraged a cheerful hymn. Then John David's walkie clicked in. "Incoming. Silver Camry. Over."

Everyone close enough to hear it froze. Zachary was the week's lookout stationed at a ridge-top campsite that overlooked the narrow private road leading to their community. Nobody used that road except members on supply runs or mission outreach trips, or the occasional wrong turn. John David brought the walkie up. "I'm on it." His hand settled on the butt of his pistol before he took off for the compound's main gate.

Maggie tried to follow. Hannah called her back, but Maggie pretended not to hear. She quickened her pace to make up for John David's strides. He had reached the gate where he met with Todd and his rifle, when Hannah caught up and held Maggie firm "You need to listen," Hannah said. Maggie shrugged her off but stayed put.

The Camry had California plates. Lucas stepped out of it, and Maggie almost jumped for joy.

"I did it," Lucas said. "I brought someone to be saved."

John David looked past Lucas to the boy lying unconscious in the car's reclined passenger seat. He wasn't just sleeping, not from the unnatural tilt of the kid's head or the loose fall of one arm over the cup holder between seats.

"It's Lucas," Todd told Zachary over the walkie.

John David shook his head. "What have you done?"

Then the door to Reverend Adonis's quarters flew open. The reverend's presence demanded attention as he crossed the compound. "Bring him inside. Both of them. Now."

Todd pulled the gate open. John David wondered how Adonis knew about the boy. As Lucas prepared to get behind the wheel, Adonis shouted again. "Not the car. The car has to go."

Todd headed to the passenger seat to check on the boy, but Lucas intervened. "I've got him," Lucas said. "His things are in the trunk." He popped the trunk open with his key fob, and Todd pulled out a book bag along with Lucas's own pack.

Adonis took the keys from Lucas and, before Lucas could gather the child in his arms, ushered John David close. "Pat him down."

John David found a gun, empty of bullets, with its numbers filed off.

"Get rid of it. Get rid of the car. Clean it of any evidence that could tie it to us." Adonis handed John David the keys and turned away as Lucas gathered the kid and began to follow. Todd fell in from behind.

"Sir, what's happening here?"

Adonis turned back. "This is your mess. Fix it. Get that car as far from here as possible. Burn it. Put it in a lake. I don't care. No trace!"

Humiliation set in. John David's brothers and sisters watched from their safe distances, and every one of them now knew that, for whatever reason, this was his mistake and that Jonas was not pleased. He turned to the community and assessed his options. "Lance? Carol?" The couple looked worried upon hearing their names. But they stepped up. "Can you get rid of it?"

"Get rid of it where?" Lance said.

"I don't care, as long as it can't be traced back here." Lance said that he could; he had friends in Michigan who worked in scrap metal yards, and John David gave him and Carol the job. "Take a stop at the Chicago mission while you're at it. A couple of days." The outreach mission was where Adonis had found Lance and Carol before they officially joined the fold.

Lance disconnected and destroyed the Camry's GPS unit, fearing its potential as a tracking device. He promised things would be taken care of and, if for some reason the car was found or traced to Michigan, it wouldn't matter because it was a far cry from their refuge in Sangre De Cristo.

John David secretly wondered if Lance and Carol had been eager to accept the charge because of Temple rules. They were married, but not allowed to bunk together per the reverend's decree. Leaving the Temple would give them opportunity to sin to their hearts' content. He instructed them to avoid major routes before he headed for Adonis's door. Hannah met him before he made it. "The boy is in the dorms," she said. "His name is Jacob."

The name was familiar. "He's alright?"

"They found Ambien in Lucas's things."

"Anything else?"

"Jonas is enraged. I've never seen him like this."

"Keep me posted," John David said. He continued to Adonis's door.

Todd answered his knock. John David tried to glance past him. He spotted Lucas leaning over his knees with his head in his hands. Adonis had his widescreen paused on video of a face: Alec Lowell's face.

Everything clicked as Adonis motioned John David in. The boy Jacob, the connection. He closed the door behind him after Todd made his way out.

"He says this was your idea," Adonis said.

Lucas cut in. "If my brother is a false prophet or...misguided, then Jake deserves to be saved."

"Is this what you told him?" Adonis waited, and Lucas filled in the rest.

"He said that if I wanted to save myself, I should save someone else."

"This isn't what I meant! You've got to know that this isn't—What did you do? Did you kidnap him? Drug him—"

"—God led me. Every step." It earned Lucas a smack across the face from the reverend.

Reverend Adonis turned on John David. "Get me an update on the boy."

"Sir, I never intended for this—"

"—There is something wrong if your intentions could be construed as this!"

John David lowered his head. He backed out of the cabin and headed for the women's dorms.

Jake leaned over the edge of a cot and threw up into a trash can. He was lucky it was there, even though his stomach was pretty much empty. All that came up was acid. Then a voice startled him, and a glass of water was thrust in his face. "This will help."

Jake scrambled back to the corner where the cot was wedged against the wall. He had yet to focus, as memories of Lucas's boney hand over his mouth filtered in.

"I'm not here to hurt you," the man said. "Children are a heritage of the Lord. And our reward." He tried to smile, but it was tight and wary, far from trusting. "I'm John David." He held out the glass one more time.

"You drink it." John David obliged with a reasonable sip before Jake lurched for the glass. He downed half the contents before cold water hit hot bile and he hung over the trash can again to spew the water back up. Jake clutched the edge of the cot and groaned.

"Sip it and it might stay down."

Jake sipped. His throat felt raw as the water trickled down it, but after a second sip, then a third, he had adjusted his swallowing to lessen the pain from it. Then John David took the glass. They sat in silence until Jake made a bold venture. "Can I go home?"

"Do you want to go home?"

A knock came at the door. A woman opened it. "Jonas wants you again." A girl stood behind the woman. She was somewhere near Jake's age, and she held an eager curiosity in her expression. She offered a slight wave.

John David called the girl in. "Maggie, keep Jacob company while we try to locate his parents?"

"Yes, sir," Maggie said, and John David slipped out of the room. The brief sound of a tensely whispered discussion came from the other side of the door before the pair moved away from it. Maggie continued to smile. "Are your parents missing?"

Jake curled up to face the wall. He wanted to crawl in a hole and die.

Maggie tried again. "Did Lucas find you? Did he save you from something—"

"—He's a fucking psycho, okay?" He sat up and turned on her, and he noticed that it made her flinch. And then she waited. Jake tried to steady his breathing. "Where am I?"

"The Sacred Temple of Adonis. We're a commune."

He scrunched up his face. "Is that like, Russia or something?"

It was Maggie's turn to screw up her face. Obviously, he wasn't in Russia. But he was terrified and still foggy from Lucas's drugs, and they had learned about the communist party in history class, so that's where his mind led him. "It's a haven for the blessed."

That made Jake even more confused. "Like some Bible camp?"

"We live here," Maggie bounced over and sat beside him. "Where are you from?" Jake braced himself, his knees drawn up. He didn't answer, and he grew irritated by her persistence. "Lucas isn't some psycho. He's nice."

"Leave me alone."

"Why would you call him—?"

"—He's not nice!"

She stared him down, and he trembled. *Just stop*, he thought. *Stop looking at me.*

"Okay," Maggie said. It was as if she had read his mind. She scuffled her feet over the floor, then came up with something new to talk about. "Do you love God?"

"What?"

Then Maggie went on about God and His glory in a way that Jake equated to girls he'd seen go crazy over pop singers and TV actors. He'd even seen it happen to Alec, and as she piled on her fan worship for Jesus, he grew more irritated. "Being here brings us closer to Him. He loves us. He cares for us. He waits for us and for the day of Judgment when we can be with Him forever—"

"—Shut up! Freak."

This time Maggie flinched from what Jake assumed was the name calling. He felt guilty over it. He had just used the same tactic to make her feel small as Reuben and other kids had done to him. But part of him didn't care. Lucas had dragged him to some kind of Bible camp. A Bible camp, for Christ sake! He couldn't escape the suffocating meaning of God.

"I'm not supposed to be here with you and your fucking haven for the blessed! I want to go home!"

"Maybe Lucas doesn't like you because you're mean."

"Do you even know who my dad is?" He could feel it again, the tightening of his chest, the inability to catch a satisfying breath. This was what Alec went through. This was it, and Jake felt worse for living up to the stupid saying, *like father like son.*

"Is he famous or something—"

"—He's Alec Lowell. The Perfect Prophet. Alexander the Great."

"I don't know who that is."

She honestly didn't, Jake could tell by her confused face. And then it started. Trembling overtook him. He couldn't stop. When Maggie leaned in to comfort him, he pushed her away. "Leave me alone! I want to go home."

"Maybe God brought you here. He brought Lucas here. Maybe He wants you here too—"

"—I want to go home!"

The confessional behind the stables was three feet high by three feet wide by four feet long, made from a two-by-four framework enclosed by corrugated tin. When the reverend was done humiliating Lucas, he led the way on the walk of shame to the box. Lucas's actions were deemed punishable, although oddly enough not so punishable to be banished again or to contact authorities. Weird.

"My brother is a false prophet," Lucas said in his defense before the walk of shame. "Jake deserves to be saved."

"Not against his own will!"

"In order to be true in spirit, you must shatter the shackles of your will." The words were a favorite among Adonis's teachings, and Lucas had rushed to continue. "Surrender it to become closer to fulfilling the Will of God—"

Another slap. The second time, it burned. "The boy must make that choice! Not you—"

"The Lord is my shepherd who leads me down the path of righteousness for—"

"—Shut your mouth, Lucas—" Adonis threw his hands in the air before calm overtook him. "You are an obstinate one."

"He led me. This was God's work."

"Now you assume to know the Will of God?"

Lucas remained silent. He believed it. The path had been too easy, and as Reverend Adonis had scrutinized him, Lucas could see that maybe the man was beginning to see a new light.

"Are you a messenger?" A sudden gleam had flickered from behind Adonis's gaze. "Misguided perhaps, but still…" Then the decree was made, the punishment set. Lucas would contemplate his sins in the box for three days.

Todd pushed Lucas along with apparent glee. He jammed the barrel of his rifle into Lucas's shoulder to quicken his pace.

Others gathered. Silent faces made their judgment. Lucas noticed John David and Hannah coming out of the women's barracks, confirming where Jake had been taken. There was no sign of Maggie, but maybe that was a good thing. This public indictment would only serve to put Maggie's friendship with Lucas into question, and he already missed their talks. He wondered if, after three days, he would be given up to the police. His sins were far more punishable than living three days in a box, and if that happened, losing his friendship with Maggie was a moot point.

Todd shoved Lucas down into the box. "Reverend Jonas is too lenient, if you ask me."

"I didn't."

Todd made sure to shove Lucas's ass in with the sole of his boot. The door shut. All was dark as Lucas heard the click of the padlock. A bit of light filtered in from a few slits in the roof. They allowed airflow, but Lucas couldn't see much. He curled up within the cramped quarters and took a nap. He had had little sleep from the drive, and he was used to sleeping in less-than-comfortable conditions. A blanket would have been nice, but the sun was up and the day promised to get warmer. He closed his eyes and listened to the sounds coming from who he thought was probably keeping guard: Todd.

It was dark when Lucas woke. His mouth was dry, and his stomach knotted from hunger. A few dots of starlight showed through the air slats. A conversation between Todd and John David caught his attention. It must have been what disturbed his sleep.

"Not a peep all day," he heard Todd say. "That's not natural."

"Have you fed him?"

The tin side rattled from a sudden kick. Lucas shifted, but didn't say anything. "Hey." It was Todd. "Someone thinks you deserve humane treatment—"

"—Get him some water," John David said.

An audible sigh came from Todd, and after enough time passed, Lucas had the urge to pee. He ventured. "Are you going to get me a pot to piss in, too?"

"He's gone," John David said.

"I'm serious. I need to go." More silence. Lucas shifted into a sitting position, stretched his legs as far as he could make them go. He heard John David lean against the tin siding.

"Why did you come back?"

"God sent me—"

"—No. Not you." There was a hint of struggle in John David's voice. "Jonas thinks he has something to prove now. You don't know what you've done by bringing this kid here."

"We're here to follow, not to lead. God led me—"

"—Everyone here believes that Jonas Adonis was chosen to lead us. To keep us safe from the evils beyond our gates. Every one! But you? A celebrity's son? They will scour the earth to find him—"

"—I covered my tracks. Jake needs to be saved. He needs Reverend Jonas—"

"—He doesn't need—" John David paused and leveled the timber of his voice. "Jonas has plans now. Do you understand that?"

Lucas wasn't sure what John David was hinting at, as John David lowered his voice to a whisper. "Do you trust me?"

"I still need that pot."

A new voice chimed in, Maggie. It made Lucas smile. "Brother Todd sent me with this."

"Maggie—"

"Don't speak to her."

"You trust me to share secrets but not to speak to your daughter?" It was a fair question. A moment passed, and the sound of the padlock clicked open. Lucas peered out.

John David had his gun aimed at the ground. He kept Maggie back until he determined that Lucas wasn't going to do something stupid to compromise her safety. That's how Lucas perceived it. He found John David's selective trust funny. Then Maggie placed a plate of bread and a bottle of water at the open door.

"Use the bottle when it's empty."

Thanks, Lucas thought. He reached for the bread and water as Maggie backed away. "Help me save Jake, Maggie. Alright?"

John David stepped in to close the door and secure the lock, and Lucas took the opportunity to try and secure his trust again. "I'm here to follow, not to lead."

The lock clicked into place, and Lucas prepared to ride out the first cold night of his penance.

The next day, John David brought Jake to the nice cabin to meet Mr. Adonis, or Reverend Adonis as most people called him. Or Reverend Jonas. The title seemed interchangeable, as long as the reverend part was there. Jake asked the only question that was important. "When can I go home?"

Reverend Adonis raised his eyes as he pulled Jake's backpack up from the floor behind his desk. He dumped the contents, and out came the bag of M-80s. Jake squirmed. "Your parents... haven't consented to your return." Adonis took the bag of explosives and dropped them into a deep drawer.

The excuses spilled out. "Reuben did it. He threw them at me and he ran—"

"Now, now." Adonis stepped around the desk and knelt down to meet Jake's gaze. "You are troubled. I understand. You have every reason to be."

Adonis took Jake by the arm, causing Jake to lurch free. "I want to go home—"

"—Some parents aren't equipped to lead their children along a proper path. A safe path. They're so...caught up in the burdens of their own lives that the children, they get lost—"

"—I didn't do it!"

"The vandalism wasn't yours?"

Shit, Jake thought. This guy knew everything. He was screwed. "So, I can't go home?"

"God led you here. We'll take good care of you. You're safe." The promise was ten times worse than weekly meetings with Father Grant. And the reverend's move to kiss Jake on the forehead made it creepy. Jake felt his insides crawl up through his throat.

The following days became weeks and, as Jake had expected, were filled with Bible study and prayer. The people held daily services before breakfast, and Maggie made it her job to accompany Jake to every single one. He had to sit with other kids, but they kept enough distance from him to make him feel like the outcast that he was. Just like at school. Nothing had changed.

Except for Maggie. Even after Jake called her a freak, she stayed with him, and because of it the other kids eventually tolerated him. Jake was privately thankful for that.

Listening to Reverend Adonis's sermons was worse than the few times Jake had been forced to sit in on those given by Josiah Light. Reverend Light loved his God and had nothing but faith in whatever His plan might be, but Adonis had a different message. "The world is a scary place," he began in a lesson catered to the youngest of his followers. "It's going to burn. Submission to God's rule is the only way to survive it." Jake could admit to the scary part. It was among them and no longer confined to some punishment box. Lucas was out of what they called the confessional. How was Jake supposed to find comfort in that?

Maggie's father, John David, who for some reason wasn't allowed to be called Dad, had assured Jake that everything would work out. "There are nice people here. Once you get to know us, you'll see." Then he leaned close with a whispered promise. "I will do everything in my power to keep Lucas away from you." Jake could tell that he meant it, but it didn't make him feel safer.

Maggie continued to insist that Lucas was sorry for what he did. "He knows he was wrong." Jake made eye contact with her. It was meant to intimidate her into shutting up, but it hadn't worked. Instead, she asked, "What did he do?"

Jake wanted to spill it. Therapy was all about sharing the horrible things of your past before they could eat your sanity away. He would have to tell someone eventually, but when he opened his mouth to talk about his nightmare past, he remembered how much of a rotten kid he had become. He had resisted his mother's attempt to give him a moral compass. He had outright told Alec to fuck off, and then Lucas showed up and here he was. This was his penance.

He wasn't ready to share. Maggie would have to remain disappointed.

The commune offered distractions. Kids engaged in lessons that weren't always steeped in Biblical knowledge. He learned to live off the land and to sow seeds in the greenhouse garden, although Reverend Adonis made certain to connect the lessons of farming to God's love. "Every single one of us is a seedling," he said. "We grow strong when we rise up out of the mud to seek the light. God is our nourishment. He is our light."

A nice fable, Jake thought, *like the one about some fox stealing away a hen or a gingerbread man.* In fact, all of the stories that Reverend Adonis told seemed like fables: tales of warning, but with people instead of animals for characters. And many of those tales were pretty damned scary. They explained why Jonas Adonis made certain that Jake learned how to shoot a real gun with real bullets on a shooting range. Jake liked that, especially when Maggie was by his side. He was Daryl and she was…well,

Maggie. They were two characters from that zombie show on TV. He didn't share this fantasy. Maggie wouldn't have known the show anyway.

All of the children were taught how to handle weapons by the time they reached the age of ten, and as they improved, so did the firepower. Jake honed his skills with a BB gun, a small rifle. Maggie was allowed to practice with a .22. John David was a patient instructor, and as Jake took aim at the paper targets at the end of the range, he imagined them to be Lucas's face.

Jake enjoyed learning to ride a horse, and he liked feeding the goats. He missed his parents, but he understood why they would decide to leave him here. He adjusted. It wasn't so bad. Except for Lucas.

The razor glided smoothly from cheek to jawline to cut away the month-long growth that had accumulated since the day Jake disappeared. Alec moved to his throat and worked his way up through a slow progression that ended with a nick. He winced. It was a big one. A rivulet of blood streamed out of it that fascinated him. He rinsed his blade in the puddle of soapy water in the sink, and he watched the stream of blood reach the collar of his undershirt where it left a stain. He let it bleed.

It didn't matter. He would rinse it away eventually, and the scab would flake off to leave no trace of a scar before he left the house, having downed a quick cup of coffee. Nothing much mattered anymore now that Jake was gone.

The story had changed. Reuben the bully admitted to having set Jake up after some attentive teachers had heard whispered rumors between Reuben's friends. It was true that Jake had run.

It was true that he left an offensive message. When the police had patrolled the neighborhood in search of Jake's whereabouts, they came up empty.

They did find his phone. A homeless guy two miles from the school claimed that he had found it in the middle of the street. He was going to turn it in, he said. They never found Jake.

Belinda moved out, which was funny because she was the one who told Alec not to come home. It wasn't about the house or the things, as she had called it. She needed space, and Josiah Light convinced her to take her time before she made any final decisions about divorce. "God challenges us in our weakest moments. And the devil waits for us to give in. Think about what's best for Jake." Josiah then offered Belinda a place to stay where she could pray for spiritual guidance. Who knew that Josiah Light would be the one to champion for Alec to be given another chance?

What bothered Alec most was that he had been right. He had been right to worry and to place Olsen at Jake's school. His irrational fears led him to take the right precautions, and it didn't matter. Jake was still gone, Lindy still blamed him, and he was still a neurotic mess of a human being.

The nightmares had subsided. The paralyzing panic attacks had stopped. It still didn't matter. He knew Lucas was involved but couldn't prove it. And that didn't matter either. Alec shut himself away for that month while he scoured the Internet for anything that might lead him to Jake. He berated the police on a regular basis for failing to find leads, and he hired a private firm to search for Jake, and it didn't matter.

None of it fucking mattered.

As Alec wiped up the blood from the base of his throat to the nick on his chin, he wondered how God, if there indeed was a god, could still think that he deserved to suffer.

He finished shaving and changed into fresh undershirt and clothes, determined to get out of the house and do something. He downed his coffee and headed for his truck, no driver catering to him in a limo this time. He hoped that driving himself would keep his mind occupied. He checked his nick in the rearview mirror. As expected, it was gone.

He wandered the freeways of Southern California before he ended up where he knew he would end up, the parking lot of Josiah Light's glorious and ostentatious church.

"Arthur! Can we adjust the spot?" Josiah peered up from behind the pulpit to the sound and lighting booth at the back of the church. Arthur responded with a "Yep" through the Bluetooth headset adorning Josiah's head as Josiah mentally choreographed the moves of the upcoming sermon. He walked to the center of the stage, then paced his steps back to the pulpit as he muttered the gist of the performance in his head.

Arthur's voice chimed in. "So, stage left to center? Center to stage left? What are we doing here, Josiah?"

"I'm mapping it, Arthur. The Good Lord is my navigation." Josiah smiled as his mind changed course over how to incorporate that into the Sunday plan, when he glanced to the side of the stage and saw Alec.

Josiah had neither seen nor heard from Alec in nearly a month. Blocking the sermon would have to wait. "Arthur, can we pick up on this in twenty?" Arthur proved to be eager for the break, and Josiah chose his so-glad-to-see-you smile as he headed to intercept Alec. He held his arms out for an embrace, then wrapped Alec briefly in it before Alec could turn the offer down. "How are you holding up?"

Alec got to the point of the visit. "I need…" When Alec paused, Josiah hoped that he would admit that he needed Jesus. But Alec found his voice after a quick shake of the head. "I need to keep busy."

"Of course you do. Of course." With that, Josiah led Alec to his office for a more intimate talk. It was a comfortable space lined with shelves of spiritual texts, many authored by Josiah Light himself, with the assistance of a few good editors who had admittedly done most of the work for him. His desk in the corner of the room was mahogany with a pair of ornate guest chairs cushioned in a rich, velvety green. Josiah led Alec past the desk and patted the equally welcoming cushions of the long sofa. He offered Alec a ginger ale from a mini fridge behind his desk, and was somewhat surprised when Alec accepted it. It wasn't bourbon or vodka, after all.

Alec set the glass aside. "I'm sorry I haven't been around for a while."

"No, Alec. You take all the time you need—"

"—I have to be here. I have to be doing something. Anything. Otherwise, I'm just wallowing."

Josiah let out a sigh that betrayed him. A wary expression crossed Alec's face, and Josiah cupped his hands around Alec's, ready to just run with the truth, when the warmth radiating from Alec's hands gave Josiah pause. It always did. Alec had rarely been forthcoming when it came to a touch or a handshake, but every time Josiah came into skin-to-skin contact he could feel it: an energy that vibrated through Alec. It made Josiah wonder if he himself was stricken with some malady that doctors had failed to identify.

Josiah composed himself. "I understand. I truly do. But no."

Alec broke free. "I get it. I'm a fucking PR nightmare. If you want to disassociate from me, I get it." Alec rose to his feet ready to bolt, as Josiah cursed inside his own head then made a mental note to ask for God's forgiveness later.

He snagged Alec's arm before he could escape. "You've got it wrong. Sit down. Sit." Alec broke free again and kept going. "Alec, I can't lose you. You're a gold mine for this church." Alec turned back looking confused, as Josiah cursed to himself one more time for the greed-tainted honesty. Alec's tragic chain of events had inspired an outpouring of charity from his believers, from those whose faith had been restored by his own quasi return to Jesus Christ. Josiah coaxed Alec back to the couch and approached the facts with care.

"The people here love you. They feel your pain. They pray that you will reunite with Jake, and…well. I'm not looking to sever our contract. Far from it."

"Then what?"

"You are part of our family now. So I want you to go and find yourself. However long it takes. I want you to find where Jesus fits in your life. Scream at Him. Learn from Him. Pray for His guidance. I want you to go to Belinda, and with God's help, I want you to forgive each other. And whatever the outcome with your son, whatever it is, I want you to be at peace with it."

Alec resisted spilling tears, and Josiah reeled him in like the master emotional manipulator that he was. "Let it out. There's no shame in sorrow."

Fear and frustration hiccupped out of Alec. "How did it happen?" Alec whispered. He did everything right. It was wrong. It was cruel. "If God wants retribution for my mistakes, why Jake? He's everything to me. I can't lose him. I can't."

Josiah listened and consoled and sent Alec on his way to find the answers that he admitted he couldn't give. Then he sat back on his comfortable couch with satisfaction. Alec Lowell was no longer questioning the existence of God. He was questioning the choices made by God, and that felt like a win.

Alec convinced Lindy to meet in an attempt to reconcile. He told her he was headed for Wisconsin where everything that was most horrific in his life had happened. "What are you going to find," Belinda said. "There's nothing for you there. How does it help find Jake?" She had yet to give up on understanding his motives, although she should have long ago. "You're running again."

"How is going home running?"

"What are you going to do? Where are you going to stay, at Ilene's?"

"It's not Ilene's anymore. And I own it, so—"

"—You're going to stay where your sister was killed—"

"—You're the one who killed her—"

"—That's not the point! What happens if you have a panic attack in that house with no one to help you through it? Or is Cleo going—"

"—I haven't heard from Cleo in weeks."

This surprised Belinda. "You've been home alone this whole time?"

"You could come with me. Josiah thinks that if we tried, we could—"

"—I know what Josiah thinks." Reverend Light had a pep talk with her, too. She began to wonder if he had one with Cleo, since she hadn't been in contact with Alec. Josiah Light, for all his glorious good intentions, was still a meddler. He probably considered Alec and Cleo, and even Belinda, to be a glorious challenge.

"The police are stalled, Lindy. And I know you don't believe me." Alec lowered his voice to barely a whisper. "But Lucas is involved."

"And you think he'd take Jake to Wisconsin?"

"I don't know! I don't—"

"—The last time you saw Lucas was here. In California. And he kind of did you a favor—"

"—That's right! He was here. In California. How can you dismiss—"

"—The issues between you and me are deeper than Jake."

Alec slouched. "Yeah. They are. And it's my fault, Lindy. I know that being who I am, that being what I am, makes everything my fault."

"I didn't say that," although she felt guilty because maybe he was right. Maybe she expected too much from him given the pressure he was constantly under. There was pressure from the believers, pressure from the skeptics, and there was pressure from her. Belinda knew without doubt how much Jake defined Alec's world. His failure to communicate with his son cut him to his soul. Maybe Belinda was being too hard. Maybe it was her fault, too.

Their relationship had always been tentative. Agreeing to marry Alec had been for Jake. Belinda knew it then as much as she knew it now. They were bound by tragedy, and they had survived, and Belinda thought that the bond left between them couldn't be broken. But the physical and mental scars left by Lucas ran deeper than any of them expected. Belinda couldn't blame Alec completely for seeking comfort from Cleo. His paranoia had grown constant and, to be honest, it had tired Belinda out. She had grown aloof. She wanted Alec to talk out his fears, but then again part of her didn't. She suffered from the terrifying memories too, and she wished she could forget it all and move on.

But she couldn't. And neither could he. And neither could Jake. And here they were, reliving this nightmare that would only tear them apart further.

Belinda took Alec's hand. "I'm not leaving here. If something breaks in the investigation—"

"—That's what your cell phone is for."

"I can't."

Alec broke from her grip. "Okay. I'll be in Ashland, or in Keystone, trying to find myself or whatever shit God wants me to do."

"I didn't say you shouldn't go."

"Yeah, you did."

"I didn't understand why. I still don't, not completely. Call me every day, okay?"

Alec nodded. He kissed her cheek before he headed out the door.

Alec returned home with some hope. Lindy had asked him to call. Every day. It was progress. He packed a duffle with three changes of clothes, a handful of toiletries, and a tablet to access the Internet, and he grabbed his acoustic case before he set out for the drive. He programmed his GPS for a scenic route to Ashland, Wisconsin, and he hit the road.

The route would take him through both Las Vegas and Salt Lake City, ironic considering one was the city of sin and the other a city for the devout. It would continue north and then east through Montana to Fargo, North Dakota, and Minnesota. It would take him a day and a half if he drove straight through without stopping. He expected to make it in three.

He blew through Vegas and its alluring lights and hoped to find lodging in Salt Lake. It was closing in on midnight when he found a place. He was far from tired, so he took to wandering the streets while he tuned out the city with a pair of earbuds and a national news podcast. Brisk autumn air refreshed him. It was the season of ghosts and goblins, movie monsters and serial killers, but there was little evidence of that here in Salt Lake City. Pumpkins and nylon spider webs cluttered storefront windows, sure. But they didn't carry the same brilliant and grotesque appeal of a place like Vegas. The decorations that peppered the city evoked homespun nostalgia, not an invitation to reenact some purge. The news podcast provided all the horror Alec needed. He grew tired of it and popped the earbuds out.

He found himself standing at the gated plaza of Mormon Temple Square. The place was closed, but the church was lit to inspire awe, like the castle at the center of Disneyland. Jake had never been to Disneyland. Alec turned away from the temple.

He found a bar, a place called Jr's, and the bartender immediately put Alec on notice. The place was closing in less than an hour. "Yeah, whatever," Alec said. "Pour me something smooth." The bartender obliged in silence, and Alec understood that he had just made another enemy. He downed the drink and waved the bartender over again. "I'm sorry for the attitude. I'm going through an existential crisis."

"Aren't we all," the bartender said. "A word of advice. That? Not the best remedy for an existential crisis."

"You're shooting yourself in the foot if you're in business to make money." Alec tapped the glass for another.

The bartender hesitantly poured. "I make ends meet. We have a niche clientele. So why the existential crisis? I'm sure you're important to somebody."

Alec raised his glass to the bartender and downed the second round.

"I just gave you your opportunity. You're not going to tell me your life story?"

"My kid is missing."

The bartender paused. "I'm sorry. That sounds serious."

"Yeah, no," Alec said. "I shouldn't have said it. But you asked."

The bartender poured a third round. "Last one. On the house. Only if you nurse it. I'm Greg by the way."

"Alec." He took the third round and savored a sip. When he looked back up, he found the bartender ogling him. *Shit*, he thought. *Why did I tell him my name?* The bartender backed away with a failed attempt at being nonchalant.

"Take your time," he said. "I'll call you a ride when you need it." The bartender slipped away to chat with a small group of locals at the other end of the bar. Alec felt his face grow hot as they whispered and stole glances in his direction. He downed the drink and left ample payment on the counter.

The cold night welcomed him back. He deserved it here in freaking Mormon country, where God had banned him from entering a church, then called him out for succumbing to the weakness of drink. He was a shitty example of a prophet and a healer. When he reached his motel room, he fell on the bed and turned on the TV, hoping to zone out to some dated rerun.

Instead, he found the news.

His panic welled as he listened. A grave desecration in Los Angeles. The grave of Marcus Anthony Edison. Alec startled out of his near attack when his phone dinged with a message. It was Belinda. *You haven't checked in.*

He typed. *I'm in Salt Lake City.* He waited for her comeback while he kept an eye on the news. She didn't reference the news. Instead, she asked if he was alright. *I'm in Salt Lake City*, he repeated.

It took a while for Belinda's reply. *Okay*, she texted. That was it. Alec turned off his phone. He turned off the TV. He shut his eyes tight and prayed that the news of Mark's grave wasn't the omen that he feared it would be.

The Good, The Bad, and the Jesus Freaks

REVEREND ADONIS WHITE KNUCKLED THE EDGES OF his pulpit and leaned forward. "A preacher and a criminal walk into God's house," he said—almost shouted. Jake braced himself for an awful punch line. It was too early for the Christian Comedy Club. In all honesty, it was always too early. Morning service was an agonizing part of the day. Every goddamned day.

The reverend continued as if reading Jake's mind. "Bear with me, because in this story our Father will only grant one of them entrance into the kingdom of heaven." He paused dramatically then, "Let's add a qualifier. This preacher is a righteous man who constantly brings his good deeds to the attention of the community. He expects his place in heaven. Who here expects their place in heaven? Automatic entry no questions asked. A show of hands, please." He raised his own, just slightly above the height of his own shoulder.

Nobody joined him.

The reverend grinned at that. "I'm going to be a lonely man up there in the kingdom of heaven…Alright, let's talk about the criminal, the sinner who lies to make ends meet. He's done things that he truly regrets, unforgivable things! He can't even look God in the eye. But he pleads. Oh Lord, find it in your heart to forgive me, although I deserve nothing." Adonis turned to the children, but his eyes met Jake's eyes. "Who does God choose—"

Maggie raised her hand, but the answer spilled out of her mouth before the reverend could overlook her. "The sinner."

Adonis tamed an expression of irritation before he asked, "Why. Jake?"

Jake thought he might cough up a fur ball. He wished Maggie would jump in and save him again, like she was prone to do. He gave in to a shrug, and the reverend expelled an excruciatingly long breath through his teeth. "You need to pay attention Jake. Maybe some time confessing your own sins would do you good."

Jake knew what this meant. He had already spent time in the confessional for acting out, for suggesting that God didn't exist. He survived it for half a day, not as long as Lucas had spent there on more than one occasion, but long enough. The confessional was cramped and cold, and it smelled like a litter box. Hannah dragged him there after complaining about his behavior to Adonis. She left a bruise on his upper arm because he had protested. Even more embarrassing, everyone watched and let it be.

Jake struggled to prove he was a good student, when another voice cut in, Lucas. "The sinner seeks forgiveness without expecting reward; a truly repentant soul."

Adonis settled his gaze on Lucas, again with irritation. But he nodded and carried on. "A perfect answer, Lucas." His eyes shot over the entire congregation. "Spend your day in contemplation of that, brothers and sisters. For if you are proud enough to believe you deserve entry into the kingdom of heaven, maybe you don't."

They commenced with a closing prayer before they disbanded. As usual, Lucas was the first one out the door. Jake stepped out with Maggie and the other kids and watched Saint meet Lucas at the stables. "He doesn't want to hurt you," Maggie said as if reading Jake's thoughts. "Like Reverend Jonas says. He knows he was wrong." Jake told her to shut up.

Later, Maggie quizzed Jake on his Biblical knowledge while they scoured rows of greenhouse vegetation in search of the ripest vegetables for the salad bar. It was always irritating. She had a tendency to whisper clarifications to Jake during Adonis's sermons that he didn't need to hear, and he didn't dare tell her to shut up then because he didn't want the attention.

Today's lesson seemed specific. "Can you define a prophet?"

"Why?"

"Because I want to know if you really know—"

"—I'm not stupid."

"I didn't say that. I'd never say that. I just want to know if we agree. Name one."

"Jesus."

"He is. He's more than that—"

"—No, I mean Jesus, will you stop?"

He had done it, successfully offended her. Maggie distanced herself and focused on picking the rosiest cherry tomatoes she could find. Jake closed in and picked tomatoes too.

Then he spoke with an ease that surprised even him. "A prophet can be a miracle worker. He can be a messenger or an interpreter. He could just be the miracle, I guess…someone chosen as a sign that God exists."

Maggie stared in awe. "I thought you didn't believe in God."

"So did I pass?"

Maggie seemed compelled to add her own definition. "A prophet is chosen by God to spread His word and to reveal signs of His return. But it's hard to know because of the false prophets, the liars. They want us to think that they are chosen so that they can lead us to hell instead of heaven. People will be led by them when the end times are near."

Jake wished Maggie would give it a rest. When she did, the silence became awkward. She was the first to break it. "Why did you call your dad a perfect prophet?"

Jake shrugged. "It's who he is."

"Is that what he told you?"

"No. Never. I mean…Yeah, no. Never."

"Then why—"

"—Ask Lucas," he said with a snide edge. "Maybe he can give you an answer."

"Ask me what?"

Jake sent a shower of tomatoes to the ground. Lucas stood in the greenhouse entry as Saint scampered in past him. The dog reached Jake's feet and gave a curious sniff at the tomatoes.

"It's alright," Maggie said. "He's sorry for what he did. Right, Lucas?"

"John David says you can't be near me."

"Jonas sent me—"

"—You can't be here!"

"He asked for a pepper. Just one. Red—"

"—What's special about Jake's dad?"

"Stop it—"

"—Do you mean my brother?"

Maggie turned to Jake, full of more unspoken questions. He couldn't believe it. He couldn't believe Lucas would spill so much with so few words. Jake wanted to burrow into the soft garden soil and hide.

Lucas whistled for Saint, then left Jake and Maggie alone.

"He's your uncle?—"

"—He killed my dad."

"You're dad's dead?"

"No. He…he tried." Jake couldn't stop shaking.

Maggie asked why. And he stuttered through it. He told her about the band, the devil worship, how Lucas killed Alec, and how Alec returned to become a healer for Josiah Light.

"He's a doctor?"

"No. He—he lays hands on people and he heals them." Maggie didn't say a word. "Lots of people don't believe it."

"Do you?"

Jake didn't have an answer. He'd never seen Alec do it, not in a way that was obvious. After bullies had sliced Jake's face open, Alec had held him for hours, his hands cupped over the damage. And the stitched cut had healed. But all cuts heal eventually. Right? Alec hadn't mentioned it in the book. And he never brought it up in any of the televised interviews that Jake happened to see.

What Jake had witnessed was the night Alec died, strapped by Lucas on an upside down cross then stabbed in the chest.

Jake wished Lucas had died like that. It would make up for the resulting trauma. That would be enough.

"It's not nice to ignore people," Maggie said, bringing Jake back.

"Then stop asking me shit."

"You said your dad can heal people. That's a miracle."

"I don't know! I can't prove it." Jake stooped down to gather the dropped tomatoes that Saint hadn't managed to lick.

Maggie bent down to help. "Maybe Lucas tried to kill your dad because your dad worshipped the devil."

"He doesn't even believe in God."

"Then why does he want you here?'

Jake shoved the bowl full of tomatoes into Maggie's hands and walked away.

"Everyone has bad things that happen—"

"—Lucas is not your friend! He fucking worships the devil. He is the devil—"

"—Then why did he ask me to save you?"

"Stop believing him!" The trembling returned. Jake couldn't make his legs carry him away. He was miserable and scared, just like Alec, and he couldn't stop it. Sobs hiccupped out of him until Maggie led him to a bench. She sat beside him, and she waited. "My dad isn't bad," Jake said. "He's just scared all the time. He's the scaredest person I know."

The scaredest person Jake knew had reached Casper, Wyoming. He had left Salt Lake City at sunrise fueled by nothing but coffee, and it was well past lunchtime when a caller lit up the dashboard system. It was Cleo or, according to caller ID, Claire. Alec answered. "For the record, you broke down and called me first."

"Did you hear about Marcus, hon?"

"Yeah." Alec avoided that subject. "I'm in Wyoming. Thanks to Josiah."

"Josiah sent you to Wyoming?"

"Not exactly." Alec typed on his GPS screen, looking for more coffee. A map popped up with a destination. "I'm on a pilgrimage."

"To Wyoming, hon?"

"I'm going home."

Cleo didn't chime in immediately. When she did, she claimed that she understood. "I haven't called because of Josiah," she admitted. "Then the news about Mark broke, and—"

"—Listen, I'm heading in for coffee and I don't want to be that one dick on his phone. Can you text me?"

"...Sure, hon." He could hear her irritation, but it was true. He didn't need people to hear him, to look at him, and to realize who he was. And he really needed fuel in his stomach. He pulled in to park at a little place that didn't seem too busy and he headed inside.

She noticed him instantly as he walked through the door. A brilliant aura radiated from him that no one else in the shop seemed to notice. But Ally saw it. She smiled in his direction as he checked something on his phone, then stepped up to the register. "Give me a grande. Black."

"We call it a large," the barista said. "We're not fancy."

"A large then."

"No special blend?"

"I'm not fancy either." He looked at the pastry case and pointed something out. "And one of those…things. Yeah, that." He paid for his goods, then passed Ally's table to slump at a more secluded spot near the back.

Ally tried to say hi, but the muscles that controlled her vocal cords refused to cooperate. They had stopped cooperating long ago, and she mumbled something unintelligible when he passed. She tried to wave, but her hands were balled into knots, and what she hoped would be a wave only amounted to a spastic flail.

Ally's mother turned her attention away from her weekly coffee friend. She adjusted Ally's wheelchair and offered her a sip of the orange cream soda that she thought Ally liked. Ally had liked it when she was ten, but now she was thirteen and her tastes had changed. It was difficult to tell her mom that though. Ally managed to turn her face away from the soda pop. "What is it, Baby Girl? Potty run?" Another thing she hated. The baby talk. Mom had regressed to using it since the disease took hold.

"I'm sorry," Mom told her friend. "I think Baby Girl's had her fill of socializing today." Mom's friend replied with the standard assurances, no worries. She gathered her purse, then delayed the departure with more talk of schools and bad teachers and the gossip she heard at the last PTA meeting. This was fine. Ally kept her eyes on the man at the back.

He sipped his coffee and played with his pastry without eating it as he texted. His face was perfectly proportioned, his eyes dense with color, and his hair kept getting in the way of them. He was also sad. Ally wished she could make him feel better. She wished she could get up out of her wheelchair, walk over, and say, "It's okay. I'll be your friend." And as her mother continued to gab, Ally felt a pressing urgency to make it happen.

"Mom," Ally said. "Let me talk to the man." It didn't come out the way she said it in her head. It never did anymore.

"Tricia and I are almost done, Baby Girl. I promise."

"It's fine," Tricia said. "I have so many errands. We'll catch up next week."

Tricia gathered her purse, and they said their final good-byes with Tricia heading for the door and Ally's mom pushing Ally along to the exit.

"Mom!" Ally insisted. "Mom, I want to meet him!" She twisted in her seat with a jerk and managed to look back.

"What is it, Baby Girl?" Ally could hear the impatience in her mother's voice because Ally was making a public scene. "I told you, we're heading home." She tightened her smile, and Ally persisted. "Sweetie, is it the bathroom? Is that what you need?"

Ally managed a stiff nod, and her mother turned around. Success. The bathroom was at the back of the shop. They would have to pass him. As they closed in, Ally smiled. "Hello," she said, although it sounded more like "uh-oh." He kept to his phone. She tried again, and again until Ally panicked because her mom was going to push right past him. Ally lurched and cried out, and the edge of the wheelchair knocked into the table leg.

His coffee almost spilled, and as Ally desperately tried to voice the words "Hello, I'm a friend," her mom went into her own panic.

"Oh God, it's a seizure. Baby Girl, don't do this to mommy." The man locked gazes with Ally. He looked terrified. And as mom bent forward and tried to stop Ally from rocking, the man lurched out of his seat and took hold of Ally's hand.

Success. Ally settled down and smiled.

Mom's panic dissipated. "Baby, what were you doing? You nearly gave me a heart attack." She settled a hand to stay her beating heart. "I am so sorry," she said to the man.

"It's alright," the man said back, and Ally beamed. The man's touch spread a soothing warmth through Ally's fingers that made her want to stretch them out and wiggle them.

"Baby Girl, what was that about? I guess she wanted to say hi. I'm so sorry."

"Hey. Hi," the man said. He kept Ally's gaze. "Nice to meet you."

"Alright, little angel. You can let go, now."

She didn't. In fact, Ally managed to tighten her grip.

"I am so sorry. Baby Girl, give the man his hand—"

"—It's okay. You can hold my hand for as long as you like."

Mom looked like she was going to cry. Ally saw her mouth the words thank you to the man, something that she did often when friends and strangers stepped in to help her. "I'm Charlene."

The man said that it was nice to meet mom but didn't offer his own name. Charlene tried to engage in small talk. It was awkward and lasted less than five minutes before she tried to get Ally to let go again. It wasn't happening. Ally was set on that. "Baby Girl, we have places to be."

The man assured her that Ally could take as long as she wanted before he sat back down, her hand still engaged with his. He continued to text with the other.

Mom was not holding it in well. She brushed at her eyes and faked a laugh and said, "Well, I need to visit the ladies' room. Coffee goes right through me."

"She can stay here. We're good."

Mom was hesitant to leave, but she did. Ally knew it would take a while because mom wasn't going to the bathroom to pee.

She was going to have a good cry. She did it often. "Be good, Baby Girl. I won't be a minute."

The man continued to text. Ally was embarrassed by her mom, so she tried to tell him. "I'm Ally."

The man looked up. "I'm sorry, what?"

He couldn't understand her, of course. No one did anymore. She tried again anyway. "I'm Ally, not Baby Girl."

He was silent for a long moment. "I'm Alec."

He understood her! Then he leaned in with a whisper. "But don't tell your mom. I'm kind of famous."

"I'm Alex," she said all excited. "Alexandra, Ally. You're famous? What for?" She was so happy to be understood that she didn't think about why or how. She gripped his hand tighter and she thought she saw him flinch, but he smiled the most genuine smile as he shared things.

"I was in a band," he said. "I just like to lay low once in a while."

"What songs?"

"If I told you, your mom might not want me holding your hand."

"She likes music. She sings in the car all the time. Beyoncé and Shakira and Demi…"

"Yeah? Is she any good?"

Ally scrunched up her nose, and it felt good to do it. "She sounds more like AC/DC."

Alec laughed. "What's wrong with AC/DC?"

"Mom says they gargle cigarettes."

Alec seemed genuinely amused by that, amused enough to dismiss his texts and give her his full attention. "Then definitely don't tell your mom about me. Our secret?"

Ally nodded.

"Does your mom treat you well?"

"She tries."

"Except for the nick name? I mean, what the fuck, right?" Ally blushed and giggled at the swearing, and Alec apologized by swearing some more. "Oh, shit, I shouldn't have said that." Then he glanced toward the bathroom and straightened up as if the teacher had come into the classroom. "Head's up. Mom's back."

Ally turned her head and caught her mom dabbing at her eyes. She had called it. She turned back to Alec and grinned.

"There we go," Mom said upon her return. "All fresh. Thank you for being so kind. Baby Girl, we really have to go."

Ally reluctantly let go of Alec's hand. His aura had changed. It had diminished. Or maybe Ally just couldn't see it as well as she thought she had when he first walked through the door. She felt different inside, like the knotted muscles gripping her bones had gone through a vigorous massage. Mom guided the wheelchair away as Alec shouted a quick goodbye. "It was nice meeting you, Ally."

Mom paused, and *oh no! Maybe she had recognized Alec for being famous*. "Mom," Ally said to pull her attention away from Alec, and the surprised look on Mom's face grew.

"Oh, Ally. You said my name." Mom looked back toward Alec's table. He was gone. The coffee cup was still there. So was the pastry. Maybe he had to pee too, Ally thought. Then her mom leaned in and gave her a hug and a peck on the forehead. There were tears in her eyes again, but a laugh of joy at her lips. "Let's get you home."

I'm effing serious. She's holding my hand and we're talking, and I don't think she could do it before. Cleo wasn't sure what to make of the turn in the text thread.

Alec had successfully avoided talk of the desecration of Mark's grave; Marcus, the Orange County, California, boy whose entire family had been part of a biker group whose membership was, oddly enough, comprised of a significant number of Christians. Mark's family had loved their youngest, although they hadn't been pleased with his flat-out denial of anything remotely related to God. They had buried him in a family plot anyway, because he was their son, and nothing would change that.

The grave hadn't only been desecrated. The coffin had been dug up and the body stolen. It was disgusting and impossible that anyone would have a reason to pull off body snatching in this day and age. But the former fans of The Great had been a dark and anarchistic bunch. Cleo was more disappointed than she was surprised. The idea of Satan worshipping psychopaths laughing it up as they toasted to a celebrity corpse in their living room made Cleo a bit nauseous. Alec, on the other hand, had glossed over the news. He had kept the conversation focused on his sudden commitment to find his spiritual purpose.

Maybe it is why Jake's gone, he had texted. *It's my punishment. For refusing to believe. For faking it.*

Hon, you can't fake anything, Cleo had texted back. *But if your goal is to find God, then I'm glad.*

Thanks.

Just don't go all Josiah Light on me.

LO-EFFing-L, he had texted. Then, *I'm sorry about us.*

Cleo had been lost for a reply. She had changed the conversation back to the news. *Mark's brother is freaking out.*

Sean is a dick. It was true, but an unnecessary observation. Then Alec added, *If Mark could see this, he'd think it was hilarious.*

Doesn't make it any less disturbing. She waited for him to respond, but for a long time there was nothing. *Hon? You there?*

He wasn't.

Cleo tucked her phone away and knelt before Paddy's headstone. The news of Mark's grave desecration had inspired her to visit Paddy. It was stupid, but she feared that Patrick's grave might have been desecrated too. It hadn't, which was a relief, but then the loss of Patrick hit her like a drunk driver, and she found herself weeping like she had on the day of his funeral.

She wiped away tears and sensed someone closing in from the edge of her peripheral range. Cleo tried to ignore the presence. She dabbed at her mascara, when the stranger engaged. "Are you alright, miss?"

Rats. She turned and found, to her surprise, that the man was a clean-cut type in a blue collar shirt and khakis, not some metal head fan. She imagined him to be a nose-to-the-grindstone dad who made it to an occasional Sunday mass at the insistence of an equally conservative wife. "I'm fine, hon. Sad memories. Thanks for asking."

The man referenced the grave marker. "O'Shaugnessey. A tried and true Irishman?"

Cleo had to laugh. The guy was obviously not a fan. "His daddy's name is Carlos."

"Really, it's a strange world we live in." Okay…maybe the man was not so tolerant of the strange world they lived in. But he offered condolences, so Cleo dismissed her judgment.

Her phone vibrated. Alec was back on the text thread, and his response threw her for a loop. *I think God just gave me a sign.* Cleo excused herself and texted back while heading for her car. Alec carried on in truncated sentences about a handicapped girl at the coffee shop. They were together and talking, and he was fucking serious. He thought maybe it was a sign.

Cleo slid into her driver seat and asked for details, and again the responses stopped. She waited, but there was nothing. She tossed the phone on the passenger seat. At least Alec was excited about something. She was happy for him even if it wasn't what he really needed, which was to find Jake safe. She started her car, about to head out of the cemetery when a knock on her window startled her. It was the clean-cut guy. He motioned her to roll down the window.

"I'm sorry to bother you," he said. "But you are Cleo LeCroix, aren't you?"

She sighed. "Yeah. I am, hon."

"Can you step out of the car, please?"

Alright, Cleo thought. *Not a fan, not a working-class man. Undercover cop.* She stepped out of the car.

It was getting dark as Alec headed for Fargo. He wouldn't make it by midnight, not without a break, so he found a place to lodge in northern South Dakota, in a tiny town called Faith. It was home to the bones of Sue, the most complete T-Rex skeleton ever unearthed within the United States until a legal dispute relocated them to a museum in Chicago. Alec found it funny that a town called Faith would be the home of something in existence long before the idea of a Christian God. He found it funnier that he would end up there.

The inn where he took refuge was across the street from an information center where a machine-parts replica of a T-Rex stood guard at the parking lot. Alec was bleary eyed when his headlights hit the thing, and he initially mistook it for a deer. He applied his breaks and swerved in anticipation of it darting in his way, and he wound up in the parking lot of the motel across from it. After gathering his wits, Alec determined that it was indeed a dinosaur at the side of the road. He also decided that he was too tired to continue on for the night if he was mistaking dinosaurs for deer.

The desk manager was a kind woman named Roxanne who set him up with a room, then happily told him about the dinosaur once he asked. "Get a good look at it come morning," she said. "It's a John Lopez original." Alec admitted that he had no idea who that was but promised to look him up once he was settled in. He asked about a place to eat, and she laughed. "Not at this time of night. But darling, you look famished. You wait right here." She left the counter and came back with two slices of moist banana bread. "Homemade. Something to tide you over until morning."

Alec thanked her after a mouthful of the bread. He returned to his truck and grabbed his things before he settled into his room. A quick text to Belinda let her know that he was safe, and when he added that he was nearly run off the road by a T-Rex, she responded with, *What?*

He kept the conversation short. Belinda was already up to speed with any news, and Alec was tired. Not long after he turned out the lights, he flipped them back on. The damned T-Rex kept intruding. It was an odd little piece of Americana, something parents might take their kids to see on cross-country road trips just because it was there. It was something Alec wished Jake could see because Jake might have still been young enough to think it was cool. It was another missed father/son opportunity, and Alec wondered why God had to rub it in.

He imagined that this stop might have been another lesson to remind him that he wasn't there yet, at the point of accepting, no questions asked. Don't question the dinosaurs that lived before time. Don't question the loss of Jake. Just accept Me. Accept that you're nothing but a cog in My machine, and carry on. Alec closed his eyes and prayed for a reason to accept it.

He couldn't. Who was to say that his gift, his ability to self heal and to foster healing in others, wasn't some kind of evolution? Maybe the brilliant minds behind the Marvel superhero universe were the prophets, and maybe he was the first step toward a future mutant, X gene world. He grabbed his acoustic and strummed it, feeling less inspired by God and more lost over the disappearance of Jake than his heart could stand. *It's not over. He's missing, not dead.* He supposed there was some grain of faith built into believing that.

He eventually found sleep, maybe four hours of it. He got up early, enjoyed another free handout of fresh baked goods from Roxanne, then drove straight through to Fargo in time to stop and find lunch. The radio was off, his phone was shut down. He punished himself with his own brooding silence.

Fargo was a metropolis compared to Faith. But it was nothing near a metropolis compared to Los Angeles. Alec exited the main highway and explored the city after asking the Internet to find the best lunch spot in town. He opted for a place called the Vinyl Taco because it offered everything that a guy like Alec needed: hip food, hip music, hip ambience, and cerveza. Alec hadn't had a real drink since Salt Lake, and he supposed that was a good thing. But he needed it, and he decided that one good cerveza was a reasonable compromise.

The place was everything the Internet had promised it would be. The music was tight, Hendrix was depicted in mosaic on the wall, a life-size buffalo hung behind the bar, and the cerveza was ice cold. The street tacos were five star-review good, but the beer was what Alec savored. He hung over it at the end of the counter after he turned his phone back on and texted Belinda. *Made it to Fargo. I'm staring down a buffalo.* He thought it would be funny considering his last check-in involved a dinosaur. Weird coincidence, that he would have another run in with an extinct or near-extinct beast.

Belinda didn't respond right away, which gave Alec time to enjoy the beer. When she finally dinged in, it wasn't about the buffalo. *Did you catch the news?*

Alec cringed. He had a feeling it was bad news, so he didn't respond.

He didn't have to. *There was a miracle in Casper, Wyoming.*

Nope, he texted back. *Hadn't heard.*

A girl can speak again. Her mom says it was you. Wants to thank you.

What did the girl say?

Says she didn't recognize you as anyone she knew. Alec smiled at that. Ally had kept her promise, but her mom had figured it out.

Can she walk?

So it was you.

Can she?

No. Just talk. Disappointment settled in. The girl deserved more. More than anything, Alec was disappointed that he hadn't finished the job. *Josiah's happy. She donated to the church.* Alec sighed, not exactly thrilled that Josiah was the one to reap the reward. The man's foundation did good work, it was true. But it wasn't all good work. So much of their donation revenue went to production costs and comfortable living expenses that it was hard to determine if the balance was adequate. Alec guessed that it wasn't. *Have you heard from Cleo?*

That came out of the blue. Alec's thumbs hovered over the phone. *No. Why?*

Belinda didn't follow up with a text. Instead, his phone chimed in with a ringtone familiar from his days as an anarchistic death metal punk. The song was his, *Looney Bin*. He answered. "I'm not with Claire. She's not with me—"

"—Josiah's been trying to get in touch with her. She's not answering her phone."

"Maybe she needs a break from Josiah too."

Another stretch of silence, the kind that Lindy was famous for. She disapproved of his apathy. But then he realized that he had read the silent treatment wrong. "I should fly out and meet you in Ashland."

"Kind of defeats the point of the trip—"

"—Alec, they found something." He braced himself. Belinda's voice was hesitant, and whatever she was going to say, Alec knew he didn't want to hear it. "There was this…murder in Arizona—"

"—No."

"And this…string of car thefts. Camrys and switched plates, I don't know. They tracked the guy who they think killed the Arizona student to California. This student had a roommate, and he said this stranger was at some party…It was Lucas."

Alec went short of breath. That grain of faith he'd found in South Dakota slipped out of his grasp. "So he's dead."

"That's not confirmed—"

"—Our son is dead and there's nothing we can do about it."

Belinda let a sob escape. "Let me meet you in Ashland—"

Alec disconnected the call. He sat in numb acceptance before he fished out more than enough cash for his meal and dropped it beside his plate. His legs threatened to crumble beneath him as he made his way to the exit, and as he quickened his pace he realized that anyone watching might have mistaken him for being drunk. Once he reached his truck at the curb, Alec doubled over and tossed up the street tacos that had tasted so good. Now they were literally street tacos, hahaha.

He landed with a thud on the walk and failed to hold back a sob. Jake was likely dead at the hands of Lucas, and here Alec was sitting on a curb in fucking Fargo trying to find himself. Fuck God. God could go to hell.

The old groundskeeper of the rural cemetery somewhere between Ashland and Keystone was now connected to the world. The organization responsible for the upkeep of the place and for the sales of plots and funeral packages was quite pleased with the service he provided; he'd lived on the premises for years and raked leaves and trimmed lawns and maintained the property with impeccable regularity. But contacting him at the spur of the moment had been a pain in the ass. That's how the representative from the main office had worded it. He had not possessed a phone, no television, not even a transistor radio. He had no desire to stay connected to the outside world after his daughter died. The world beyond his cemetery gates was cruel and loud and uninviting.

But Valerie, for that was the name he'd read off the tag perched over the pocket of her navy blazer, had arrived to tell him that it would no longer do. She had come bearing gifts, a laptop computer and a Wi-Fi router. Now, every morning and every afternoon he opened the lid of his sleek little computer, and he checked his email, gkeeper@wimortuaryservice, for messages. He rarely had any, and this morning was no different.

The groundskeeper continued his morning by adding water to a pot and putting it on the stove for tea. He glanced out his window and saw a visitor among the headstones. Alarming, since he had yet to unlock the cemetery's front gate. The visitor must have climbed over it, something he found irritating. Most after-hours visitors who stormed the gates were high school kids who did it on a dare. But the visitor's location disturbed him. It was near his daughter's grave.

The groundskeeper set the flame beneath the teapot to low. He found his coat and set out to meet the visitor.

"Well, well, well," he said as he recognized the slender built, long-haired man from behind. "You've decided to visit after, what? Two years?"

Alec tried to smile, and the groundskeeper understood that this was not a casual visit. Alec motioned to the headstone with his father's name on it. "He shouldn't be here. Next to her. He shouldn't—"

"—You can change that, Alexander. It's your decision."

"It's not yours? Since when." Alec sniffed back the run from his nose, possibly from being poorly dressed for the cold weather. But the groundskeeper knew it wasn't that. He threw an arm around Alec's back and guided him toward the house.

Once Alec settled in and accepted some tea, he unburdened himself from the things that had happened since he left Wisconsin. The groundskeeper listened, although he was aware of some of it. The new celebrity as a healer, the murder of Dr. Carver, and Jake's disappearance were all things that the groundskeeper knew. He did have an Internet connection after all, and he was guilty of having spied on Alec once he figured out the unlimited potential of the thing they called a browser. The scope of the investigation in Jake's disappearance was new, although he assumed that the police had not publicly announced the information.

"I'm sorry," the groundskeeper said. "The loss of a child is something we never get over, although we try."

"Have you seen him?"

"Now why would Lucas come here? Why would you come here?"

The lost expression on Alec's face hardened. "You know how to find him."

"Do I?"

"You can do it. The black magic shit he uses on me. You knew how to do it before he was born. Teach me. I want him to bleed from his eyes."

"That's not you, Alexander—"

"—You could have done it when he killed Paddy. And Mark. And mom. You could have stopped it. You could have stopped all of it—"

"—Your father's prophecy was not written that way—"

"—Fuck his prophecies!"

The groundskeeper waited for Alec to take a breath. Then he laid out the truth. "I got scared, Alexander. When your mother died, I got scared. You know how that feels. It's easy to be enticed by the kind of dark power Lucas knows. But it's manipulative. It's wrong."

"You have the book. The thing that changed him. Burn it like he burns my bullet—"

"—One could argue that your father's book of prophecies is a thing that changed you, too. But it didn't belong to Lucas, not the one I have."

Alec slumped in his frustration.

"I thought you found your way past the bullet. It was no longer a thing that defined your change—"

"—He took what defined the change. He took Jake." The groundskeeper couldn't counter that, and Alec continued. "The one thing that holds meaning in my life? Gone. I found a purpose when I found Jake. And then God ripped it out of my hands. What does that say?"

"I don't have answers. You know that. Where are you staying while you're here?"

"Ilene's." It was his dead sister's house, the one where he grew up under the strict religious torture of their father. The house had been on the market since the horror of the satanic attacks on Alec and his family, but there were no buyers. Local families were aware of the property's sordid past, and it was no place for Alec to find refuge.

"Stay here. For as long as you need."

Alec thanked him before he went into deep contemplation over the cup's contents. The groundskeeper left Alec's side feeling like he had failed his grandson, but what could he do? It was true. He knew things. He knew how to take a cup and fill it with ingredients to torment the right soul. He had helped teach it to Alec's father. He was partly responsible.

When he returned to the house after his morning routine, he found Alec on his computer. Alec turned to the groundskeeper with an amused expression. At least he had found something to distract him from the sadness. "You've been stalking me."

The groundskeeper suddenly understood what it was like to be the grumpy, out-of-touch codger that people poked fun at. Alec pointed to something called a browser history, then highlighted an address at random from it. Pictures of Josiah Light and his church popped up that reported on Alec as an addition to their spiritual family. The groundskeeper grumbled, then avoided admitting to anything. "That Reverend Light is an interesting fellow. Do you like him?"

"Not really," Alec said. "But he's been good to me."

"I'll bet you're making him money, what with your unique skills and all."

"Are you Marcus, now?" The sarcasm hadn't gone unnoticed, and the groundskeeper smirked. The remark had been a respectable dis. Mark Eddison would have been proud. "When did you get technology?"

"Well, you know. One has to keep up with the times if they want to stay in touch with family."

"I'm not really good at that."

"It's alright. You grew up never having a reason to try." The groundskeeper pulled up a chair. "I can't make your choices, but if I'm going to believe that you have a destiny, then it's not my place to define it or get in the way."

"What?"

"I'm trusting the path that led you here. Lucas has no business trying to hurt you by using your son. If you want to learn what Lucas can do, I will show you."

The upside-down cross was still in the clearing in the middle of the forest. Lucas had killed Alec there. He had left Alec to burn. Alec remembered the dying part. He remembered leaving his body and floating above it as Lucas pulled Jake away to a shack deeper in the woods.

He hated that memory. But he'd done more. He had re-inhabited his body and had suffered through the healing in order to rescue his son. He had done that. And here the cross was, a testament to his suffering. Decorated by random graffiti carved by strangers. A piece of odd Americana, but not for a fun family road trip. It existed for drifters and the disenfranchised who needed their own dark tourist attractions.

Alec headed into the woods. His grandfather had shared the details of Lucas's favorite ritual, and if Alec could find anything that might have been significant enough in Lucas's life to define who he was or what he had become, Alec could use it. He could make Lucas writhe until the flames of the chalice were put out, and Alec had a full canister of lighter fluid in his pocket.

Alec hoped to find something, anything at that shack. It was a long shot, but it was the only shot he had. The pack on his shoulder had other items, a chalice, a knife that had been defiled, and a sealed container of urine. He would use his own blood for the final mixture rather than kill or hurt an animal. He wasn't a sociopathic little shit like Lucas.

He was so ready for Lucas to die.

He pictured Marcus waiting for him in hell. Yeah, Marcus would be there, and Marcus would laugh his ass off while telling Alec what a useless prophet he had turned out to be. Alec imagined himself saying, "Yeah, sure. Now go play with this punching bag." Then he would lift Lucas onto a meat hook, and he would tell Mark to pummel the prick into an unrecognizable mass of blood and bone.

Alec neared the shack with caution. The location had once been littered with hunter's traps. He found that out the hard way, too. He pushed open the hinged piece of plywood that served as the shelter's door, expecting to find nothing.

His expectation was close. The place didn't seem to be as popular a hangout as the upside down cross. There was a table, a broken chair, the bones of a cot made of metal springs. Its mattress was gone. He found a tackle box in a corner. It was open and raided of most of its fishing tools, and the few plastic bobbers that were left were scattered in the dirt. Alec bent down and wondered if fishing had been special enough to cause Lucas pain. He picked up a bobber and noted that it wasn't caked with dirt. It was caked with a thick coating of dried blood. How did the police miss that?

Fish blood. Would a fish bleed that much? Closer inspection of the tackle box proved that it, too, had been stained with blood. Lucas's blood. It had to be. After all, this was where Alec had shot him, had left him to die. Alec pulled a tray out of the box and found hooks and fishing line underneath. Lucas was a resourceful one. He could have used the tools in the tackle box to remove the bullet and sew himself up. He had the skills.

Alec scoured through the dirt. He picked through leaves and empty food wrappers that had been left behind by strangers, and when he came up empty he pushed aside the cot and searched there, and—*No fucking way*! He found the bullet.

He didn't know whether to thank God or the devil, because it was there in his hand, a bullet that changed Lucas's life forever. Alec dumped the contents of his pack: chalice, knife, the container of urine, and the lighter fluid. A Latin incantation raced through his mind, and he practiced pronunciation of the more difficult words. He dropped the bullet in the cup, emptied the urine and some lighter fluid into the mix, then poised his open palm over the top of it with the knife in the other hand. He was about to engage in a pact with the devil. A breath. He winced as he cut against the grain of his skin then squeezed the blood out like he was squeezing a lime.

When he set the contents on fire, he dropped to the floor in agony.

Lucas didn't drop, not immediately. He helped John David repair the goat pen. The damned things tried to eat through anything, including chicken wire. Saint yipped for attention before Lucas tossed a ball that kept both of them amused enough to get through the day.

Lucas caught a furtive glance from Jake as he and Maggie crossed the compound. The two kids entered the stables before John David pulled Lucas's attention back to the job. "Reverend Jonas is taking them riding," John David said. He held his hand out for wire cutters.

Saint returned with the ball and Lucas tossed it again. "Does Jake like riding?"

John David didn't give him a direct answer. Instead, "It gives Jonas the chance to talk about scripture. Jake needs ministering almost as much as you."

Lucas took the ball from Saint again. He didn't throw it right away. As Saint begged, John David turned a concerned eye on Lucas's pause. "Is there a problem?"

Lucas shrugged. Reverend Adonis had absolved Lucas after a time, after Jake grew more comfortable among them. But it seemed like John David never would. He stared Lucas down as if he was guilty of criminal intent.

Maggie came out of the stables, heading for them. John David stepped ahead of Lucas, a barrier to protect her. "John David," she shouted. "Reverend Jonas wants to see you."

That's when Lucas dropped the ball. Sharp pain pierced through him. He grunted and gradually sunk to his knees. He cupped a hand over his gut to keep his innards from spilling out. That's how it felt. His fingers found blood at the point of the scar left by the bullet; the one that had wounded him and Alec together.

More pain shot through him with the burst of a gas-fueled flame, and he crumpled. He knew what it was. Someone had found the bullet that had changed him.

One person closed in to help him, Maggie. "Lucas? Lucas!"

Alec took a spastic swipe at the flaming chalice, knocked it off the table. Its contents spilled to the floor and the flames scattered out, and the debilitating ache that had burned through Alec's gut vanished. *Shit.* He couldn't even get his revenge without suffering. He figured it out once he managed regulated breathing. The bullet that had changed the world for Lucas was tethered to Alec, too. He had to share it with that black-hearted waste of a soul.

But he had seen things through Lucas's eyes. A girl about Jake's age had called Lucas out by name. Alec found the slug again. He gathered up the rest of the paraphernalia, and he returned to the cemetery.

"I saw a girl."

"So it worked. You can get your revenge."

"You don't get it! I saw a girl through his eyes. She was Jake's age. What if he's going after other kids? What if Jake's not the only one?"

"There's not much you can do if you don't know where he is. I suppose you can try again."

"I can't."

"Good," the groundskeeper said. "You've learned the cost of courting the devil."

"I can't because of the bullet." The groundskeeper waited for Alec to continue as if he already knew what Alec was going to say. "The bullet went through both of us. The ritual took me down with it."

The groundskeeper nodded, and Alec understood what the old man didn't need to say. *Ironic, isn't it.*

Alec moved on. "Maybe I can identify her. Maybe..." He headed for the groundskeeper's computer and did an Internet search on databases of missing children. There were state sites, dedicated organizations, and even a listing by the FBI. The groundskeeper's hand settled on Alec's shoulder, and when Alec looked up, he noted intense fascination in the man's face. Maybe he was coming around. Maybe his grandfather was beginning to see that this, too, had been part of some divine plan. Alec still had a hard time coming to terms with the idea of a divine plan, but if this was it, saving a girl from the same kind of victimization he imagined Jake had gone through, maybe there would be a bittersweet outcome. Maybe Alec was meant to save her.

He scoured websites for pictures of missing girls across the United States for hours. He focused on California, then Wisconsin and every state in between, hoping that a picture of the girl would match the image from his mind. The groundskeeper made snacks and provided lemonade and puttered, and by midnight Alec had grown dejected. The number of missing children throughout the nation was staggering. He came up empty. None of the girls in any of the databases matched. God, be it He, She, or It, had led him to another dead end.

The groundskeeper's voice pulled Alec out of his depression. "There comes a time when we have to accept what is and carry on."

"Lucas doesn't deserve to win! Or to live. I almost felt sorry for him once, because I thought that maybe he'd been misled. But no. There is no fucking forgiveness for him."

The groundskeeper threw up his hands. "Keep searching, then. I'm going to bed."

Alec stared at the computer screen. He heard the click of the groundskeeper's bedroom door closing and he sighed. There was nothing he could do. He should move on.

It was past midnight in Wisconsin, past ten in California. Alec fished his phone out of his pocket and turned it on. It had been off since Fargo because he anticipated calls from publicists and agents and Josiah Light since the news of the girl in Casper broke. He didn't need to be inundated, not after Belinda's bomb drop about Lucas, so he had turned the phone off. More than fifty text messages waited for him and almost as many voice messages and missed calls.

None of them were from Cleo. Not a one. A few were from Lindy. He thought he should at least answer those, but he didn't want to. He imagined Belinda would give him the same advice that the groundskeeper had given him—finish your grieving and move on. He should have called Lindy. He called Cleo instead.

The call went to voicemail. "I made it to Keystone. Hit me back when you get this." It wasn't instantaneous, but after a short scroll through more pictures of young faces that didn't belong to the girl, a response text from Cleo dinged in. *What's up?*

Alec texted back. *Screening your calls?*

Can't take calls at the moment. Where are you?

Home.

With your wife?

Alec cringed. He didn't want a passive aggressive fight with Cleo too. *No, not with 'my wife.' She wanted to come. I said no.* There was no follow up for the longest time. Alec couldn't bear it. *Lucas took Jake. It's over.*

More nothing. Alec fidgeted, wondering what had her preoccupied. It was staggering news. The least she could do was excuse herself from whatever she was doing to call him. She finally texted, *I'm sorry.*

Alec stared at the text for what felt like eons. He didn't have the words to reply. He tossed the phone aside and focused on more missing children. Then he typed in a search for Jake. His kid's face had made it to several lists; the last school picture he'd had taken, and it didn't include a smile.

That was it. Alec was done. He was exhausted and couldn't take the lack of progress anymore. He shut the computer down and went outside to brood over his mother's grave.

Adonis paced. The fresh wound in Lucas's gut that had split along the scar left by his own butchered attempt at self surgery years ago had healed over. A day had passed and now, as John David peeled back the bandage to re-dress the wound, the damage was minimal. It was yellow and tender, a scabbed-over gash, but not the open hole that had sent everyone into a panic earlier.

"Did you do this to yourself? Is that it?" Adonis had rejected Lucas's explanation of black magic. "I'm not fond of games. I will cast you out. No second chances—"

"—Don't you mean third?" Lucas found the tipping point.

"John David? Give us a moment." John David finished applying a fresh bandage before he stepped out of the infirmary. Adonis leaned close. "Why should I believe in you, Lucas?"

"I didn't ask you to."

"You weren't led by God. The devil is still in you. You threaten our—"

"—I know I can't be saved." Lucas added a shrug. "But I know Alec did this. He's looking for me, and he's using satanic ritual to do it." Adonis had no comeback. "Isn't this what you wanted? Because if it isn't—"

"—Our time is near. Our tribulation is at hand—"

"—I'm ready."

"To be chosen or to be left behind?" When Lucas didn't answer, the reverend leaned in. "Everyone is born into sin. My father was a Jew. My mother insisted that they didn't cut me." *Too much information*, Lucas thought. It was odder that it brought memories of his once-severed tendon at the wrist. He started flexing fingers again, agile, perfect fingers.

Adonis moved on. "We'll be ready." He smiled at that before he called John David back into the room. Adonis let John David finish up before he took his leave.

"It's healing well," John David said. Lucas hopped off the bed, when John David held him back. "Promise me. When things hit the fan? Stay out of the way."

Lucas wasn't sure what this meant. "Why," and with a single word, Lucas caught the man flinch. John David was afraid of him. Lucas hadn't held that kind of power for a long time. "You don't trust me near your daughter. You want me to follow, not to lead." He lifted his shirt again. "This was from Alec."

"Trust me, Lucas—"

"You ask me that, to stay out of your way, because you're the one losing faith—"

"—You've led the apocalypse to our door. You. And you're right. I don't understand why Jonas is keeping you here; why he isn't punishing you—"

"—Maybe he has more faith than you—"

"—This was our haven. We were the good ones. Maggie and I…among the chosen when the time was near. But…"

"Now you don't believe him? So what are you going to do?" John David didn't reply, so Lucas gave him a suggestion. "Let God lead?"

"What is your brother to you?"

"We have a mutual distrust of each other."

"Okay, then. Okay." It was John David's turn to pace. His thoughts bubbled up and spilled out. "I can change this. I can be the difference." He turned to Lucas one last time. "Promise me you'll stay out of the way."

Lucas shrugged and gave John David a nod.

The groundskeeper woke to his morning routine. He opened his computer and grumbled as he tried to figure out how to exit from Alec's missing child search and navigate to his email. He managed it and found his inbox empty. Task one done. He pulled the lid closed and heard an unfamiliar ding.

It was Alec's phone beside the laptop. A text message lit up the screen. *Do me a favor. Talk to this man.*

The groundskeeper puzzled over it. If he knew where Alec was, he could pass the message along. *Sleeping*, he thought. His grandson had finally given in to sleep. He wasn't about to knock on the guest room door to disturb him. He found his teapot, lit a burner, and set the flame to high. When he looked out the window, he found Alec. Sleeping.

Alec startled awake when the hand settled on his shoulder. Then he realized he was freezing. He had gone out to his mother's gravesite the night before, laid on top of it to stare up at the night sky and wonder why things had to be what they had to be, and he had fallen asleep. The groundskeeper draped a blanket over his shoulders. "I am constantly confused as to why you haven't died from plain stupidity." He handed Alec the phone.

The text was attached to the end of the thread with Cleo from the night before. It included a phone number he didn't recognize. "Two four eight. Where is that?" Alec flashed the screen at the groundskeeper so that he might identify the area code, but the old man shrugged.

"You could call, I suppose."

Irritated, Alec texted Cleo for more information. She didn't reply. He called her, but the call went to voicemail. "Got your text. What man? Call me."

She didn't call. The groundskeeper led him inside and provided sustenance with some kind of potato and egg hash doused with a blend of delicate herbs. Alec was thankful for the old man who didn't deserve his absentee grandson. He fretted over the phone until the groundskeeper nudged him. "Just make the call. What are you afraid of?"

He was afraid of another curveball. He gave in and made the call.

"Hello," said a man's voice on the other end.

"Yeah, I got a message to call this number. From Cleo—Claire? Claire LeCroix?"

"Mr. Lowell?" Alec admitted that it was indeed him, and the man got flustered. "I represent the Mission for Lost Souls. I'm so sorry about…about the disappearance of your son. I… was hoping we could meet."

A business call. Alec cut in. "You can contact the Josiah Light Foundation to schedule me for an event—"

"—It's not that. I need to speak with you face to face."

"This isn't a good time—"

"—Please. It's extremely important. I have—" The man cut himself short then continued in a hushed tone. "I have information about your son."

And there it was, the curve ball. "Who is this again? What information? Who are you?" He listened to the man, Lance, repeat the name of the organization, but his brain must have been partially frozen from his graveyard nap because he wasn't processing. He shot out questions without time for the man to answer. "What about Jake? Is—is he alive? Is he—Who are you?"

"Your son is safe. But it's complicated."

The instructions were simple. Meet face to face somewhere between Keystone, Wisconsin, and Detroit, Michigan. Lance's number began with a Michigan area code. Alec had done a search after the call ended. The guy hadn't been lying about where he was from. But he had begged Alec not to contact anyone about the meeting. That was the complicated part. "We are a discreet Christian organization. We don't need media attention or to be branded for our unorthodox lifestyle."

Alec wasn't thrilled by any of this. But Lance was so adamant about Jake being safe that the circumstances almost didn't matter. He still asked questions. "Why is he with you? Why didn't you call the police?"

"One of our brothers found him. And we have a limited connection to the outside world. We don't want the kind of media attention that other churches crave."

"Jake was abducted! The guy who did it needs to be caught."

"I understand, sir. If you'll meet with me, you'll see that no harm has come to your son."

The proposed location to meet was a public place, and Alec felt safe that he could decide how much he could trust the guy then. He promised not to share the news, but the first thing he did after finishing the conversation was text Cleo.

How do you know this guy? He had done an Internet search to find the Detroit area code while he waited for a reply.

Through someone in Los Angeles, Cleo texted. *They don't like publicity, unlike Josiah Light. Just do it. They have Jake.*

She was right. Alec thought about contacting Belinda, but he refrained. She deserved to know, but there was still the potential for the whole thing to be a sick lie, a ploy for a stranger's opportunity to meet Alec and touch him because of a broken toe or an acne condition or, God forbid, an autograph. Alec didn't want to let Belinda down if this turned out to be nothing.

He gave the groundskeeper a huge hug before he headed out. "You've got email now," he said. "We can stay in touch."

"I suppose." The old man footnoted it with a sigh. "Trust your hunches."

Alec promised that he would and was met with a skeptical raise of the old man's brow. Grandfather and grandson finished their goodbyes, and Alec headed out. The man named Lance had agreed to meet in Chicago at an address in a sketchy neighborhood within the city. GPS tagged the address with a name. It was The Mission for Lost Souls.

It was late afternoon by the time Alec reached the dirty little storefront on a rundown street populated by the homeless and the addicted. It didn't deter Alec. He had been close to living that life during his early days with the band. If anything, the location of the too-obviously named mission gave the place credibility. Inside, the place was laid out like a chapel: benches lined up before a podium, a simple cross gracing the wall behind it. A donation box showed signs of having been broken into at least once. A padlock secured the lid closed, but its hinges were bent and loose.

A table had pamphlets fanned across it advertising drug-rehab centers, second-hand stores, and suicide-prevention hotlines. There was also a stack of pocket-sized versions of the *New Testament*. Alec leafed through one until a gentleman stepped out from a side room. The man opened his mouth upon spotting Alec but failed to follow through.

"Lance?"

"…Mr. Lowell, of course!" He shook Alec's hand, and Alec made certain to keep the contact brief. "It's my pleasure to meet—"

"—I'm not here for anything but my son."

Lance asked Alec to follow him to the back, when the front door opened again. A pair of anarchist types wandered in. They were thin and pale with angry piercings. One had scratched the skin of his arm raw. Tracks betrayed the habit. The kid shivered from bones made of ice.

"He needs his Dolophine," the other said in panic. "He's freaking out."

"Rehab is two blocks north," Lance said before he was cut off.

"He's not gonna make it. Come on, man! You've got a supply."

Lance shouted. "Carol! We need assistance!" He turned back to the anarchists and held his hands out in an attempt to calm them. "God has led you here, and we can shuttle you to—"

"—Fuck that! He's in a hurt! He needs it now!"

Lance whispered an apology to Alec, then left the room in search of Carol. The guy suffering from withdrawal grew more agitated. He hugged himself to dispel tremors, and Alec cursed. Memories of Paddy floated through his mind, and the night the kid had overdosed on Molly. It had been Alec's fault for giving him the drug, but it had also been Alec who brought him down just by holding him. He had held Patrick for hours, and now… now he knew that he was the one who had saved him.

The sober one of the two addicts tried to talk the shaky one through it, but the kid wasn't calming down. He paced and sweated and pushed away any attempt at being reined in. "Don't touch me. Don't—don't—don't touch me!"

Alec understood that feeling. The friend shouted. "You people, you set this place up and you don't do nothing! You got the shit he needs. He won't make it down the street!"

"I'm sorry," Alec said. He closed in thinking that maybe this was another test, another opportunity from the god he failed to believe in.

The addict didn't like it. "What's he—Don't touch me!"

"You got what he needs. Just share the shit—"

"—I don't know if they got your shit. I don't work here. But if you let me hold his hand, he might feel better." Alec held his hand out, feeling stupid for doing it. The addict took refuge behind his friend, and the friend pulled a gun.

Alec stepped back, hands raised. The addict pleaded. "Don't do it, Nico. We don't want this mess—"

"—Give up the meds."

"Nico. Let's go. We can walk—"

"—Yo, get him the meds!"

A noise alerted Alec of Lance's return. The more telling sign was the shift of Nico's shaky aim. "Get him what he needs. Or I shoot somebody."

"You don't want to do that," Lance said, and when Nico's aim grew steady in Lance's direction, Alec gritted his teeth and stepped into the line of fire.

"Oh, is it you, then?"

"Call 911, Lance—"

"—You got a death wish?"

"I get it, I've been there. Your friend is crashing, and you're in a panic to get him what he needs, but this isn't it—"

"—You want to get shot? Hey—don't you move!" Nico shifted his aim toward Lance again, and again Alec eased himself into the line of fire. "You want to get shot—"

"—I am fucking tired of getting shot." Bitter frustration hardened Alec's jaw line, and for a moment he thought Nico was going to drop the gun and run. When he didn't, Alec softened his stand. "What's your friend's name?"

"You don't need—"

"—It's Dante," the addict said. "I'm Dante."

"Meet me half way, Dante." Alec extended his hand. "I'm not gonna preach. I promise." The kid hesitated. He reached out, and Alec reeled him in. Alec cupped a hand against the base of Dante's skull. A sob escaped the kid as they sank to their knees together.

Nico broke for the exit, and Lance gave chase. Lance was also armed. Once Nico slipped out the door, Lance locked it. "That was impressive." Alec heard enough surprise in Lance's voice to become irritated.

"You couldn't have pulled that thing sooner?"

"You were kind of in the way."

Dante rested his head against Alec's shoulder like a child finding comfort in a parent's embrace. His tremors decreased to a point where Alec could feel the kid's heart beat a steady rhythm.

Lance called Carol again. When she arrived, she tugged at Dante's shoulder. The kid clung to Alec, a magnet to steel. "We're going to get you to the clinic, but you have to cooperate."

Dante clung tighter. Confessions spilled out of him. "I do this to myself. Ain't nobody's fault but mine. I got no home. I got no place. Momma, she prays for me. Pop says he'll cap my ass if I show face. I'm sorry for the things I do, but I can't stop. I can't."

Alec fretted over the kid's need to share. He was no priest, no saint. Shit, he had once been a fuck up too. The kid spilled it as if doing it would absolve him. Then Carol finally eased Dante away, and Lance led Alec to a back office.

The discussion elevated to an argument. Alec Lowell wanted answers. He wasn't placated with the idea of some blind reunion. "He wants proof," Lance said over the phone. "He wants to know why it took so long to contact him." Lance listened and watched the self-proclaimed perfect prophet pace with his feet on fire. At one point, the man tried to intervene and reach for the phone.

"Let me tell him. Hand it over."

Lance dodged the reach and held a finger up for patience. He didn't like this assignment. He and Carol had joined the Sacred Temple to disconnect from the evils of the world, not court them. Lance had mentioned that to Mr. Lowell at one point, but Lowell became belligerent and demanded to see his son.

"He's at our refuge. In the mountains."

"What mountains? We're in fucking Chicago!" Lance said he couldn't be more specific, and Alec Lowell threatened to call the police. Lance appeased him by calling Reverend Adonis on his Temple-supplied prepaid phone instead.

"He doesn't believe we have him." Then with a whisper, "He doesn't hold much faith."

Adonis agreed to send Lance a picture of the boy. "One picture. Show him, then remove it from your history."

The picture was of Jake sitting on Moses. The boy was new to riding. His grin was huge, and Maggie stood beside the horse to steady Jake in the saddle. Lance turned the phone toward Mr. Lowell.

Relief swept over the man. He expelled a breath. Lance felt it too. Everything was going to work out like the reverend had promised. Then something changed in Lowell's expression.

"Like I said, he's fine."

Alec handed the phone back. He pulled out his own phone.

"What are you doing?"

"Calling his mom. She should know—"

"—That wasn't our agreement—" Lance ripped the phone from Alec before he could hit send. The number glared up from the screen, 911. "I don't understand," Lance began to say before Alec lurched forward.

"Give me my son!"

"I'm trying to—"

"—You think I don't know who's behind this? Your fucking little cult leader who wants to see me burn?"

Lance pulled his weapon. The self-proclaimed perfect prophet didn't cower. He shook his head and cursed again. Lance heard Carol returning from her rehab run, and he called out to her. She paused in shock when she reached the door. "I don't like doing this," Lance said.

"Then don't—"

"—Jonas knows the truth."

"Shit." Alec said it again, and then he lunged. Lance was caught off guard, and Carol screamed. Lance struggled to keep possession of the gun. If this had been any other attack, Lance would have shot Alec. But Adonis didn't want that. Alec Lowell was special. Carol left the doorway and returned with a baseball bat. Alec Lowell never knew what hit him.

Judgment Days

MEMORIES FILTERED IN. COLD DAMPNESS INVADED his senses. He was in a cellar, an ice box, a morgue. He wasn't certain. But he wasn't alone. A face popped in and out of view. What was her name again? Carol. That's right. "He's coming to. It's wearing off." Panic filled her voice, and Alec had the faint sense that they were moving, the steady hum of a passing landscape.

But wait. That was then, and this was now. The sting of a needle was then, the familiar sense of floating in a black sea of nothing was then. It hadn't lasted long enough; it never did, and it had been interrupted a few times by Carol's stricken face. That was then, and now had changed. He was waking up, becoming woke as the cold, damp cellar morgue became cold, damp earth. Okay, maybe not fucking woke, but he was wakening to a delicate circumstance, one that was really, really bad. The smell of dirt invaded his nostrils, dirt and something else. A funeral parlor.

Noise pulled him closer to his reality, a voice from on high. "He's moving. Get the reverend," followed by the garbled static of another voice.

Alec opened his eyes, focused and— "Shit—Jesus!" He shot upright and scrambled back against the wall of a pit. He'd found the source of the funereal ambience. Jesus, it was Marcus, lifeless and stiff, wearing an ugly chocolate suit. It had probably belonged to his father. Alec had recognized the suit before he recognized the face because Cleo had pointed it out at the funeral and because Mark's face…it hadn't aged well after two years in the ground. Apparently, chemical preservatives didn't last forever.

Alec gagged. He rammed his heels in the dirt to push himself farther away before he realized that he was sitting against another body in a much finer suit: Patrick. His parents had splurged on a Tom Ford. *Jesus. Fuck…Jesus.* Then Alec realized that his hands were bound behind his back and he lost it. He let out a scream that he couldn't control. Total freak out mode.

"That won't help." A woman peered down. It was hard to see her face, cast in shadow with the sky at her back, but it was a woman. She held a rifle and said nothing more.

Alec breathed. He ratcheted down the beat of his heart from some Metallica guitar solo to something more in keeping with, say, The Sex Pistols, and he eased himself away from Patrick. He was going to puke, he knew it as he took in shuddering breaths of rancid air. *Shit. Fuck,* he thought. Then, *alright. Assess.*

The pit was just deep enough to be difficult to climb out of, especially with bound hands. An iron grate covered the opening, and the face that belonged to the voice continued to peer down. *Where am I* came to mind, but no. That was a stupid question to ask. He was in a fucking pit. Alec doubted they would share more. "Is that you?" *What was her name again?* "Carol?"

"No."

Alec nodded at that. He took in the shriveled, split face of Marcus laughing at him. And he couldn't do it. He couldn't maintain some brave composure anymore. He barreled his way through a stutter. "C-can you let me out? C-can you-you tell me what you want?"

The woman gave him nothing.

Alec continued. "Please. My kid was abducted and he—"

"—Jake likes it here."

Alec processed this. Rage bubbled out. "He likes it here? Where is here?" He'd said it, dammit. "Where—Is it the mission? In the mountains? Is that what this is, some kind of fucked up God cult? Have you brain washed my kid? Or was that a lie? Maybe you just want to get rid of me! Bury me alive because, what? You didn't fucking like my music? What do you want?!?"

Nothing. When Alec looked up, he saw the silhouette of a second person peering in. "Open it up." The woman passed off her weapon before she and a third person bent down to remove the grate. Bits of dirt showered down, as Alec rolled onto his knees and pushed himself up onto his feet. He tried not to shiver, but it was fucking freezing.

Alec said it again. "What do you want?"

"Reverend Jonas, should I—"

The one named Jonas silenced the woman with a raised hand. He squatted down at the edge of the pit and he studied Alec, and Alec couldn't help but wonder if the guy was trying to pay homage to the singer in an A-Ha music video, except he was too old to be one of those guys. Well now, maybe. That video was an ancient thing, after all. He was old enough to be Alec's father, if his father had kept fit instead of wasting away in some mental ward. The man's hair was too perfect. Strands fell out of place over one brow as if they were choreographed to do so. "Rumor has it that you're not a believer," he said.

God cult. Alec had called it. He felt himself go pale, which wasn't a thing, it couldn't be a thing and he wished his own mind would shut the fuck up.

"When you die, this is where you end up if there's nothing to believe in. This is it."

The guy's point was lost on Alec, irrelevant even. He tried once more. "What do you want—"

"—You're a miracle worker. This generation's Jesus. Its... perfect prophet." The way he emphasized the title made it sound like a dirty joke, which it was as far as Alec was concerned. Jonas continued. "Go on, then. Work your miracles. Raise them up. Once you do that, we can talk." The man got to his feet and signaled the other two to put the grate back in place.

"Wait," Alec shouted. "You want me to... What? Raise the dead? I can't do that!"

"To those who believe, will He give the power to become the sons of God."

"What? You can't leave me here! You can't—" The reverend named Jonas kept walking. "Let me see my son!"

Alec craned his head back, hoping to catch a glimpse of the man, but he could see nothing. He waited. He trembled. Not from the cold. Then he screamed Jake's name. Over and over and over, he screamed. The guard above him said nothing.

He screamed until his throat went dry and he needed to give it a rest. He managed to thread his butt and his legs up over his wrists so that his bound hands were in front of him. But the restraints were made of a strong cable that managed to rub his wrists raw, as raw as his throat felt.

It was the least of Alec's concerns. Both throat and wrists would heal. "Jaaake! Can you hear me? I'm here! Jake!" A bird screeched back. Was it an eagle? A falcon? Alec didn't know, some bird of prey. Other than that, there was nothing.

He curled up tight and he shivered, and when he brought the day's chill to the attention of the woman above him, she ignored him. So he stared at Mark and at Patrick without touching them until he decided that Mark's shit brown suit coat looked mighty inviting. Mark was the bigger one. Paddy's coat would have been too small. Alec wrestled it off of Mark's stiff shoulders. It smelled stale and old, and he had to flip the body over to work the arms out of the sleeves. But he did it. He pulled the coat free, and that felt like a win.

Alec curled back up into his corner, the coat draped over him, and he called up to the woman guarding him. "Do you have kids?"

He didn't expect an answer, but she gave him one. "No."

"My kid's the only thing that matters to me." His voice cracked as he said it.

"Raise your friends up, and he's yours."

Alec didn't budge. Instead, he worked at slipping his hands free from his tight bindings under cover of the jacket. His wrists became slick with blood. When he looked up to catch the woman watching him, he saw her sigh. She stepped aside, and Alec heard her walkie in a request. "Ask the reverend if the prisoner can have some water."

Not only did they bring him water, they brought him food.

Day two. John David arrived on horseback and greeted Hannah with a freshly baked muffin. He hazarded a peck on her cheek and offered a second muffin to Mr. Lowell. When he handed it down through the grate, he noted the man's blood-caked wrists. "We should have those looked at," John David said. It was meant for Alec, but he directed it at Hannah. Alec retreated to the farthest point of the pit and ate the muffin.

"Talk to the reverend," Hannah said.

"I have." John David bent down for Alec's benefit. "This would be easier if you tried. Pass or fail. The test would be over and we could move on—"

"—Fuck you."

John David signaled Hannah to leave. She took the horse, and John David tried again. "Our reverend thinks he can change your mind…Make you see the error of your deceptive ways." When Lowell refused to join in, John David sighed. "Your son is a good kid. But he's got problems. I can see where it stems—"

"—You don't have the right to judge my kid." Alec came out of his corner, rabid in his decree. "You don't have that!" He stood tall, and a part of John David was glad that the metal grate served as a barricade. Then John David bowed his head. The man was right.

"I'll be honest. This isn't the way I would have handled it."

"Then let me out."

"I'm not in charge."

"Not in charge? You're not in fucking charge. Wow—"

"—Jake has done well here." That silenced Lowell for a moment.

"Let me see him."

"He doesn't know you're here."

"Just let me see my son. Let me see him." He was breaking. John David could hear it in Alec's tone.

"He was a miserable kid when he first got here—"

"—He was kidnapped by a sociopath."

"—But now he's better. He has adjusted—"

"—Fucking give me my son!" Alec leaped up and grabbed the grate with a force that made John David back off. John David rested his hand on the butt of his pistol. The move made Alec curse, more out of frustration than fear.

"We know everything that happened before Jake arrived. His school, everything. Lucas...he came here seeking guidance, and...well, I'm not going to justify his actions. But you, it turns out, are part of the problem." John David paused to let that sink in.

Alec took his bound hands, stained with blood and mud at the wrists, and he swung them over the dead men at his feet. "I can't bring cadavers back to life."

That was it. John David was going to have to talk with Adonis. He wasn't looking forward to it.

"He won't even try, sir."

"Because he can't do it." Adonis caught a glance of himself in a mirror on his mantle, then adjusted his posture.

John David proceeded with caution. "I believe in our purpose. But this—"

"—A caged rat is what he is. But we'll break him. Who's watching him now?"

"Lucas."

The reverend scrutinized John David in surprise. "Let's go, then."

John David gave Adonis a stiff bow and stepped out of his way. He didn't mean it, the respect that the bow inferred. There was a time when he had, but now that respect felt misguided. Since the day when Adonis allowed Lucas back into the Temple, the reverend's choices felt wrong. John David struggled with it, he was the one who brought Lucas here in the first place. But Adonis justified his decisions. "There is something bigger here that God wants us to witness." And Adonis had spoken.

The reverend took long strides toward the stables. The shepherds and foxhounds paced in their runs as they passed, and Adonis chose Moses for the ride. "You must be coming around," he told John David as they made their way at a slow trot.

"What do you mean?"

"I know you're not happy about Lucas. But you've let him guard his brother." They drew closer to their destination.

The pit was located in surrounding wilderness, far enough from the commune proper to render Alec Lowell's calls for help pointless. Lucas sat at the pit's edge with his legs crossed. Saint rested his snout on Lucas's knee, and Adonis signaled John David to slow his approach. Adonis wanted to listen, and this is what they heard.

"You're not good for Jake. If you were, he wouldn't have left you the message."

"He's fucked up because of you, Lucas. Not me!"

"Open it up," Adonis said alerting Lucas and Saint to his presence. Saint scrambled to his feet with a wagging tail as Adonis dismounted. He rewarded the animal with a scratch behind the ears before the dog returned to Lucas's side. "God must think you're special," Adonis told Lucas, "to let you take my dog." He said it with a deceptively joking demeanor, but everyone knew it irritated him. He whistled for Saint to come back to him as John David joined Lucas to pull the grate from the pit.

Alec Lowell refused to make eye contact. He stared ahead, covered by a corpse's coat, his jaw set. "You're not helping yourself. If anything, you're proving my point—"

"—Are you the reverend? Jonas?"

"I am." Lowell seemed to make mental note of that. He said nothing more, so Adonis filled him in. "This is a Christian community. We are a haven for the blessed—"

"—I'm in a fucking pit! I don't care how Christian you think you are."

"Do you want Jake to see you like this?" This time, Alec looked up with the slightest flinch. He pulled his bound hands out from under the jacket, exposing his bloody and raw wrists, and he pointed to the bodies that shared the pit. "They're dead. I can't bring them back—"

"—You came back from death. Was that a lie?"

Alec said nothing.

"Maybe you could give them a piece of your soul."

"What?"

"Perfect prophet. Perfect soul. Maybe you could share."

Alec seemed perplexed. "I'm not...perfect. Nobody is perfect...You're persecuting me because I'm not what you want me to be—"

"—What is it that I want you to be?" Alec stuttered through the beginning of a retort, when Adonis cut him short. "I don't want you to be anything because I know what you are. Christ works through you! That's what your book claims. It's what Josiah Light claims—"

"—I don't know why Christ works through me!"

"But you do claim that He does. So prove it. That's all you have to do."

John David could see a fresh bout of trembling work through Alec. "I don't…I can't…" The man gestured to the two bodies as John David watched him crumble from the inside. "I couldn't save them. When they died? I tried. I tried to…They deserved to live more than me, I tried…"

"Help me in," Adonis said.

Alec Lowell rose to his feet and pressed back against the dirt wall as John David and Lucas helped Adonis in. "No," he said, "don't touch me."

"Give me your hands—"

"—Don't touch me!" Alec tried to slip away, but stopped when Adonis pulled a key from his pocket. Adonis opened the lock that secured the cable around Alec's wrists. He traced the man's dirt-stained hands. Even John David had to admit that they were uncommonly elegant for a guitarist. He had expected fingers that were knotted, calloused, bent like the legs of a tarantula and designed for wide-spanned reach. Maybe the dirt hid the attributes.

Adonis quoted biblical relevance as he caressed those hands. "They shall rise to show great signs and wonders to deceive the believers, but they do not serve our Lord Jesus Christ. They serve their own hunger, and by good words and fair speeches, they will deceive the simple minded."

"What?" Alec said with more confusion.

Jonas Adonis looked Alec in the face with fierce conviction. "I am not among the deceived." His pocket vibrated. Irritated, Adonis pulled out a phone. He read the display then showed it to Alec. "Your whore gets a lot of calls from Josiah Light."

It took Alec a moment to register what that meant before he lunged. Adonis sidestepped the attempt and signaled John David with a raised finger. And John David did what he was trained to do. He took the shot, one shot that buried itself in the dirt wall behind Alec's ear. Alec flinched then froze, his breath coming out in short gasps that betrayed the rapid beat of his heart. "What did you do? Where is she?"

Adonis stuffed the phone away. "You have work to do." He left Alec with free hands, and as John David helped Lucas pull the reverend back out of the pit, he questioned why it had been so easy to do what he was told. Alec Lowell may have been a liar and a fraud who courted sin from the day his life began, but here he was unarmed and provoked by words that were clearly meant to provoke. John David had shot at a desperate and unarmed man, and for that he felt a need to serve penance.

Once they secured the grate back over the pit, John David and the reverend rode home in silence. It seemed like a good time to privately pray, for forgiveness, for guidance, for a sign. By the end of the journey, it had started to rain, and John David hoped it was God's way of washing him clean.

The rain lasted through the night as Jake fought boredom. He wished that he had access to a good old-fashioned first-person RPG, but a board game would have to do. Some board games were fun. *Adventures of the Bible Man* was not one of them. But Maggie enjoyed it, so Jake pretended to be happy. The mission of the game was to rescue the most children from the enemies of God while being the first to make it safely home to a cave, of all places. The hero was a pumped-up Power Ranger of sorts with the equivalent of a Jedi light saber, and Jake wondered if having lived in movie town for two years had stolen his innocence, because Bible Man wasn't cutting it.

"He's the best," Maggie said. She moved her piece across the board. "I watched his show all the time before we came here."

"Never heard of him." Jake tried to change the subject. "Do you miss the way things were before you came here?"

"Sometimes. But we're safe here."

"We're not safe here," Jake said, annoyed, and he regretted stating the truth because now Maggie had something to go on about.

She quoted their lessons verbatim. "When the end times are near, God will come for us. We will lay ourselves down, and He will raise us up through our dreams into heaven."

"I don't believe that." Yes, two years in movie town had stolen his innocence.

Maggie glanced over her shoulder. There were others in the hall, including adults engaged in discussion or reading their bibles. She lowered her voice. "You should. I heard Lance and Carol talking with John David. Something's going on."

Jake had noticed the strange behavior too. "Whatever it is, it scares them."

"Lucas knows. John David sends him out to do stuff. Just like Hannah. And Zachary—"

"—And Todd?" They had both noticed. People left camp on horseback and didn't come back for hours. Some had left camp altogether, and hadn't come back for days.

Maggie continued. "They're preparing the shelter, checking inventories. We're canning more food than we're eating."

"The shelter?" Maggie explained that it existed under ground. "You guys have a cave like Bible Man?"

"I guess we do," Maggie said with a smile. She rolled the dice and took her turn.

"Like Doomsday preppers."

"Like what?" Again, Maggie's limited knowledge of the outside world made her look dumb.

Jake skipped over an answer. "I want to see where they go." When Maggie kept silent and drew a card, Jake nudged her. "Don't you?"

"If we were supposed to know, Reverend Jonas would tell us."

"No, he wouldn't."

"Yes, he would—"

"—Scared people hide things. They tell you everything's okay when it's not, so you don't panic. And then when shit goes down—"

"—stuff."

"Whatever! When it happens, you're not ready because you didn't know. That's why you're in danger, because you didn't know in the first place."

"You're not making sense."

"Wouldn't you want to know so you could be ready?"

Maggie shook her head. "It's your turn."

Jake took his turn as thoughts churned. Then, "Your dad is hiding something—"

"—John David isn't hiding anything." But he was, and she knew, and Jake knew she would cave.

Mud, urine, and cadaver juice frothed as the rain beat down. It didn't wash anything clean, rather it stirred up a fresh hell of foul aroma. Alec threw up twice, adding to the mix. The third meal that had been sent down to him was some kind of sausage with rice. He couldn't eat it. The sausage floated about the muddy water like a turd. The rice brought maggots to mind.

Someone aimed a flashlight into the pit. No words were exchanged until Alec heard the short conversation between Lucas and the new arrival that Alec had come to recognize as John David. "Head home," John David said. "Not the horse. She stays."

"I'm supposed to walk? In the rain? In the dark?" The bitterness in Lucas's reply was dangerous. Someone was going to feel the brunt of his wrath one day, and at the moment Alec hoped it would be John David.

"You have Saint." Then they were done, and Alec heard John David settle into what he assumed was a tent.

Alec listened. He got to his feet to assess his chances. His hands were free. The grate above him might have been heavy, but it was not locked down. If John David had retired in a tent, there was the slim chance that Alec could climb up the bodies of Mark and Patrick, move the grate to one side, and slip out unseen. He reached up to test the weight of it when John David's flashlight blinded him again. "Don't get ideas. I've pulled night patrol more times than I can count." The man's rifle was slung comfortably over his shoulder; Alec could barely make it out in the dark. John David didn't seem particularly bothered by the rain. But then, he wasn't the one stuck in a hole that smelled like rotting flesh in a sewer.

Alec backed into his corner.

"You're not some divine answer here. That's all Jonas wants to hear. You can't heal…Admit those things and this will be over."

"It's not that I can't," Alec said. "I won't. Not for him. Not for you."

"You're saying that you can, then?"

"Jesus. Why would you think I could do this?"

The beam of light went out, and Alec massaged his eyes with dirt-stained fingers. Big mistake. Minuscule grains got caught under one lid and scratched at his cornea. "I have to admit," John David said. "Our leader may have…overstepped here."

It was Alec's in. he took a long stride back to the center of the pit. "Then help me! Help my son." Silence. "Hello?"

A moment passed, and the flashlight was back. It illuminated a sea of blue that billowed down over half the grate. John David had laid out a tarp to block the rain. The patter of it played out a calm rhythm that Alec shattered with a shout. "Fuck you! Fuck you and your fucking people! Let me out! Let me the fuck out!"

Nothing. Not a peep from John David. Alec jumped and caught a piece of the tarp through the grate. He yanked and pulled until he threaded the entire thing through the bars, and he wrapped himself in it. At least he was warmer. He was also exhausted. Restless sleep came as his mind kept one single thought on loop: militant Christians. This could only get worse.

On day three, Alec woke to sunlight. His breath clouded the air. He huddled inside his glossy blue cocoon, and he noted the splitting skin on the faces of Mark and Patrick. It left Marcus resembling more and more like some demonic joker. He would have loved it if he was alive and on stage. Noise descended into the pit, and Alec had a sinking feeling. There was a crowd up there.

"Bring them up," Adonis said after Zachary and Todd removed the grate. John David watched Lance and Carol throw down a fresh tarp as Zachary dropped into the pit, and as Todd hovered at the edge. Adonis slapped a pair of work gloves against John David's chest and motioned for him to join in.

Alec pushed as far back into his corner as he could, while John David helped Zachary and Todd lift the cadavers out. The filth covering the man and the exhaustion in his eyes weren't enough to temper his desire to fight.

They laid the bodies out on the fresh tarp with space to walk between them and when Todd jumped down into the pit, Alec made demands. "Don't touch me. Don't fucking touch me." He struggled and got a face full of foul puddle water once Todd took control. John David helped lift Alec out and dump him before Reverend Adonis.

Alec landed on his knees, a miserable bedraggled thing looking to do whatever penance the reverend suggested, except no. It couldn't be that easy. Alec proved John David's suspicion when Adonis lifted his face up by the chin. Alec jerked his head aside, and Adonis introduced him.

"Alec Lowell. Alexander the Great. Who knows this man? A show of hands." Hands went up, several in fact. "You are popular," Adonis said with half a grin. "But popular for what? A filthy mouth? A filthy soul. And a God-given gift to heal. Apparently." Adonis circled Alec. "So why, when you are given this opportunity to prove your…talent, when you are given this chance to raise your friends up from the pits of hell, why then do you refrain?"

"I want my son."

Adonis bent down for an intimate face off, a piece of scripture on his tongue. "Children are our gift from the Lord. Our reward."

Alec stuttered. "So you—you'll let me see him? If I do… something, I can see him?"

"Not parlor tricks. This." Adonis cast his hand toward the bodies in an extravagant swoop. He stared Alec down until the man became a trembling mass of doubt.

"They're dead. I can't do this—H—how am I supposed to—to do this—"

"—Spoken like a true nonbeliever. Or something else." Adonis rose to his full height. John David wished that the reverend would move on. But that was not Adonis's way. Everyone present stood in silent reverence of his pacing before Lucas elbowed his way to the front of the group. Alec saw him. And everything changed.

The sight of Lucas, the former demonic pack leader of satanic miscreants, now a follower of some mad Christian preacher, was all Alec needed to find his fight. Flight was not an option, and Lucas needed to die. Alec roared. He became a mad mountain cat, and he took Lucas down.

He got a good punch in to Lucas's face before the hands of strangers pulled at him, every touch an assault upon contact. He kicked and screamed, and Lucas rose up nursing a bloody nose. "Don't touch me," Alec screamed. "Don't touch me don't touch me DON'T TOUCH ME!" Alec heaved in ragged breaths as John David restrained him from behind. *Fucking John David.*

Who went by two names anymore? Racists and school shooters, that's who.

Jonas Adonis got in Alec's face one more time. "Look at me," he said. "A man who has rejected God in every way possible." A quote from Alec's autobiography, "Still He chooses me to spread hope, faith, healing throughout the world. In a way, I am the perfect prophet for our times." Adonis cocked an eyebrow. "But are you?"

Every gaze weighed on Alec. He stuttered nonsense through stinging tears that refused to spill. "I don't—please. I—I—I'll do whatever you want. My kid...please."

"For false Christs and prophets shall rise up to show the world great signs and wonders in their attempt to deceive the true people of God—"

"—I will kill you, Lucas! I will rip your fucking lungs out through your throat!"

Adonis carried on, unfazed by the tirade. He aimed a finger at Mark and Patrick, and John David brought Alec to them. "Show us your signs, prophet! Dazzle us with your wonders."

Alec, on his knees, continued the struggle. Fight, not flight. Adonis stepped in and grabbed him by the hand. Alec fought until the barrel of an AK got waved in his face. The reverend clasped Alec's hand over Mark's. When Adonis let go, Alec did too. Adonis reached for him again. He pulled a pocketknife from his coat and slammed Alec's hand back over Mark's, then slammed the blade through both.

Alec grunted. Every observer flinched. Every one, except Lucas. Alec reached for the knife with his free hand until Adonis uttered a soft warning. "Leave it." Blood oozed and mixed with the dirt and grime caked on Alec's skin. He left the knife in place.

Adonis signaled his followers to keep silent as he paced. They waited for something to happen. Nothing did.

Then Lucas spoke. "They're embalmed. Organs cut up, desiccated. This isn't a good test."

Damning silence. Adonis straightened out the drape of his jacket, then cursed lightly when he noted a blood stain left from his hands. Alec's blood. He leaned over Alec and yanked the blade free. Alec clutched the hand to his chest.

They put him back in the hole, back with Mark and Patrick and with a challenge to meet. "Two more days," Adonis said. Two more days to resurrect the dead, to relive the same torture that his father had put him through as a child because the man had so much fear of the devil. And here Alec was, way down in a fucking hole because no one believed that he could ever be one with God. He watched them replace the grate above his head, and then he did what he had done as a kid. He shut everything out and he shut himself down.

Following the Light

"I HAVEN'T HEARD FROM HIM SINCE HE LEFT," JOSIAH told Belinda. "Honestly, he doesn't keep in touch with me for any reason."

"He's not good at it," Belinda said. "But he promised. He's supposed to text me every day, and it's been almost a week."

"Where was he last?"

"Wisconsin."

Reverend Light pulled out his cell phone and engaged an app. "Well, he's in Chicago now." He showed Belinda the screen that pinpointed the location of Alec's cell phone, and Belinda grew irritated.

"You have a locator on his phone?"

"Everyone who works for us has one. It's a safety precaution. Our church, as glorious as it is, still has enemies. Your phone has one, too." Belinda and Alec had acquired their phones through Light as part of the arrangement for working with him.

For some reason, Belinda felt that Light was less concerned with safety and more concerned with keeping an eye on his people.

Belinda dismissed the urge to tell Josiah where to go. She took advantage of the potential use of the app. “Have you heard from Cleo?”

“I haven’t. Not since this whole grave-robbing situation. Honestly, Belinda. Your husband carries some extreme baggage. Don’t get me wrong. We’re blessed to have him, but…” He tapered off once he read the impatience on her face, and he referenced the app again. “You can dismiss your concerns,” he said. “She’s in Colorado. Or is it New Mexico…”

Josiah showed her the screen a second time. Cleo’s phone pinged from a generalized area along the border of Colorado and New Mexico. But the app indicated that the signal wasn’t strong enough to pinpoint the exact spot. “Why would she be in the middle of nowhere in New Mexico?”

“I’ll admit that she’s better at keeping in touch than Alec, but—”

“—It’s not your business? You’ve got a tracker on her phone.” Belinda was deeply worried. The last time Alec had checked in, he was staying at the cemetery with his grandfather. Then there was nothing. She assumed that Alec was spending the time to emotionally heal, for that’s what the old man seemed to provide. But the groundskeeper of the little cemetery near where Alec grew up was an odd man. He kept to himself. He had a satanic past of his own that he rarely talked about, and he had been adamant about cutting himself off from the world. No phones or computers, not even a TV. “How long has he been in Chicago?”

“Do you think I check on him every day? I don’t know—”

“—Right now, Alec is your headliner.”

Josiah scoffed at the implied suggestion, then gave in. "He's been there for a few days. First Wisconsin, then Chicago. And the girl in Wyoming who went viral with her improvement after meeting a stranger? It was him. I love him for that. Jesus loves him for—"

"—Josiah. I'm worried."

Light sighed. He made a call. "Alec! It's me. You haven't gotten in touch and it has people concerned. Call someone. We care about you. God bless." He disconnected. He held up his hands to indicate that there was nothing more he could do.

"Call Cleo, too."

"You can call Cleo—"

"—She'll ignore me."

"Forgiveness is a powerful thing, Belinda—"

"—Do you understand what I'm going through? Do you?" Belinda reined in the outburst and pinched her fingers deep into the bridge of her nose to stave tears.

Josiah got the message, "I'm sorry. I'll just…" He engaged his phone and texted Cleo instead.

Cleo didn't get that message either. As Adonis scrubbed at Alec's blood on his jacket, the phone buzzed in its pocket.

A text from Josiah Light. The Josiah Light. *Is Alec with you? He hasn't checked in.*

Adonis sneered at that. He answered, and he chuckled.

Cleo's response was inappropriate and filthy, and Josiah briefly wondered how he could have missed the signs that Cleo might have those kinds of intentions toward him. The response had nothing to do with his text to her, and it made him blush. If his wife had happened to see it or, God forbid the media, his career as the mega church preacher might have officially been over.

"What does she say?" Belinda asked after she heard the ding from the reply.

"It says that he must be in Chicago." Josiah deleted it.

"He's not answering—"

"—What else can I do, Belinda. He's somewhere in Chicago."

"What's in Colorado? Or...New Mexico?"

"Mountains. Looks like a wilderness area. I'm surprised she even has service."

"Cleo hates the wilderness. Bugs are not her thing."

"If they're not going to answer, there's not much I can do." Josiah fidgeted under Belinda's glare. He knew he was right, but he also knew that he wasn't really trying. Belinda had legitimate reasons for her concern. Josiah liked Belinda. She was a far more stable person than her husband. In spite of her more liberal beliefs in what did and did not constitute sin, she had a rationale that Alec needed in his life. She accepted God, but didn't really need God, unlike Alec who fought the idea with every ounce of his being.

Josiah could have abandoned Belinda. He could have left her to search for Alec on her own. He had so much on his plate: upcoming services, meetings with lawyers and financial advisors, preparing for their next tour. God kept him busy every day. But he knew that what needed to get done could get done without him. He gave in. He settled his hands on Belinda's shoulders, and engaged in solid eye contact. "We'll call the authorities in Chicago. You're right. It's weird. But we will find him with God's guidance."

Belinda gave him a reluctant nod. Josiah prayed that his hesitation hadn't put her faith into question. Because he liked Belinda. He liked her a lot.

She couldn't believe her own stupidity, how vulnerable she had let herself be. She had rolled down her window because she thought he was a fan. But he carried himself more like a cop, and after he'd asked a few cop-like questions regarding her relationship to Paddy, she stepped out of the car. He had taken her phone, asked her to unlock it, and had scrolled through her texts. And while it crossed her mind to object because the man didn't have a warrant, she knew she had nothing to hide. And now here she was, locked away in a windowless room by three men who could have raped her at their discretion, but who hadn't.

The two who abducted her were Zachary and Todd, although she wasn't sure who was who. The third man appeared after a long trip where she was blindfolded, gagged, and restrained in the locked-down bed of a pickup truck. She heard them call him Reverend, sir.

Her prison cell was as inviting as an underground parking garage. The flickering light of a fluorescent bulb added to the ambience. The room had a cot and a desk, and a shelf full of spiritual reading material, including the Bible. Cleo knew from her own Baptist upbringing that the Reverend, sir leaned toward the Evangelical. There was a separate bathroom with a toilet and sink, and she thanked God for that.

"Let me out! Please," became her daily plea. "I'll give you whatever you want."

What the Reverend, sir wanted became clear by day three. Cleo heard the creak of a heavy door. She heard footsteps tapping down stairs, and she backed away from the locked door because the routine would include the shout to do just that, to stand in full view.

The door opened, and the Reverend, sir held a sandwich on a plate. Zachary or Todd was behind him and he was armed. The Reverend sir spoke. "Do you accept Jesus as your—"

"—Yes," she said. It was part of the routine. "Yes, I do."

"The world as we know it is coming to an end."

She squeaked out an "Mmm, hmm," to appease him.

The Reverend, sir extended the plate. When she didn't take it, he took a bite of the sandwich. Cleo then accepted the offer. "When will you let me out?"

"When you trust me."

"I trust you. I do." She hadn't been convincing enough, probably because of the hesitation to take the sandwich. They hadn't poisoned her yet, but she still needed to be sure. She was at least grateful that they hadn't physically abused her.

After the Reverend, sir and his armed escort vacated her prison, Cleo picked at the sandwich. She was starving by the time they decided to feed her. The bread seemed safe, so she always started with that. She rinsed off the lettuce and tomato slices before thanking God for the vegetables, and she flushed the condiment-slathered meat and cheese down the toilet. She didn't trust the mustard. It looked spicy enough to mask the aftertaste of a drug.

Cleo wondered what was in store for her. She wondered how it was connected to Jake's disappearance, to the robbing of Mark's grave, and possibly to Patrick's, too. She didn't like where her assumptions were leading, and as she pressed the last crumbs from her sandwich into her fingertips to bring to her lips, she burst into tears.

"Are you coming or not," Jake said as they brought their dishes to the kitchen area. Maggie handed her plate over to the on-duty clean-up crew and didn't reply. It was a bad idea. She didn't need to say it.

"It'll be dark," was her excuse after they stepped out of the kitchen.

"They change shifts every night. We can follow from a safe distance—"

"—They go on horseback. We won't keep up. And what if they bring Justice." Justice was the biggest of the shepherds they used to patrol the grounds at night.

"Lucas walks," Jake said. "And it's his night." Jake was right. Whatever was going on beyond their camp was far enough away to go on horseback, but they made Lucas walk. Jake continued, "You're just scared of what we'll find."

"No, I'm not."

"What if it's a spaceship?"

"It's not a spaceship."

"What if it's Jesus? Or the devil—"

"—Stop it—"

"—Because it's as impossible as a spaceship?" Jake snickered as Maggie rolled her eyes.

"If Reverend Jonas wanted us to know, he'd tell us. Sneaking around will get us punished."

"Does it say that in the Bible? Thou shall not sneak around?" Maggie told Jake to shut up, which wasn't a thing Maggie was prone to do. Jake pleaded with her to be dangerous, and later that night she found herself tip-toeing out of her quarters and meeting Jake behind the confession box. The path taken by the adults into the woods always started there.

Saint was with Lucas when he showed up. The dog let out a curious yip and pointed his nose toward the shadows. Maggie cringed and squeezed Jake's arm in fear of being caught. For some reason, she was more fearful of Saint than of being found by Justice. Justice was on the opposite side of the grounds on this night. She knew the patrol team's routine, but it would have served them right to be caught. In her heart, Maggie knew that what they were doing was wrong. She silently prayed for forgiveness when Lucas called for Saint and the two kept going.

Jake took the lead. It was darker than dark in spite of the brilliant half moon and the crisp, clean sky, and Maggie wished they had been smart enough to bring a flashlight. She supposed that the beam would have put them in danger of being discovered, but she also worried about getting lost. Lucas had a long, quick stride, and there were more than a few times when they had to catch up to find him again. Then he was gone again. After time spent hoping that they were still on the right path, Maggie tugged on Jake's arm.

"We should go back—"

"—I'm not lost. Just keep going."

Maggie protested as Jake turned in circles, and she knew he was lying. A hand dropped onto her shoulder, and she screamed.

"What are you doing out here?" It was Lucas.

Jake froze without saying a word.

"What are you doing? You shouldn't be here."

Maggie shielded Jake once she heard the stuttered terror of his breathing. "We're sorry."

"Go home then," Lucas said. "Go on."

"We're lost."

Lucas got behind them. He settled a hand on each of their shoulders and pointed them back in the direction of camp. It was Jake's turn to take tight grip of Maggie's arm. She thought he was going to break it. "Keep straight. That way. You'll see the light on in Jonas's cabin after ten minutes. He stays up late." Maggie gave him a nod. "Don't come back. I mean it."

"Why?"

"Go!"

Jake was the first to move. He dragged Maggie along without looking back.

But Maggie looked back. She caught Lucas watching them, not budging from his position until they were nearly out of sight.

The old groundskeeper hadn't heard from Alec, which wasn't necessarily a surprise, but after a few days passed he was curious to know if the reunion with his son had gone well. He sat in front of his computer and composed a simple email asking how things went. He read the thing twice before he clicked on the send button. There was no immediate response, but the groundskeeper hadn't really expected one. He was of the generation when mail was on paper and took days to be delivered. He decided to check the message's status at the end of the day, but even then there was no reply.

So he searched the Internet. He had been guilty of doing it before, putting Alec's name in the search finder to see what would come up, and he had been amazed at the wealth of information the computer offered. There was no need for Alec to keep in touch with his grandfather regarding what he'd been doing. The world was doing that for him.

Still, no news of a reunion. The old man scrolled and clicked and scrolled. He found nothing. His instincts told him that Alec wasn't avoiding keeping in touch this time. Something was wrong. So he typed and scrolled and clicked some more until he found a website for The Josiah Light Church and Foundation.

"Do you know a Piquette?"

"I'm sorry?" Belinda was in the middle of packing a bag when Josiah called.

"Touissaint Piquette? He or she sent an email to the foundation asking for you by name.

"I don't know a Touissaint Piquette."

"They asked for you specifically."

"What's the number?"

"It's an email address."

"Well, what did the email say? Why are they trying to contact me?"

"It doesn't say, Belinda. I thought you might know. But if it's an unfamiliar name, I'll ignore it. We can never be too careful with the people who try to reach out to us."

Belinda found bitter irony in that notion. The security measures that were in place to protect Josiah and his staff seemed counterproductive to the church's cause.

Besides, she was busy. After contacting the Chicago authorities to be on the lookout for Alec and his truck, she decided that she would head to Chicago herself because, while the police had agreed to put a bulletin out, she got the feeling that it wasn't their priority. She also knew that going to Chicago in hope of finding Alec on her own would probably be fruitless, but she had to try. Sitting around waiting for bad news was killing her. She didn't know any Touissaint Piquette. It was one of those names you would never forget.

"What's the email address," she asked out of habit.

"It's a mortuary."

"A mortuary?"

"It's gkeeper@wimortuaryservice. It's in Wisconsin."

Belinda suddenly knew who Touissaint Piquette was. She had never known his name. She hurried to find pen and paper, and she had Josiah repeat the address as she jotted it down.

She was in tears once she contacted the old man, and when his emailed response told her that Alec had found Jake. But more than a few days had passed since the discovery, and he assumed that he would have seen news about it by now. Belinda asked Touissaint for a phone number, and when he responded that he didn't have a phone, she suggested a video chat. Touissaint had no idea what that was, so Belinda gave him instructions on how to set his computer up to connect with her.

Touissaint seemed giddy over the technology when they saw each other on screen. "Well that wasn't hard, was it?"

"Who contacted him," Belinda said with no time for pleasantries. "Where is he now?"

"Chicago, I suspect. They said they were affiliated with a mission. I'm not sure which, but..." he hesitated as if afraid to share it. "Claire…I'm sorry, Belinda. The contact came through her."

She didn't care. News that Jake was most likely alive filled Belinda with a hope that made her tremble. "A mission? Do you have a name?"

"I don't. Your husband doesn't like to share things."

"It's in Chicago. You're sure?"

After the groundskeeper assured her that it was most definitely in Chicago, Belinda contacted the authorities again. They weren't as helpful as she wished. "He's found our son, and he hasn't been in contact since."

"If he's found him," the officer said on the other end, "then there's no need for alarm. The boy is with his father—"

"—He hasn't reached out to me! I'm his mother—"

"—Aren't you going through a divorce, Mrs. Lowell?"

Belinda gritted her teeth. There were no official divorce proceedings between her and Alec, but the fact that the authorities were aware of the tabloid rumors was more than irritating. She chose her words carefully. "If my husband and I are going through a divorce, and he's gone missing with my son, then we have a custody issue. Would you like to be part of that story? Because I will tell my side of it."

The detective on the other end saw her point. He set an official search for Alec's truck in motion, and the police focused on neighborhoods with missions and church-run shelters.

The truck was found not far from a methadone clinic in a less-than-desirable neighborhood by the time Belinda landed in Chicago. The truck's wheels had been jacked. The passenger window had been smashed, and the electronics in the dashboard were gone. There was no cell phone, probably stolen by whoever took the tires and the dashboard head unit, Belinda thought.

Her hope was crushed. The news hit the airwaves quickly, and once Belinda shared information with the police about the general location of Cleo's phone, a federal investigation was set in motion.

Then they found a closed-down storefront called the Mission for Lost Souls. The organization's website had sparse information. It included outreach locations and phone numbers, but no one was available to answer those phones. All calls went to voicemail. Still Belinda was told that federal authorities had some leads. They were going to find Jake. They were going to find Alec.

John David kneeled at his bedside, his mouth and nose cupped by his hands in prayer. The warmth of his breath accosted his fingers, and he wished that God would break His silence. He did not trust Alec Lowell. The man's attack on Lucas, while arguably justified, was a reaction reserved for people who had something to hide. John David knew the behavior from his tour overseas. It was the behavior of the unscrupulous, of insurgents caught in a lie. But Alec Lowell was not the true problem. Reverend Adonis was.

Jonas's tactics to out the man for being a fraud were extreme, and while John David had seen results from using such tactics, had even engaged in them, this time it felt wrong. Maybe Adonis was a genius, a gifted prophet with far more knowledge about their ultimate fate than John David understood. But John David had doubts, serious ones. So he prayed.

He prayed to Naomi. As he asked for guidance from a woman who had left this world feeling lost, he gazed at the letter she had left behind. A pregnancy test rested on top of it. The indicator read positive, and John David would never forget the day he found it.

I almost lost our daughter. Pray for me. I am weak in my faith and not built to protect her.

We were shopping. I was so afraid of the possibility of a second child, that I took this test in the restroom. The wait had been too long. Maggie wandered. She was being taken away by a stranger when the store greeter recognized the situation and stopped it. The stranger ran. Our daughter is safe. But I failed her.

John David had returned home from a long shift on that day. He told Maggie to run and find her mom to start dinner before he made his way to the bedroom to change out of his work clothes. The letter had been on the bed, and when he spotted the little plus sign on the pregnancy test, he smiled. *A boy maybe*, he thought. *A perfect set.*

But the letter itself sent John David into a tailspin. Naomi suffered through postpartum depression after Maggie's birth, and although she had gotten through it, John David never felt like she fully recovered. And he knew. He had weathered his own hell of post-traumatic stress after his time in-country, and Naomi was the one who saved him. Not his devoutly Christian parents or his brothers who had also served their country, but Naomi.

On that day, John David had called his wife's name in a sudden race to find her. Maggie found her first in a tub of water that had turned crimson from slit wrists.

Adonis came to John David's rescue after Naomi's death. Not intentionally. The Mission for Lost Souls was a charity recipient of donations by John David's church, and John David met the man on a delivery run to their Chicago location. Many of Naomi's things were among the donations, things too painful to keep. Maggie was with him. He no longer trusted leaving her under the care of others for long, not even family. They had failed to understand Naomi's depression; there was a disconnect since the suicide, so he drifted from them. It was easier.

The reverend singled Maggie out at the Chicago mission. "Who do we have here?" She was helping unload boxes of canned goods at the building's back entrance.

The mission was not in the best of neighborhoods, and John David's protective nature kicked in. "She's my daughter. Who are you?"

Lance and Carol, who were not yet members of the Temple but who had helped run the mission, froze in dismay. But not Maggie. She smiled at the stranger. "I'm Maggie."

"Maggie. A beautiful name. Come inside." With a nod of the head, the man had Maggie following him. John David barked at her to stay, and Jonas Adonis turned with well-honed scrutiny. "Lance? Carol? Can you take over?" Lance and Carol obliged, and the man introduced himself. "I'm Reverend Adonis. Come inside. Come on."

John David hadn't initially perceived this man of jet-set casual fashion to be a preacher. He especially seemed out of place for Chicago, more 1980s throwback to hip Los Angeles or Miami than Midwestern Man of God. He wore no socks, just loafers that looked comfortable for a price.

John David kept Maggie close as Adonis walked. "It's not often that I visit one of my own outreach centers. I'm admittedly a bit of a recluse, but with a bold presence. So I'm told." Adonis smiled at that. He looked amused with himself. "Your name again?"

"John David."

"We appreciate what you do, John. Every single church is a blessing to our cause."

"His name is both names," Maggie said. "John, like the Baptist, and David like the boy who slew Goliath."

Reverend Adonis paused. "Is it, now? Hmmm."

John David found himself compelled to draw Maggie close. "She knows her Bible. Her mother was a good teacher."

"Was…How did she die?"

That simple perception ripped through John David's paper-thin wall of coping like a sniper's bullet. "She…" He couldn't say it with Maggie present, even though she was well aware.

The reverend seized that moment. He ushered Maggie to a room where she could find coloring books and puzzles, before he took John David's hand and pulled him to the floor in the adjacent hall. John David's emotional resolve crumbled. They sat across from each other, the reverend with his legs crossed like some Bohemian guru and John David crouched, ready to spring in retreat if the worst hit the fan.

"Sometimes God takes the brightest among us because they have proven their worth," Adonis said. But when John David mentioned suicide, the man's tone changed with a disappointed, "Oh."

John David stuttered through Naomi's story, and Adonis took time to reinforce what John David already knew to be true. "A stranger with candy. A pedophile. It's a sad world we live in." It was truer than true. John David's own experiences supported it: the war on terror both foreign and domestic, the degradation of moral values, the nation's divisive stand on every single issue. The world had taken a speedy uptick to its own demise.

"You're a military man?" Adonis continued once John David nodded. "When storms crest the horizon, we shelter in hidden harbors; we ride it out in wait for the coming of the

Savior. And there's nothing wrong with that because for the righteous, He will come."

John David's faith had been eroding, but he left that day feeling like his eyes had been opened. The world was a cruel place, and the idea of hiding from it rather than fighting against the increasing flood was appealing. The reverend had given John David his private number and, after regular intervals of cell phone chats over the course of six months, John David was ready to seek his refuge.

"Your wife was led to her death," Adonis had said. "For that's how the devil works. He's in the fabric of our morally corrupt society, and yes. Your wife was weak. She succumbed. She gave up before her time was due."

John David had feared heading down the same path, so he did it. He did it for Maggie. He gave up his material connection to the world. He donated his truck and the sales from his property to the mission and became one of the blessed souls of the temple. "I'm extremely picky about who I invite. But you, John David, and your daughter belong with us, among the chosen."

It was a wild idea, absolutely insane as his brothers and his family told him. "Where is this place?" his parents asked. "We know nothing about it."

John David quelled their concerns with vague answers. "It's a wilderness retreat. An escape from that," and he pointed to the television news airing a story about a police officer accused of brutality. The nation's protectors were no longer perceived as the good guys, one more thing that cut to the core of John David's beliefs. John David was a good Christian, a protector of the likeminded of his nation. But that notion was under attack. The good guys were being accused of bad things every day.

So, he did it. He donated everything. He promised his parents that he and Maggie would keep in touch and visit on holidays. But they didn't. The temple isolated its members from the rest of the world, and it became easy to disconnect from his family. They hadn't really supported his decision anyway. Adonis postulated that maybe this happened because God didn't think they were worthy. And John David accepted this. He and Maggie were even happy.

But he kept the letter. And the pregnancy test. He couldn't let those go.

Adonis eventually gave John David a position of command because of his military expertise. Regular outreach runs to the missions were assigned, and John David took Maggie along because the trips to Chicago or Los Angeles were the only times he could have quality talks with his daughter…or sister. That idea was harder to accept than others.

But he understood the reverend's intention. He did. Contact with the outside world became an increasing disappointment. From the war-torn streets of countries controlled by their insurgents to the streets of America in decline, the Christian, the patriot continued to have a target on his back. John David would do his Christian duties, he would praise Maggie for her strength and bravery, and he would anticipate their safe return to the commune every time.

Then John David found Lucas. Lost. So in need of refuge and care that Jonas should have been proud. Lucas was the reason for doing God's work, a crowning achievement for the ministry, a saved soul. What Lucas ended up being was a thorn. And he went deep. His sins triggered something in Adonis that brought fresh concern to John David's plate. And it was John David's fault. All of it.

Trust the path. Let God lead. The advice parroted by Lucas terrified him. Naomi certainly wasn't answering his prayers. If Alec Lowell would just admit to being a fraud, it would be over. John David wouldn't have to consider the thing that he thought God was leading him to do. *Let it play out,* he thought. *Trust the path. Take the reins when God hands them over. For it will be over soon. It has to be soon.*

John David folded the pregnancy test back up in the letter and placed it with care among the socks in the top drawer of his dresser. He pushed back the thought of what Naomi had done. She had robbed him of a second child, maybe a son. He thought of how Jake might fill that void. Then he headed for the reverend's quarters.

My daddy walked with Jesus, now he's in the looney bin,
Put your faith in God We Trust, a masquerade for sin…

The abrasive lyrics spilled out past the doorframe of the reverend's cabin so loudly that John David's knock went unheard. He hazarded opening it and was met with a brutal glare when he called out the reverend's name. There was a glass in the reverend's hand and a bottle of spirits on his desk, something expensive by the looks of the bottle. John David wasn't a drinking man, so he wasn't sure. But the reverend wasn't supposed to be drinking either; Temple rules.

John David closed the door behind him as the music video assault continued on half of Adonis's TV screen. The other half framed the paused image of a smiling girl in a wheelchair.

The god you praise, the rapist loves his virgins, kills his sons…

"May I speak, sir—"

Adonis raised his hand for silence then gulped down the rest of his drink. And the grotesque video images were hard to ignore.

My daddy's in a padded room insane for the wrong one—

Adonis fiddled with controls on his computer keypad and shut the video down. The image of the girl stayed. John David kept silent, as Adonis slumped into his seat then spoke. "I'm weak." He shoved his empty glass aside, where it clinked against the bottle.

"Everyone has moments of doubt," John David said. "But sir…You saved me."

"Did I?"

"Who's the girl?"

He didn't answer. Instead, he posed a question. "Do we remember Lazarus?"

"Yes—"

"—Four days after his death, John David. Four days! Jesus commanded him to rise up! He did this for those who had accepted Him. For those who believed in their rebirth! Do we believe?"

John David watched Adonis rise up and pace, and he was hesitant to answer. "Alec Lowell has denied being anything more than a man with a gift. And barely that—"

"—The devil works through him. Don't let your hesitation to believe it lead you astray."

"He still refuses to prove anything." The two-day extension was up, and John David watched Adonis reflect.

Then the reverend caught sight of himself in his blasted mirror. He combed through his locks and smoothed over the wrinkles radiating from the corners of his eyes. "Where's my dog? Where's Saint?"

"You know where your dog is, sir." That seemed to disturb Adonis more than anything else.

The man found his wits. He smoothed out his jacket and bent down to lift a throw rug off the floor as he laid out instructions. "Gather our witnesses. Todd, Zachary, Lance." He pulled up the trap door, exposed now that the rug was gone: the entrance to Adonis's private emergency bunker.

"No women?" Adonis gave him a sideward grimace. No, no women.

Not everyone knew about Adonis's bunker, although the commune's barracks each had their own bunkers designed for the final days. John David was one of the few to have the privilege of knowing Adonis's secret, along with Zachary and Todd, the appointed guardians of the commune. Adonis's bunker was a safety protocol, a separate unit built to monitor and regulate efficient operation of the other two.

John David followed Adonis down the metal steps and through a short hallway dotted by closed doors. A surprise awaited him behind locked door number three. It was the singer, Cleo LeCroix, and she was not happy to see them.

"Who do you think is in the hole," Jake asked after time went by. He refused to give up on his quest after Lucas had turned them back, and now after retracing their path during the early-morning hours, they had found it; a pit that Lucas guarded. Saint was by his side.

Maggie made sure that they were tucked far back among the trees so that Saint couldn't catch their scent. She watched Lucas engage Saint in a game of fetch. The dog was happy. Maggie thought she even saw Lucas smile. But Jake's question left her annoyed. "Why does it have to be a person? Maybe it's treasure."

Jake rolled his eyes. "Nobody puts bars over a hole with treasure."

"Maybe it's a bear," she countered. "Or a mountain cat." She was pleased with her comeback. But it didn't last long because if it was some wild animal trapped in that pit, then Saint was pretty calm about it. Dogs and wild animals didn't mix well. Saint should have been barking up a storm. Maggie was enjoying the mystery until Reverend Jonas arrived on horseback with a woman sharing his saddle. Her hands were bound, and John David was among the few men who rode alongside him.

Jake locked fingers with Maggie. She could feel a rapid pulse course through him. "What's wrong?"

"It's Cleo," he whispered. Maggie did not know Cleo. This woman didn't belong to the temple. Her wild hair and clingy clothes hinted that she was unclean, a sinner. And Maggie understood. The pit was a confessional, like the box behind the stables but for serious offenders.

"How do you know her—"

"—We should go," Jake tried to pull her along, but she didn't budge.

Reverend Jonas addressed the group as if it was a sermon. Maggie wished she could hear it, but they were just out of range and missed most of what was said, only faint mumbles that didn't amount to words. Then Todd carried a bucket to the pit and dumped it in.

Icy water washed Alec clean. "Jesus!" He was already fucking freezing.

The reverend looked down through the grate and gestured at the rotting bodies of Patrick and Marcus. "I'm disappointed," he said.

And Alec lost it. His mouth spilled out every complaint, every frustration that had been trapped inside him for however many fucking days he'd been in the godforsaken hole, for however many fucking months he'd been labeled *special* in the eyes of God. He couldn't hold back. "Do you know what it's like to be hunted? To be shot and stalked and stabbed and…burned from the inside out? You can't see it. I'm scarred on the inside. That damage is never going to heal! So please. Please, please, please absolve me of whatever sin you think I have and let me go home with my son. Please! Please."

Adonis scrutinized him for an excruciating amount of time then said, "Bring him up."

Two of them lifted the grate. They dropped in and cornered Alec, and they suffered the consequences. The one called Todd cursed without really cursing, then socked Alec in the face. It dazed him. He felt blood stream out of his nose. At least it felt warm.

When Alec regained his senses, he was above ground. The reverend stood in front of him with Cleo hugged tight, the muzzle of a pistol pressed deep beneath her chin. Alec trembled. "I'm sorry," he said. He hadn't mentioned Cleo in his plea to be set free, and that leaden ball of guilt and self-loathing sank deeper into the pit of his stomach. The one named John David kept sentry by his side, as Todd stepped in beside the reverend.

"But you can save her," Adonis said. "Isn't that right?"

"Please—"

"—Lord, if there be iniquity in my hands; if I have rewarded evil unto those that were at peace with me, let my enemy tread down my life and lay my honor in the dust—"

"—She's not part of this—"

"—It was your brother who lobbied for a better test. So let's do this."

Alec lunged forward and threw his hands up. "Don't! I'm your deceiver. I'm a lie! Nobody puts their faith in me!" His whole being trembled as John David pulled him back.

Adonis paused. He reached out and took Alec's outstretched hand, the one that had been stabbed through two days earlier. It had been rinsed clean from the downpour of freezing water, and the wound...was gone.

The Reverend Adonis marveled over it, and for the briefest moment Alec thought he had been saved. Then Adonis raised his gun and shot Alec in the face. The blood spray coated John David's jacket.

Alec thought he heard a scream, a distant one that had almost been drowned out by Cleo's. He was certain he heard the Reverend Jonas Adonis have his final say. "A false witness shall not be unpunished. He shall perish..." And it was true. As he rose up out of his crumpled body like he had the first time when he had died, he saw everything. He saw the source of the second scream, and his no-longer-beating heart sank.

Saint yelped and scampered to Lucas's side as Adonis turned, and Lance cried out. "Holy mother of—" He dropped to his knees and lost his breakfast.

The reverend's eyes were elsewhere. He took in the forest as Cleo sobbed for mercy and as John David tried to keep it together. Lucas was stunned to see Alec drop, a useless sack of meat and bone, but he knew what Adonis was looking for. Someone else had cried out.

Adonis motioned for Todd to silence Cleo. Then, "Lucas. Check that out."

"Check what out?"

"—I heard something! Check it out!" Adonis was on the verge of losing it, too. Lucas knew the signs. He did as he was told, for he was a follower, not a leader, and as Adonis took hold of Saint's collar, Lucas hoped that gaining distance from what had just happened would alleviate the strange numbness that had settled in him.

He reached the tree line and found Maggie with her hand over Jake's mouth as she hugged Jake tight. She was terrified, but she was keeping it together better than Jake.

Something broke inside Lucas. He had never recalled feeling truly guilty about anything. Until now. Odd. The only two people who had ever offered him true friendship would be forever damaged by this. For Jake, it was twice. Maggie glanced past Lucas when she heard Todd scream at Cleo to shut up. Her terror transformed to angry judgment once her gaze reconnected with Lucas.

Lucas lowered his voice to a whisper. "Go."

Maggie pulled Jake deeper into the woods.

"Oh, God," Lance muttered repeatedly at the ground as Zach urged him to his feet. Todd kept Cleo restrained and John David had recovered enough to take aim at Adonis.

"Put it down," Adonis said with his own gun aimed. A standoff.

Zachary was the most confused. "What are we doing? What are we—"

"Stand down, Zach!" Todd warned, and Adonis spewed a biblical rant.

"Judge me, O' Lord, according to my righteousness! My defense is of God, which saves the upright in heart! In My name they shall cast out devils. They shall lay hands on the sick, and they shall recover—"

"You shot a defenseless man—"

"Defenseless without God! He leads the world astray, but not here! Not anymore."

Cleo sobbed and struggled until Todd struck her with the buttstock of his gun. She sunk to her knees as blood flowed from a gash on her cheekbone.

"What…what are we doing?" Zach repeated.

Adonis lowered his weapon first, eyes still set as John David pulled himself out of the depths of fresh fodder for nightmares. He hadn't expected this. Not this. He tried not to think of the blood and brain matter staining his clothes, and he lowered his aim. He was complicit, complicit in killing a man who…the hand. *There's no wound in the hand. Or the wrists. Nothing…*

Cleo continued to sob and, as Lucas returned, Saint tried to escape from the clutches of Adonis. "Anything?" Lucas said nothing. The reverend got down on one knee and tried his best to sooth Saint in a tone reserved for newborns. "It's alright. Forgive me for the assault on your ears—"

"—What happens now?"

Adonis scrutinized John David again, as Saint escaped to be with Lucas. "Why, John David, are you questioning my judgment? You saw the man's vile message. And God spoke—"

"—Look at his hand!"

The reverend shrugged at that. "An illusion. A trick to tempt us into believing that he's the One. He's not! He wasn't. Does everyone else understand this?" He got a yes, sir from Todd. Zachary hesitantly followed Todd's lead, and Lance hugged himself while keeping his eyes averted from the mess. Lucas said nothing and Cleo moaned. John David acquiesced with a slight bow. He didn't mean it, that false gesture of respect again. But the consequences for standing against his leader were a threat.

The reverend turned to Lucas. "Take care of this," he said, and with his foot he rolled Alec's body into the pit.

John David discarded his stained jacket, and he weathered the cold on the ride back to the commune. He didn't need Maggie to see him in it. He slipped into the barracks, stripped off his clothes, and showered after he threw the clothes into the wash with too much bleach.

He tried to block out the events at the pit, but he couldn't do it. He couldn't believe how easy it had been for the reverend to kill an unarmed man. Alec Lowell was not that kind of a monster. *Was he? Would the rest of the commune blindly follow Jonas after this?* John David noted a tremble in his hand that wouldn't go away, and he thought about Lucas. *Lucas and his left hand that he constantly flexes. I brought him here. God, forgive me.*

And what the hell were they going to do about Cleo LeCroix? As he stepped out of the barracks with too many troubles to sort through, Hannah met him. "What happened," she asked. She had been aware of people keeping secrets since the day they met.

"The perfect prophet is dead."

"The reverend?"

"Yes, the reverend," John David said irritated. "He says he was doing God's will."

Hannah let this churn. She kept pace on their way to the commissary. "You don't believe him."

"It doesn't matter what I believe, because nobody here will challenge it."

Hannah stopped him in his tracks. She looked him in the eye. "Then this is your moment." John David knew what she meant. It scared the life out of him.

Let God lead. Was this that moment? Before he could entertain whether his time had come, Carol rushed up to meet them.

Her news was more disturbing. "Jake and Maggie are missing."

"For anyone who might have spotted anything," Belinda said to the Chicago news reporter who shoved a microphone at her, "please step up. My son is alive. He and Alec are missing." Behind her was a closed-up storefront, with a sign in the window, *Mission for Lost Souls. Jesus saves. Ask us how.*

The reporter chimed in. "Is it true that Cleo LeCroix is also missing?"

That's when Josiah stepped in. He had been itching to dominate the conversation, Belinda knew. "We haven't been able to contact Cleo since the time of the desecration of Patrick

O'Shaughnessey's grave, and we hope for the safe return of all three. We ask that the public send their prayers, and—"

"—The authorities dragged their feet on this, and they know it," Belinda said, hoping to steer the interview toward a more useful end. "Alec last contacted me to say he was headed to a mission. This is the closest mission to where his truck was found, but we have been unable to contact anyone representing this organization. If anyone knows anything, we need your help."

She was relieved once the cameras were off. She didn't like public scrutiny and had to admit that Alec, who hated the spotlight far more than she did, was a pro at it. She was so close to finding Jake, and she wondered if her level of anxiety was anywhere near what Alec claimed to experience every single day. She hadn't expected to get much feedback, with the exception of the fans and well wishers from Josiah's church. Then a neighborhood punk stepped up to her with a terrified expression on his face after the news crew packed up from the shoot.

His name was Dante. "I don't want to be on TV or nothing, but hey…I saw your guy—I mean I think I did."

"You saw Alec Lowell?"

"They're saying he's famous and shit?"

"He was in a band—You saw him? In the neighborhood—"

"—In there," Dante said as he pointed toward the mission. But the kid wasn't good at keeping eye contact. "You know…these people, they're never here. The place is closed for like weeks. Then someone shows up for a couple days, and they're gone."

"But you saw him?" Josiah asked. He kept close to Belinda's side, his hands pressed over his hips and his coat tails fanned back to make him look like a well-pressed TV show detective. Belinda assumed that was the look he was going for. In fact, she was certain.

The kid sniffed. Belinda noted a tremor in one hand. *An addict, not a reliable witness.* He lowered his voice. "He…he took me, and he held me. And I felt better. Something about it…"

"That's him," Josiah said. "Praise you, son. Praise Jesus."

"He didn't preach. He just held me. Two days later, and I ruined it. You find him, tell him I'm sorry."

The kid wanted to run, so Belinda grabbed that trembling hand before he could escape. "Dante, what did you see?" She pleaded with him to talk to authorities, and what they learned was a beacon of hope for Belinda. Dante had one name, Carol. She had cosigned admittance papers at the nearby drug clinic. That lead would develop into several.

WTF—WJD

Once Reverend Adonis and the others were gone, Lucas took the shovel sticking out of excavated dirt and began dumping it back into the pit. With every pitch, he felt the increasing weight of a burdened soul. He had wanted to change, to make up for his misguided past. He had wanted to save someone else.

Far from done, he tossed the shovel and slumped down to his haunches like some modern gargoyle made of flesh instead of stone. Saint rested his nose against Lucas's thigh and implored him with concerned eyes. And Lucas brooded. He hadn't saved anyone, least of all Jake.

Jonas Adonis was no savior. Alec had never been a threat. Lucas understood it now. He had sought divine guidance, had asked God to lead the way, and the way brought him here. He did have a purpose, but that purpose had eluded him. Until now.

Would you kill for me? Adonis's challenge echoed through Lucas's mind. Maybe God did speak through the reverend.

Killing was Lucas's gift, after all. He hadn't really learned anything about redemption. He had accepted the fact that he couldn't be saved, although part of him had hoped for it. As he stroked Saint's head and stared down at the gaping hole left at the back of Alec's skull, he tried to think of a thing that was most significant to Adonis, a thing in the man's life that represented a change.

"Hey, Saint," Lucas said with a smile, and Saint bounced up to slap Lucas's nose with a wet tongue. "Yeah, you." He pulled Saint in with affection. "I'm sorry," he said.

Lucas returned to the commune, Saint wagging his tail beside him. The compound was quiet, everyone at communal lunch in the cafeteria, so Lucas slipped into his room and laid out his paraphernalia. Saint sniffed about the room, maybe in hopes of finding some dropped morsel before he abandoned the search and joined Lucas at his bedside. Lucas scruffed up Saint's fur, even rewarded the dog with an affectionate kiss on the snout before he focused on the task.

He would slash Saint's throat, pull a tooth or a claw, and set a mix of blood and urine on fire while reciting his Latin incantation. Adonis would burn. He would crumple into a ball of searing inadequacy and he would pray to the God who owed him nothing.

That seemed fair.

Lucas pulled Saint in and Saint managed to squirm. "Stop," Lucas said. He soothed the dog with whispers, then hung his head. He couldn't do it. Saint met his face with more sloppy affection, and a shudder worked through Lucas.

"What are you doing with my dog?" Lucas looked up to find Adonis watching him from the doorway. Adonis waved a hand at the chalice. "What is this?"

Lucas set Saint free before Adonis grabbed the dog by the collar. Adonis yanked Saint into a sit. "You're done at the pit?"

"No, sir."

"Then why are you here?" When Lucas didn't answer, Adonis leaned close with a whisper. "I read your brother's book. I know why you're here." He flicked his hand at the chalice on the bed. "Now that he's out of the picture, it's time to silence me—"

"—No."

"It had to be done. You know that. He wasn't the one—"

"—I'm not doing what you think I'm doing."

Adonis kept silent for a time. "Do you really think I'm a changed man because of a dog? I'd snap Saint's neck if God told me to do it."

"I'm not doing what you think." Of course it was a lie. Lucas hoped that he had sold it this time.

Adonis backed down. "Go finish your job. Dump your Satan shit in while you're at it."

"That was the plan, sir." The reverend did not look convinced. He left with Saint anyway.

Lucas had no doubt that Adonis could take Saint's life on a whim and attribute it to the Will of God. He had made a mistake believing that some kind of redemption might come from changing sides. But what now? What could he do to atone? For everything. He dumped his wares into the backpack where he stored them, and was at a loss for what to do next when he was moved into stillness by a metallic click.

"Where is she?" Lucas turned slowly. John David had his Armalite aimed, the safety disengaged. "Where is Maggie—"

"I don't know—"

"—If you've hurt her, so help me God—"

"—When has God ever helped you?"

John David closed in until the barrel of his AK met Lucas's chest. Lucas could have panicked. He continued in a measured tone instead. "I know what you want—"

"—I want my daughter."

"You want more. God brought me here for a reason." The thought came without consequence. If Adonis could believe it, why couldn't he?

"What are you saying—"

"—You know what I'm saying. Jonas was just here. You missed him."

John David pursed his lips. His mind worked behind his unwavering aim, although the trigger finger went slack.

Lucas continued. "Maggie saw everything. And then she ran."

The finger returned to the trigger. "Why didn't you stop her?"

"What would have happened if I brought her out for Jonas to see? I thought she'd come back here. I guess she didn't."

John David lowered the weapon. "What would you do?"

"Do you really want to know?"

John David didn't answer that. "I'm not complicit."

"That's fair. Go look for Maggie."

John David wasn't yet at a point to blindly trust whatever Lucas planned. It took a moment for him to stand down. But he did. He backed out of the room and left Lucas alone.

It was a simple plan. Lucas reached Adonis's door, then knocked. When the door pulled open, "We need to talk. About the body."

Adonis straightened into a wary stance. "What about the body—"

"—You need to come see it, sir. Just you."

Adonis laughed. "Do you think I'm a fool, Lucas?"

Lucas managed a shrug. "There are leaders and there are followers. Sometimes the leader has to do what the follower can never understand." It was enough. Jonas Adonis found his coat and followed Lucas out the door.

They went on foot. Saint followed, and this pleased the reverend to no end. He engaged Saint in stop and listen games, then sent the dog off on wild searches for nothing with an enthusiastic, "Go get 'em, boy! Go get 'em!"

Lucas ventured. "Why is Saint so important to you?"

"I've told you," Adonis said. "He saved my life."

"But how?"

Adonis shrugged with a smirk. "Alright. It's a lie. There's nothing special about my dog other than I found him roaming on a street in Chicago and I decided to take him in. Much like you."

"Did he have a collar?"

"He did."

"So, lost. Not a stray."

"Is there really a difference?" There was, but Lucas knew that Jonas Adonis would never admit it. Saint had blindly followed him, and Adonis had taken advantage of that blind loyalty.

They reached the pit. Lucas peered in, half hoping that Alec had risen up and left. He had done it before after having been shot and stabbed and burned at the stake. But not today. Alec remained face down in the foul muck, the hole in the back of his head exposing brain matter. He wasn't coming back from it, not this time.

Adonis motioned to the mess. "I know you suddenly think that your brother didn't deserve this, that he wasn't meant to be fodder for the forest. And maybe that's true. Maybe it's not. You think that it's all about me. I need control. God must surely want you to kill me because here we are. It's your calling, after all."

"I seem to be good at it."

"So this was your plan?" When Lucas didn't oblige him with an answer, Adonis grinned and pulled a gun out of his pocket. "Then you're a fool. Different from your brother, for a fool from his heart says there is no God. But a fool who—"

Lucas lunged. Adonis, caught up in his moral piety, mistook the simplicity of Lucas's plan. He simply went for it. He caught Adonis in a gripping hug then plunged in the knife that he had hidden up his sleeve. He ripped the blade up, probably through the appendix and likely through some bowel, and he twisted before he pulled it out and plunged again.

The reverend slumped into the hug. Lucas felt the warm trickle of the man's blood on his hand and Adonis, who could have raised his weapon and shot Lucas through the skull just like he had done with Alec, didn't.

Lucas pulled the knife free then claimed the weapon in Adonis's hand. Adonis wobbled, a faint smile on his lips. He still had things to say. "Do you think you've won? God watches everything you do."

Lucas shoved him into the pit.

Saint took up post at the edge. He barked and wagged his tail and barked some more, while Adonis spit curses and fragmented scripture. And Lucas felt nothing. As it should be. He shoveled dirt and drowned out Adonis's rant with a quote in his head from another black book, the one written by his and Alec's satanic high priest father:

Death to my son, the misguided one
New life for the unholy spirit

He still wasn't sure what those words meant. But Alec was dead, and Lucas would never be whole. So he went with that interpretation and kept filling the grave. He stopped when Saint stopped barking, and when Adonis stopped ranting. The reverend was left sitting waist deep in the soft fill, his hair and clothes powdered by it. The other bodies, including Alec, were mostly covered, visible as bumps under the soil. Lucas heaved in air. His sweat and toil had left him feeling cold and clammy in the thin atmosphere, and he needed a break. As he settled down on his haunches, Saint met him with a whine of discontent.

And Lucas wondered if the end of Jonas Adonis would make John David happy. He realized that he might need to prove to John David that the deed was done, so he left the rest of the pit unfilled. Other things were more important, namely Jake and Maggie. He wondered if he could track them with Saint's help, so he took Saint in the direction where he had seen Maggie and Jake run. If he found them, they could run together.

The trail ran cold fast, and Saint proved to be nothing more than a mutt. "Go find Maggie. Find her." Saint made the motions, but in the end it was just play, like Adonis faking the poor dog out with the throw of a stick. They returned to the pit and found Todd.

Todd had a foxhound on a leash and his beloved semiautomatic slung over his shoulder. The foxhound betrayed Lucas's presence before he could slip back under cover of surrounding brush, and Todd slung his rifle off his shoulder with the immediacy of a pro. "What did you do?" He advanced on Lucas and repeated himself.

The lie came with ease. "I just got here." But it didn't matter. Todd had made up his mind. He struck Lucas down with the butt of his gun.

Late afternoon sun gave way to clouds that threatened to burst by nightfall. "Come on," Maggie said. "We need to keep moving."

"I'm cold."

Maggie tried to pull Jake along, but he had stopped again to catch stuttering breaths. There wasn't much she could do. She had already made him walk through a frigid stream at one point because she knew there would be a search once John David or Hannah realized they were missing, and she remembered from some story that dogs lost your scent if you walked through a stream. Jake later complained that his feet were freezing, even though they had taken their socks and shoes off to keep them dry while crossing. And then he dropped to the ground, hugged his knees to his chest, and shivered.

Maggie hugged him, too. She could feel his heart beating at a rate faster than her own, and a math problem danced in her head. If one train heads east at sixty miles per hour, and the other heads west at eighty, when will the two trains collide? It was an incomplete math problem, but the impact was the same: inescapable panic.

Still, she knew things. Two bodies held close kept you warmer. The sun rose in the East and set in the West, and if you looked out for significant landmarks it would help find your way back home. But she didn't want to go home, not now. Not ever. Maggie looked to the sky to witness an aggressive cloud pileup, and she tugged on Jake's arm one more time. "We need to find a place to stay dry."

They found a ravine where the earth had caved in and an uprooted tree provided cover. It wasn't much, and when the rain came down it was more like sleet. It stung when it struck exposed skin, and it chilled every inch of her. Jake shivered too, his head resting against her shoulder, and she was glad for his warmth. It would only get colder as night fell, and by the looks of the light, that time was soon.

They hadn't really eaten. They had packed some snacks in Jake's book bag, but those snacks were gone. The only things left were water bottles and a knife for cutting apples. Maggie wished that she had better thought things through, but then she hadn't expected to be on the run. As daylight dimmed to dusk, Maggie cuddled into Jake.

Dogs came barking. "Over here," came a familiar voice in the distance. It was Hannah. Jake stirred then tried to run, but Maggie held him tight.

"Where can we go? We'll freeze." She hated admitting it. They were better off being found.

The dogs cornered them as Hannah rode up. She pulled Maggie and Jake out into the frigid sleet, and she wasn't kind. "What were you thinking!?!" She shook Maggie by the shoulders. "You have explaining to do—"

"—No, they don't," John David said as he arrived with Zachary. He dismounted before the horse came to a stop, and he scooped Maggie up. Maggie went rigid. "We'll talk when we get home." He draped a blanket around her, and he instructed Hannah to do the same for Jake. Zachary boosted Jake into his horse's saddle, while John David boosted Maggie into his own.

The horse provided warmth on the ride home. Night had fallen, the sleet had turned to snow, and John David was greeted with problems upon their return. Todd broke the news at the stables. "It's Jonas."

John David made a point to silence him in front of Jake and Maggie. "Meet me in the chapel," he said.

"I guess this puts you in charge."

Maggie noticed John David's silent warning alarm go off. It was in the raise of the head, as if his ears had picked up the sound of a lurking predator. "Lucas?" And that was troubling too.

"That needs to be dealt with." Todd put a special emphasis on the word *that*. "Are you ready? Because we can vote—"

"—I'm ready."

That's when Todd leaned in for a more private conversation. Still, Maggie could hear him. "Maybe other people don't think you're ready—"

Hannah cut in. "—What's wrong with Reverend Adonis?"

Maggie didn't find out. John David ordered Zachary to bring her and Jake to the infirmary for Carol to assess. Jake had not stopped shivering through the trip home. Then John David pulled Hannah along as Todd led them to the chapel. Maggie watched Hannah's reaction to something John David said. Whatever he had shared, it wasn't good.

Carol accidentally spilled the news. She was already impatient, but Jake's unwillingness to be examined caused her more stress. Jake batted her hands away and broke into tears. "Don't touch me! Don't! They killed my dad. You all did—"

"—Jonas killed your dad. There was no they. And now he's dead too—"

Maggie straightened up. "Reverend Jonas is dead?"

Carol almost cursed. She'd let something slip. The woman opted for a different truth. "John David is in charge now." She took Jake's hand. "Have faith, okay?"

Jake refused to look at her, and Maggie was not comforted by the news.

"This is your moment," Hannah whispered. John David took in Adonis's corpse laid out on a pair of benches. Todd had retrieved the body and brought it here for the rest to mourn. Women carefully removed Adonis's clothes and mopped dirt and blood from his exposed skin. Men bowed their heads in whispered discussion as others gathered in clusters and wept. But not Hannah. She reeled John David in and kissed her forehead against his. "You've got this. God knows that your time has come."

Todd had other thoughts as he bounded across the room in answer to a conversation he surely couldn't have heard. "This wouldn't have happened if you hadn't brought Lucas here."

"Jonas made that choice," John David replied in a heated moment. "Maybe Lucas did us a favor!" Heads turned. Silence fell. Some made gradual reaches for guns at their hips. John David swallowed his true feelings and he preached. "Jonas was a good man. Once. We know that…this refuge…was founded on a real need to save the truly blessed. But he changed. We all saw that."

"He was chosen," came one shout.

"Who chose him, God? Because Jonas said so?" He felt sweat bead his forehead from a stifling lack of support, but he pressed on. "The hand. Alec Lowell's hand…those who saw it? Who can deny it?"

Silence overtook the congregation. John David continued. "Jonas Adonis killed a miracle worker—"

"—A false prophet," Todd said. A handful of murmurs agreed. "A false witness! That's what they do. We've seen the videos. The man praised Satan, and rumors say he failed to believe in anything—"

"Which is it, Satanist or Atheist," John David shouted, but it was too late. Arguments broke out and no one was heard, no sides vindicated. "Everyone! Stop!" John David held his breath until he thought it was safe to continue. "Lucas…once said—"

"—Lucas once said?" It was a bad starting argument, and Todd had called him on it.

John David pushed it anyway. "Jonas knew everything! When Lucas led his brother here, Jonas failed the test. Jonas. Failed. He took the bait because he thought he was anointed. Chosen. He wasn't. His soul was blacker than Lucas's. But there's a difference. Lucas knows what he is. He believes God led him here to erase two sides of a bad coin. His actions are our wake-up call."

Horrified faces stared back. But they didn't counter. John David stood a little bit taller. "Hannah?"

She dutifully stepped up. "Yes, sir?"

"How is my daughter?" It felt good to say the word daughter. He thought he caught Hannah flinch from the use of it, but he didn't care. He didn't have time for that.

"Alright. Still with Carol."

He motioned to Adonis again. "We'll hold a memorial. Jonas deserves that." Although he didn't believe it, he sold it well.

But Todd wasn't appeased. "What about Jake? And the woman? And Lucas—"

"—Jonas chose me to replace him! If something like this happened, he chose me."

Todd backed down, but John David understood. Todd was going to be a problem. "Lucas is confined?" A few nods confirmed this, and John David ran through a quick checklist of what needed to be done. They would bury Jonas where he died, and they would move on. There would be changes to temple rules: husbands and wives could lie together. There were logistics to figure out, but in time it would happen.

"I will handle Lucas. We will handle all of this! But right now, I need to see Maggie."

Jake slept. Maybe he was pretending, Maggie wasn't sure. Carol refused to let them leave the infirmary until John David arrived. He crooked his finger for Maggie to follow, and she obeyed out of habit.

They found a private spot, and John David pulled her into an embrace. "What were you thinking—"

"—I hate you." She pulled away and braced herself before he cast his eyes to the floor.

"You don't know what led to it. I'm sorry you had to witness it." He reached out for her shoulder, and when she flinched away, she noticed it. John David was trembling. He tried again. "The world outside is a horrible place. We've seen it before we came here, and today it found us. Sometimes we have to make hard choices in order to save the people who deserve to be saved."

"He was Jake's dad."

"He was a bad man—"

"—Could he heal people?"

"—I know what Jake wants to believe, but Maggie…" His voice turned thin when he said, "Please trust me."

"Is Reverend Jonas—"

"—Dead…I didn't know it would happen." Maggie refused to look at him, and he added one final thought. "I pray for your mom every day. I pray that God has forgiven her."

Maggie didn't understand why he had to bring up her mom. He had avoided talking about her for so long.

"We've gone to great measures," he said, "to keep the outside world out. We can save Jake. But his father…I don't know what you know. He was misguided, a disciple of the devil."

"What about Lucas?"

"We failed with Lucas."

"What happens to him? And to Jake? And to that woman—"

"—The woman is an adulterer. But she has a choice."

"And Lucas?"

John David sighed. It was his way of telling her that she was too naïve to understand. But she understood too well what John David had become. This was what was meant by innocence lost. "I love you," John David said. "Trust me."

"Yes, sir." Her eyes stayed cast to the floor.

"No, no. Not sir. Not John David. I'm your father…Say it, Maggie."

"Yes, Daddy." She said it. But she didn't smile.

Adonis's cabin was theirs for the night. It was theirs now that John David was in charge, and he hoped that Maggie would soften with its comfort. It was the only place that was close to feeling like the home she had once known. He thought that maybe she would be swayed, but little things prevented it, the first being Hannah. Maggie had never warmed to the idea of Hannah taking the place of her mom, and John David had taken precautions to downplay the growing relationship in her presence.

Hannah had made herself at home in Jonas's quarters when John David and Maggie arrived. She had stoked the fire and rose from the nicest chair in the room with a hopeful upturn of the lips until she saw Maggie. "Can we talk? Alone," she said.

John David had Maggie sit tight, and Hannah led him back out the door. "Where do we stand now?" She was nothing if not blunt.

"She witnessed an execution. Give her time—"

"—It happened because she was sneaking about. If you can't discipline your own daughter, how are you going to handle the likes of Todd?"

John David shook his head. The direction of the conversation had him confused.

"John," she continued. "You are the right choice to lead. But you need to handle this."

"Maggie's not the problem! Todd is a problem."

"Todd is necessary."

"What are you really trying to say?"

"Your daughter is being led astray by a messed-up boy. He sits through service after service and learns nothing. We've heard his smart mouth. His denials. Jake was the one who brought her there. He witnessed the execution too. What message was God trying to send him?"

"That's...a cruel lesson for a child."

"God's lessons are cruel. It's what we take away from them that make us better Christians."

Hannah stared him down. She was a strong woman who didn't really need a man in her life, not like Naomi had needed. John David felt guilty for comparing the two. It wasn't fair to Naomi. The progression toward a marital union with Hannah seemed clear except for Naomi. Her memory was the one thing he had yet to give up. And then he realized. "I thought you brought me out here to talk about us."

"If you expect me to replace her mother, she's going to need to understand discipline. It needs to come from you first."

He didn't believe her, that she could think Maggie some kind of delinquent. He wanted to lash out. He wanted to make Hannah take back her words and to admit she was jealous of how well Maggie had been raised. Instead, he put distance between them. "I will take care of my daughter."

Hannah gauged him through a squint. He hadn't pulled off hiding his disappointment, and she added to the distance between them. He stepped around her and headed inside where he found Maggie in front of the television.

The beam of a high-powered flashlight cut through the blackness of the confessional and seared Lucas's retinas. Hands reached in and grappled him. He caught a glimpse of blood on his shirt from the gush when Todd had smashed him in the face, and it was Todd who dragged him out of the box. Lucas struggled, struck his temple against the doorframe, and was rewarded with another sock to the face for resisting. He found himself in a chokehold, and he wondered if Todd had once been a dick cop, the kind who favored the enforcement half of law enforcement. But this was Lucas's fate; he had always known it would end something like this. The struggle was just a reflex. Lucas grew still, then allowed Todd and his buddies to pull him toward the chapel.

Once inside, they forced him to his knees beside Jonas's body. Todd took the same steel cable that once bound Alec's wrists and used it to chain Lucas to Adonis. Lucas was now holding hands with a corpse, fingers entwined like lovers do. *Okay,* Lucas thought. *Todd's execution plans just got kinky.*

Todd smacked Lucas across the back of the head and got in his face, "Meet your new grave mate, psychopath."

Lucas sniffed a clot of blood out of his nasal passage. He watched one woman collect Adonis's filthy clothes in a bag. Others washed him clean. More supported each other in a prayer circle. Aside from being tethered to a corpse, Lucas was invisible.

He wondered if John David had found Jake and Maggie. He hoped the two had found shelter. Or a well-travelled road. He hoped that strangers in the big scary world were compelled to offer them granola and fruit and a nice blanket to keep them warm. That would be nice. As he imagined the possibilities, Todd stepped up to the podium and solicited everyone's attention.

"Who thinks that John David is fit to lead us," Todd said point blank. "Who thinks that he has what it takes to fill our reverend's shoes?" He referenced Lucas with a sharp toss of the hand. "This is what he brought us. This! We can't stand here and reward a gross mistake. No. Reverend Jonas united us. What John David is doing is a power play. It's sabotage."

Lucas listened to Todd's rant. He watched the man's audience take it in like dried-out sponges; resistant at first, then willing to soak up the outrage until they were bloated with despair. The women cleansing Jonas's body distanced themselves, and the repercussions washed over Lucas like a frigid ocean wave. He felt himself drowning in them. He pressed at his nose with his free hand. It was tender, and warmth radiated from it, not a bad sensation considering that it was probably broken. And as he imagined himself being pulled deeper and deeper into an abyss, he wondered what it was going to feel like to breathe in dirt.

John as in John the Baptist

MAGGIE PLOPPED DOWN ON THE SOFA, ANGRY THAT John David had tried to justify Reverend Adonis's actions, angrier that Hannah had been waiting at the cabin. While she didn't hate Hannah for anything in particular, she didn't like her either. Hannah wasn't her mom, but she often tried. Even more frustrating was the fact that Maggie couldn't change anything or help anyone, not John David, not Lucas. Not Jake. She had made a promise to follow Jesus's way so that others could find joy through Him, but lately there was no joy to be had.

Only despair.

She had thrown up her hands after John David and Hannah stepped out. She landed on the couch with a thud and she turned on the TV. Images passed before her eyes: scenes depicting things that she knew she shouldn't see and that made her anxious before she had settled on an entertainment news show with a familiar face. It was the man that Reverend Jonas had executed, Alec Lowell. The woman was mentioned, too. Her name was Cleo LeCroix, and there was a federal investigation into their disappearances.

Jake's mother, who was accompanied by the familiar evangelist Josiah Light, spoke. "If you know anything about the Mission for Lost Souls, please contact us. If you've seen anything, particularly in the Chicago area, please call."

A toll-free number flashed along the bottom of the screen, and the Reverend Light made sure to let the viewing audience know that his foundation had set up the number. Maggie turned her head and caught a glimpse of John David and Hannah watching from over her shoulder. She reached for the remote to turn off the TV, but John David pushed past her and swiped it away. He stood there and stared at the interview. Panic.

"Daddy?"

He shut down the TV, took long strides to Adonis's desk, and supported himself with a straight-armed brace against its surface. A long moment of silence, then… "Where's Lance?"

Hannah said, "John—"

"—Get me Lance! Get me Carol. Now." Hannah closed in on him, and he repeated himself. "Now." Hannah hurried out the door.

John David stared at a spot somewhere between the farthest wall and the ceiling before the mania hit. He disassembled Reverend Adonis's laptop computer. He took out the battery pack. He ripped the cord out of the black-boxed antenna that allowed the computer to search for everything on the Internet, and he stalked over to the TV and unplugged it.

Maggie had questions, but she stayed quiet, and John David returned to the desk. He searched every drawer before he spilled the contents of one: cell phones. Maggie watched her father count them. There were five.

"Where is it?"

"John—Daddy?"

"Where is her phone?"

Maggie backed away as John David headed to the room's center. He rolled aside a throw rug to reveal a trap door in the floor. Once he scrambled down it, Maggie inched toward it. She heard her father shout "Away from the door." Sobs and pleas came from Cleo LeCroix as he demanded to know about the phone.

Maggie inched away. She found herself drawn toward the mess of phones on the desk. She pulled open drawers. The lower one had a baggie full of explosives.

Maggie closed it up and backed away when she heard John David returning. "Daddy?"

A sad smile found him before he caught her in an embrace. The hug was too tight. His collarbone pressed against her throat almost enough to make her choke. "We're going to the shelters," he said and kissed her on the top of the head. He proceeded to dismantle the phones.

Josiah Light was not particularly fond of cemeteries. It was an irrational reaction, he knew, but they represented a finality that even the promise of the Second Coming couldn't erase. Everyone died. Everyone. It was probably the most difficult obstacle to hurdle when trying to bring new members into the fold. Cemeteries were also creepy. Their reputation grabbed him and spread fingerlike chills through his spine. Every time.

But here Josiah was, standing outside the gate of a closed cemetery in the middle of a frigid night, in what Alec had often referred to as Fucking Wisconsin. "Money is no option," he reminded Belinda. "We can find a nice motel."

Belinda ignored him and waved at a figure approaching from the inside.

The old man, Toussaint Piquette, greeted Belinda with a warm hug once he opened the gate. He offered his hand to Josiah. "Reverend Light. Who knew an old geezer like myself would hobnob with so many celebrities." The smile was the most welcoming smile Light had ever met.

"You're too kind." Josiah shook the hand, but when Belinda stepped through to follow Piquette inside, Josiah held back.

Quick scrutiny came from the old man. It was clear that his wits hadn't aged. "Is something wrong, reverend?"

Josiah found solace in self-encouragement. "The good Lord has my back…Hallelujah." He stepped through. A breath of relief came when nothing happened from it; no bony hand shooting up out of the dirt, no burning hell pit cracking the earth to swallow him. He caught sight of the old man's smirk.

"You're one of the good ones, reverend." The old man added an odd chuckle to that then led the way to his little house on the hill.

After finding the Mission for Lost Souls in Chicago, Josiah and Belinda were shut out of the investigation by federal authorities. This irritated Belinda to no end, and she convinced Josiah to visit Piquette in hopes of unveiling more leads. Although convinced wasn't really the correct word. She had decided that she was going, and Josiah felt obligated to tag along. He feared that the stress of what they found in Chicago might undermine her otherwise rational mind. He half admitted to himself that this belief was probably a conceit, but he still felt protective enough of Belinda to stay for moral support.

The old man's house was just as Belinda had described it, quaint and cozy. Remnants of an old spouse's touch inhabited the place: a hand-crocheted throw over the sofa, a needlepoint quotation about home being where you hang your hat framed and on the wall. A small collection of well-read books stood on a shelf, the great works of many religions. Josiah was pleased to see the Christian Bible among them, its binding betraying the stresses of use. He was less pleased to see the Koran and outright suspicious to see the Satanic Bible.

Piquette caught Josiah looking. "Knowledge is a dangerous thing," he said with a smile. "Isn't it. What's your poison, coffee or tea?"

"Water," Josiah said. "It's pure. Life giving. It's enough to feed the soul." He helped Belinda out of her coat as he watched the old man pull a pitcher from his refrigerator with a shake of his head. He was getting the slow impression that he and Toussaint Piquette were not really going to be friends.

They settled around the kitchen table and got straight to the business of the visit. Mr. Piquette said, "He had a vision. He saw Lucas with a girl, one who was about Jake's age."

"A vision…Like a dream—"

"—I'm not going to go into the specifics of how he saw the girl. Frankly, Mr. Light, you wouldn't approve."

"The girl," Belinda said. "Did she have a name?"

"Not that he said. He thought maybe he'd recognize her as a missing person, but no luck."

"Who called him," Belinda said. She was met by a shrug and a shake of the head.

"So the only lead we have is this couple from Michigan and the general location of Cleo's phone," Josiah said in summary. He regretted saying it. He watched Belinda visibly age in her seat. "I'm sorry, Belinda. But we haven't lost faith. We can pray—"

"—Prayer does nothing!" Belinda reined in her tears. Then she apologized and stepped away from the table. Josiah was compelled to follow until Piquette settled a hand over his arm.

"Give her some room."

Josiah couldn't do that, because he liked Belinda. Maybe more than he should. He followed her to a guest room that she seemed more than familiar with, and he found her sitting on the edge of a soft bed with a frilly comforter more in keeping with the taste of a contented grandmother than a solitary old man. "I didn't listen," Belinda said as she blotted at her eyes. "The entire time, he said Lucas was involved, and I didn't listen. I pushed him away and now they're gone. Both of them."

Josiah took her hand. He was relieved that she let him. "We will find him," he said. "We will find Jake. I need you to be strong in that belief." He didn't bring up divine intervention, and she sniffled with a nod. She rested her head on Josiah's shoulder, and she thanked him.

If the truth were told, Josiah Light didn't want to be here. Alec was an investment, not necessarily a friend. And Josiah probably needed to atone for that. He probably needed to atone for liking Belinda as much as he did as well. But it didn't matter. The moment she rested her head on his shoulder, Josiah Light became truly invested in the mission. His words had put Belinda at ease, and now he was invested.

Belinda slept in the guest room and Josiah on the comfy sofa. He awoke to the crisp smell of crackling bacon and he offered to lend the old man a hand once he reached the kitchen alcove. Mr. Piquette politely declined, then hummed along to a song in his head without saying another word.

Josiah couldn't place the song. And he couldn't handle it anymore. People liked him, especially old people. "I'm not trying to put you on the spot," he said. "But have I offended you in some way?"

Toussaint paused with a curious expression. Again with the wry smile. "Have I given you reason to assume I'm offended?"

"Well, you…don't share much."

"I didn't realize I needed to, other than my home and my food, of course."

Josiah felt like an ass. "I'm sorry."

"Don't be." The old man flipped his bacon to even out its crispness. "But you could keep in mind a well-worn proverb. When you assume, you make an Ass out of U and Me." Toussaint Piquette chuckled and continued about his business, and Josiah Light felt small. He decided that he really did like the old man after all, in spite of the embarrassing exchange.

Then a song chimed in from somewhere in the living room, *Awesome God*, by Rich Mullins. It was Josiah's ringtone, a classic gospel tune written by a man whose music and ideas had a profound impact on him growing up. Rich Mullens had questioned the evangelical path to enlightenment. He had questioned the Catholic and the Protestant methods of worship too, and yet he had never lost his faith. Mullins never strayed from spreading good will until the day of his death in a sudden and unfortunate car accident. Maybe Josiah had strayed. He felt a pang of guilt about that as he caught a curious expression from Piquette over the ring tone choice. He answered the phone.

His wife was on the other end. "Lorena! My darling—"

"—You must be jumping at the news," she said. "Where are you?"

Josiah wasn't jumping at any news, and he looked around frustrated when he noted that Toussaint Piquette didn't have a TV. "Wisconsin. What news?" His wife told him about leaked information from federal authorities, because Los Angeles was Los Angeles, and the Hollywood gossip reporters were ravenously good at their job. She told him about the Mission for Lost Souls branch that was found there, and she told him about its connection to another church, the Temple of Adonis. Josiah had never heard of the Temple of Adonis.

"No one has," Lorena said. "But there were flyers there, sweetie. The church is run by a Jonas Adonis, and the authorities are asking for people to step up if they know anything about the church or the man."

"And?"

"Sweetheart. Why don't you know this?" Josiah didn't feel like explaining why he didn't know this. He glanced at his watch: eight in the morning. He was curious to know why she was up so early on the West Coast to know this. Then he remembered how enamored Lorena had been by Alec on the occasions she had met him. He had seen in his wife's eye her desire to covet much in the same way that he himself had been guilty when he admired Cleo. But Lorena would never follow through on those desires. Alec wasn't her type. She made that clear when they had played the game of what celebrities would get a pass if you succumbed to infidelity. Lorena proved to be fond of men with some muscle, an Idris Elba or a Chris Pratt. Alec Lowell wasn't even close.

He glanced up to find Belinda arriving for breakfast, and he pushed thoughts of infidelity games to the back of his mind. "Just tell me, Lorena. What did they find?"

"A father and daughter from Illinois went missing a few years back," Lorena said. "According to his family, the man wanted to live off the grid after the death of his wife. She committed suicide, Josiah. It was heartbreaking—"

"—Lorena—"

"—I'm getting to it, Josiah. Let me tell it." And she did. The family knew the name Jonas Adonis. They knew the location of the temple—sort of. It was in a place called Sangre De Cristo.

Josiah snapped his fingers at Belinda to get her attention once he saw the laptop folded down on Toussaint's desk. "Look up Sangre De Cristo." When he asked Lorena where that was, she said she wasn't sure. Josiah thanked Lorena and told her how much he loved her before promising to be home soon. He watched Belinda do an Internet search while Piquette set aside his frying pan to join her.

"It's a mountain range," Belinda said.

"Where?"

"Colorado. Or New Mexico." Josiah and Belinda exchanged worried glances. They said Cleo's name together.

"She's the one who contacted him," Piquette said. "She set up the meeting."

Josiah returned to his phone again. He clicked on his tracker app, and sure enough, Cleo's phone pinged from the same general location as the map on the laptop screen. His grin was as broad as the Golden Gate Bridge. "My my, we have a lead."

Dawn filtered through the trees as John David pulled Maggie along. They headed for the chapel in search of Lance. When they stepped inside, they were met with fervent discussion that died down to nothing. Heads turned.

Maggie saw Lucas shackled to Reverend Adonis by the wrist. She pulled free of John David. She didn't want to be here, a witness to Lucas's death, for she knew this was the plan. John David renewed his hold and pulled Maggie toward a bench close to the doors. He sat her down and gave her a flat-out order. "Stay put—"

"—Yes, Daddy." He didn't look convinced by her obedience. But he left anyway and strode toward Todd as if on a mission.

"Are you ready to face what's out there? Are you, Todd? Lance?"

Hannah pulled Lance out of the crowd. "I don't understand—"

"—They found the man's truck! In Chicago. They have your name."

Hannah shoved Lance as if she had gotten lessons from Todd. "You said you got rid of the truck."

"We moved it! We ran out of time—"

"—Our day of judgment has come. Because of Jonas. And because of him! And the rest of you are standing around wondering who should lead us? This isn't a time for deliberation. It's a time for action. We need to prepare."

"You're the one who brought him here—"

"—I did! And I will atone! And Lucas will answer for it."

Lucas perked up, and Maggie locked gazes with him. John David quickly stepped between them, severing their connection. "That's right, Lucas. Make your peace." Lucas met John David's ultimatum with a sniffle and a smirk, his teeth licked clean behind a face stained with dried blood.

John David turned away to continue addressing the others. "The reverend had a phone, LeCroix's phone. Who has it?"

As he waited for anyone to step up, Maggie noticed it again, Lucas staring at her. He gave her a pointed nod, a signal toward a bag full of mud and blood stained clothes sitting next to her. The topmost item was a folded coat.

Blank faces met John David's plea. Lucas was almost amused, especially when the man had to further explain himself. "GPS! Her phone could lead them right to us!" Understanding dawned on a few faces. One of the women who had been washing Adonis's body clean closed in on Lucas and searched the pockets of the trousers still left on the reverend's corpse.

She came up with nothing, as John David closed in too. "Where is it?¨ John David searched Lucas roughly. The other woman who had been helping cleanse the body chimed in.

"His clothes are over there." She pointed to the bag, and Lucas was impressed by how clueless Maggie looked as the woman headed toward her. She looked in the bag with a puzzled expression before she stepped out of the way to allow the woman to search. The woman came up empty, and when she turned to Maggie, on the verge of an accusation, Lucas spoke up.

"Maybe it fell out at the pit."

Todd landed his boot against one of Lucas's kidneys, and Lucas groaned. He would get even with Todd for that one. *One final stipulation before making my peace*, he thought. He grinned some more.

John David held Todd back from further assault, but the suggestion seemed to bring him focus. He pointed at Todd. "Go look for the phone."

Todd reluctantly accepted the charge. He grabbed a pair of friends, Caleb and Joseph were their names, and he left the chapel. Lucas said, “Do I get a thanks?” John David ignored him.

Lucas snickered. Not because it was funny. It was clear. He was going to die with Jonas fucking Adonis chained to him and, while the others followed John David to the opposite side of the chapel to discuss their new problems, Lucas glanced down at his pending grave mate.

Blood welled up from the ragged gash along the length of Adonis's belly. The reverend's chest rose and fell, just barely, and Jonas Adonis opened his eyes. His gaze drifted then locked on Lucas before a rasp of laughter escaped his throat. “Fuck,” he said.

Lucas let his eyes dart about to see who might have caught the exchange. No one had. Everyone was caught up in the frenzy of dealing with a potential outside invasion. Everyone except Maggie. And Maggie did nothing.

Lucas reached down to slip his free hand over Adonis's mouth and nose, as he noted Maggie turning away. “My kid,” the reverend said before Lucas could follow through. “Where is he?”

“You have a kid?”

“Where is he?” Adonis's voice gained strength and volume. “Where's Jake, you Sonofa—”

Lucas clamped down. It was sudden. It was violent. And it brought attention. *Shit.* The action was meant to avoid a scene, not court it. The wound kept bleeding; the man was alive, and shit this was impossible. It couldn't be true, not this.

A commotion ensued, the miracle witnessed and before Lucas understood what was really happening, his brothers and sisters surrounded Adonis. “My God, he's breathing!” And, “Can you hear us, Jonas? Glory to God, praise Jesus.”

They unbound Lucas's wrist, bound the stab wound tightly, and tried to coax the man to say more. He didn't. He had passed out, but he was breathing, and they might have forgotten about Lucas if Adonis hadn't kept a tight grip of his hand. The man had slipped into unconsciousness, but he still kept a solid grip on that hand. Weird.

John David swooped in. He secured Lucas's wrists tightly behind his back and shouted orders to Zachary. "Lock him up." John David led others to bundle their leader up and carry him away and, as Zachary dragged Lucas along to be confined in the cold confessional that reeked of piss, Lucas realized that none of them knew.

Not a one. Of that, he was certain. But Lucas knew, and he was confounded about how. Lucas noticed that one person didn't follow the rest taking Jonas Adonis out the door. Maggie didn't even try. And that was a significant thing.

"We're not equipped for this," Carol said after they made Adonis as comfortable as possible in his own bed. He remained unconscious as she rechecked the damage, and the damage was bad. "We should transport him—"

"—A public hospital? No—"

"—He'll bleed out. It's just a matter of time—"

"—We can't do that!" Carol shook her head and kept silent, but John David wasn't ready to dismiss the botched-up job she and Lance had done. "We were untraceable until now. We were safe! The man has no pictures of himself! Anonymity. An outside hospital? No—"

"We can't close up this kind of wound."

"Then maybe he's meant to die." Carol was aghast. John David regretted his outburst.

"What about the bigger question?" Carol countered. "Killed by a wickedness that could only be conceived in the devil's mind, and now he's alive." Carol waited for John David to answer. He shook his head before he caught his own harried reflection in one of Jonas's damned mirrors. *They remind me of the man I am, not the man I was,* Jonas once said.

The reverend had been aggressively disturbed by news from the outside world on that day. John David vaguely recalled something about a synagogue shooting before Adonis flipped the television off. When John David asked Jonas to explain, Jonas said that he was a mongrel, like Saint. He had grown irritated after that because Saint was never around anymore, and where the hell was his dog!

John David turned away from the mirror. He didn't like the look of the man he had become. But Jonas was in no condition to lead, and John David reminded Carol of the decree. "If ever he's too sick or injured—"

"—You're next in line. I understand. Do we know his blood type?"

"No."

"What's yours?" It was B positive, and Carol shook her head. "Someone with O negative might give him time to express his final wishes."

"You and I both know what his final wish will be."

Carol let out a breath. "Lance told me about Alec Lowell's hand. In Chicago? At the mission? When we were held up? Mr. Lowell got in the way. He stepped in the path, and—"

"—He's dead, Carol. I didn't pull the trigger. And by some miracle, Jonas is alive."

Carol dropped it. "Maybe he will pull through." She smiled at the potential. "Maybe everything will work out fine." Carol could have her dream. John David knew better.

Zachary shoved Lucas back into the confessional, and the lock clicked into place. Lucas's spine rested against corrugated tin cold enough to stick to his skin without the barrier of his thin cotton shirt. But the cold wasn't what bothered him. It wasn't Zachary's treatment either because he knew that if it had been Todd, things would have been worse. The kick to his kidney still ached, but the nose, it didn't feel that bad. Maybe the swelling had made it numb to pain. It didn't feel swollen. He wasn't breathing through his mouth out of some necessity to do so. He tucked the thought to the back of his mind then focused on his real problem, John David.

"Hey Zach."

No answer.

"Zach?" Lucas rammed his shoulder against the door. The move rattled the lock, but the door didn't give way. Still nothing from Zachary. Lucas tried again. And again. The lock refused to give way, and his shoulder ached, so he took a brief break. Maybe Zach was waiting for free target practice.

He rammed the door again anyway. This time it brought attention. "Did you really do it? All the things Jake says you did?" It was Maggie.

"Is Zach—"

"—I waited until he left. Did you—"

"—I'm lost, Maggie. I'm following God's lead, and here I am in a fucking box." He expected to hear Maggie tell him not to swear.

Instead, "What's God telling you to do now?"

He wasn't going to answer that one. "How is Jonas?"

"John David hasn't said much."

Fucking John David. It was the moment when Lucas realized that he couldn't kill the man even though he wanted to. "He's your dad. Just call him your dad."

"I don't want to."

A response that Lucas hadn't been ready for. The most wholesome spirit Lucas had ever encountered wanted nothing to do with the man who raised her right. And she wasn't wrong. "I'm sorry if I led you to misjudge me," he said.

More silence.

Lucas, who had never been prone to fill in those awkward moments, found himself doing just that. "Alec—Jake's dad? He never believed in this idea of God. But me? I just thought that God was wrong."

"Seek the Lord, and he shall deliver you—"

"—Not for me, Maggie."

"I don't believe that; that His forgiveness has limits."

"That's what makes you special." He changed the conversation. "Do you still have the phone?"

"Yes."

"Get it to Jake."

"It's locked. Five numbers. Or letters, I don't know."

It was in Adonis's possession last, and Lucas thought about it. "Try Saint."

It worked. He shouted before Maggie was gone, and she complained. "The power says ten percent. I have to hurry."

"Do me a favor. Keep an eye on the reverend."

"Why?"

"I think he's going to pull through. You might need to help him—"

"—He killed Jake's dad."

'I know...I think this all might have changed him." He didn't know how else to put it without sounding like a loon. "God's forgiveness has no limits, right?"

No response.

"Maggie?"

A moment passed before he heard quick footfalls diminish.

He wasn't pulling through. He felt numb and tired and cold. Memories existed in a haze; he knew they were there, but he couldn't quite reach them. They were shady images behind a barrier of fog.

Hands groped him. A burning in his gut came and went in waves. He needed to puke, but he had no energy to roll over and do it. He couldn't even open his eyes as he listened to unfamiliar voices having heated arguments from somewhere far away. They were closer than that, much closer. They just seemed far.

His bones sank into the comfort of a plush mattress. At least it seemed plush. It wasn't a fucking pit. He tried to remember the moment, to push past the numb cold and focus on how it happened. He had floated. Just like the first time when Lucas killed him and left him to burn. And he had seen things. He had risen up and away from the chaos, driven out by one shocking blow, and he had seen things.

He saw Jake and the girl he had seen through Lucas's eyes, and he saw Lucas heading toward them. And as he ascended, he lost sight of it all. The world below was fast becoming a dot. And no no no, he couldn't lose consciousness. He fought the urge to evaporate into oblivion like brain matter from a point-blank shot, and he focused. He tried to return, to laser in on the pit and re-inhabit the vessel. But he couldn't do it. He couldn't find himself. So he floated again, trapped in a stream of vague memories that slipped away on a steady current. He was losing himself.

He let it happen. He slipped through the stream until something snagged him back, the blackened roots of a long-dead tree. It snagged him with gnarled tendrils, and it pulled him in. He was descending, drawn back through the weight of the world at a fast clip, through rooftops and rafters until he felt the weight of his own existence trapped again in a cage of flesh and bone. When he opened his eyes, he found Lucas. He remembered it all, and he wished that he had the strength to reach up and rip out Lucas's throat. But he hadn't had that strength, and before he knew it, Lucas was clamping down on his mouth and nose. He had been too weak to fight it, and he must have passed out.

He found the resolve to open his eyes again, and this time he found the man, John David. "Ah, Jesus," he managed.

John David's silent scrutiny was unsettling. The man reached for a glass on the nightstand and offered it. The water going down refreshed him, until it seemed like John David was feeding him too fast. He choked, then spluttered. John David set the glass aside without apology. "I'm not going to get your hopes up," he said. "You're bleeding out. We've made you as comfortable as we can, but…" He shrugged without the slightest hint of sympathy.

"I'll recover. I've got a track record." John David said nothing to that. "So what's next?"

"What's next?"

"Your man tried to kill me. But here I am—"

"—Lucas acted of his own free will. I had nothing to do with it."

What a boldly stated lie. Alec decided to sit up as a show of his own strength. He pushed up onto his elbows with an effort that ripped through his belly. It left him so lightheaded that he almost rolled out of bed to land face first on the floor. Almost. John David caught him, and as Alec rested in the embrace, his head heavy against the bone of John David's shoulder, he caught his reflection in a mirror.

He wasn't himself. He—what? As the reverend stared back from his reflection, Alec felt his breath catch in his throat. He slipped off of John David's shoulder, and the contents of his guts hit the floor in strings of saliva and blood. He was fading again. He was fading fast, and as John David braced him to prevent the fall, only one thing played out in his head. "Don't touch me. Don't don—don't touch me…"

"Carol!" John David's shout brought more hands to touch him. But he was fading. He was fading fast, and he slipped into the comfort of unconsciousness one more time.

Maggie returned to the shelters where her brethren stocked blankets and food and tallied ammo supplies. They emptied the upper stores of goods to make the place look abandoned, a Christian retreat that was closed for the season. Maggie's presence went largely unnoticed, and she found Jake holed up in a room with two bunks. He was on the top, his face turned to a vent in the wall. It was how she first remembered meeting him, and she wondered if there was some cyclical revelation behind it.

She prodded him. "Wake up." He rolled over, and she handed him the phone. His eyes lit up. "Call your mom before someone checks on us." She helped Jake unlock the phone, and he eagerly dialed.

A moment, and he looked at the screen in disappointment. "It can't find a signal." He pulled his arm back reflexively to whip it, but Maggie stopped him.

"How do we get one?"

"Outside? They won't let me out of here. They follow me to the bathroom."

"They're preparing." Jake nodded sadly at that, and Maggie scrambled to find better news. "Your mom is looking for you. I saw her on TV."

Jake burst into tears. "What if she gets here? What if they kill her, too?"

Maggie took the phone back. "I'll do it. I'll call her and warn her."

Jake still sobbed, but he managed a nod. Maggie took his hand and promised him it would happen. She slipped back out through the shelter, almost going undetected until she reached the stairs that led up through the women's dormitory. Hannah's voice made her wince. "Maggie. All hands together—"

"—John David needs me." She gained two more steps before Hannah grabbed her arm.

Hannah said, "Why—"

"—He wanted me to check on Jake."

Hannah shouted over her shoulder for someone to look in on Jake. She didn't let go of Maggie's arm until she got the answer.

He was in his assigned bunk sleeping. "You're sure?" Hannah said. "He's not just pillows stuffed under a blanket?"

"It's him."

Hannah let go. Maggie could feel Hannah's hawk-like gaze on her as she scurried up the steps. She was relieved when she broke out of the dorm into the chilly air. She took refuge in the stables. No one was there except one of the horses left behind by Todd. She checked Cleo's phone, and she could see it—a single bar of reception.

They said goodbye to Toussaint after they finished the breakfast that the old man insisted on before they left. Toussaint gave Belinda a long hug, and Josiah a firm handshake before Belinda settled in the passenger seat of their rental. Josiah took the wheel and refused to give it up for the bulk of the drive. Belinda was fine with that. She didn't want to bruise his chivalrous ego. It gave her more time to browse routes along the Sangre de Cristo Mountains.

The range encompassed 17,193 square miles of land and was traversed by what seemed like a million unmarked roads. Finding Jake or Alec or a little-known commune among the mountains and trees would be monumental. But Josiah Light, the infinite ray of sunshine that he was, refused to lose hope. "Her phone is pinging from this region here. That narrows it down considerably." And it did. But not enough.

The drive from Piquette's graveyard refuge in Wisconsin to Sangre de Cristo would take the entire day and the better part of a night. And Josiah turned out to be a slow driver. He was pleased to point out how the Midwest was God's country whenever he spotted a billboard that shouted the sentiment. He pointed out highway exits to towns where his church was popular. Belinda watched him fondly ponder over it every time, and she quietly marveled over it. The man's simplistic view of the world was sometimes unfathomable to her.

Once night fell, they found a reasonable motel that Belinda assumed was the equivalent of slumming it for Josiah. He took it upon himself to pay for two rooms, although he didn't have to, and he made a point to thank the concierge and her family with a "May God bless you," before he handed Belinda her room key. Once they reached their rooms, she said goodnight, then shut the door with a deep sigh and her own thanks to God for the break.

She didn't sleep. Instead, she paced between bouts of tossing and turning and searching the Internet for any shred of news. She searched and magnified images of the land comprising Sangre de Cristo. There were trails throughout the range: hiking trails, biking trails, and secluded camping areas. There were clusters of homes and there was wilderness. So much wilderness.

And then there was Cleo's phone, its signal still hovering in the general vicinity of Colorado or New Mexico. Belinda wished Cleo would answer her damned phone.

When morning light bled past the motel room curtains, a knock came at the door. Belinda had showered at that point. She was wrapped in a towel when she opened the door a crack. Josiah blushed and averted his eyes in spite of the fact that she was covered. "I wasn't sure if you were up. There's a continental breakfast in the lobby."

"Let me finish up," she said. "Then we can go."

"Would you like me to grab you something? Coffee? A pastry?"

"Whatever's easy."

Josiah said he would check out for them then waited for her to hand over her key card. Belinda watched him head down the hall, realizing that this trip was as awkward for him as it was for her. She closed the door thinking that maybe she'd been unfair to the man. His constant sunny disposition and praise to the glory of God was annoying as hell. But he was here, willing to help however he could. He had his flaws, like Alec had flaws, but he was a good man as much as Alec was a good man. How was that possible when the two were so drastically different?

The second half of the drive began with Belinda at the wheel and Josiah on the phone with his wife. He kept her up to date on where he was and where he expected to be, and he promised to check in before he might possibly lose cell service. His wife put their daughter on the phone, and Josiah praised the girl for what sounded like good grades. His daughter was seven, the pride of her teachers. They chatted about her for a bit after he ended his call.

"There was a time when raising a family was the farthest thought from my mind," Josiah admitted. "Don't get me wrong, I knew it would happen eventually with a good and strong woman of faith by my side. It's our duty to bring children into the world, to teach them, but to learn from them too…It really is God's way of humbling our arrogance, don't you agree?"

Belinda kept her eyes on the road and appeased him with an ambiguous "hmmm."

"I wish your husband could have seen that sooner."

"What does that mean?" She glanced at him, aware of the edge in her own voice.

Josiah was smart enough to recognize it. "I'm sorry, Belinda. I thought I knew Alec. I judged him accordingly. But when your son disappeared, and when Alec came to me, I realized I was wrong. Forgive me."

She stared. It wasn't what she had expected to hear. She returned her eyes to the road, partly because the honest sentiment left her at a loss. "Thank you," she said.

"I pray this turns out well," Josiah said. "But if it doesn't, and I'm not suggesting it won't, I hope that you'll stay with us. I sense that maybe you only do it because of Alec, and that you think some of our ideals are…archaic. But you're an asset. I don't want to lose you."

Belinda felt her eyes well up. She did her best to blink tears away. She kept her focus on the road. Josiah Light was making it difficult to dislike him, and somehow she hated him for it.

Then her phone rang in the cup holder. Josiah scooped it up before she could reach it. "Cleo?" Belinda's eyes fell off the road, and as Josiah listened, she found a spot to pull over. He said, "Who is this?" Belinda motioned for him to hand over the phone.

"It's—I'm Maggie. Can you hear me?" The reception was poor, but Maggie didn't want to raise her voice. She crouched behind hay bales and took glances over the top, hoping no one would wander in. The voice on the other end had changed from a man's to a woman's, and the woman wanted to know why she had Cleo's phone. "Is this Jake's mom?"

The woman wasted no time. She spoke in an even tone. "It is. Who is this again?"

"He wants to go home—"

"—He's okay?"

"Yes." She barely heard an exchange between Jake's mom and the man.

Then mom returned to the conversation. "Is his dad with him?" Maggie froze. She couldn't answer without choking up, and Jake's mom seemed to sense it. The woman hurried through the next question. "I very much want Jake to come home. Maggie, is it?"

"Yes."

"But I don't know where he is. Are you his friend?"

"Yes."

"Where are you?"

Maggie hesitated to answer. She was going to say it. They were at the Temple. But Jake's mom needed an address, and Maggie didn't have one.

"Maggie—"

"—I don't know. We're in the woods? It's not on a street. It's not a house. I don't know."

"Is it near a town?"

"No."

"In a state? Colorado? New Mexico? Maggie, you don't know where you are?"

Maggie slumped to the floor. Straw scratched her back as her shirt hitched up. She had never felt this anxious talking to a stranger. She prayed that Jesus would help her through this then she blurted out the first thing that came to mind. "I've been to California."

"You're in California?"

"We drove there…my dad and me."

"Can I talk with him? What's his name, is it… John?"

Maggie was in tears. "He—he loves me. He does, but…"

"Maggie, you've got to give me something. Do you know Cleo? This is her phone—"

"—She's under the floor. My dad is a good dad. He loves me, he's—"

"Honey, I need—"

"160." It was a sign; one of the ones that she remembered from her Los Angeles trips. It wasn't the only one, but it was along one of the longest routes. She remembered it as they made their way closer to home along a steep and winding pass. On more than one occasion, Maggie had imagined John David missing a curve and sending them past the guard rail to plummet to their deaths. It was far more frightening than the overcrowded highways of Los Angeles. "Route 160. Pa...pagosa Springs."

"You're in Pagosa Springs?"

"We stopped there. We pick up supplies sometimes." Maggie heard Jake's mom relay the information. She heard Jake's mom tell the man to write it down.

"Maggie," she said again. "You need to tell me more."

That's when Maggie heard the shuffle of hooves. She let out a gasp, then sat perfectly still before she hazarded a glance up and over her shoulder. Todd leaned over her. He took the phone and crushed it under his heel.

"Maggie? Maggie!" No reply. And Belinda couldn't breathe. Like Alec felt when he suffered his attacks, she couldn't breathe, and when Josiah reached out, she pushed him away because she didn't want to be touched. Not now. Not by Josiah who would smother her in a caring embrace and tell her that God had some plan. She opened the driver's side door and pushed herself out only to be nearly mowed down by a passing Audi on the highway.

"Belinda! Get in the car! Get in the car now." Josiah had launched out of his own seat and staggered to meet her. He pulled Belinda to the safety of the passenger side and forced her down into his vacated seat. He stayed beside her, his hand on her knee, and let her sob.

"He didn't make it. Whatever happened, Alec didn't make it—"

"—We don't know that."

"We do. And Cleo? Under the floor?" Belinda struggled with her feelings. The woman had been fucking her husband. She shouldn't have cared what happened to Cleo. But she did, and it was wrong. Sickening and wrong.

Josiah grabbed her hand, and maybe he had managed a quick prayer in his head, his lips were moving. But it was brief before he left her side with his own phone wedged to his ear. It gave Belinda time to recover. When Josiah returned, he had news. "We are meeting with authorities in Pagosa Springs. Alright? We can make it by two—"

"—We're overshooting it. The girl said they went through Pagosa Springs coming from California—"

"—It's a point, Belinda. It's progress."

"Give me your phone."

Josiah held it up, halfway through asking why, when she grabbed it. The device was still unlocked due to the recent call, and she checked his locator app. The marker indicating Cleo's general location was gone.

Josiah gave her a decree. Her turn behind the wheel was over. She was no longer allowed to dwell on worst-case scenarios. They had made contact. It was from the girl whose name was in the news, Maggie and her father John. They had narrowed the field down to a location off of Route 160 and close enough to Pagosa Springs for a church or a ranch or a communal living facility to make supply runs. Jake missed his mother, which meant he was alive. "Alive, Belinda. Federal agents will meet us in Pagosa. We will find them. Jake is coming home."

Belinda nodded with a numb feeling in the pit of her stomach. Jake was alive. They were going to find him alive. But not Alec; there was no hope for Alec.

Maggie's feet tripped over the threshold as Todd shoved her through the cabin door. John David rose, and Todd dumped the busted cell phone on the desk. "It wasn't at the pit," he said with a scowl.

When Maggie winced from Todd's grip, John David said, "Let her go."

Todd pointed a finger dangerously close to John David's face. "You need to step down. You need to discipline your kid and—"

"—Jonas is still with us, Todd." John David threw up his arms. "He's alive. And if you think he's the one to save us, from ourselves, then I can't help you."

"You're lying—"

"—Maggie, where did you find it—who did you call?"

"No one." She could tell he wasn't convinced, and she stuttered through a better lie. "Jake—his mom. She never answered—she, she wasn't there—"

Todd said, "Now she's lying—"

"How did you know which number to call?"

"Her name's Belinda. She was the only one—"

"—Okay." His eyes rested on her face in a lingering moment of disappointment. "I don't know what to do here, Maggie. I don't—"

"—She needs time in the box—"

"—The box is occupied!" Todd backed down from the outburst. Maggie was thankful to have her dad sort of on her side. Until an idea dawned on him. "Did Lucas have it?"

"No." The lilt of her reply was pathetic, but after John David went through some kind of mental checklist, he dismissed the possibility with a shake of his head.

He took her hand and pulled her aggressively to a seat. "You need to sit. And you need to stay. Do you understand?"

Maggie appeased John David with a nod. She watched him brush the remains of Cleo LeCroix's phone into a waste can before he led Todd toward the reverend's bedroom.

And Maggie was alone. She was alone beside Adonis's desk and its drawer full of fireworks. She could slip some into a pocket if she was quick. She was becoming a bonafide delinquent, and she didn't care. She reached for the lower drawer. The zip-tite bag was too bulky to stuff anywhere, so she snapped the bag open hoping that the little noise would go undetected.

It did.

She scooped out three fat sticks of dynamite about the length of a grownup's thumb, and the lighter that accompanied them. She stuffed them into her pocket, and she pushed the drawer closed. She felt good having them, except for the fear of getting caught. That possibility terrified her.

As she waited for Todd and her father to return, her gaze drifted to the front door. They were taking their time.

And the door beckoned.

Apocalypse

A HINT OF SATISFACTION DANCED THROUGH JOHN David's mind as he noted Todd's expression of disbelief. Carol mopped the reverend's forehead and monitored his pulse. An infection was surely setting in, she had said.

"How long does he have?" John David knew why it was the question Todd chose. Todd adored Jonas Adonis, but Todd had his own conceits. He wanted to lead. He was better at it, at least in his own mind. And he never got over Adonis's decision to pass that leadership on to John David if anything should happen.

Todd would challenge the decision. Bringing Lucas into the fold was already a mark on John David's record. Maggie in possession of Cleo LeCroix's phone was strike two, and that was a deeper problem. She was slowly being led astray. By Lucas, by Jake, by the exact kind of people John David had tried to shelter her from. It was his fault. Every bit of this mess was because of his decisions, and—

"Reverend Jonas?" Carol squeezed the man's hand as Adonis opened his eyes. "You gave us a scare."

Adonis squinted at the three of them before his gaze drifted to his beloved mirror across the room. His eyes rolled up, oddly like those of teenage disdain. "This isn't happening." He chuckled, although it was apparent that it triggered some pain. "It's kind of funny, though." The chuckle faded into a sigh. "Aaahhh, fuck me…Jake?"

John David and Todd exchanged glances, while Carol answered, "He's still with us."

"And Cleo?"

"Jonas, we have other problems," John David said. "You're not going to live through tomorrow—"

"—We don't know that." Carol patted Jonas's hand, and John David spoke over her without pause.

"Don't sugarcoat it. You're not surviving this, and federal authorities are on our trail. I need you to say it. Who should lead us?"

Adonis said nothing, and John David feared that he had passed out again. Then the man drifted back as if speaking in a dream. "Federal authorities? They're coming?"

"For you, Jonas."

"Then it's over." He smiled at that. "Your time has come… tell Jake I love him. Have him…give Lindy a kiss for me." He smiled at that, too. Then he was out, his mouth slack, his breathing shallow. He had made his decree.

Shaken, Carol laced her fingers together, head bowed in silent prayer. Then she rose and headed for the door.

Todd locked eyes with John David. A silent challenge.

"Trust me, Todd."

"Trust you?"

"If this gets to that point, we have options. Jonas killed Alec Lowell. Lucas killed Jonas."

"You think it's that easy? We are dead here! They will swoop in and take away everything we've worked for. They'll take our guns, our freedoms. We'll be labeled the decade's latest religious freak show, and we will be incarcerated for the rest of our lives because of one mistake made by you—"

"—Keep your hands off of me." It was in response to a shove, and Todd threw out his chest in defiance of it. John David pulled in as much calm as he could muster. "We have the bunkers—"

"We have a body! We have a psychotic piece of—sh…and we have two hostages who will never understand our cause. And we have your daughter."

"My daughter isn't—"

"—We need to get rid of our immoral burdens. Bury them. Fast."

John David went cold. "What are you saying?" Todd didn't have to answer, and he didn't. "That's insane! No. That's…" He huffed and backed away from Todd and his monstrous idea. "You're not thinking clearly," he said as he headed back toward the living room with Todd on his heels. "I will figure this out—"

"—When it's too late?"

John David turned on Todd in the hallway and put down the law with a harsh whisper. "We are not killing innocent people. We can save them."

"What about Lucas?" And that was the problem.

But it could also be a solution. "Everyone shelters in the bunkers," John David repeated as he led Todd to the living room. Maggie was gone.

"Maggie?"

Panic curled around his chest in a tight embrace. He checked the rest of the cabin as Todd shadowed him. The kitchen, the bathroom, she wasn't there. When he lifted the trap door to Adonis's cellar a scratch came at the front door. Todd investigated, and Saint scampered in from the cold.

"She's outside," Todd shouted.

Footsteps went to and from the porch through the fresh snow, but one strayed away from the beaten path. They were smaller prints, and they headed for the confessional.

Thud! Lucas slammed his shoulder against the door one last time before he decided that he was doing irreversible damage to his musculoskeletal frame. It ached, and he massaged it.

"Hey!" The shout startled him as Maggie's face blocked incoming light from the rooftop slats. She wedged something through; four cylindrical items scattered to the floor. Lucas gathered them up, filled with renewed hope. Another shout. It came from John David, and Maggie stole away from the slats in the roof.

"Maggie! What are you doing?"

The door to the box clattered, and Lucas stuffed the explosives into the darkest corner he could find. He heard the hasp of the lock unlatch. Hands reached in, and Lucas squinted from the stark daylight.

Todd threw him to the ground. He landed a hard kick to Lucas's gut, then bent low to peer into the box. John David continued to demand answers from Maggie. She didn't oblige, at least not with answers he wanted to hear. "I didn't do anything! I hate you!"

Lucas smiled at that. Then Todd stomped on his hand, the one with the scar along the wrist, the one that Alec had once healed. Finger bones snapped. "What are you smiling at, you worthless piece of—" Another stomp and two more snapped; the pinkie and the ring finger. There would be no roast beef for that little piggie. And the other was squealing in agony. Or was that meant for toes? It was funny where Lucas's mind could wander. He managed another grin.

"Stop it," Maggie screamed. "Stop!" Lucas cradled his freshly crippled hand in the other as Todd pulled him to his feet.

"What's the matter," Lucas said with a grin reserved for sociopaths. "Things not going as planned?" And with that, Todd socked him in the face. A white hot flash blinded him before everything went black.

Alec drifted. He wasn't coming back from this one. He felt weak, and he had failed: as an anarchist, as a rebel, as a healer, and as a husband. He'd failed as a dad. He supposed it was time to die. Leave it in God's hands be it he, she, or it.

He waited to be lifted up and out, to dissipate, when something wet slobbered across his palm. His eyes rolled open and he managed to turn his head. It was the dog—the incessantly barking mutt from the pit. Lucas's little fetch buddy. The animal sniffed at the hand that hung limp over the bed's edge, then curled up its lips and snarled.

Great. The dog knew something was off, and the hand was about to get mauled. Add insult to fucking injury, Jesus. Or, Whoever…Just do it.

The dog sat back on its haunches and let its tongue hang loose. Maybe it was the laugh that Alec let slip that put the dog at ease. More important, the whole thing gave Alec focus. He pulled his arm back to the confines of the bed, then managed to push up into a sitting position.

Okay. Alright. He breathed. He felt nauseous doing it, and his head pounded, but he hadn't passed out. The dog yipped with a little jump and a wagging tail. Okay, alright. Friendly dog, his own personal cheering squad. "You're getting used to me? Because I'm not." Alec swung his feet to the floor. He took another breather as he stared at the image of Reverend Jonas in the mirror, and the dog leaped onto the bed. It settled beside Alec and rested its head in his lap. Alec absently let his fingers stroke through the dog's fur. He found comfort in it. "Saint? Is that your name?" He vaguely remembered hearing it when he had been in the pit. Saint bounced up and lashed his tongue across Alec's nose.

It was enough for Alec to think he could do this; to get out of bed and to do, he didn't know…something. Find Jake. Or Cleo. He was the Reverend Jonas, after all. He was the authority.

Alec nudged Saint out of his lap, then rose to his feet. His legs trembled, and he hunched forward like an ancient man due to the pain burning through his gut. But, okay. He managed. He managed more steps at lengthy intervals to reach the vanity. One, two three, four, step. Another count to four, and step. His feet were bare, the floor was chilly, but he made it. He braced himself and stared his reflection down.

The throwback to the eighties' hair was disturbing. Alec tousled his fingers through it to make it less obvious. The man who killed him, who kidnapped his kid and held Cleo hostage, stared back through haunted eyes in a face with a bloodless pallor. How could this be anything but disturbing?

He grasped for focus again. Jake. Cleo. They were here somewhere. What he needed was a phone to call for help. He pulled open the top drawer of the vanity in hopes of finding anything useful.

It held socks, the thin ankle ones not designed for the freaking cold weather of the place. They were color coordinated and neatly folded. Not a single pair was white. The boxers were folded, too. They were silk with fancy patterns. High-end boxers. This guy had money. Alec hazarded a glance below the waistband to see what he might be wearing. "Well," he said aloud. "Not me either." Inhabiting another man's junk freaked him out more than the face.

Saint barked, and Alec found his focus again. He rummaged through the essentials. No weapons, no phone. Just a wallet with a good amount of cash and an ID. The name read Nathan Shein, from Austin, Texas. The face was still the man who killed him. "I thought your name was Jonas," Alec said aloud, and Saint replied with another bark. *Who the hell is Nathan Shein?*

It didn't matter, not at the moment, and Alec went to pocket the wallet until he realized he had no pockets. He was in a loose pair of sweatpants, probably dressed by the reverend's nurse. He didn't have a shirt either, and he made note that the binding holding his guts in place had soaked through with fresh blood, wet to the touch. He'd probably opened the wound by getting out of bed. Would they have sutured him up? He didn't even know. He searched other drawers for a warm layer, then opted for a blazer hanging in the closet because it had pockets and it was easy to slip on. He had to find Jake. He had to find Cleo. He had to find a phone.

As he headed toward the bedroom door, he felt faint. He grabbed at the wall for support as Saint threatened to trip him up by bouncing along and yipping at him. "I'm working on it, okay? Where's Jake?"

Saint's ears pricked up.

"Jake? Is he here?"

Saint coiled up as if preparing to bolt to find Jake. Alec imagined the dog doing some Lassie shit, and he would have been thrilled except that he was in no condition to keep up with a search and rescue. But it was a sign. Saint recognized the name—that's what Alec chose to believe, and it renewed his energy.

They made it to the living room. A laptop sat on a desk, the kind that housed a compartment for a battery pack, and it was disassembled. It gave Alec hope as he settled into the swivel chair beside it so that he could put it back together and fire it up. His fingers trembled. Sweat painted his forehead and the pain in his gut had gotten severe. He refused to pass out.

Success! He switched the device on and waited for it to power up when he noticed the open trap door in the floor. How could he have missed that? Then the computer beeped that it was ready, and a welcome screen popped up. It read, *Are you Jonas Adonis?*

Alec stared at the screen. He wasn't, but he was, and shit the thing was password protected. He tapped enter because he didn't know what else to do, and the computer went to work. The device's camera kicked in, and he saw Nathan Shein's—or Jonas Adonis's sickly face stare back at him as a program centered an oval on it and analyzed it.

And he was in! There were no apps to log in to social media, but there was an icon for mail and another for a web browser. Alec clicked on each to discover no Internet connection.

Fuck.

The pain in his gut was getting worse, and he cupped a hand over the spot in an attempt to soothe it. It didn't help. More blood stained his hand. He wiped it clean on the leg of his sweatpants. He wasn't healing, not like he was used to doing, and it worried him.

The trap door beckoned, but he wasn't feeling strong enough to leave the safety of the chair, not without passing out. So he opened a desk drawer. He found burner phones, five of them, all with their batteries removed.

He found a clump of keys for doors, padlocks, and cars. Those might come in handy. He dumped them into his pocket with the wallet that identified him as Nathan Shein then opened a lower drawer and found a baggie with explosives.

His heart sank. Jake was most definitely here. It hadn't been a lie to scare him.

And the open trap door waited.

Alec pushed out of the chair. He shuffled to the opening and eased down to the floor fearing that he would black out and break his neck from the fall before he reached it. "Hello?"

No answer. Saint wagged his tail. Alec called out again. He dangled his feet over the edge. He was going in. He scooted his butt down the steps until he reached the bottom floor.

A short hallway led to five doors, all locked. Alec searched through the wad of keys. It took a few tries to find the right one. The first door opened to a storage room; a pantry stocked with canned and dry goods to last a man through a couple of winters. Behind door number two was something more disturbing, a control center with a bank of surveillance monitors. The console controlled other things, too, by the look of the setup, heat and air, lights, but the monitors kept his attention. They showed people in a confined space. A bunker. There were four displays on a single monitor, and on one of them, Alec found Jake.

An audible gasp escaped him. Jake was alive, and in some bunker, and Alec shot up on his feet ready to look for him. Bad move. The speed of his ascent drained what blood he had left in his head. Woozy, he stumbled and crashed into the doorframe. Curse words slipped out as he closed his eyes and supported himself there.

Just fucking breathe. He lurched out and toward the stairs when a noise made him pause. Sobbing came from an unopened door across from him. Alec tried the handle. Locked. Dead bolted. "Cleo?" A pause. Alec pawed through the jumble of keys, almost lost them, then found the one that worked. He threw the door open, braced himself against the frame, and peered in.

She was backed into a corner like an abandoned pet at a shelter. Alec felt a grin invade his entire being. "I don't have it," she said. "You took it from me."

"What?" Alec was lost before he remembered that he wasn't Alec anymore.

"You're bleeding."

He barreled through an explanation. "I'm not who you think I am—I don't know how to explain—"

"—Are you alone?" Her eyes darted past him to the hall.

"Cleo, listen—Oh, Jesus. Fuck..." He winced and leaned against the doorframe. The tear in his gut burned like acid, but the rest of him felt cold. *Jesus, don't pass out.* "I'm sorry. For everything I've done. To you. To Lindy..." He panted, unable to wrap his mind around words.

Cleo crept closer and took continued glances toward the hall. "Are you letting me out?"

Alec motioned to the keys still dangling from the dead bolt. "Get help…Find Jake…" He slumped to the floor and faded. Cleo roused him with a nudge. She had the keys in her hand by then. "I'm not healing like I could… I'm not… Tell Jake I love him? Tell Lindy, too."

Cleo didn't say yes or no. Or maybe she did. He never heard it. He sensed Cleo stepping over him, leaving him behind. As it should be. Then he drifted into the numb place where nothing mattered. He expected to float again, and that was good. He looked forward to dissipating.

Cleo bolted for the steps. She didn't know what happened to the Reverend, sir and she didn't care. She had keys, and she had to move fast. A part of her feared that this was some cruel game; that at any second, someone would leap out of a hidden corner and punish her for failing to have faith in the plan. Because the reverend, Mr. Jonas, Nobody's Real Name Is Adonis, had said it more than once. *God wants you here. Do you have no faith in His plan?*

Apparently, God had other plans, or the man wouldn't be bleeding out in his basement. Still, his final words were odd. Before she could dwell on it, she reached the top step and was startled by Saint. Cleo let out a yelp, and Saint obliged with a full-on bark. "No, no, no, hon…Ssshhhh—I love dogs." She froze in place then closed her hand into a fist to let Saint take a sniff. He seemed satisfied, and she rewarded him with a scratch behind the ears.

Cleo peeked out a window. The compound outside looked abandoned. What were the chances that she could waltz out the front door unnoticed? She peeked out again, still no people. She tried the door, first with a crack and then wide enough to slip out. When Saint tried to follow, she whispered, "Sit. Stay," and the dog obeyed. She closed the door and tiptoed off the porch. Tiptoed. Like she might wake someone. She attributed it to idiotic panic before she slipped around the side of the cabin and kept close to its wall.

There was no one around. Absolutely no one. At least on her side of the building there wasn't. She thanked God for that and set her sights on a garage that was more like a carport. A small number of trucks waited for her in a line.

"Stop it! Stop! Daddy, make him stop!" Maggie clawed at John David's attempt to hold her back as Todd continued to kick, beat, and bash at Lucas. Todd took out his frustrations with a vengeance that didn't matter. Lucas was out cold. A disturbing look of satisfaction remained on his bloodied face.

"Todd! It's over!"

Todd stepped over Lucas and turned his rage on John David before he pulled himself together because of Maggie. Maggie shivered through tears, devastated beyond reach. "You need to step down," Todd warned.

"And you need to trust me! Adding to the body count isn't it!" The two men glared at each other as Maggie continued to tremble in John David's arms. He kept firm hold as he turned her around to face him. "Go to the bunkers."

She sniffled and shook her head.

"Do it! Now." He shook her when he said it, and he regretted his actions when he saw how much it rattled her. But she nodded. Maggie scrambled for the women's quarters, and when Todd started after her, John David lurched for his arm and held him back.

"You don't know she'll go there—"

"—Listen to me!" John David crowded Todd and gave him no room to speak. He threw his hand out to indicate the bloody mess that was Lucas. "He is our only chance of beating this! He has a history—"

"—How does that matter?"

"It matters a lot. Go to the bunkers. I will take care of this." When Todd stood fast, John David engaged his walkie. "Hannah, locate Maggie for me."

"She's here," Hannah said over the crackling airwaves.

"Keep her there. No one leaves the bunker. Radio silence unless you hear from me." It took a moment for Hannah to respond with an okay, but she did. "We need to work together," John David said to Todd. "Can we do that?"

"What's your plan?"

John David would have told him the plan if it weren't for the squeal of tires that grabbed their attention. They turned toward the central compound and spotted the truck speeding toward the closed gates. Cleo LeCroix was behind the wheel.

Todd went running as Cleo jumped out of the cab to pull the gate open. John David saw Lucas stir, limp hands attempting to push himself up. He grabbed Lucas by the shirt collar and dragged him back to the box, shoved Lucas in, and snapped the lock in place when Todd opened fire and when Cleo screamed.

Cleo abandoned the gate. She ducked back into the cab, put the truck in reverse, then rammed forward through the half-open gate. Everything moved too fast, but John David didn't have to tell Todd anything. The man headed for Adonis's cabin, probably in search of keys for one of the other trucks. John David met Todd coming out from the cabin entrance.

"She has the keys. All of them—"

"—The spares?"

"Look inside! He kept them in one damned wadded mess! They're gone. We're screwed."

John David pushed past Todd. Saint got under foot, and John David stepped on a paw. The dog yelped. "Git! Go!"

Saint scampered away as John David got his bearings and took in the nightmare. A trail of blood led from hallway to Adonis's desk to trap door. Paw prints traipsed through and spread the blood trail like a virus, and John David had the sickening thought that they would have to get rid of the dog too. But that was Todd-like thinking. He refused to give in to that level of panic. He peered down the bunker steps and caught a glimpse of Jonas, passed out beside the open door to Cleo's cell.

John David headed down then squatted beside the listless preacher. His heart sank. "What did you do?" He heard Todd fly into a rage up top, and John David was back on his feet.

Todd had pulled out every drawer from the reverend's desk. Failing to find spare keys, he'd whipped a drawer across the room. "I'm not going down without a fight."

"Go to the bunkers—"

"—She's heading straight for—"

"I know!" John David took a breath and held it. Then, "I will take care of it."

The ramifications of what that meant hung between them as Todd silently worked through how. "On horseback?"

"Go to the bunkers. If I'm caught, I'll stand alone. At least there's a chance for the rest of you."

"That's not a plan—"

"—What's yours? A shootout? Go out like Koresh?"

Todd backed down looking less than convinced that John David could handle this. He left without argument, and John David found the resolve to return down the hatch. He knelt beside Adonis and searched the man's pockets in hopes of finding another set of keys. What he found was Nathan Shein's wallet. He read the name on the ID and was appalled. They had been led by a man who wasn't even who he had claimed to be. A Jew. And suddenly too many things made sense. The bunkers, the ultimate plan. They had been duped by a false prophet. They had been had.

John David checked Adonis's condition. Still alive. Barely. He slipped the wallet back into the man's pocket and he brooded. Jonas Adonis, Nathan Shein, whoever he was, could go to hell. He abandoned the body and stepped into the surveillance room where he knew he could check on Maggie. Not everyone knew about this room. Todd didn't. Adonis, or Shein, or whoever, hadn't trusted Todd enough to follow the plan. "This is God's way," the fraud had confided to John David. "And when the day comes, we will cross over. Do you trust me?"

I did trust you. He looked over to the pressurized tanks lining the surveillance room, the ones connected to the duct system of the main bunker. The reverend's plan had been to keep tabs on the rest of the members of the commune from his own private bunker when the end times were near. The following would shelter underground, and Adonis would be the face of an otherwise empty retreat. This central hub controlled heating, air quality, and electricity. The breaker panel for the entire underground facility was built into the console where John David stood. Built in alarms would warn of fires and carbon monoxide, which was ironic, because...well, that was the thing of it. The emergency systems were wired separately from the rest of the bunkers.

He prayed for God's guidance. Catching up with Cleo LeCroix on horseback was possible but improbable. Jonas Adonis was the man she witnessed executing Alec Lowell. He reached to flip the breaker switch to the emergency systems off. He touched the monitor where he saw Maggie pacing alongside Jake in his bunk. Then he stepped over the body of Nathan Shein and hurried out of the shelter.

There were three well-hidden exits in and out of the commune bunker, and John David began by blocking the door that led in from the women's dorms with a sofa. He would take the entrance through the men's dorms when the time came, and he would eventually block that one, too. He didn't bother with the entrance through Jonas Adonis's private hideaway. That door was locked with a bolt, and the keys were probably in Cleo LeCroix's possession.

He headed for the confessional.

Lucas's body and mind had shut down from the beating. When he startled awake, he was lost for where he was. Then he remembered. He braced his broken fingers with his useful hand, then tried to wriggle them and found that he could still move them. They were sore but apparently not broken. He was vaguely aware that gunshots had roused him, rapid gunfire and the roar of a truck's engine. Now there was nothing but silence.

Lucas waited. He listened. It was unlikely that there would be no activity outside, not even the shuffle of some guard's feet. "Hey," he shouted. "I think you might have bruised my bladder because I really need to piss." It was a lie. Still no response. He slammed his shoulder against the locked door surprised that he had strength to do it. The door still didn't budge. "Shit."

The M-80s. The lighter. How could he have forgotten those? Lucas prayed to the powers that be, whether Satan or God, that having them hadn't been some hallucination. He wasted no time once he found them.

He had to position the little stick of explosives in the right place for maximum effect—right against the locked latch. He ripped his shirt along the seam then tore a strip long enough to tie one end around the stick. He stuffed the other end into the crack along the doorframe. The fuse sparked to life. He curled up in the farthest corner of his confines to shield himself from the blast, and he covered his ears.

BOOM! John David shielded himself from a spray of exploding wood chunks. Lucas bolted out of the box, then stopped cold when John David pulled his gun. They stared at each other for what seemed like an eternity before John David broke free from the shock of it and closed in. He slammed Lucas against the confessional and kept him still with the muzzle of the gun at his ear. Lucas groaned from the hit. John David found himself huffing like he'd reached the end of a climb to a stony peak.

"How did you—" he cut himself short, still breathing heavy when he pieced it together. Maggie. The M-80s from Jake's stash. Rage. "I tried to save you! To help you find the right path! And you corrupt my daughter?"

"I didn't corrupt her. You failed her—"

"—Shut up!" He shook Lucas so hard that it was a miracle the gun didn't go off and shatter Lucas's skull. John David squeezed his eyes shut and refocused on the plan. He swung Lucas around and shoved him toward Adonis's cabin.

"Where are you taking me—"

John David shut him up with another shove. Lucas stumbled briefly then limped along.

"He wants to see me? Why?"

They closed in on the porch, and John David stopped him at the base of the stairs. "You killed him."

"Now he's alive—"

"—You killed him! He killed your brother, and you killed him. But not before he killed you first."

"Okay," Lucas said looking thoroughly confused from behind the goatee of dried blood staining his face.

"That's what Cleo LeCroix knows. Jonas killed your brother. He was dying when he set her free. Who did it? Who killed him? You."

"Is Jonas dead—"

"—You're sick! Perverted! With an unhealthy attraction to your nephew. And my daughter. Then you learned about Jonas's plan, so you killed him. But not before he killed us, too."

"What…what was Jonas's plan?"

"It doesn't matter." And it didn't. Not for Lucas. He pulled Lucas, tripping up the steps and inside.

The main room was a mess. Blood everywhere, thanks to Saint. Lucas tried to keep John David talking. "Jonas killed you?"

"Maggie and I? We'll start over. We'll find a way. But you?" John David shoved Lucas toward an open trap door in the floor.

Lucas resisted. "I'm not going down there—"

"—Get moving—"

"—If you're going to kill me, you're doing it here—"

John David shoved harder before Lucas turned and head butted him in the face. Shit, it hurt, the movies depicting it were a lie. John David cursed for what Lucas believed to be the first time ever, as blood spurted from his nose. Lucas shouldered past him, but John David managed to trip him up with one swipe of the leg. He struck the floorboards hard. Saint came running from Adonis's bedroom with a litany of barking.

"It doesn't matter where they find you," John David said as he took aim. "They will find you, and they will blame you." He pulled the trigger.

Lucas shifted just enough for the bullet to miss and bury itself in the floorboards beside his head. He rolled and swept John David's leg like John David had done to him, then scrambled to his feet and bolted for the front door. He reached the porch and thought he might make it, when a second bullet punched into his back. He crashed down the steps, landed face first against the frozen ground. The shot was high, lodged into the muscle and bone of his shoulder blade. He tried to rise, but his own roar filled his ears as he collapsed back down in agony.

John David landed beside him. Lucas felt sharp cold sting his lungs with each intake. He knew it wouldn't be long before another bullet exploded through his head and he would breathe no more. Cold steel met the base of his skull, and as an incessant buzzing filled Lucas's ears, John David leaned in.

"You don't deserve forgiveness. Or redemption or absolution...Not everyone can be saved."

The buzz that filled Lucas's brain took to the sky. He looked up, and John David did too.

A drone hovered. *A drone.* John David shifted his aim and took the thing out.

Stupid move. A chill worked its way up from John David's toes. He closed in on the machine for a better look, but he already knew. It wasn't some toy or mass-market device for a model plane enthusiast. It was a military or police grade unit, and it had a built-in camera. He shot out the lens.

That was it. John David had failed. He had failed because he thought he could find redemption for the irredeemable. And now, he was no better than Lucas, worse even for believing that he had been better. He turned to face Lucas and he roared. He took aim again, but Lucas lay there. Unconscious. Bleeding out. John David nudged him with his foot. Nothing. If he wasn't dead, he would be soon enough. What was the point anymore?

There were only a few things left for him to do.

John David headed for the cabin to do what was always the plan. He ignored Saint's wary gaze and headed down the trap door steps. He stepped over the false preacher's slumped body and ended up in the surveillance room.

His fingers touched the screen that showed Maggie in the room with Jake. "God, be good to her," he whispered. He turned to the tanks lining the wall and he unscrewed the valve on each one. Then he sat down in front of the bank of monitors, placed the muzzle of his gun in his mouth and blew his brains out.

Lucas was faking it. It had proved to be a smart move. He was probably bleeding out, sure. But John David had assumed, and he had assumed wrong. It gave Lucas a fighting chance. The pain in his shoulder blade had bubbled down to a dull throb until he tried to push himself up. Bad move. He shifted his weight to his good arm and managed to sit.

He puzzled over the pile of electronics. *Huh,* he thought and nothing more. The compound gate, now bent and broken, beckoned. Lucas could walk away if he wanted to. He could go somewhere and bleed out from the bullet in his back in peace. But he couldn't do that. He couldn't leave Jake and Maggie behind.

He also wondered what was so important for John David to return to Adonis's cabin when he heard the gunshot. He staggered to his feet and stared at the open door. If Jonas Adonis, or more accurately Alec, wasn't dead before, he was dead now. Lucas edged toward the porch thinking that he had a better chance of surprising John David with a weapon than he did of running. There was a poker by the fireplace. If the coast was clear and he could reach it, he could skewer the bastard and they could both die side by side. Brother beside brother. It seemed to be Lucas's destiny after all.

He tested his weight on the first step. He managed, was thankful for the rail and, when he crept inside, Saint bounded from his sentry behind the desk to greet him. Lucas welcomed it then shushed the dog and crept toward the fireplace. He grabbed the poker then slowly searched the cabin. John David was nowhere to be found. Neither was Adonis, although the blood trail clearly had its start in the man's bedroom. Lucas braced himself then made his way toward the trap door steps.

He found Jonas Adonis lying crumpled on the floor. Except it wasn't Jonas. Not anymore. "I'm sorry," he said, and he believed that he was. Once he slid to the floor, he wrapped a hand around the base of Adonis's skull and pulled him close. "It's my fault. I'm sorry. I am." Lucas rested his forehead against Adonis's forehead, or Alec's, if the truth was to be told.

Lucas laid the body down when a thud caught his attention. It came from a room down the hall, and the door was open. Lucas used the poker like a cane to push himself up to his feet. He took measured steps toward the open door. What was left of John David lay on the floor. His body must have shifted and toppled. Bits of brain matter speckled the headrest of the swivel chair he had been in. Lucas supposed the discovery should have made him sick. Instead, he was drawn to the monitors.

His gaze flicked from image to image of the bunker as he noted a pattern. People slept. Or they napped. Lance and Carol lay in a lovers' embrace, fully clothed. Others who were known to be couples did the same. As Lucas flipped from camera to camera, he saw people passed out on sofas or slumped to their knees in prayer. Except they weren't praying.

The strong ones, Zachary, Todd, Hannah, lay slumped beside bunker exits. They had been trying to get out. Then Lucas found Jake in a bunk and Maggie passed out on the floor. Lucas turned to the cylinders lined along the far wall. They were marked CO. Carbon Monoxide. He lurched for them, twisted each valve shut. Then he grabbed John David's blood-spattered handgun from the console and bounded out of the room, the bullet in his back a faint annoyance.

A hide-a-bed sofa blocked the bunker entrance. The thing was heavy, but Lucas managed to shove it aside. Todd and Hannah fell out when he pulled the door open. They were either dead or unconscious; Lucas wasn't sure. He took cautious aim, and when Saint nosed through them, Lucas shooed him away. If they were alive, he didn't need Saint to give them a nudge. He vaulted inside, his mouth and nose shielded by the crook of his arm. Saint stayed behind. *Smart dog*, Lucas thought.

Lucas found Jake. He shoved John David's gun into the waist of his pants and lifted Jake out of the bunk. Maggie's head lolled as he tried to gather her up, too. He couldn't do it, carry them together, not with a bullet in his back. It was a challenge to even carry the one. He had to choose who deserved the better chance at living. Instead, he sank to his knees and hugged them both.

Alec had been right. Alec had refused to accept God or Satan, or any other superior entity ruling over his life, because if they existed they were self serving, petty, and cruel. No one was saved through blind allegiance to anything. This place, the weight of unconscious children in Lucas's arms that aggravated the dull throb in his back, was proof.

"Don't punish me like this," he heard himself whisper. "Not like this."

"I feel sick." Maggie's breath warmed Lucas's cheek, and a laugh skittered out of him.

"Walk with me, alright? I need to carry Jake." Maggie stirred a little more, and Lucas felt her forehead snuggle deep against his neck. She wasn't getting to her feet. She didn't even try. He grabbed her hand and coaxed her some more. "Come on."

Once he got Maggie to move, he dragged her past the aftermath and toward the door where he had entered. He halted. Todd and Hannah were gone. Lucas kept Maggie back while he poked his head through to see if the immediate surroundings were clear. He eased the gun out of his waistband.

Jake was coming to. Lucas felt the boy hold on tight, which aggravated Lucas's back but made Jake easier to carry. He nudged Maggie along. They made it halfway down the hall when retching from a nearby room caught Lucas's attention. He signaled Maggie to proceed quietly, and she tried, but when he pushed her forward, she stumbled. The noise alerted whoever was in the room. Lucas heard Hannah. She must have been the one getting sick. The one who lumbered out was Todd.

"Run!"

Adrenaline kicked in. Maggie ran. Todd roared. "Luuuuccccasss! You evil shit!" The effects of the carbon monoxide had yet to wear off, and the esses were slurred, the vowels elongated. Lucas hoped to outrun Todd because of it. He couldn't shoot at Todd and carry Jake at the same time. Then the bratatatattat of an assault rifle ripped the wall beside him to shreds.

Lucas ducked around a corner and slumped, spreading blood from the shot in his back down the length of the wall. He held Jake tight. John David's gun had fallen out of his reach in the attempted escape. His bleeding shoulder had compromised the use of the entire arm down to the fingers. At least Todd was too messed up to aim. Heavy footfalls closed in, accompanied by the thud of collisions against walls. Lucas tried to get up, to reach the gun that had been bowled ahead of him, but pain shot through his leg. It crumpled beneath him. It was drenched red. He'd been struck in the thigh and hadn't even realized it.

"You can't run, Lucas! Today's your judgment day!"

Getting closer with every stupid word. Lucas felt a flutter in his gut. The door to the outside was in reach. Maggie had left it propped open, and Lucas could see the light powder of snow on frozen ground. A waft of crisp air beckoned. He pushed Jake back and wrapped his hands around the kid's head. "Jake! You gotta run. Jake—"

Jake didn't open his eyes. Lucas freed his hold, and Jake wrapped his arms so tightly around Lucas's neck that Lucas struggled to breathe. He pushed through the leg pain and made a break for that door, then crashed to the ground, a sprawl of arms and legs with Jake still latched around his neck.

Todd rounded the corner. He freed a slack-jawed grin and raised the assault weapon. Then, BANG. Todd looked confused as his rifle slipped away. He wobbled, then hit the ground. Lucas glanced over his shoulder to find Maggie with her father's gun. It trembled in her grip.

"Take Jake," Lucas said. Maggie laced Jake's arm up over her shoulder and led him outside. The kid convulsed a few times once he hit pure air, but he was going to survive. Lucas was a hero.

He still couldn't put weight on the leg, though. He pulled himself forward, wrapped his hand around the barrel of Todd's weapon, and there was Hannah, woozy, pale, and aiming a .38 at his head. He was going to die after all, just like Alec. Sort of. A bullet to the brain, then thrown in a pit. He accepted his fate.

"You killed him, didn't you," Hannah said.

"He killed himself."

Hannah clenched her teeth from the news, but her tears didn't ring true. Then she screwed up her face as if she'd sucked on a lemon and took aim.

Another shot rang out. Hannah dropped, her blouse stained by an increasing spread of crimson at the breastplate.

She tried to raise her gun in one final act of judgment as Maggie closed in and put the woman out of her misery. Lucas flinched from the lack of hesitation. The light in Maggie's eyes that Lucas had always admired was gone. "We've got to get out of here, Maggie. Understand?"

She helped him to his feet.

Cleo had no idea where she was going. The roads were narrow dirt paths, unmarked and dusted with snow. She'd made a left, then a right, then took a winding turn alongside a deep cut of land before she hit an ice patch and slammed the truck into a tree.

She shivered. Her nerves refused to rest, and she sat at the wheel sobbing for a good five minutes before she gathered her wits and opened the door. She fell out of the cab, because frazzled nerves and an empty stomach were a bad combination. The day had grown long, the shadows a testament to it, so she took a breath and figured out which direction was north...which didn't mean shit, because she had no idea where she was.

Just follow the freaking road. Keep moving, hon. Keep moving before they figure out which turns you took. It wouldn't be hard. All they had to do was follow her tire tracks through the recent dusting of snow. She was the only vehicle out here, it seemed.

She began walking. She wasn't going to die in this hellish nightmare. She wasn't the one. She refused. And she wished she had a decent pair of shoes. She walked, and she shivered, and she refused to dwell on Alec. There was nothing she could do about that, he was dead and he hadn't deserved it and he was a goddamned fucking martyr, that's what he was, because of his beliefs, and Jesus Christ, stop dwelling on it…He was persecuted, a martyr without a god.

What would she say to Belinda? She supposed that thought betrayed some hope that she would escape this and actually have the opportunity to see Belinda. And why would Jonas Adonis bring up Lindy? Not Belinda. Lindy. Alec was the only person who called her Lindy.

She picked up the pace as best she could in her weak excuse for shoes, the kind meant for LA weather and for accentuating a skinny girl's alluring posture. She swore to herself that she would never wear a pair of shoes like these again. Then the sound of a motor came from somewhere, and *shit*, she fell into a panic. She searched for cover until her brain processed the sound. It was the flap-flap-flap of helicopter blades, not the roar of some engine. She looked up.

"Oh my God, I'm here! Right here!" Cleo danced in her crappy but fashionable shoes. She waved her arms over her head, and she screamed for attention. The helicopter began to circle. She had been saved.

"You can do this." Lucas handed Maggie forceps found in an infirmary drawer and gritted his teeth.

"I can't." The wound in Lucas's leg continued to bleed. Suture thread and a needle blackened by a recent flame waited their turn to sink through Lucas's flesh.

He had to coax her. He would have removed the bullets himself, but Jake continued to cling to him, and he wasn't capable of reaching the one lodged in his shoulder blade anyway. "It's just meat. Like stabbing a fork into steak. You can do this."

Maggie's breath quickened. Then she did it. She screwed up her face and dug deep. Lucas groaned until she pulled the slug out. More blood poured from the wound, and this worried Lucas. If the bullet had hit an artery, he was dead. But he found words to let Maggie know she'd done good. He had her douse the mess with a whole bottle of peroxide. The wound bubbled and burned and Lucas fought the urge to pass out, but once the two of them sutured it and bound it tight, Lucas managed. The extraction of the bullet from his shoulder hurt like hell, but not near the pain he'd endured with the leg.

They had to move fast after that. Jake was no help, but Maggie was a godsend. She gathered warm clothes, canned goods, sleeping bags, and a small tent. Lucas collected knives and a fishing rod, and ammo for John David's gun. It was far more than he had survived on through frigid nights in the woods of Wisconsin or soul-chilling nights on the streets of Los Angeles.

They saddled Moses, Lucas steadying Jake in front of him and Maggie wrapping her arms around him from behind. Lucas kicked the animal into a trot and Saint bounded along behind them. "Did he really do it," Maggie said after a stretch of silence. "Did he kill himself?"

Lucas held his breath. It made the shoulder ache. "I'm sorry, Maggie." She hugged him tighter from behind, and they continued to ride.

Agent Karen Burroughs had not been looking forward to meeting with Josiah Light and Belinda Lowell in Pagosa Springs. Family involvement in these things was always a hindrance, especially when it involved the loss of a kid. That wasn't necessarily fact.

But it was probability, and she didn't need a distraught mother making unrealistic demands or hysterical accusations about the inability of the bureau to do its job. Belinda Lowell proved to be the exception to the rule. She passed on valuable information in a measured tone, and she accepted the fact that Burroughs didn't have much hope. Josiah Light, on the other hand, was a problem.

When news surfaced about the potential location of a fringe church somewhere near Pagosa Springs, residents with leads came calling. They shared rumors of a wilderness commune, recollections of a precocious little girl and her straight-laced father. Mostly, they remembered the girl. Then the Reverend Light shared the approximate location of Cleo's phone. Burroughs assigned flyover surveillance of the area using drones. What they caught was video of one man shooting down another.

"We brought you this. My people filled in the blanks." By that, Light meant that the witnesses of the girl and her father in Pagosa Springs were patrons of Light's church. "We want to be there. You owe this to us, because, when you find Jake—and his father…well, Jake is going to need a familiar face—"

"—Josiah. Let them do their job—"

"—The good Lord hasn't brought you this far to leave you in despair, Belinda."

Good God, shut up, Burroughs thought. She didn't have time for this. She didn't put much stock in the idea of a faith healer, much less in a heavy metal punk turned faith healer. She had even considered the whole disappearance to be some stunt conceived by an attention-starved celebrity. But as it turned out, there was something very wrong going on deep in the Sangre de Cristo range, and the drone's camera transmission was proof. Surveillance footage led the way for an air team investigation, and what they uncovered was a hysterical woman waving them down from a winding dirt road. The woman was Cleo LeCroix.

Burroughs hadn't mentioned LeCroix yet. This would have bolstered hopes, sure. But the flyover also sent back images of what looked like a pit or possibly a grave about two miles from the facility proper. This wasn't going to turn out the way Reverend Light was praying for.

Either way, having the two underfoot was a problem. Burroughs had brought them into Pagosa Springs because they had a significant lead. She was thorough with more questions. The additional demands made by Josiah Light were just an added perk. "I can tell you this," she said. "We have evidence to believe that your husband and your son may have been, or still are at this mountain retreat—"

"—Where is it," Josiah said.

"I can't bring you there—"

"—Give us directions. We'll go ourselves."

Fat chance, Reverend, she thought. *Your money has no pull here.* "I'm not putting civilian lives at risk. You're going to have to wait this out, like the rest of your followers on social media."

"It's a cult we're dealing with, isn't it." Josiah held up his phone to show one of those social media threads that Burroughs had grown to hate. "Like the Branch Davidians or the Children of God." The witnesses of the girl and her father had spoken. There had been a fringe Christian vibe from the two.

Burroughs confirmed that it was possible they were dealing with such an organization. She kept it at that. Then she ushered the two out of the office that the Pagosa Springs Police Department had set up for her and her people. She sent the two to a motel where they could stay until further notice, and she had them followed by a police escort to make sure they didn't try to follow their agents up through the mountains.

Because that's where she was heading. The investigators in her charge were already on their way to pick up Cleo LeCroix.

Helicopters were the best way in. Agents were dropped down at significant points outside the retreat's perimeter, where they could advance from all sides. It turned out to be more manpower than they needed. Burroughs was met with the grim findings over the radio. People were dead in what looked like a mass murder/suicide. The grave did have a body. In fact, it had three, and preliminary reports claimed that one did indeed look like Alec Lowell, at least the half of his face that was left to identify did. There were no kids. There was one survivor.

"It's Nathan Shein," said the agent over Burroughs' radio. "We need to evac him."

Her first inclination was to say, *who the hell is Nathan Shein*? But his relevance bubbled up from the back of her mind because he was a hot topic several years ago, a wealthy man gone missing. So the question, who the hell is Nathan Shein became "What the hell is Nathan Shein doing there?"

"Maybe a hostage," came the reply.

A hostage. A weapons stash. A controversial faith healer dead and the kid still missing. This was going to be a PR nightmare, especially with the discovery of Nathan Shein. He had been at the center of his own religious controversy before his disappearance. Burroughs's research team filled her in on the details, which she clicked through on her tablet during the drive.

Shein had an adventurous spirit and hadn't returned from a sailing expedition out of Corpus Christi more than five years ago. He had set sail for the Caribbean, and then South Africa and Australia on a fancy Catamaran yacht that betrayed his wealth. Mr. Shein had reached his Caribbean destination but had failed to check in at the Cape, or anywhere Down Under. The yacht had never been found. He would have been presumed lost at sea had it not been for banking activity that investigators found in offshore accounts. Mr. Shein's attorneys insisted that the man was simply a reclusive individual who travelled the world, and his mother, who asked reporters to stop bothering her because Nathan didn't keep in touch, had frankly admitted to being disappointed.

He was the sole heir of his father's estate. It was a lot of money, more than any individual with no heirs had a right to own. At least Burroughs thought so. Transfer one zero from the placeholder of his worth and add it to her own, and she could retire. Transfer two, and she could put her kids through school debt free. Ivy League schools, not some four-year state institution.

Shein's father had been a real estate developer and a prominent figure in the Austin Jewish community, which was an incredibly small group of people. Nathan's mother was an Evangelical, and she raised Nathan as a proper Christian after the divorce when Nathan was five. She refused to get her boy circumcised when he was born, and she was proud of that. It was all right there on the Nathan Shein WikiPage. Nathan's father apparently still loved his only son enough to leave him everything when he died, and Nathan took that wealth and invested wisely.

Nathan had lived his life as a bachelor and prominent figure in the rise of a Texas mega church before his disappearance. Burroughs imagined a rivalry between Shein and Light. The man with the Jewish name had helped the Cross on the Rock Christian Community build its foundation with a generous property donation about fifteen years ago. He had been involved in the financial end of the church's meteoric rise, until a rumored disagreement with the church's pastor surfaced and Nathan removed himself from its board of administrators. Then he set out on a trip to recharge his heavy soul, and he disappeared.

How the man ended up here was a true mystery, one that Cleo LeCroix did not have answers for. When Burroughs reached the retreat location, the dangerous work had been done. A forensics team was in the preliminary stages of assessing evidence. Photos were taken and bodies were being pulled from bunkers. Cleo LeCroix tried to answer questions, but she was beyond shaken. Her answers were contradictions, often within the same sentence.

Burroughs questioned her as she watched Nathan Shein being pulled out on a gurney from the central house on the property. "Did you know him? Nathan Shein?"

"Yes—No. I didn't…didn't know him, no."

"You sound uncertain."

"What they did. To Alec…" she swiped tears both left and right, then pulled in a breath.

"You witnessed what they did?"

"I don't know what they did. I don't know why—I mean, yes? They shot him in the— face, and oh my God…"

Burroughs waited for LeCroix to pull together. "Who pulled the trigger?"

LeCroix glanced toward Shein before she shook her head. "I'm not sure. I don't—I don't know."

"What about the dead man found with him? And the ones in the bunker?"

LeCroix didn't know anything about a bunker, with the exception of the one where she had been held prisoner. She didn't know who else was dead, but she did know some of the names of her abductors. There was Zachary, and there was Todd. There was a man named John David, which was the most significant connection to already-known leads. She remembered seeing Lucas, the "satanic little shit" who, as it turned out, was Alec Lowell's half brother.

"Our evidence suggests that he was the one who kidnapped Lowell's son. Did you see Jake? At any time?"

Two solid answers came from Ms. LeCroix. "No," and "no."

"How did you escape, Ms. LeCroix?" Again, the woman's gaze drifted toward Shein.

"Something changed about him." Burroughs pursued the odd reply, but the helicopter kicked its rotors into gear and she had to pause. Then Cleo burst with information that Burroughs failed to completely hear. "I don't know w— —et me go. I don't under——. He wanted — prove some—, — Alec — — lie, and — killed —. But he let — go and—Nath— Shein? I heard — — him Jonas. — don't know. I don't know."

The helicopter lifted off, and Cleo drew herself up into a trembling mess. Burroughs reached deep for a proper amount of empathy and resigned herself to the fact that some things would have to wait. "We're going to get you to a hospital and get you treated."

Cleo seemed grateful for the reprieve, and Burroughs decided that she would eventually prove to be their best witness. But it didn't help that she hadn't seen Jake, or that she had seen the brother Lucas who had yet to be identified among the dead. Burroughs tasked her research team with finding information on the half brother. They came up with sketch-artist renditions and photos of the guy when he was a teen. It wasn't much to go on, with the exception of reports that the guy had a crippled left hand. And even that was muddled by a history of conflicting reports. Then Burroughs made the call for a search and recovery operation to find the boy, Jake.

It was going to be a long night.

Lucas truly had a gift. He never really thought about it, the ability to be invisible when it benefited him. It wasn't in the superhero-with-superpowers sense. Rather, people failed to notice him in crowds. It's how he got away with shooting Alec, which had made Alec a star. It's how he got away after killing Dr. Carver at the Light Fest. He had simply blended in and walked away without people taking note. But as he heard the slow pass of a helicopter overhead, he thought maybe he wasn't going to slip through shadows unseen this time.

The thwap thwap thwap of its blades hummed somewhere in the distance, and Lucas navigated Moses toward a dense thicket of trees with hope that the looming dusk would finally drop. Jake twisted his head up to face the sky at one point, but he was dazed, still not shaking off the effects of the carbon monoxide hangover. A search beam cut through diminishing light, but the pilot failed to circle far enough to reach them. Maybe he hadn't calculated the distance a person could travel by horse as opposed to on foot. They continued under cover of night until Lucas felt Maggie's grip around his waist slip. She was getting too tired, so he stopped.

He pitched the pup tent in the dark, no flashlight or fire to alert sky patrol, and he sent the kids inside with the sleeping bags and Saint to keep them warm. Lucas stayed outside, kept close to the horse, and shivered beneath thinner blankets until he heard the rustle of the tent's flap. "Go back inside, Maggie."

It was Jake. "What happens now?" He was groggy, but his senses were returning. Lucas didn't answer, and Jake tried again. "Where—"

"—Do you trust me? I don't blame you if you don't."

Jake looked down into the palm of his hand, then squeezed it into a fist. It was the one that Lucas had sliced open once, when Alec was the enemy and when Lucas had coaxed Jake to be blood brothers.

"You saved me, Jake. You and Maggie."

"Maggie said you got shot."

Lucas twisted his shoulder around, then squeezed his thigh at the wound. "I'll live."

"I trust you," Jake said.

"I'll get you home. I'll find a way."

Jake climbed out of the tent and snuggled up to Lucas. For warmth, he supposed, although the sleeping bag should have been far warmer than Lucas and his well-worn blankets. Jake took Lucas's hand, the one with the broken fingers that didn't seem that broken after all. He hugged the hand to his face *like the kid from those cartoons hugging his security blanket*, Lucas thought. As Jake drifted to sleep, Lucas thought that this might be what contentment felt like. He took hold of Jake's hand and held it tight.

Grant Me the Wisdom

ON THE DAYS WHEN THEY WERE FORTUNATE ENOUGH to have a bed in a motel, Lucas would wake up early and slip out the door to do whatever it was he did for food or cash. Sometimes he took Saint with him, sometimes he didn't. On this morning, he took the dog. Jake would normally curl up tight under his covers and pretend to sleep. But Maggie would slip out of bed and turn on the TV.

She was interested in any news she could find about Jonas Adonis, who turned out to be some guy named Nathan Shein, and about the continued search for Jake. Finding information had been hit and miss. The story was old by the time the three of them made it out of the Colorado Rockies. That's how Jake had put it. And the places where they found shelter rarely had anything but local channels with local news.

Sometimes Lucas scored funds and splurged on a Motel 6, and this morning that's where they were. Maggie flipped through cable stations until she found national news. Stories of war and rebellion and mistrust in the government played across the screen, and Maggie couldn't help but think her father had been right. The world was a scary place.

But she didn't want to think about John David. He had been led astray, and he hadn't given himself the chance to atone. Lucas was trying to atone for his mistakes, although most of what he was doing was still wrong.

Maggie knew how Lucas was getting money. He never shared it, but she knew, and he didn't seem particularly ashamed about it. Stealing was a sin. Sodomy was a sin. Or prostitution. Maggie wasn't sure which act Lucas was engaged in, but she got the impression that he wouldn't have been ashamed about either one.

John David would have judged Lucas. And Jonas Adonis would have found fiery words before sentencing Lucas to the box. She decided that her father, and especially Reverend Adonis, had gotten some things wrong.

Maggie wished she could have seen John David after he died. But Lucas said no. He was honest and said that it was like how Alec Lowell had died. She didn't need to see it twice.

The morning TV hosts got to the news she was waiting for. The police were no longer just looking for Lucas and Jake. They were looking for her, too. An image of Maggie with her parents, from the last year when they were a family, came up on the screen. Then an interviewer sat down with her grandparents who sent out a public plea for help. "We want our girl home."

"Do you want to go home?" Maggie caught Jake peeking out from under the covers. She left the question unanswered, and Jake climbed out of hiding to join her. They watched more updates before Jake shared what was really on his mind. "Have you noticed how fast Lucas got better?"

"What do you mean?"

He shrugged. "I don't know. Maybe I'm stupid." Jake crawled back to the warmth of the covers while Maggie scrutinized him. "What."

She wasn't going to let it go. She had noticed things too, the bruises around Lucas's face and nose left by Todd were gone. The broken fingers of his hand…well, he still had the habit of flexing and stretching it, but the fingers weren't a problem. Or perhaps Maggie had no concept of how fast some people could heal.

But then there was the leg. And the shoulder. Maggie had helped Lucas dig those bullets out. Those kinds of injuries took more time to heal. She had caught sight of his leg that very morning before he had slipped on his jeans and slipped out the door. A scar was barely visible.

Maggie closed in on Jake, who cowered as if he didn't want anyone to invade his safe space. "When did your dad know?"

"Not right away." He shifted his gaze to the TV. Then he held out his hand, palm open. "I used to have a scar down the middle of it."

Maggie remembered. Now, there was nothing there. They stared at each other. "Should we tell him?"

"Look how it ended for my dad."

Together they watched the updates on the murder/suicide investigation. It had been well over a week since the raid happened, and the investigation had taken a strange turn. Nathan Shein was recovering in a Colorado hospital. He was in stable condition, but not good condition, and the talking heads on the TV were calling him a victim, not a leader. No one identified him as Jonas Adonis. In fact, Jonas Adonis was a mystery. There were no pictures to identify the man, and the only witness authorities had who knew him was Cleo LeCroix. Her statements were confusing. So were Mr. Shein's, who had turned out to be a rich man who had disappeared and had been assumed dead.

Psychology experts weighed in. Nathan Shein's behavior exhibited qualities of post-traumatic stress and abuse. Some believed him to be Jonas Adonis, but others sold the idea that he had been kidnapped and imprisoned, a hostage whose money helped fund the commune's accounts. Jake called the coverage "a bogus fucking circus," and Maggie turned the TV off.

"Lucas is trying not to get caught," Maggie said. "That's why it's taking so long."

"I know." Jake rested his head against Maggie's shoulder.

She didn't like it. His lethargy and mood brought back memories of her mother. "Hey," Maggie said. "Don't leave me, okay?" When Jake gave her a vague nod, she insisted. "Promise."

"I promise."

Josiah Light was back to work. His wife, Lorena, was in charge of floral arrangements for the event, and bless her heart for her involvement, but he could tell that they would eventually have an argument over it. She wanted everything lilies, white lilies, and nothing else. She directed assistants to drape white fabric over the stands where the lilies would go. "Alec was not some pure, innocent heart," he tried to tell her. "I'm not trying to disparage the man, but I know he'd agree. We need color, darling. Something to reflect the flaws that he carried, that we all carry, to be honest."

"White lilies are traditional, dear."

And Josiah knew this. It was pointless to argue with his wife. Then he noticed Belinda's arrival at the back of the hall. Arms crossed, she was not pleased, and he went to greet her.

She got to the point. "I said no memorial until we find Jake—"

"—I know you did. But the masses have spoken. They want this—"

"—How much money did Alec bring into this church?"

Josiah was stung by the inference. "That's not fair."

"I don't want this. If you have any regard for me, you'll wait."

"Belinda? Is that you?" Lorena abandoned her decorative arranging and headed toward them, and Josiah noted tension working its way through Belinda's shoulders.

He turned to his wife to stage an intervention. He didn't like the all-white motif anyway. "Darling, Belinda has spoken. We're delaying the service."

Lorena didn't register the decree. She pushed past her husband and locked Belinda into a heartfelt embrace. Josiah knew it was heartfelt. Belinda seemed less convinced. "We know in our hearts that Alec is in a better place. And we know in our hearts that Jake will return. You cannot give up on Him." And she pointed to the heavens.

Belinda stepped back without a direct answer as to what her feelings were about Him. She motioned to the stage and said, "We're not doing this yet." Then she backed out of the main hall and into the concourse in retreat. Josiah kissed his wife on the cheek, then followed.

He slowed as Belinda gained distance and as he watched those rigid shoulders slump. She was crying. He quickened his pace until Cleo rounded the corner from the opposite end. The two women assessed each other like Daniel and the lion, and

Josiah decided that he did not want to be in the middle of that, even if things did turn out well in the story. He retreated to discuss lilies with his wife.

"Hon, I've been looking for you." A simple-enough statement. But when Cleo took a step closer, Belinda propelled her back with waving hands. She didn't want to be hugged or touched or consoled, especially not by Cleo.

Cleo kept her distance. But she didn't stop talking. "I feel... horrible. Stripped of any safe space. I feel like it's my fault, and I need to accept that part of it is—"

"—It's not your fault. Claire." It was petty to resort to Cleo's true name. But it made Belinda feel better, just the tiniest bit. And Cleo, bless her heart, freed a smirk. "You were a victim too. I'm not going to pretend you weren't—"

"—He made me watch. This Jonas Adonis, he..." Cleo drifted through the memory without sharing, her gaze seeming to take in an abyss. "Then he saved me. He set me free, and I swear to God, I don't understand why."

"So you defended the man—"

"—No, hon. It's not like that. And I'm confused, because I don't know what to think, and... I really need to talk with you."

"The damage is done. Your testimony, your witness statement, whatever...it's vague enough to let the man walk. But right here, right now you're telling me that he made you watch—"

"—Hon, he told me to *tell Lindy that I love her*...That's strange, isn't it?"

Belinda glared, hoping to make Cleo feel small, a bug to be squashed by the sole of her shoe. "Is it supposed to make me feel better—"

"—Hon, no one calls you Lindy, except..."

It dawned on Belinda what Cleo was saying. "Why would you think that? Why would you say it—"

"—Because—"

"—Because it's not possible. Jake is still missing, and you ran away from it, and you think I'm going to entertain some wild theory that Alec is...someone else?"

"I want him back, too!" Cleo brushed away tears. "He was a mess, and I don't know. Maybe I deserved...the mess, but I can't shake it. The man spoke your name as if he was Alec. After the things we've seen, why isn't that possible?"

Belinda elbowed past Cleo and kept walking. She hoped Cleo would leave her alone, and Cleo did. Belinda pushed through the doors of the Light Foundation church and heaved in a deep breath of cool, Southern California air. The idea cut through her grief in a way that burned. *Why would Cleo push a story like this?* She didn't care if she had witnessed Alec's healing miracles. It wasn't the same as jumping inside another person's skin. That idea was absurd.

Belinda resorted to pacing. She wasn't going to do it, to turn back and ask Josiah for a favor. Josiah would accommodate her. He had the connections. But he wanted this memorial service now, and he would most definitely use it as a bargaining chip.

If nothing more, she could face the man who killed Alec. She could tell him what she thought of him, maybe break him enough to make him slip, a chip to expose the lie. It might give her some closure. Some. She cursed under her breath and headed back inside.

Lucas couldn't risk getting caught in dangerous behavior, so he refrained from shoplifting and outright thievery to survive, and he relied on taking early-morning strolls through nearby truck stops to be the lot lizard. Like the driver who had picked Lucas up when he had set out to kidnap Jake, he encountered many a lonely man who had a similar preference. He made enough money for occasional motels and short bus hops, and Lucas supplemented the income by begging at strip malls and street corners. This is where Saint proved his worth.

People ignored Lucas on most days when he was alone with his cardboard plea, but on the days when he had Saint, people responded. They had no heart for a skinny young loser down on his luck, but they had all the sympathy in the world for his mongrel dog. They dropped change as if it was a fee to give the dog a scratch behind the ears.

Saint played his part. He wagged his tail and sometimes danced in excited circles before he pressed close to Lucas as if to say, "Don't worry, I'll never leave you." If Lucas happened to be sitting, Saint would curl up beside him and rest his snout on Lucas's knee. Lucas could not be the lowlife that people wanted him to be if he had such a loving dog.

On this day, a clean-faced seven-year-old in a paisley dress and white leggings came out of the super center in Gallup and strayed from her mother and older siblings. "Hello, doggie," she said. Saint sniffed at the remnants of some snack on her fingers and proceeded to lick them.

"Go with your mom," Lucas said without hesitation. Stranger danger was not a foreign notion to him. As expected, the mother came running when she realized that her youngest had hung back to chat.

"Melissa Ruth!"

Ruth? Lucas thought. *Poor girl.* "Saint. Get down."

"He likes me, Mommy." Melissa Ruth giggled, and Lucas nabbed Saint by the collar.

"Go." He tried to shoo the girl along until the mom reached them and pulled her daughter back like Lucas had done with Saint.

"Come here, Saint." The girl was fearless. Lucas decided that she had well-off parents. The way it should be. Saint tried, but Lucas held firm.

The woman scrutinized him, then ordered the oldest of the siblings to take Melissa Ruth back to the car. "Your dog's name is Saint?"

"Yes, ma'am." Lucas imagined what Jonas Adonis would say. "He saved my life."

The woman sighed. She didn't seem happy about breaking down and handing him a couple of bucks. He thanked her. After a couple of steps, she turned back. "I'll give you fifty for him." Lucas pulled Saint closer. "You'd be doing him a favor."

Fifty bucks might have covered a bus ticket to Flagstaff. Maybe. For one. But—"A hundred then."

"No." He averted his gaze and buried his face into Saint's fur. The woman huffed and dropped him another twenty. He felt guilty for being so selfish, but he couldn't sacrifice Saint for the cause. The dog seemed to love him; no strings attached.

Lucas abandoned the entryway of the super center and decided it was time to be more dangerous. But not here. This parking lot had cameras. A residential working-class neighborhood would be best. It was noon by the time he reached the right neighborhood. Lucas had Saint on a leash, giving the illusion of an average dude on his day off taking a walk with his dog.

Other dogs barked with discontentment as they passed house after house. Some howled from behind closed doors, others from inside gated yards. It was the silent homes that Lucas paid attention to, the ones where apathetic cats observed with disinterest from living room windows. Lucas found the right one, a silent house with silent ones surrounding it. An older model car sat at the curb, one that hadn't been moved in a while based on the debris collecting at the gutter. Lucas studied the house. "What do you think, boy?" He headed for the gated drive, lifted the latch, and stepped through to the back yard.

Out of sight from the main road, Lucas checked windows and doors until he found his way in, an air conditioner propped in a window. It was off, another good indicator that no one was home, although this was New Mexico in late autumn. Lucas pulled a patio chair up to the window, removed the portable unit with care, and climbed in.

Keys hung on a rack by the front door, convenient for the perpetually tardy. He let himself out the back and herded Saint back through the gate. The cat never left its perch along the front sill. Lucas scooted Saint into the passenger seat as a car drove past. He played it cool, hoping that it wasn't an immediate neighbor, and it wasn't. He slipped into the driver's seat, started the engine, and pulled away from the curb.

God was with him again. Jake was one step closer to making it home. When Lucas reached the motel room, he made the kids hurry. Checkout was at one, and Lucas wanted to be gone. He would need to change the vehicle's plates, but not yet, not with the cleaning service going in and out of rooms or with other guests milling around the parking lot. He figured he had until five o'clock before the car would be reported stolen. "Come on," he said. "Let's go."

Maggie said, "Where did you get a car?"

"Don't ask stupid questions." She didn't like the response, it was clear. But she got in anyway. They drove into Arizona in silence. The only one who kept a chipper mood was Saint.

Lucas glanced into the rearview mirror as the sun was setting. He found Jake curled in a ball, Maggie holding his hand. "We're getting close, Jake. You're halfway home."

Maggie asked, "What will you do when we get there?"

"What do you mean?"

"The police."

"Let me worry about the police." Then after some silence, "It doesn't really matter." And it didn't. If he was caught, they would try him, convict him, and probably sentence him to death. He was okay with it, a fitting end.

"Can you do something for me?" Jake asked. "When we get there?"

"That depends. What is it?" Jake stuttered through what he wanted and why he wanted it. And Lucas didn't know how to respond.

"Ah, Jesus." Alec eased out of bed, taking into consideration the colostomy bag hanging from his side. He was healing, sure. But with a fucking drainage collector. He wasn't used to this, not healing in record time, and he still wasn't used to finding Nathan Shein staring back from his reflection. When he had first come to consciousness at the hospital, out of surgery and into his new reality, he was terrified. People asked him questions that he didn't have answers to, primarily because he wasn't Nathan Fucking Shein. Attendants and doctors were touching him, poking and prodding, propping his pillows, and offering to help him pee.

It was a waking nightmare. He didn't even have the luxury of avoiding the spotlight because he was no longer Alec Fucking Lowell. No, now he was Nathan Fucking Shein. If there was a God, he or she or it probably thought it was hilarious. Alec had been questioned, no interrogated, as Shein as soon as possible post surgery. The fact that he didn't know anything—anything!—made the ordeal worse. He couldn't piece together a truth or a lie without knowing much about Shein's backstory, and that led to him expressing the only true emotion he ever felt, panic. Well, maybe not the only true emotion, but it was the one that chose to be his life's tour guide more often than not. "I don't know who the fuck Jonas Adonis is. He—he kidnapped me, and what does he look like? He looks like me. But he's not me. I'm not him—" And then he was saved, not by God or an entourage of angels, but by a well-paid staff of attorneys.

Four known persons of interest might have been able to give testimony to the identity of Nathan Shein as Jonas Adonis. One of them was Cleo. The other three were Lucas, Jake, and a girl named Margaret Grace Laurent. The girl was the same one he had seen in his vision, the one from the picture on Lance's phone. Every other witness was dead. Cleo had seen Adonis kill Alec, but her statement to the FBI had been vague. Alec wasn't sure why she had hesitated to identify the reverend as Nathan Shein, but she did. The only other living witness was Lucas, and Alec wasn't sure if this was a blessing or a curse.

What he was most concerned about was Jake. Alec hadn't seen Jake at the commune other than in pictures, but he'd been there. He hadn't been among the dead. The likely conclusion was that he had escaped with Lucas, and maybe the missing girl, but mostly…with Lucas.

Alec tried not to dwell on it. He took slow steps toward the bathroom to empty the bag. He let it drain in the toilet, and he cringed from the smell. His insides were dying. That's what he concluded. Then he sealed up the bag and washed his hands while staring at Nathan Shein's haggard reflection.

This was his life now. He needed to accept it. He braced himself against the marble sink and he ached. A slow, corrosive acid was eating him from the inside out. *How did people do it?* The pain meds helped, but if he was prone to addiction as Alec, he most certainly would acquire a habit now. Plus, the pain meds had to be modified due to the damage left from the tears. Lucas had ripped through Nathan Shein's colon with the kind of expertise that should have left him dead. Alec had cobbled that truth together and he puzzled over one thing. If Alec could sustain himself within Nathan Shein's skin, why couldn't he heal faster? His gift was literally gone, lost, maybe because of his new DNA structure. He didn't know.

If consciousness was separate from physicality, Alec supposed it made sense. But what the hell did he know about science other than occasional episodes of Star Trek? He was never that kind of nerd. Belinda might have known, and Alec wished that he could call her. But that would be weird, and his advisors and attorneys told him so. "There will be no personal contact with Belinda Lowell until you are cleared of suspicion in the investigation," they had told him. They didn't understand why Nathan Shein wanted to speak with the woman, and he didn't try to explain. He thought that maybe Lindy, and Cleo, and everyone would be better off if Alec Lowell stayed dead. Part of him was glad of that, just not the part that was so slow to heal.

Alec dressed with care. Nathan Shein's wardrobe was a bit too tailored for his tastes, but he managed. He chose the most neutral colored slacks and button-down shirts, and he left his hair messy while not worrying about the stubble growing on his face. He did note a few gray patches, which was odd. He was too young to think about gray, although Shein wasn't. Maybe it was why the guy had so many mirrors, because whenever Alec caught the reflection, he found himself stroking over the grays. He pushed the obsession out of his mind and made his way down to the main floor.

An in-home caretaker greeted him in the kitchen. Her name was Luz. "Good morning, Mr. Shein. Rise and shine." Alec hated the pun, but Luz was a pleasant older woman who could sell it. "Your mama called." She handed him a cup of decaf.

"The Internet tells me that I don't get along with my mother, so I guess she can wait."

Luz chuckled at that as she pulled a stool out for him beside a counter. "You should be thankful for your mother. She's alive and she cares about you, and that's a blessing. You should count all your blessings, Mr. Shein."

"You're pretty bold considering I'm a man under suspicion for mass murder."

Luz placed poached eggs and white toast in front of him, as bland a meal as you could eat. "I've known you too long, Nathan, to believe you did those crimes. You are no murderer." Alec found this funny. The woman had apparently known Nathan, had taken care of him even, before his disappearance. She had been part of his parents' household staff when he was a boy, and had carried on with Shein when he had grown. And she knew beyond a doubt that Nathan Shein was no murderer. *Fucking hilarious*. But Alec liked Luz. He let her believe what she wanted to believe. "You have changed since I last knew you, though."

"For better or for worse?"

"I haven't decided yet." She patted his hand and gave him a wink that made Alec think of his grandfather.

"Are you married, Luz?"

"Lord Almighty, Nathan. You know that didn't end well. It was before you were gone."

"I've lost a lot of my past…I'm sorry?"

This time, she patted his knee, and Alec tried his hardest not to flinch from another unwelcome touch. "It's probably best. He wasn't worth the memories." She slid a note beside his plate. "I was told to give this to you. A list of interview requests."

"I'm not doing interviews."

"I was only told to give it to you, Nathan." She patted him on the shoulder. "I'm leaving to restock your pantry. Any problems, you can call me. And don't waste your day in front of your computer! Get out. Get the fresh air. You will thank me."

Alec gave the woman an appeasing "Yes, ma'am," which tickled her in amusement before she headed out the door. He scanned the list of well-known names that Nathan's public relations representatives had given Luz over the phone. Their intent was to help Shein earn some money with appearance fees, which would help offset the cost of his legal fees. Not that it mattered. Nathan Shein had money. He was assured of that by his financial managers. Also, a book deal was just a matter of time.

But Alec didn't want to think about book deals and interviews just yet. He needed time to adjust within Nathan Shein's skin, and to flesh out the story that he only knew from Wikipedia pages and Internet news. There were already questionable holes in his story to the Feds, and the whole ordeal was more than a drain on his emotions.

Alec was about to crumple the list into a ball and do a free throw to the wastebasket at the far end of the kitchen, when the last name on the list grabbed his attention. The Reverend Josiah Light.

Goddamn it. Not again. Josiah had changed Alec's life once, or helped shape his path. "Come talk," the man had said after Alec's first life-changing tragedy went public. "Share your story, and I will help you find and understand God." It hadn't worked, not really, and although people could argue about the better life Alec had after becoming Josiah Light's top draw, the fact remained that Alec still hadn't found that moment where he could say that he had seen the light. It didn't exist.

What existed was people. Maybe this whole body swap should have been the obvious eye opener, but only one thing stayed on his mind. Evil wasn't some demon led by Satan. Good wasn't some gift handed down from God. All of it was people who were scared of what might be. The good ones were there, sure. But the others tried to protect themselves, and their fears blinded them until they became the evil that they claimed to hate. Good intentions coupled with fear equaled evil. And Alec was guilty. Totally fucking guilty.

He needed to relax, to take life one day at a time, and maybe he could do that once the investigation was over. No more Alexander the Great. Just Nathan Shein, reclusive rich dude. He could deal with that. The thought made him happy. Almost. He headed for his study—no, Nathan's study, where he found the acoustic that he had made Luz purchase for him days ago. He strummed it. Shein's fingers proved to be something else that Alec had to get used to, but he could play the thing well enough to give Luz pause. "When did you pick up the guitar?" she asked. Apparently Nathan had shown no interest in a musical instrument when he was a child. "You're not bad."

And Alec strummed. His attempt to not have a care in the world was not going to last. He set the guitar aside, rubbed at the growing tension in his face, then got up to find his phone. He was going to schedule an interview with Josiah Light, and as he talked to his attorney about how to make that happen, he said he'd do it with one condition.

"Well that…that's interesting," Josiah said over the phone. "Because I know that she wants to be there." Arrangements were made, and Josiah disconnected his phone to let his legal representatives prepare the non-disclosure agreements and consent forms that everyone would need to sign before the actual meeting could take place. Josiah learned that he was the only person Nathan Shein had granted an interview to, and he chalked it up to the will of God.

Rorie stepped through the gates of her high school campus and kept walking. She left early most days because her mother's illness had taken a turn. Mom wasn't expected to last through the month, and Rorie's grandparents wanted her to have as much time with her mother as possible before the woman was gone. Rorie was indifferent to it. It amounted to a missed P.E. class with time to walk alone and contemplate the unfairness of life before she spent time sitting at her mother's bedside, not talking but listening to the woman moan. There were the occasional interactions where she got to adjust her mom's pillows or get her some water. Mostly, Rorie ended up doing reading assignments while her mother slept through episodes of "Wheel of Fortune," and Grandma and Grandpa found excuses to do other things.

It hadn't always been that way. Rorie's mom didn't really deserve her daughter's indifference. There was simply nothing more to say, nothing that hadn't been said, good or bad, nothing that could be fixed. The rest of Rorie's time left with her mother would involve waiting for her to die and leave Rorie with nothing, not even fond memories.

Her earliest memories of her parents were of them fighting. Dad had been the kind of guy who made promise after promise because he was the shit, and he knew how to get things done. He hustled his ass between construction jobs and part-time gigs with set-building crews on non-union shoots. At least that's what Rorie remembered about him when she was younger and he was around. Her parents had gotten married out of high school because, as Rorie's mom had put it, her little Power Puff Girl was on the way. A Power Puff Girl. Ugh! But it was better than being compared to a Gilmore Girl. She was nothing like that TV character either. But then Dad abandoned them before the birth, and Rorie's mom had her own ideas about how life was going to be.

What a fucked-up delusion. Yes, Rorie thought her mom was stupid. Dad returned and abandoned the family on many occasions, showing up when he'd had a windfall and wanted to prove he could provide, then gone when some half-baked scheme to get rich fell through. Most of that time was spent living under Rorie's grandparent's roof, and most of that time included Mom being judged and condemned for her choices. Mom had never been good enough in the eyes of Rorie's grandparents, and maybe that attitude had rubbed off on Rorie. No, not maybe. She knew it had. As Rorie walked home, contemplating her own influence in undermining her mother's self confidence, her pace slowed. She was losing her mom, and she hadn't done enough for her, and nobody else cared. She was going to cry.

Grandma often complained that if her daughter, who hadn't a brain in her head, had tried to be pretty instead of slutty, she would have found a better man. Grandma was also the kind of woman who left the important decisions up to Grandpa. Maybe Rorie's mom wouldn't have put her trust in a steroid-dependent loser if Grandma had stood up for herself once in a while. And yeah, Rorie's dad had bouts of rage. It's why he eventually disappeared for good, probably because he was rotting in corrections, but not long after Mom's diagnosis was deemed terminal.

That's when Grandma resorted to prayer, and discipline for a granddaughter who was just like her mother. Suddenly, in her mind, Rorie was the thankless and promiscuous preteen with no brain in her head. The slipping grades and withdrawal from the right friends proved it.

But it was more. Rorie's grandparents would never understand. Nor would they try. Her bestie, Juana, would understand, or Juan depending on Juana's mood, and that was another thing Gram and Gramps were best left not knowing.

Jake would have understood, she thought. The kid had been surprisingly nonjudgmental for a middle schooler. She missed him. She hated herself, because the last time she had seen him, she had judged him. The kid had gone through far worse shit than she had gone through, and now he was gone, part of a nationwide search after his famous father was found dead execution style. Jesus, she felt bad. Maybe she was more willing to keep watch by her dying mother's bed because of it.

Rorie made an effort to walk a little taller when she noticed the car. It was a silver two door that she didn't recognize, and it was following her. She had caught sight of it from the corner of her eye after a full block of walking, and it should have passed her by now. She stopped in her tracks.

The car stopped too, so Rorie turned to face it. No shouts, no hand gestures. She glared. The window rolled down, the driver a college student maybe. He was the kind of guy that her grandparents would immediately disapprove of, yet Rorie wasn't sure why. He stared back at her, a lion assessing the lone gazelle across the Savannah. "Are you Rorie?"

Shit, who was this guy? And like the lone gazelle, she turned and kept moving. Flight, not fight. She quickened her pace as the car inched alongside her.

"Rorie? Rorie!" Different voice. Jake leaned in view from the back seat.

"Jake?" Rorie abandoned her terror and met him through the window. A mutt bounced up from the front seat and tried to lick her face. The animal thumped its tail as the driver pulled it back by the collar. There was a girl in the back with Jake, and Rorie had a vague recollection of the missing child reports in the news. "What are you doing here?"

"Get in the car, okay? Before somebody sees! Come on—"

"—People are looking for you."

"Come on!"

The driver raked his fingers through greasy, unkempt hair and checked his rear- and side-view mirrors. Everything about him told Rorie to run. But there was something more. If Gram and Gramps were to find him knocking on the front door, they would most assuredly call the police. She looked down the street, and she got in the car.

"Where's your mom?" Jake asked.

"You know where my mom is. How did you find me?"

"You told me where your school was—"

"—Jake, the police are looking for you."

"I know—"

"—And probably you, too."

"I'm Maggie."

"What are you doing here?" She turned to the guy behind the wheel. "Who are you?

The guy didn't answer. He glanced at the rearview mirror again. "This is stupid, Jake."

"Because you don't believe it," Jake said. "But I'm not leaving. Not until you try."

Rorie said, "Try what?"

"Tell us where your mom is," Maggie said.

"She's at home."

"Tell us how to get there." It was Maggie again.

"I don't like this. Let me out of the car."

"Too late," the guy said, and all the inner alarms that she had ignored when she first got into the car sounded again. She reached for the door and pushed it open, and the guy slammed on his brakes. "Shit!"

Rorie escaped with a leap that could have hurt her. She found her feet and ran, as she heard the dog bark from behind. She heard Jake shout. "Rorie, come back!"

"Let her go, Jake—"

"Saint! Get Saint!"

Rorie got knocked down. She thought she was a goner, but as she struggled to get up, she was assaulted with licks to the face. The guy got out of the car. "Saint! Come here. Let her go."

Saint wagged his tail and bounded back to Lucas. And Rorie understood. If the guy had meant her harm, he wouldn't have been willing to let her go. She had judged him from sight, like her grandparents would have done. Like strangers often did with her.

The guy restrained Saint by the collar. "Jake has this insane idea that I can help your mom," he said. "I'm Lucas."

She knew the name. "From the news? And the book?"

"You can't tell anyone we met." He didn't plead or threaten with it. It was just a matter of fact.

"How can you help my mom?" He didn't answer. But based on what she had read in Alec Lowell's book, and from what she had heard in the news, she imagined that he was good at putting people out of their misery. Maybe that's what her mom needed. Rorie choked back the finality of it then followed him back to the car.

Lights clicked on and blinded Alec as he protested from a makeup artist's touch-up job. Josiah Light was seated across from him, and it was awkward. The man held his chin high to allow his own groomer access to his jaw line as he prepared Nathan Shein for the interrogation. Attorneys and advisors lurked along the outskirts. And there was Lindy. No one was giving Alec the chance to talk to Lindy. She paced without making eye contact with him. They were protecting her.

"I beat the polygraph," Alec blurted. It wasn't relevant to anything Josiah had said.

"We'll let you share that, Nathan. I promise. But keep in mind that I'm going to ask about the discrepancies—"

"—They don't matter. Otherwise, I'd be on trial."

"But the public has weighed in, and they have mixed feelings."

"In spite of the charity. The funds I've set aside for victims' families…I know. Story of my life." When Josiah gave him a curious look, Alec tried to change the subject. "Look, when can Lindy and I—Ms. Allen and I. When can we talk?"

Belinda was within hearing range. She stopped pacing and glanced over. She had words with an advisor that Alec wished he could hear. Then he noted Josiah's curious scrutiny again.

"Mrs. Lowell will accommodate your request when she's ready."

Shit, Alec thought. *I called her Lindy. Nobody calls her Lindy.*

"Are we ready, now?" Alec gave a reluctant nod, and they were rolling. Josiah freed his sincerest smile. "Mr. Shein, thank you for being with us so soon after your ordeal. How are you feeling?"

"Like I've been to hell and back." Alec followed up with a nervous laugh, and he caught Belinda studying him.

"An interesting start, I must say. So, Nathan. Where do you think you stand before God?"

You sonofabitch, Alec thought. Josiah sat there with his gotcha grin, and he waited. *You motherfucking*—Alec scoffed, because this was the question. This was always the question that Josiah Light needed to have an answer for, always the first and final question.

"I'm not sure I like the sound of that," Josiah said, still smiling. He couldn't not smile when a camera was running. "You have your doubts about God? After He brought you home? I'm surprised." Alec could tell that the man was primed for a theological debate, and Alec was always blindsided by them. He never knew what to say.

Unless it was a challenge. *I dare you*, shouted from Josiah's eyes. He wanted Nathan Shein to falter so that he could lift him up with the rhetoric of The Word. It was Josiah Light's call to heroism, and it was the one thing Alec had always hated about the man.

Alec could have said fuck you and been done with it. But he found his voice like he often did when under pressure, and he ran with it. "It's not that…I mean, what is God? I guess that's the question." Josiah attempted to interject, but Alec threw up his hand. "We are supposed to be created in God's image. We. Not me, not you. Or her." He made an indiscriminate motion toward Belinda off camera, and his eyes lingered there for a moment.

"You sound—"

Alec cut Josiah off again. "Maybe God exists because we exist." He made a point to air quote the word God. "And that would be a perfect way to define it, except that we exist. We are one entity, except that we're shattered and scattered. Broken pieces of the whole with sharp jagged edges, every one of us flawed in some way. And…I don't know. Maybe we'd become something perfect if we tried to find each other, if we tried to fit the broken pieces back together to rebuild the whole. Instead, we try to polish away each other's rough edges. We'll never come together as one again because of that. We just knock each other around like balls on a pool table. We'll never be the perfect whole that we aspire to be."

Josiah nodded at that, speechless. Alec leaned back satisfied. He had just given Josiah Light a run for his money. Maybe he could have been some prophet, if he'd still been in his own skin. Instead he was this, Nathan Shein with a colostomy bag wedged under his shirt. No, Alec Lowell had to die. Too many people had put their faith in him instead of putting faith in themselves. He needed to stay dead.

But should he share the truth with Belinda?

Once the interview was over; where he answered questions regarding his abduction and torture with the truth of his own experience and not Nathan's, he was allowed to sit with Belinda. It was the one requirement agreed to by both sides prior to the interview. Alec lobbied to sit privately with Belinda, but legal representatives on both sides refused. Alec didn't have the flair that he proved to have when addressing Josiah. He had nothing.

Belinda dabbed at an eye before the tears could fall. She sat tall. "Did you kill my husband?"

Legal counsel leaned in. "Don't answer that—"

"—No." It came easily, and Alec was irritated that Shein's attorneys apparently didn't hold stock in his innocence. Belinda was quick with the next question.

"You're not Jonas Adonis?"

"He's not me."

"I'm here because Cleo has doubts—" Her legal counsel leaned in this time, and Alec couldn't make out what was whispered between them.

"Doubts about what?"

"I'm not supposed to discuss Cleo or her testimony."

The stretch of silence that came after was agonizing. Alec closed his eyes and pursed his lips searching for what he wanted to say, for what he was allowed to say. He was losing her, she would be better off not knowing, this had been a horrible idea. What had he thought was going to happen, he couldn't remember. "I'm sorry," he said. I was in this pit—I was…with Alec for a while? Not long…He knows—or knew that he was a burden—"

"—A burden? Who do you think you are?"

He started again. "That's not what I mean. He...confessed things. He said that he needed you more than you ever needed him, and that Jake—" Alec stopped short when he noted the flinch that rippled through her. He was doing this poorly, an outright massacre to be honest. Lindy didn't even deserve his shitty apology.

He started one more time. "These people hid in their little refuge thinking they would be safe from facing the end of the world. No one knew about them, but what the fuck? How does that make sense? When the world implodes, we're all going down with it. Like Sue in fucking South Dakota. When our world ends, we cease to exist. Not even a sculpture left behind to memorialize our bones."

Belinda shook her head in confusion, and Alec suddenly felt sick. His proclivity for panic had lain dormant throughout his recovery, but Jesus, it was back. "I need some air."

He lurched out of his chair and out of the room with his legal counsel trailing, until he waved them off and staggered to the front door. The guards posted outside gave Nathan Shein a nod and let him pass through. He crossed an expanse of lawn that was too green for the season, and he stumbled to the solitude of an Anaqua tree, where he sunk to the base of its trunk. He shuddered.

The hand that settled on his shoulder made him jerk. It was Lindy. "Why would you mention a dinosaur in South Dakota?" She waited. She knew, and he knew that she knew.

"Alec is dead. He has to be. He can't come back. And...I pray every day that Jake is found safe, but I can't live on hope anymore. I can't."

"Alec—"

"No."

"Alec, listen—"

"It's Nathan. I am Nathan Shein. And I'm Jewish." He laughed at that, because he didn't know much about being Jewish.

"Should that matter?" Belinda asked.

"No. It shouldn't. It doesn't…Maybe I'll learn something."

Lindy gnawed at her lip, and Alec wanted to draw her close and kiss her. She said, "It's funny how you tear God down at one moment then ask why he's abandoned you the next."

He laughed at that. "I'm never going to change." Then he lifted his shirt enough for her to see the damage. "Alec is dead. And the people who put their faith in him need to move on."

Lindy leaned in and gathered Nathan Shein up in an embrace. Her words fell softly upon his ear. "The world doesn't know what it will be missing." She kissed his forehead. "I don't understand this. And I don't understand you. But I hope you find peace. I really do."

"Belinda?" It was Josiah. He closed in with wary steps. "Is everything alright here?"

"We're done." Belinda rose to her feet and took Josiah's hand. She glanced back once as Josiah led her away, and Alec believed that she would be alright. Whatever the outcome with Jake and with Lucas, she would be alright. He had never questioned that, really, and he took solace in that one small constant in his life. He decided to hold onto that truth that everything else would turn out alright. *Alright, alright, alright*. Matthew McConaughey, the celebrity noted for the phrase, flashed through Alec's mind with a wink and a nod, and Alec chuckled at that. He closed his eyes and focused on nothing. And he let himself float.

Rorie's grandmother did not like Lucas. Rorie had passed him off as a senior from her school who also belonged to the youth group led by Father Grant. She had concocted a story that he had offered to drive her home after he picked up his little brother and sister from their middle school, and well, here they were, slightly late but not by much.

"A senior?" Gram eyed Lucas with full-blown skepticism. Rorie thought that Lucas could pass for eighteen even though he was older. "Are you planning on college?"

"Arizona State," Lucas said without pause. "Undeclared, but I'm interested in religion. Theology."

Rorie's gram scoffed at that. "Tell me what you know about your Savior, son."

As it turned out, Lucas had plenty to say about the Lord Jesus Christ. He had the Catholic rules and regulations memorized, and he said that he had once aspired to be a priest. Then he began rattling off the Apostle's Creed like it was the words to a popular song, one by Flo Rida, maybe. Gram nodded, not necessarily impressed but convinced.

"He's going to help me with my math," Rorie said. "Okay?"

"Not in the bedroom," Gram said. She turned to Jake and Maggie. "And what about you kids?" Rorie hated how quickly her grandmother made any of her friends feel unwelcome. But Maggie smiled and asked if they could let their dog play in the back yard. "You got a dog? Straight from school?"

Maggie faltered, but Jake ran with it. "He's my support dog."

"Support dog? For what." Gram's skepticism challenged Jake, and Jake froze. He opened his mouth, and nothing came out.

Lucas filled in the blanks. "We talked about this. You don't need Saint as much as you think." He pulled Jake into a hug.

Rorie watched her grandmother cave. The woman didn't like it, but she was sold. "Go on, then. Go get your support dog."

Maggie pulled Jake along as they bounded back out of the house. They returned with Saint, and Gram pointed them in the direction of the back yard. "You pick up after it!" Gram turned back to Rorie. "Dinner's at six. We don't have enough for company." The woman headed for her kitchen. Rorie pulled Lucas along.

"Let's go meet my mom."

Rorie's gram paused upon hearing that. "Your mom isn't up for company! Especially not strangers." Rorie kept going. She hoped that Gram would do like she usually did, shake her head and leave it alone. She reached her mom's bedroom door, and she knocked. The TV was on, but that didn't mean she was watching it. She slept with it on constantly.

"Mom? Can I come in?"

"Rorie!" Gram wasn't taking this strange friend lightly. "Your mom is—"

"I'm awake," came her mom's voice. "Come in, baby." Rorie pushed the door open before Gram could say another word. She was hit by an acrid stench as her mom pushed herself up into a sitting position with arms that threatened to snap from the modest weight. This was stupid. Why had she let Jake talk her into this? Nothing was going to change, except that her mom would now have to live with the humiliation of some highly suspect stranger having seen her in this sickly, vulnerable state. Her mom tried to smile in the most gracious way possible. "Sweetie, who's this?"

"Stupid girl," Gram said. "Leave your mother some dignity—"

"—I'm a friend," Lucas said. He stepped in and held out his hand. "It's nice to meet you, Rorie's mom."

Rorie bit her lip. Her face flushed. The way that Lucas shut her grandmother out by refusing to acknowledge her was beautiful. Her mother took Lucas's hand. "I don't get to meet Rorie's friends. To be honest, I didn't think she had any."

"Is that true?" Lucas turned to Rorie with a huge grin. "Get out!" He still had a hold of Mom's hand. "Well, we're friends." He continued to hold the hand, and Rorie sensed that her mother was growing uncomfortable from it. Lucas wouldn't let go. In fact, he cupped his other hand around hers. That's when the woman noticed the scar. She reached over with her free hand and traced it.

Gram spoke up again. "You've said your hellos. Now let your mom rest—"

"—I'm feeling okay, Mom. I'd like to get to know Rorie's friend." She patted the edge of her bed for Lucas to sit. Miffed, Grandma dismissed herself. "What's your name again?"

"Oh." Rorie faltered. "It's—"

"—Ever heard of Alec Lowell?"

Rorie's mom screwed her face up. "The televangelist from the news?"

"I watched him die."

Oh! Not what Rorie expected. Her mom stiffened and tried to pull away. Lucas didn't allow it. He reeled her in and wrapped his arm around her head and shoulder like a tentacle, her face smushed against his chest.

"What—Rorie, make him stop." Her plea was muffled by the fabric of his plaid shirtcoat. Rorie's thoughts raced through what she knew. Lucas was a killer, an antisocial manipulator who terrorized his victims, but mostly just a killer. He had kidnapped and terrorized Jake and had made him watch the murder of his dad. What had she done? Why would Jake think that Lucas could save her mother? Jake was beaten down, that's why. The one who tortured him became his savior. It happened in movies all the time.

Rorie lurched forward to stop Lucas, then froze. Lucas was going to kill her mom, and maybe that was a good thing. She would no longer have to suffer. She would be at peace. Insufficient breaths escaped from Rorie. She did nothing.

"Rorie—"

"—Ssshhh," Lucas said. He freed the woman's hand and he slipped his palm up her nightshirt to rest it beneath her belly. Rorie's mom gasped at the touch.

"Don't hurt her." But Lucas wasn't hurting her. Rorie watched her mom sob and free her pinned arms enough to wrap them around Lucas in an embrace. She wanted his touch, and suddenly Rorie felt like she shouldn't be there. She left the room and lingered in the hall outside the door. Steady breaths continued to elude her as she checked on her grandmother in the kitchen then slipped outside to check on Jake and Maggie.

Maggie hurried to meet Rorie when she saw tears. "Why do you trust him," Rorie whispered.

"Did he do it?" Jake joined them. His wide-eyed expression betrayed an eagerness to know.

"Tell me why—"

"—My faith," Maggie said. That was it.

"Your faith? Oh my God!" Rorie's panic was loud, and it got her gram's attention. The woman peered out the sliding glass door then headed in the direction of the bedroom.

The woman's breathing slowed. Her arms slipped away from Lucas, who continued to hold her. She had peed herself. Lucas laid the woman back against her pillows and let her rest. So much for Jake and Maggie's crazy idea.

Still, they were right about the leg. And the shoulder. Both wounds had healed too quickly. He wouldn't have given it much thought on his own. Healing takes time. Everyone recovers at their own rate. But the leg. The shoulder… Alec hadn't recognized his gift until he was older. *Could it be true?*

Anyway, the experiment failed. He rose to slip out of the room, when Rorie's mom reached for his hand again. She pulled it to the base of her belly and moaned. It was oddly sexual the way it came out.

"What are you doing?" Grandma had returned. Lucas yanked his hand away, a damning move that made the old woman close in with fury. "You stinking pervert! Get out of this house! Get out before I call the cops!"

Rorie called out her grandmother's name as she returned with Jake and Maggie and Saint, and Lucas pushed his way through them. "Let's go," he said as Rorie's grandma kept pace.

"Are they really your siblings? Do you fondle them too? Hah? Do you touch your little brother and sister? Does he touch you, girl?" Rorie got in her grandmother's way, but it didn't stop the woman from hurtling more threats. "This is what you bring to your mother," she said to Rorie. Then, "I'm calling the police!"

They had made it out of the house. Lucas hurried Maggie and Jake along. Maggie said, "What happened?"

"Nothing happened." Lucas got a whiff of piss lingering from his fingers, and he wiped them against his pants. He had parked the car down the street so it was less likely to be identified if things went wrong, and he was glad.

Then Jake posed the question that made Lucas stop. "What happens now?" That was it. The whole reason that they came here was to bring Jake home, to do it in a way that wouldn't get Lucas caught. The window of opportunity was closing fast because of this failed experimental detour. But Jake and Maggie had been willing to walk out that door with him, no hesitation or remorse. They shouldn't have done it.

He said, "Listen to me. Go back. Take your time. Lie about the car—"

"—No!" Maggie latched onto him. "What about me?"

"Your grandparents will find you. It'll be fast." Lucas tried to walk away, but Maggie wouldn't let go. She hugged him tight until Jake pried her loose.

"He's right." Jake pulled her off of him, and Lucas quickened his steps. Saint followed at his heels and scampered into the car when they reached it.

And Lucas drove. He drove out of Los Angeles and into the desert where he found a quiet campground to spend the night. He wiped tears from his face throughout the trip, and he even told Saint to shut up once, when the dog yipped at him. Tears were new to Lucas. He didn't like them.

Come morning, Lucas waited for the few campers in the grounds to finish their breakfasts and load their packs for day hikes. Once the coast was clear, he found food tucked away in a cooler and car keys tucked away in a hauler. He and Saint were back on the road with a half tank of gas.

There wasn't much choice on the radio, but the news was good. The two missing kids had been found. Belinda Lowell was reunited with her son hours after returning from an interview with Nathan Shein in Texas. Maggie would reunite with her grandparents, and they had praised God for her return. Lucas worried the most about Maggie, and that was weird. He couldn't remember a time when he truly worried about anyone.

And he drove. He changed up cars several times and hit truck-stops on occasion to pimp himself out for food and gas money until he reached the place where it all started, a rural cemetery outside Ashland, Wisconsin. Morning sunlight had yet to crest the horizon when he arrived. It was freezing. The gates were closed.

The lights inside the little house on the hill were out, and Lucas remembered a time when that would never have happened. Not when he was around. The old keeper had always been aware of Lucas's unannounced presence. He was a vigilant bastard with the premonition skills of a master occultist who had never shown fear of Lucas when he should have. And Lucas had never crossed into the grounds. Something had always compelled him to hold back, something that he couldn't explain.

But here he was drawn to this place, drawn to the keeper of the dead. He was so drawn that he got out of the car and dropped down against the gate where the chill of wrought iron seeped through his shirt. Saint curled up beside him and kept him warm as he reached into his pocket for a knife. It was the same blade he had used on Jonas Adonis.

Lucas shivered as he thought about the news of Jake's return, of Nathan Shein's upcoming interview with Josiah Light. Belinda Lowell had been there, according to the reports. The way that the chain of events played out intrigued him, and he wished they included more about Rorie's mother. Jake and Maggie had been right. The gunshot wounds had healed quicker than they should have, but Rorie's mom led to nothing.

Lucas toyed with the knife as he flexed his left hand, watching the tendon there pop and recede with each squeeze. It would be a fitting experiment. Either he would bleed out, leaving the old man on the hill a fine dog to keep him company, or he would heal. Nagging question answered.

But it wouldn't answer why.

Saint lifted his head and whimpered as if he sensed Lucas's intentions. Lucas gave him one affectionate stroke behind his ears. Then he slit the wrist. It went deep, along the old scar, and blood gushed out without slowing. He dropped the knife. He leaned his head back against the wrought iron slats. He closed his eyes, and he waited.

"You can't park it here."

Lucas startled at the old man's presence. He didn't remember falling asleep, but he must have. Daylight had broken, the morning fog had begun to burn away. The groundskeeper seemed unconcerned by the sticky mess staining Lucas's clothes and hand, and when Saint popped up to poke his snout through the gate, the old man tickled the dog under the chin.

Lucas climbed to his feet, found he was lightheaded from loss of blood. "Thought I'd drop in on my family," he managed.

The groundskeeper scrutinized him. The first time they met, Lucas had said something similar, and the old man had been quick to answer that his family wasn't buried there. Since then, things had changed. The old man tossed his hand at the car again. "Still can't leave it here. Come back later, if you like."

The groundskeeper unlocked the gate for the day, and Saint scampered in to try and trip up his new-found friend. There was nothing stopping Lucas from disobeying the old man and either walking or driving in. Like the first time, the groundskeeper had said he was welcome. But the first time he couldn't do it. Something had prevented it.

This time was different. It wasn't that he was scared. It was if he was worthy. He wanted to cross to the other side, but the thing that was holding him back came from within. He looked down at his blood-drenched sleeve, and he realized that he shouldn't even be standing.

"I have no place to go." The way it came out sounded desperate.

The groundskeeper nodded. "Get rid of that car. It's stolen." He turned toward the house on the hill, and he let Saint go along with him. He hadn't mentioned the blood-stained sleeve, hadn't even acknowledged it. Lucas brushed across the dried cinnamon crust hiding the gash. It wasn't gone, but it was healing over. *Was it normal to heal over that fast?* Why him?

He drove the car to a wooded area that he had known as a teenager. He had lived there, along with others in the satanic community. People had passed the dirt road entrance for years, thinking that it led to a private summer camp. Now it was abandoned. Lucas knew that the car would be found there eventually. But it would take a season. He removed its plates and chucked them into a nearby lake that had yet to freeze over. He rinsed his slashed wrist in that icy water. It came out clean, with an angry scar that looked a week old.

It was mid afternoon when he returned. Lucas walked through the gateway expecting his skin to boil and peel away from setting foot on hallowed ground. But that didn't happen. He ended up at Brent Lowell's grave. It sat between the markers for his wife and his daughter, and on the other side of his wife was a stone for Alexander Lowell. "They were quick about it," the groundskeeper said from behind him. He gave a vague motion toward Alec's stone. "He won't be buried until they close the investigation, of course. That'll take time. I heard mention of cremation. The stone is symbolic, I suppose."

"I can do it."

"Do what?"

Lucas exposed his wrist where the wound continued to heal. "I cut it open this morning."

The groundskeeper didn't seem surprised. "And you're thinking that you've been chosen."

"I don't deserve any…gift—"

"—You are brothers. Or, were." The old man patted Lucas on the back and continued with a chuckle. "It's complicated, isn't it." Lucas frowned. He wasn't sure what the groundskeeper meant, and the groundskeeper didn't bother to expand on it. "Head inside. Take the spare bed. Or the sofa. Recharge."

"Could my father…was Brent…?"

"Who knows? They kept him sedated in the sanitarium. And Alec…it took him years to realize it. So it could be a gift. Or it could be your gift to others. I don't have those answers. Only you can decide what feels right." The old man carried on when Lucas failed to come up with a reply. "Jake is home with his mother. He will be fine. The girl, Maggie, will be fine. Alec is…in a better place—"

"—What about the other girl? What about her mom?"

"The other girl?" Again, Lucas didn't explain. He could see exasperation building behind the groundskeeper's eyes before the man gave up. "Go get some rest. You'll find answers in time."

And he did. He opted for the groundskeeper's sofa, where Saint had already made himself at home. He slept with an afghan up to his shoulders and with the dog tucked under his arm. It felt good. He was exhausted, and he hadn't realized it before this very moment.

When he woke, Saint had abandoned him. The aroma of bacon coaxed Lucas, too, off the sofa. The groundskeeper set a plate on the table of his little kitchen and pulled out a chair. No words, just a silent invitation. "Why are you being nice to me?"

"Shouldn't I?"

Lucas let it be. He munched on the bacon and eggs scrambled with spinach.

The groundskeeper never pressed about anything after that. He set Lucas up in his own room, and gave him daily chores such as splitting wood for the fireplace, or organizing the tool shed behind the house, shoveling snow or tending to minor repairs. And Lucas lived there.

In his free time, Lucas took advantage of the groundskeeper's only connection to the outside world, the Internet. He relied heavily on YouTube, where he found interviews with Nathan Shein and reports on the ongoing investigation to find the young man who brought Jake home. The police were nowhere close.

One interview was with Jake's friend Rorie. The girl's mom sat beside her, and Lucas thought she looked good. Her face had filled out, the gray pallor gone. She no longer looked like a woman stricken with disease, although she mentioned it. Doctors were attributing her remission to a latent response from chemotherapy. She said that she hadn't known that the young man Rorie brought home was a fugitive. She said that she wouldn't have thought him capable of the murderous things the press claimed he had done.

The old groundskeeper was right. Everyone involved seemed to be healing. Then a panel opened up with a video chat request. The ID read Nathan Shein. Lucas could have ignored the call. He could have stepped away from the computer and found the groundskeeper. Every fiber of his being told him what he should do. His fingers had a plan of their own. They tapped the answer button, and Nathan Shein's presence filled the screen.

Shein's gaze initially focused on something out of the computer's camera range. "Have you heard," Shein began with a grin reserved for awesome news. It melted away when his eyes met the face onscreen. Nothing was said. The two stared at each other for what felt like a lifetime. Then Shein found his voice. "What did you do—"

"—Well hello, there!" The groundskeeper settled a hand on Lucas's shoulder, then reached in to adjust the camera so that the feed included him from more than the neck down.

Nathan Shein just stared. And Lucas realized that Nathan, or Alec, didn't know that he'd been staying there. He had no reason to know, unless the groundskeeper had said something at a point in time before this. And the old man hadn't. It was apparent by the icy reception.

"I'm sure you have questions," the groundskeeper began.

Lucas cut him off. "I brought him home. I escaped with Jake. And Maggie. And I brought them home." Nathan Shein let tension rule his face in a way that was distinctly Alec, and before he could let loose with a litany of curses, Lucas cut in again. "I saved them—"

"—That's not good enough!"

"Forgiveness is a hard one to master," the groundskeeper said, and Alec let it spill.

"What is he doing with you? What are you doing? You said he was afraid of you—that he couldn't cross through the gate—What the fuck!"

"Things change. Nathan." Alec shook his head. The name alone seemed to make him squirm, and Lucas wondered what kind of hell it was to be trapped inside the skin of the person who had killed you. He had caught up on the news. Nathan Shein had his own physical scars to live with, and they weren't pretty.

"Why did you help him, Lucas?"

Lucas shrugged. "I don't expect a thank you."

Alec didn't oblige. The glare that he shot through the screen conveyed one sentiment. Execution.

Lucas said, "Tell me what you want me to do, and I'll do it. Turn myself in? Kill myself?" He shrugged again and expected Alec to choose the latter.

Alec disconnected the call. The screen went blue. And Lucas decided to accept his fate, whatever it might be.

Morning after morning, Lucas woke to the routine of chores that would make the old groundskeeper's life easier, and every morning the groundskeeper greeted him with, "Still here? I thought you'd have left by now," followed by a shake of the head and a chuckle. Lucas awaited his fate. Law enforcement never came.

But Nathan Shein did. He arrived in an upscale rental a week after the chat, and he had changed dramatically from when Lucas had last seen him. He was thin, like Alec, but not from some high, nervous energy that Alec had been prone to. No, the outer layer of Nathan Shein was thin from sickness. His face was emaciated, and he walked with a tired gait. He wasted no time once he found Lucas collecting dead flowers from headstones. "Let's take a walk."

Both were familiar with the grounds. Lucas knew that Alec was leading him to a little-visited area on the farthest reaches of the property. They walked in silence until Alec stopped to catch a breath. He rested on a stone that was stained and aging. Lucas reached out to take his brother's hand.

Alec pushed the offer away. "Don't touch me. I don't need your help." Lucas slipped his hands in his pockets and kept strolling until Alec shouted. "I don't get it!"

"Don't get what?"

"You ruined my life. No matter what side you're on, Satan or God or…whatever. No matter what side you choose, you make me out to be the enemy—"

"—Not anymore."

Alec scoffed. "That's too late! You know who I am. I'm trapped in this dying man's body—dying because of you, by the way. And I can't heal! Not just physically. I can't heal up here." Alec jabbed his finger against his temple hard enough to make himself flinch. "And Jake? I can't even have a life with my son. You took that from me."

"You could tell him—"

"—I can't. What he sees is the man who killed me. You get that, right? How can you not get that?"

"Jake is stronger than you think." When Alec shook his head, Lucas continued. "What can I do to make it right?"

Alec glared through Nathan Shein's eyes. He pulled out a gun. "You can get on your knees."

Lucas held up his hands without a reply.

"Get on your fucking knees." Alec rose to his feet, and Lucas…he did what he was told. He dropped to his knees, and he waited for his fitting end as he noted the tremble in Alec's grip. "I don't understand why you're here, why my grandfather would trust you. But I don't care. The only way for me to move on is to eliminate you."

Lucas spread his hands out. He closed his eyes, and he waited. He heard Alec's labored breathing as cold steel met the bridge of his nose. He waited for the ear-splitting crack of the shot that he imagined would be the last thing he ever heard before he was sent to where he belonged. Maybe heaven. Probably hell. And he wondered if it would be more like Dante's rendition of hell or like the hell depicted in the cartoon South Park. He snickered at that, because it was a stupid and inappropriate thought. He truly must not have a soul.

The bullet failed to come. The shot, the anticipation of brief exploding pain, the blackout, and descent into some netherworld failed to come. "Do it."

The steel barrel lifted from his nose. Lucas hazarded opening his eyes in time to see Alec heaving in breaths as tears streamed down his face. The gun hung limp in his hand. Then in one determined move, Alec shoved the muzzle up under his own chin.

Lucas lunged. He tackled Alec to the ground and managed to take possession of the gun before Alec could pull the trigger. Alec struggled and wept and cursed, and Lucas wrestled with him until Alec gave in. "I hate you," Alec finally said through a whimper. "I hate you so much."

Lucas rocked with him, one hand cupped against the back of Alec's head, the other gripped firmly around Alec's own hand. Alec slumped into it. He didn't push Lucas away or insist that no one could touch him. He eventually rested his head against Lucas's chest, and he let it be. They huddled together for an indefinite hour before the groundskeeper peeked up from beyond the edge of their hill. The old man appeared to assess the situation, then left.

"Come on." Lucas pulled out of the embrace and helped Alec to his feet. They walked slowly, again without exchanging words, and Lucas let Alec shift his weight on him for support. Some color had returned to the man's cheeks.

Alec spent the night. He was given the room that had become Lucas's room, and Lucas occupied the sofa with Saint again. In the morning, Lucas caught a glimpse of Alec through an open crack in the doorway. He was staring down Nathan Shein's reflection, and his colostomy bag was in full view. Alec took a glance over his shoulder and shoved the door shut.

They sat quietly across from each other at breakfast. The groundskeeper, whose name was Toussaint it turned out, seemed to take pleasure in identifying Alec by his new persona. "More coffee, Nathan? How about some toast? Nathan, how do you like your eggs?" Alec finally shot the old man a look before Toussaint chuckled and carried on. "You should be happy. Alec Lowell and the baggage that came with him is no longer your problem—"

"—I feel different this morning… Better." Alec's gaze remained fixed on Lucas.

And Lucas shrugged. What was he going to say? His fingers danced across the one scar along his wrist, fresh now, but the one scar that never seemed to disappear.

"I don't get it," Alec said. "Is this some lesson? Some punishment—"

"So, now you want the gift."

"That's not what I mean! Why him? Why now? Why this?" Alec clutched his side where the bag was, and Toussaint responded like Lucas had. He shrugged.

Toussaint said, "The Lord works in mysterious—"

"—Shut up." Then Alec settled.

"All wounds heal with time. Nathan." Toussaint smirked at the name again. "As long as we don't pick and scratch in consternation, they heal." Alec reacted with a roll of the eyes, and Toussaint added. "It's a metaphor." Then Toussaint noted Lucas's preoccupation with the wrist. "Of course, some scars never seem to disappear, do they."

"A reminder of the things that change us," Lucas said. Alec picked at the egg that the old man slipped onto his plate. A moment passed, and he reached for Lucas's hand to grip it tight.

And Lucas was good with that. He was good with whatever the future had in store.